S0-AAA-440

I'LL SEE YOU IN MY DREAMS

Hell Yeah!: Book V

SABLE HUNTER

Copyright Pending Sable Hunter All
rights reserved.

ISBN: 1482736519
ISBN-13: 978-1482736519

Illustrating and Technical Advising by Barb Caruso
http://www.addedtouchesllc.blogspot.com

Take a Moment to check out Sable's current and upcoming projects.
Visit her on:
Website: http://www.sablehunter.com
Facebook: http://www.facebook.com/authorsablehunter
Email: sablehunter@rocketmail.com

Check out all of Sable's books on Amazon
http://www.amazon.com/author/sablehunter

CONTENTS

ACKNOWLEDGMENTS

Thank you to all my Friends that support me and Fans that can't get enough. Also, thank you to Ryan and Jess for the above and beyond. Love you all.

This is a work of fiction. All names, characters, places and incidents are either the product of the author's imagination or used fictitiously, and any resemblance to actual persons, living or dead, business establishments, events or locales is entirely coincidental.

Presley

"After you do the dishes, make sure you iron those sheets. If you're going to live here with me, you have to make yourself useful."

"Yes, mam." Presley had heard the same explanation a thousand times. She had lived with her grandmother for as long as she could remember, but it was never like the television shows. Grandmothers were supposed to be loving and kind. Her grandmother wasn't loving or kind, she was harsh and demanding and never failed to remind Presley of her place. The shabby trailer they lived in could never be described as a home, yet it was all she had ever known.

"I have company coming. It'd be best if you drug the ironing board in the bedroom. Children shouldn't be seen or heard, especially when they look like you."

Presley had heard offhand remarks like that so often from Mabel Love that they didn't really wound her as much as one would think. "Okay." She had learned long ago that arguing was a waste of time. There was no escape for her from this situation. She wasn't abused physically and Mabel sent her to school She had even seen to it that her cleft lip was repaired, after a fashion. Mirrors didn't lie however, and Presley could still see that she didn't look like everyone else. None of the children at school ever let her forget that sad fact, not for a single day.

"By the way," her grandmother stood over her as she gathered the iron and the spray starch from underneath the sink, "I heard from your mother, today."

"Really? What did she say?" Presley sprang back up. Hope was an odd thing; it could still spring up midst the ashes of despair. Kelly Love hadn't made an appearance in her life since before she began elementary school. At fifteen, Presley fantasized about her mother driving up at the school and going to the office to demand they get her out of class. She would walk in with the principal and this beautiful woman would embrace her and tell her they were leaving together and she would begin a new life faraway from Houston, a new life with her mother.

i

"She wanted money from me, just like always. Worthless slut."

Presley ignored the name-calling, it might not mean anything. Mabel called Presley names all the time. "Did she ask about me?"

Her grandmother laughed out loud, a phlegm filled laugh that spoke more of derision than it did of humor. "No, I don't think she remembers you are alive, or she doesn't want to. Face it, Miss Hare-lip. Nobody cares anything about you; not me, not your mother – hell, no one even knows who your father is. You are lucky to even be alive. If I were you, I'd get down on my knees every day and thank God that someone like me wastes my time and money on the likes of you."

As Mabel continued her tirade about Presley's misplaced gratitude, she hung her head and made her escape. Ironing was way more preferable than being berated. When Mabel's friends came over to watch television and drink beer with her, the safest place for Presley was out of the way.

Closing the bedroom door, she sat up the ironing board and plugged in the iron. With a flip of the sheet, she draped it over the rickety wooden structure. What should she think about today? Escaping her reality through day-dreams was her favorite thing to do. Presley smiled, she knew exactly which one. Her favorite. As she let the hot iron glide over the cheap, thin sheets, she imagined how life would be like for her one day. Oh, it wouldn't come true, but it was a joy to live it out in her mind.

One day, her prince would come. He would be tall and strong, he would be smart and funny and he would kind. Her hero would take one look at her and fall in love. As she rehearsed what they would say and what they would do, Presley left reality behind and during those precious moments, she was happy.

Zane

The blackness engulfed him. It was palatable and thick – impenetrable.

And the pain!

The burning, searing pain was excruciating. Zane covered his eyes and screamed.

One second he had been riding his tractor, spraying herbicide on the hay meadow – the next, a strong gust of wind had made the trailer carrying the tank of Weedrid sway and he had been afraid it was about to turn over. So, he had turned to look.

Instant Agony. . .

Looking back at that exact moment had been the worst mistake he had ever made. The same freak wind that had jostled the trailer had blown a cloud of the caustic chemical right into his eyes. Why was this the one day he hadn't been wearing protective gear? He had no answer to that, other than his mind had been preoccupied with other things - like planning how he was going to propose to Margaret.

One stupid mistake had cost him his sight, his woman, his happiness and his future.

Fear. Despair. Rage. Emotions he couldn't control washed over him. With a gasp, Zane sat up in bed, breathing heavily.

It was dark.

God, what a dream.

He ran a big hand over his head, ruffling his too long, unruly hair. Opening his eyes, he saw only darkness. It was still night. He started to reach for the lamp by the bed – and then he remembered. The dream was real. It had been a memory.

He was blind.

It would always be dark. A tidal wave of sorrow caused him to groan out loud.

As if cursing fate, Zane tried to see. He looked; he strained to pierce the darkness. This was not new, it never changed, every moment his eyes were open he tried in vain to see, peering into the inky blackness as if searching for a shaft of relieving light. He found no relief at all.

Knowing he had no choice if he were to go on, he rose, resigned to his fate. Zane threw back the covers and headed for the shower. Walking through his home was an instinctual process; even sighted people could maneuver through their houses without turning on a light, but Zane had developed special skills. He had eidetic memory, what would be photographic memory if he could see with his eyes. Since he couldn't see, he processed information, catalogued it and stored it for future reference. Of course, he occasionally stubbed his toe. Unfortunately, Zane was at the mercy of others. Rachel was good about picking things up, but sometimes a dog toy would get in his way. That was okay, Rex was worth a stubbed toe.

The big black lab whimpered at his side. "I'm fine, boy. I'm just hot." His body was covered in a fine sweat. It wasn't the weather, his big, rustic ranch home stayed at an optimum temperature. Zane's perspiration was caused by sheer unease. When would he become accustomed to existing in a world that was void of sight?

What he would never see again haunted him.

Zane leaned on the stone bathroom vanity and gazed into the arched mirror. He knew it was there, he could feel it. And he knew what it looked like, he had picked it out. It was cold and smooth. His face was reflected in that mirror, a face he hadn't seen in five years – a face he would never see again.

Closing his eyes, Zane mourned for what could never be. He would never see a sun rise again, or a horse prancing through tall grass. He would never see a woman's face contort in ecstasy as he made her cum, or gaze at the erotic beauty of a naked lover as she offered him her body.

He would never see the face of his twin, the face that so closely resembled his own. And he would never see the face of his wife or his children – not only because he was blind, but because he'd never have a wife and children.

At the time of his accident, Zane had been in love, head over heels in love with Margaret Farrington. He had longed to have children and build a home with her.

His family, other than Kane, left something to be desired. They were cold and distant, for the most part. Money and social standing took precedence over hearth and home. Oh, his Dad had come around after Kane and Lilibet's crisis. Grandchildren tend to make a difference in those situations. Now Lilibet was pregnant, and she and Kane had adopted Dwayne. The whole family loved the little boy. Yes, they all realized he had been the product of Kane's ex-wife's twisted sense of revenge, but he was a little boy and they adored him. The family had even forgiven Preston, their cousin, for his part in the scheme. Preston was Dwayne's real father, but Kane would be his dad.

Estelle, their mother, was still a pill. She couldn't get her nose down out of the air long enough to enjoy life. Other than Kane, Zane's favorite family member was a cousin. Not Teresa – oh no, not Teresa. She was two-faced and entirely too close to Margaret. No, he meant Willow.

Willow, who had run and played with him, chasing baby alligators in the swamp and prowling through the French quarter, playing tag in the St Louis cemetery. Willow was his and Kane's childhood companion. She had grown up to be a doctor; graduating from Tulane with honors. Zane had pulled all-nighters with her, quizzing her for anatomy tests. Now, she was a premier surgeon and had made him a promise that she had not been able to keep, so far. Willow had solemnly promised that one day she would restore his sight. One attempt had failed. He had undergone a corneal transplant, but his body had rejected the tissue. It wasn't Willow's fault, maybe darkness was his destiny.

Zane was blind and alone.

Margaret hasn't wanted him, not after he lost his sight. Her words would forever ring in his ears. To give her credit, she had waited till he was released from the hospital before she had dropped the bomb. They had been in his bedroom. Margaret had never moved in with him, her family would have never gone for that, but she had stayed over frequently. With her own apartment in town, her folks weren't able to keep constant tabs on her whereabouts.

All Zane had been able to think about was holding her again. He had longed to touch and hug, to feel her body mold to his. Instead, she had stood by the bed they had shared and delivered the killing blow. That was one time Zane had been grateful he couldn't see. The revulsion he knew was on her face would have killed him. "I can't do this Zane. You're not the man I want any longer. I need someone who can look in my eyes, who can tell me I'm beautiful because they can see and appreciate my beauty. I need a man who can protect me, who can walk beside me down the street without tapping one of those disgusting canes ahead of them like their eternally dousing for water. I need a whole man, not a sightless shell of a man who can do no more than stumble through life and fumble around as he touches my body."

Actually, he had to give Margaret credit for being honest. It would have been far worse for her to have stayed with him for his money or for the prestige of his family name. He could just imagine the shame of her enduring his lovemaking, allowing him to take her – him thinking they were in love and all was well, and all the while she is repulsed by his handicap and merely tolerating his touch.

Zane had changed that day.

For months, he had mourned Margaret, even calling her several times. The only time she had responded with anything close to a positive response was when he had thought there was a chance to regain his sight with the transplant. After it had failed, he had never heard from her again.

As he looked into the mirror, he saw himself clearly. He was a man, a strong man. He had accomplished many things that most seeing men could not. But there was one thing he would not do – he would never make himself vulnerable to a woman again.

Chapter One

"Will you zip me up, Zane?" Tricia moved into his space and turned in front of him, so close that he could feel her heat. Blind or not, there was no way he could miss the signals this little hottie had been sending him. When she had grabbed him by the hand and pulled him behind a closed door, Zane had fantasized that it was for a bit of afternoon delight. Instead he found himself playing ladies maid – not that he was complaining.

"You do realize I have to feel my way," he located her hips, felt his way to her waist, rubbed the soft skin of her lower back – all in the magical pursuit of a zipper. "I like your perfume," he dusted the back of Tricia's neck with a kiss and felt her shiver. Avery had ushered Tricia into the McCoy fold. They were best friends and operated the neighborhood florist together.

"Me next!" Skye Rogers flounced next to him, the rustle of taffeta giving him a clue to her whereabouts. He would know Skye's husky voice anywhere. From what Joseph McCoy had told him, she was exotic, strong-willed and the family's best hope to bring Noah to his senses. "All of our fingernails are still a bit wet. We can't do each other." It amused him that the women thought they had to change their clothes and nail polish color just to go the reception dance.

"I want to 'do you', Skye. You bring out my lesbian tendencies," Avery's voice came from his right side.

Zane was surrounded by half naked women!

He loved it.

"Does Isaac know you swing both ways?" he teased one of the sweetest women he had ever met. Avery Sinclair, destined to be Avery McCoy, had a heart of gold and had won the heart of the Badass of Kerrville County.

"Ha! Isaac is possessive! The only way he'll let me swing is on that contraption he has hanging in that kinky playroom of his. I've ridden that a few times." Avery giggled as she waited patiently for Zane to zip her up. He accommodated her, gladly, thankful that she was well and happy and back with her beloved. Avery had narrowly escaped a madman's clutches.

"TMI!" Cady protested. "Zane is sweet to come in here and help us. Don't scare him off." Cady was Joseph McCoy's angel. She was always the voice of reason.

"I don't mind," Zane drawled. "We blind people have to enjoy what few advantages we're given." Despite his blindness, Zane could see more than one might think. When he walked into a room, he would pause and listen. What he could hear would paint a picture for him. He memorized voices, footstep patterns – if he concentrated he could even use the vibrations of the noise in the room to sense furniture and the placement of walls and doors. He called it echolocation even though he didn't do the clicking noises – he sought to be patient and absorb what went on around him and visualize the scene.

"Zane Saucier, you have more advantages than you know. Sexy, smart, handsome and funny are just the first things that pop in my head." Tricia was sincere. Everyone in their circle of friends was urging him to ask her out. The chemistry was definitely hot between them, but Zane didn't date anyone within his circle of friends. Actually, he didn't date – period. It was just too hard to maintain the charade around people he cared about. He had been known to escort a woman to a social event, but he never followed it up with more. And since the drinking water at Tebow seemed to be infested with orange blossoms and wedding-itis, it was time for him to hit the road.

"Anyone else?" He hated to zip and run, but he had a legitimate excuse. A few minutes ago he had received a puzzling phone call from his secretary. Chloe never called him unless it was an emergency. She had asked him to meet her at the office and he had agreed.

"Just me," it was Libby's soft voice.

"Ah, the blushing bride, it was a beautiful ceremony, Mrs. McCoy. Aron is a lucky man."

"No, Zane, I'm the lucky one. Aron is my heart."

A knot of sadness formed in his throat. "I think you're both damn lucky." After zipping her, he stepped back needing a bit of air. It was time to get out of here. "This has been a sweet distraction. There's nothing I like better than spending a few minutes with a bevy of beautiful women."

"You're a sweet talker," Cady said. "Joseph has told me so many stories about you and Kane. He says you are so silver tongued that you can talk a coon down out of a tree."

"I'll take that as a compliment." He spoke into his phone, "Sherwood, meet me out front please." Lifting his face to the ladies, he thanked them. "I enjoyed spending this time with all of you, it was a privilege. And as much as I hate to leave good company, I have to go. If any of you see Kane, tell him that I'm headed back to Austin. I have a late meeting at the office."

Every one of the ladies had to give him a kiss. And Zane accepted them graciously. He had wanted to come to this wedding, Aron and Libby McCoy meant the world to him.

"Rex," one word was all it took and the faithful dog was at his side. The black lab had an uncanny instinct and was completely devoted to him. They moved effortlessly through the crowd of people who had come to Tebow to witness the elder McCoy brother tie the knot with Libby Fontaine. Zane said a few final goodbyes as they made their way to the door.

"Mr. Saucier," he heard his name as he exited the ranch house. "Over here, sir." Rex was already pointing his body in that direction. The car door opened and he found the cool steel easily. "Where to, Sir?"

"My office, Sherwood. Please."

The drive from Tebow Ranch to Austin took a little over an hour, so Zane used the time to make some notes for Chloe. "First, please confirm my reservations at Eagle Canyon Resort. Remember, I'm speaking at that conference. If you'll begin to get all the notes and PowerPoint presentations ready, I'd appreciate it. And you might as well book an extra room; I'll probably need you to go with me. Second, confirm our firm's attendance at the premier of Burning Love. Make sure we have a table big enough for the partners and a few others." As bad as he hated to do it, there was no way he would get out of the movie studio's big shindig. Vision Star was one of the firm's oldest and best clients, "Third, call Shelly Taylor and tell her we'll take the case." Laney Taylor might be dead, but her sister deserved to know what happened to her. And if suing Rayford Kendall to reclaim Shelly's stolen property would get their foot in the door, he was all for it. This was exactly the type of case that Zane loved to sink his teeth into. He had no doubt they would get to the bottom of the mystery, but it would require some investigating to bring the truth to light. Putting the mini recorder in his pocket, he settled back to enjoy the remainder of the ride.

Rex rode in the seat beside him, his big head on Zane's leg. "Sherwood, tell me what you see," he asked while absently patting the dog.

They played this game regularly. Sherwood had been with Zane for years and there was great affection between them. "Well, sir – the leaves have turned to mellow golds and russets and many of them are falling and flying through the air like confetti. All of the storefronts have big pots of mums in front of them and people are wearing sweaters and hugging themselves as they walk. The sun is going down and the sky is pink and orange. Day is dying in the west, but the moon will be huge tonight. It's a blue moon, you know, the last one this year."

"Thank you, Sherwood." He felt the car slow down and he knew they were at his office. Downtown Austin was one of his favorite places on earth.

"We're here, Mr. Zane." His door was opened and he and Rex departed. The streets weren't deserted, he could hear the swish of tires on wet pavement and an occasional car horn sounded. If he listened closely, he could hear the sounds of music from Sixth Street. Tonight there was no time for lingering, however, Chloe wanted to meet and he had a bad feeling that he wasn't going to be happy with the topic. His dog didn't slow down and Zane knew that the doorman had pulled back the double glass doors for him.

"Evening, Mr. Saucier. You're out late."

"Yes, I am, Norman. I hope you're well. Is Ms. Jacobs here, yet?"

"I am well, Sir. Thank you. Ms. Jacobs is waiting for you. She arrived about ten minutes ago."

Zane and Rex stepped into his domain. There was a certain smell about a law office. He didn't know if it was the books or the furniture polish that every cleaning service used to buff the heavy wooden furniture – but they all smelled alike to him. Of course the books were for his staff and their research; he couldn't use them any longer. He had collected everything he needed, however. For his own use, he had a massive library of audio eBooks and audio files, plus he had access to several university library systems where his secretary or clerk could request case information, rulings or briefs.

The reception area was beautifully decorated, or so he was told. When he had met with the interior designer, he had told him to erase Margaret's influence. So now instead of French austerity there was a western flair. Rich pecan wood was paired with saddle leather and photos of Whispering Pines and his horses decorated the walls. If the five-star Driscoll hotel could decorate in Texas chic, so could he. Turning to the left, he went to his private wing.

Because of his handicap, or as he liked to think of it, his unique perspective, Zane wanted his secretary or assistant close at hand. It just made things easier. So Chloe's desk was on one side of the huge L-shaped room and his was on the other. A sitting room with two couches, a fireplace and a wet bar connected at the back and they enjoyed their own private bathroom and dressing facilities.

Zane liked the idea that someone was nearby. He didn't feel so alone. So, it was important that he have a good relationship with his secretary/assistant. Many people had marveled at the way Zane preferred to operate, he talked through his work and he expected his assistant to follow along and participate. Chloe served as his sounding board. Maybe it was because he couldn't make notes and read them, or perhaps he just liked to hear a smart man's opinion. That thought made him smile, he wasn't an egomaniac and he wasn't overly humble. Zane liked to think of himself as a realist.

"Zane, I'm here."

Chloe Jacobs wasn't a young woman, but she was an attractive woman. He had never seen her of course; she had only been with him for four and half years. But he knew how other men treated her and he could sense the confidence with which she carried herself. Having been widowed for over five years, her work with him defined her days. "Chloe, what's up?" Zane was in his comfort zone so he released Rex and made his way to one of her side chairs and sat down.

"I have something to tell you and it's going to be hard to do."

"I'm not going to like this am I?"

Her voice was soft and gentle. Zane could sense hesitancy and an apology. But there was also a hint of excitement. What could have that type of an effect on the indomitable Miss Jacobs? "Is this about a man?"

"How do you do that?"

The shock in her voice told him volumes. It was a man. Doom. "I could read it in your voice." What was he going to do? He didn't think he could function without Chloe – not even for a week! But she would never know that. He wanted her to be happy. "Who's the lucky man and when's the big day?"

"The man is Fraiser McGee, owner of The Horseman Club and we're eloping in ten minutes."

Eloping? "Congratulations! How long will you be gone?" Needy much?

A deep sigh. Hell! He knew what the answer was going to be.

"I won't be coming back, BUT . . ."

He didn't like the sound of any of that, but least of all the 'but'.

"I am not leaving you uncared for." She laid a small digital recorder on top of his hand that lay on her desk. "Here is the number for an employment agency – a temp agency. Call them Monday and ask for Presley Love. She is exactly what you need. Presley is smart and capable and she needs you as much as you need her."

That sounded odd. What could she mean by that? Zane chose to ignore the strange inference. He'd think about that later. "If she's so good, why is she with a temp agency?"

"Presley has had challenges in her life, like you have. Despite those challenges, she has exactly the talents you need at this firm."

Ah, a mystery. He liked mysteries. Okay, he'd play along. Challenges didn't bother him. After what he had been through, it was Zane's philosophy that those challenges only served to make you stronger. "Should I call her direct or go through the agency?"

He trusted Chloe. He was mad at her, but he trusted her. How dare she choose happiness over taking care of him? Yea, he was pitiful.

"Go through the agency, that way if it doesn't work out, she'll still be on their role for employment opportunities."

"You don't think she'll work out?" Zane knew what was coming.

"If she doesn't it it will be your fault."

Ouch.

Before she left, Zane gave her a five thousand dollar bonus, kissed her cheek and told her to call him if she needed anything. Now, he just wanted to get home.

Home was his ranch, Whispering Pines, located in the rolling hills between Austin and Bastrop. The pine trees in Bastrop County were as unusual as the stand of lost maples near Kerrville. Both were marvelous accidents of nature – unexpected gifts. His father had owned land in a dozen counties and parishes in Louisiana and Texas, but this little spot of heaven on earth had been all of his family's holdings that he had ever wanted. And it hadn't been just given to him, either, he had earned it. From the time he was twelve, Zane had worked – after school, before school and weekends – delivering papers or working in a restaurant so he could have money to purchase the only thing of his father's he had ever wanted.

Every summer, he had spent here in Central Texas, learning the ropes and helping the hands. When he had turned eighteen, it had become his, the only legacy from the Saucier Empire he desired.

"We're here, Sir."

"Thank you, Sherwood." The car slowed to a stop in the circle drive in front of the lodge style Hill Country home. It was a big house, constructed of natural local stone and wood. A wide front verandah ran the entire length of the front of the first and second story. Zane knew the wood trim was painted dark brown, but he wasn't sure about the landscaping, all he had requested was that Margaret's ornate shrubs be removed and that Cape Jasmines be planted everywhere – he loved the smell.

"Are there any kittens on the steps?" He had to ask because they had no fear of him or Rex and Rex wouldn't bark at the little mites. Stepping on one of the little fellas was the last thing he wanted to do.

"The coast is clear, Sir."

"Good, thank you, Sherwood. Would you like to come in and see if Rachel left us any cookies and milk?"

"No sir, she brought me a batch of my own to the cottage." As soon as he had said the words, Sherwood coughed, as if he had let the cat out of the bag. Zane just smiled.

"Enjoy," he wondered if Rachel were waiting on Sherwood at the Cottage. Oh well, he wasn't about to interfere. He and Rex walked into his home. The smells comforted him. The sound of his boots on the wooden floor comforted him.

Heading for his room, he intended to change clothes and go check on Shalimar. The progress he had made with her was encouraging. With sure steps, Zane moved down the hall and into his bedroom. There was no need to turn on the light, of course. Rachel had helped him organize all of his clothes by season, function and color. There was a place for everything and everything in its place.

By nature Zane hadn't been very organized, but all of that had changed after the accident. He became what was necessary to survive. Stripping off, he stretched his arms over his head and flexed. What he needed was a massage – hell no, what he needed was sex. His body was starved for a woman.

Donning blue jeans and a comfortable long-sleeve shirt, he padded to the back door and slipped on his well-worn work boots. A few minutes later, he and Rex were on the way to the barn. Around his property, he didn't even make Rex wear the harness. They had developed such a rapport that the dog merely walked by his right side and if something was amiss or in the way, the lab let him know with soft barks or pushing on his leg. But at home, he could have a little more freedom.

Several whinnies greeted him. "Listen to them, Rex. They're glad to see us." We'll go check them all, but let's see Shalimar first. He made his way to the corral, opened the gate and went inside.

"Come here, girl." Of course, she didn't come to him – so he went to her. He could tell where she stood trembling, Zane could hear her breathing. Making soothing, crooning, noises, he ran his hand down the long length of her back. "You've had a hard time haven't you?" Ridged scars stood out on her flesh, left from the bite of a whip.

Zane was proficient with a whip. He could wrap the curled, flexible end around one of the special-made vibrating tin cans he practiced with and once he had taken the head off of a rattlesnake – as long as he could hear his target – he could find it. But one thing he didn't use the whip for was to punish, tame or torture his animals. Zane was also a martial arts expert. He had won tournaments and was called upon to give demonstrations. The fact that he was blind and a black belt fascinated people.

The thin horse seemed to want to respond. She allowed herself to enjoy his touch for just a few seconds before she skittered away.

With all the patience in the world, Zane held out his hand to coax the frightened filly closer. "I promise you, you're safe now. Never again will you have to return to that hell you were in."

Zane didn't use force, he used love. Maybe it was because he was blind, but he believed in the healing power of touch. There had been a time when a loving touch would have healed his soul. If he could just get the broken spirited horse to accept the comfort he offered, half the battle would be won.

The animal had come to him from an owner who prided himself on cruelty. Shalimar was lucky. Three other horses had starved to death. The idiot had literally corralled them up next to his house and waited to see how long it would take for them to die without food.

"Are you hungry?" The horses had all already been fed, but he liked to walk through the padlock and the stables handing out treats. Shalimar would follow, she always did. His employees made sure that nothing was left out in his designated paths. A stray pitchfork or bale of hay could cause him to fall, so a check was made every afternoon to ensure that Whispering Pines was Zane-friendly. Every horse received a treat and Shalimar watched. She didn't approach for hers, but if he held his hand out far enough, she would take it – quickly. And every day, she stood a bit closer. Soon, he'd try to ride her. Coaxing her back to trust was a long process, but well worth the effort.

Zane Saucier wasn't your typical cowboy, but he did love his version of ranch life. No longer could he operate machinery or compete in the rodeo, but there were other things he could do to stay active in this important part of his world. Keeping this life from changing completely after the accident had been his goal. At first, he had felt lost on the ranch. For a time, he had given up, he had even gone so far as to try and sell his spread and his herds of Beefmaster cattle to Kane, his brother. But Kane wouldn't hear of it. He had kept telling Zane to give it time. And he had been right.

Blindness hadn't hampered his law practice; Zane had adjusted by using audio books and the many programs available for the visually impaired. But his sex life was a different story. Women seemed to gravitate to him – the bridal party dressing room fest had proven that. But he couldn't get past what Margaret has said to him. A couple of times when he was out of town at a conference in Houston, he had given in to his friend Dylan and let him hook him them up with a pair of women who Zane swore were high priced escorts. He hadn't been with a woman in so long that he didn't question it too much – God, he had needed the release. But it wasn't the same, she wasn't enjoying him or needing him. Undoubtedly, she was tolerating him – for money.

So, Zane Saucier led a relatively celibate life. He came regularly, but it was by his own hand and if he mourned his sight a hundred fold, he mourned his passionless existence a thousand fold. Sometimes he wished he could just push aside his doubts and find a woman who could love him, long for him – but so far, he hadn't met a woman he felt was worth the risk.

To make up for the absence of female companionship, Zane had thrown himself wholeheartedly into his law practice and Whispering Pines. Now he was glad he had listened to his twin because Zane had turned his home into more than just a working ranch, he had turned into a shelter for abused animals. One day his foreman had brought home a young stallion that had been mistreated in a traveling show. The poor thing had been beat so badly it had turned vicious. No one could come near it, and people were afraid to try.

The authorities had shut down the show and jailed the owner, forcing a sale. Unable to control the horse, the new owners had made arrangements to have the horse destroyed, but Frank had found out and bought the animal – not knowing what Whispering Pines would do with it. At first Zane had been unwilling to even visit the abused animal, much less work with it. But hearing Frank talk about the frightened creature made Zane think about what could be done to help it. Finally, he had made his way to the holding pen and met Onyx. A sense of kinship enveloped Zane and he knew he had to try and help the horse.

Night after night, Zane would walk to the corral fence and talk to Onyx, whispering to him softly. Both of them – he and Onyx - were the victims of circumstances beyond their control. Both of them had been thrust into a storm not of their own making. One warm summer night, as he had leaned on the fence with his hands through the railing telling the animal all of his problems, he had felt the nudge of a warm nose in the palm of his hand. So, Zane had discovered he had a gift. He might be blind, be he could help and heal others that were hurting. Maybe his inability to see with his eyes increased his capacity to see with his heart.

Morning came sooner than he would have liked. He got up, showered, shaved and dressed for work. Zane loved the law. Both he and Kane had chosen it, but in slightly different respects. Kane was the sheriff of Kerrville County. Their parents were Louisiana royalty – richer than God, but he and Kane had walked away from the ties that would bind them to big oil, bayou politics and a lifestyle of acquiring more and more and enjoying it less and less. Oh Zane made a good living, but he chose cases that meant something to him and did just as much pro bono cases as he felt like he could afford – which was quite a bit.

Saucier and Barclay had the reputation of being a generous firm. Zane was lucky to have found Adam Barclay for a partner. He brought talent, vision and compassion to the firm. The Taylor case would be perfect for him. Bringing justice out of tragedy was his specialty. One of his goals was to take on an associate with the same passion he had, but as of yet, he hadn't found one with the same zeal for justice that he had. Most young lawyers were, understandably, interested in making a name for themselves and racking up the billable hours. Now, what he dreaded was starting over with a new secretary. This was not going to be a picnic any way you looked at it. Change was not something that Zane Saucier dealt with very well.

Rex was ready to go before he was. When Zane came out of the dining room after his usual morning fare of Rachel's sausage biscuits and gravy, the welcoming bark met his ears. "Patience, dog, I'm on my way." Sherwood greeted them with enthusiasm and Zane was glad to hear the lilt in his voice. "Good morning, it sounds like you're looking forward to the day."

"I am, Sir. I'm thinking about taking up dating again."

"Marvelous!" He started to ask if it was anyone he knew, but he decided to get off the topic. He knew Sherwood's opinion of his penchant for solitude. A twinge of jealousy flashed through his heart. Damn, he hated to be alone. Was this what his whole life was going to be like? Zane had the reputation of going where angels feared to tread, but putting himself in a position to be rejected by a woman again was where he drew the line.

Settling himself in the back of his prized Mercedes sedan, he knew there was no use putting off the inevitable. As soon as Sherwood pulled out on the highway, Zane called Work Force. A hard, agitated female voice answered. "It's early, but I'll accommodate you. This is Earline Felts, owner of Work Force, may I help you?"

Zane wondered if he should apologize. He was going to work; he thought everybody else should be open for business, too. "Hello, my name is Zane Saucier of Saucier and Barclay. I find myself without a secretary this morning, but one of your people has been highly recommended to me. I'm wondering if you could send Miss Presley Love over for an interview."

There was a pause, a pregnant pause. "Mr. Saucier, thank you so much for getting in touch with us."

The abrupt attitude change amused him. "Can you help me, Ms. Felts?"

"Of course, we can help you. Presley Love, you say? Are you sure? We have many very qualified people to choose from. Miss Love is adequate. In fact, she is very talented. Did you say this was for the position of your secretary?"

Zane wondered why the woman was balking at his suggestion. "Actually, my personal assistant has resigned. She was more than my secretary. Chloe gave me the name of Miss Love. Is that a problem? Has she accepted another position? Did I miss out?"

A wry laugh came over the speaker. "No, she is still available. The thing is, Mr. Saucier, Work Force prides itself on matching the right employee with the right job. And while Miss Love is adequate for the task, she is not what I would call 'front office' material."

Zane was confused. What did that mean? Something told him that it wasn't an explanation he cared to hear. "Thank you for your insight, but I trust Ms. Jacobs. Let me be the judge of Miss Love's qualifications. Could you send her over this morning?"

"Fine, I guess you can judge her suitability for yourself." Earline cleared her throat and gave a half-laugh. "Excuse me, Mr. Saucier – I forgot about your uh, condition. Perhaps you and Miss Love will suit one another just fine."

What in the hell did she mean by that? Women, he'd never understand them if he lived to be a thousand. Regardless, Mrs. Felts was not someone with whom he wanted to prolong a conversation. "I don't know what you're talking about, Ms. Felts, but I don't have time to discuss this further. When can I expect her?"

"I'll give her a call right now and she can be there within the hour. You can let me know how it works out by the end of the week, if you keep her that long."

"Fine, thank you." Zane was glad to hang up, the whole conversation disturbed him. He hoped to high heavens the day got better as it went along.

Presley was nervous. Saucier and Barclay was a very reputable firm. The call from Work Force had not been totally unexpected, however. Sweet Miss Chloe had confided to her about Fraiser's proposal and how much she wished for Presley to go to work at Zane Saucier's law office in her place. Working at the law firm would be a dream come true for Presley. While she enjoyed her part time job at The Horseman, she didn't like Work Force. Ms. Felts wasn't an easy person to work for.

Working at The Horsemen's Club had helped supplement her income. She had started out as a dishwasher, then moved on to helping in the kitchen. Now, she worked mostly out of her own kitchen preparing specialty desserts and pastries that Mr. Fraiser especially enjoyed. He paid her well for her creations. And that was a good thing, what she made at the temp agency was barely enough to pay the notes on her student loans. People just weren't apt to give Presley much of a chance. So, she wouldn't get her hopes up too much about this job, either, despite Chloe's assurance that Zane Saucier would welcome her talents.

Mr. Frasier had been a widower for years and Chloe Jacobs was perfect for him. When they had first started dating, he would bring her into the restaurant and Presley would occasionally share a cup of coffee with her. As she and Chloe had gotten to know one another, it wasn't long before they found they had the law in common and a bond was forged that soon became a close friendship. Chloe's encouragement gave Presley hope. This opportunity she had been granted was not one she took lightly. Presley did not intend for Chloe's faith in her to be in vain.

The front reception area was impressive and she hung back, watching employees and clients as they moved about. It was easy to tell the two apart. The clients had an anxious expression and the law firm employees looked to be on a mission. For the most part, they were young, good-looking and filled with confidence – unlike her.

Presley ran her hand over the smooth wood of a table and thumbed through a Texas law review magazine, trying to look busy. As she waited for the woman at the desk to get off the phone, Presley inspected the photos on the wall. They were all of a very good-looking man. He was working with horses. One photo in particular captured her attention. A golden palomino with a scar on its right cheek, stood with its head bent to touch the chest of the man in front of him. The man was the same as the one in the other photos – a tall, well-built man in typical western dress. But there was nothing typical about the handsome cowboy. Presley felt her pulse pound. His expression was so kind and loving. At that moment she knew he had instilled in the horse an absolute assurance that it was loved. This man could be trusted.

Presley smiled.

She envied the horse.

"Excuse me, may I help you?"

Presley turned to greet the receptionist. At first the woman was smiling, but when Presley drew closer and the woman got a good look at her, Presley saw the woman's countenance change. Her eyes narrowed and she sneered.

A reaction like this always made her want to sink into the floor, but she squared her shoulders and faced the music. "I have an appointment with Mr. Saucier. I'm from the temp agency, Work Force."

"Really." With one word, the woman projected skepticism and disapproval. She wasn't prepared to go against her superior's wishes, however, so she pressed the button and announced her. "Zane, the woman from Work Force has arrived."

"Thank you, Melody. Send her in."

Presley thought this was probably a useless endeavor; there was no way she was going to fit in here. Saucier and Barclay was filled with beautiful people and she – wasn't. Nevertheless, she marched forward.

"Come in, Miss Love." The voice that called to her was deep and authoritative, but something about it warmed her heart. It was a kind voice.

"Yes, sir."

The room was huge, yet comfortable. There were two work areas, one larger than the other – comfortable chairs, computers, a credenza – everything one would need to conduct business. Another room sat off to the side, but her gaze passed over it. Clearly, that was the inner sanctum. Presley's eyes moved quickly around the room before they settled on the man behind the larger desk. Her breath caught in her throat. It was the same man pictured in the photo with the horse. This was Zane Saucier? He stood up to greet her.

God Almighty! The man was fine! Dressed in a perfectly cut grey suit, he dominated the room. Presley wanted to run and hide. She didn't do well around really good looking men. With a reflex born from years of hiding, she jerked her hand up to cover her mouth. There was no way in hell this was going to work.

A movement next to the desk caused Presley to glance sideways. It was a dog! She was a little shocked and a gasp escaped her lips. "Are you okay?" he asked. A beautiful black Labrador sat there with the prominent halter and handle that a blind person would require.

She looked back at the gorgeous man standing in front of her. "I'm fine; your dog startled me, that's all." Was he blind? No! Impossible! Not him. The tragedy of it all took her breath away.

Presley stared at his handsome face, hoping to see some indication that she was wrong. It didn't matter if he looked at her with disdain – she just wanted him to be able to see. Zane appeared to look right at her, seemingly right in the eye. However when he held out his hand in greeting and she extended hers in return – he didn't take it, rather he waited for her to touch the tips of his fingers with hers. It was obvious he could not see her hand approaching his. The breath lurched in her throat. God, no - he was blind. She closed her eyes in abject sorrow and let her fingertips graze his. When she did, he grasped her hand warmly and Presley felt kindness, strength and security. Still, it hurt her soul. If she could have changed things for him, she would have – in a heartbeat.

"Welcome, please sit down. My previous secretary held you in high esteem."

Presley's heart pounded. "Thank you. I am grateful to be considered. Miss Chloe is a good friend." She forced herself to say the words carefully. When she became excited, Presley had a tendency to let a lisp slip in when she pronounced her s's.

Zane listened carefully and tried to formulate an image of the young woman. Her voice was beautiful. He could detect a deliberate control in the way she said her words. She didn't speak haphazardly. He admired that. It also made him wonder what she would sound like when she lost all of that cool control. Smiling to himself, he wondered where that had come from. He knew nothing about this woman – yet. How she looked, what her personality was like, how they would work together, all of that was still a mystery. But he soon would, and for some reason, he looked forward to it.

Sitting down, he leaned back and asked. "Do you have experience with the law? Have you worked at a law firm before?"

Ah, a touchy subject. "I am familiar with all of the law office management programs like Abacus, CaseFox, Practice Master and Legal Track. I'm also up to speed on the online law libraries as well as the subscription ones at UT and Tulane. Whatever you need, I'm sure I'll be able to help you."

"If you don't mind, let me ask you a few questions so I can gauge the depth of your knowledge." Frankly, he couldn't hope she was as knowledgeable as Chloe – but it would make such a difference if she was.

"Certainly."

"Let's say, my step daughter is thirteen. She has been with my wife and I for fifteen months without seeing her real father. I'm being deployed in three weeks and our daughter doesn't want to go back to her dad because they are having disagreements over school. Does she have the right to tell a judge that and stay with my wife while I'm gone? What do we have to do legally to keep her home?"

Presley knew this like the back of her hand, and before she realized what she was saying, she answered like a lawyer. "Statue 25-415 will guide you in how to file for custody and Statue 25-405 states that the court can interview the child to determine her wishes."

Damn! Was that a fluke? He'd try again. "Let's say we had a client that was in a relationship with a guy who was verbally and emotionally abusive. After a few months, the yelling and arguing had escalated and she was scared. The guy would tell her when and where she could go and wouldn't let her leave the apartment. But she gets away. Now he's breaking into her email, calls and threatens her and her friends. She's afraid he's going to get violent. What can she do?"

"She should close her current email and get a new account. As for the telephone, she should report his threats as harassment and file a report with the police. It would be wise to tape record all of his calls and make at least two copies of them. I'd also copy and save all threatening emails. According to Statue 13-2923, this is stalking and she needs police protection. Criminal jurisdiction would apply either to location of calls made or received. The victim's rights unit would be a good place to start. I'd strongly suggest that she get a domestic violence protective order and be ready to write down everything the man has done to her. She should be specific and have dates, times, and quotes."

By this time, Zane had sat straight up and moved forward in his chair. He was hanging on her every word. It was a shame Laney Taylor hadn't known Presley Love. Lane could have used Presley's advice. "You realize you could be an attorney, don't you?"

"Well, I. . ." She was saved from explaining when his cell phone rang.

"Excuse me, Presley." Zane stood up and walked to the window. He listened for a moment, then began to speak. "Laura, I'm surprised to hear from you." His silhouette stood in direct contrast to the bright rays of sunshine coming through the window. In the distance she could see the pink dome of the Texas Capitol. But the sight of that remarkable landmark was nowhere near as impressive as the set of shoulders that all but blocked the light from the room.

"I enjoyed myself, also. You are an incredible woman." Presley watched him bow his head, as if listening intently. She felt uncomfortable eavesdropping. "I'll have to check my calendar, but I think I'll be at a conference that weekend."

She tried not to listen as he made small talk with a woman that he obviously had dated at one time or another. She was sure that Zane Saucier could have any woman he wanted. God, Presley was so nervous, her fists were clenched so tight that her fingernails were digging into her palms. Not only was this a wonderful opportunity for her, but Zane Saucier was an extremely attractive man. His face was fallen angel beautiful with long dark brown hair that touched the top of his collar and warm golden brown eyes. And his body! He wasn't wearing the jeans and tight western shirt she had seen in the photo outside, but he looked equally devastating in his business attire. And she couldn't help but notice that his tie was loosened and the top two buttons of his shirt were undone, showing a smattering of dark hair on his chest.

What would it be like to touch him? Presley felt her nipples tighten. She couldn't help but indulge. It probably wasn't fair, but since he couldn't see her looking – she could ogle him to her hearts content. Oh, Lord – he was speaking to her; his phone call must be over. She had to pay attention.

"Sorry about that, I just have a few more questions if you don't mind."

"No, of course not, I'd be glad to tell you what you need to know." She scooted back in her chair and got ready to sell herself to the best of her ability.

"I'm going to ask questions that I would know if I had read your application or if I could see you – so bear with me. How old are you?"

Easy enough. "I'm twenty seven."

"Where did you grow up?"

Okay, this topic was not so comfortable. "I grew up in Beaumont. My grandmother raised me. She passed away while I was in college. I've been on my own ever since." What she didn't say was that her mother had left her at her grandparent's house when she was two days old and she hadn't seen her mother but a handful of times in her life. Presley didn't know where her mother was living, nor did she even know her father's name.

"I know Beaumont well. I'm originally from Louisiana. Texas is my adopted home. Are you married?"

He couldn't see, but Presley blushed. "No, I don't think marriage is in my future."

"Famous last words, but I have no plans to enter the bonds of holy matrimony, either." Before Presley could mourn the idea that he didn't want to marry, he moved on to even more precarious ground. "Where did you go to school?"

Careful, Presley, she admonished herself. "I went to The University of Texas, on scholarship."

"I went to Tulane, but I did graduate work at UT. What did you study?"

"Pre-law." That was the truth, not the whole truth – but close.

"Ah, that explains it. I advise that you get back in school and pass the bar." Before she could attempt to explain her circumstances, he continued. "Do you think you would like to work here with me? We'll go through Workforce for now, to see how it goes. It would be on a trial basis to see if we're a good fit, of course."

A good fit? "Of course." Now, he had given her an image. She was bent over the desk and he was showing her what a 'good fit' they were together. Great Scot! She was almost squirming with arousal. Looking down, she noticed her nipples were big and swollen. Presley crossed her arms over her breasts and couldn't help but glance behind her to make sure they were alone. It would be her luck if there were hidden cameras and someone was monitoring her lust factor for the hot boss. "If you give me a chance, I'll work very hard for you."

In spite of her momentary lapse of lust, she knew she wanted to work here. They had the reputation of taking on meaningful cases and doing their part to end injustice in the world.

"All right – good. Chloe's recommendation of you and your obvious knowledge is good enough for me. When can you start?"

"Now?" she offered.

"Excellent. Your desk is right behind you and I think Chloe left you all the instructions you'll need to get started."

Presley was happier than she had been in a long time.

In the Caymans

"Would you take me snorkeling?"

Libby lay on a large beach towel. She was wearing a red two piece with fluttery sheer panels that hung down from an otherwise regular bikini top. It was floaty in all the right places, but still managed to show off her sexy maternity curves. Aron lay by her, and was spending a lot of time kissing her stomach. "Snorkeling? Do you think that's wise, Pregnant Lady?"

"I checked with the doctor. He said watching the pretty fish would probably reduce my stress."

"I have an idea how to reduce your stress," he nuzzled the swell of her breast.

"And you're very good at it, too." Libby flounced over to face him. "It would be fun. Please?"

"Let's think about this," Aron tried to reason with her. "Motorcycles, horses – bars – does any of this adventure sound familiar?"

"Yes, I know," Libby persisted. "I have a tendency to get into trouble, but this is our honeymoon and being with you is the most exciting thing in the world – but I would love to do something extreme." She made a little face that emphasized her request.

Aron blew on her stomach. "You know I don't swim very well. Tubing down the Guadalupe and soaking in the stock tank hasn't gone a long way to preparing me for the deep blue sea."

"I'll make it worth your while," she whispered in his ears, telling him of untold bedroom delights "Avery taught me that move. She learned it in the brothel."

Aron laughed, he couldn't help it. He loved Libby McCoy more than anything in the world. "How can I tell you 'no' about anything?"

She threw her arms around his neck and hugged him. "I love you."

"I love you, too. I'll check into renting the gear."

"Good. Thank you. You've made me happy."

"That's my job, baby. Whatever it takes."

Presley spent an hour or so reading through Chloe's notes and familiarizing herself with the files. This wouldn't be too hard. She could handle it. More than anything, she would love to delve in and really practice law. But this would be close. It would all depend on how much leeway and responsibility Zane would grant her.

"Presley would you like a cup of coffee?"

His question coming out of the blue made her jump. "I'm sorry," she rose. "I'll get it for you."

"No, no," sit back down. "I wasn't hinting. This coffeepot is a dream. I can put in a little K-cup, fit my mug under the spout, push a button and there you go." He showed her how it was done. "What do you take in yours?"

"Two sugars and a cream." Deftly, he prepared it for her.

"You like it sweet," he smiled. "So do I." Zane set the coffee on her desk – never spilling a drop, then fixed another cup for himself. "Have you been able to make sense of the notes?"

"Yes, I think so." Surprisingly, she had been able to concentrate. Zane's presence was soothing. True, she did glance up at him from time to time when he would move around. There were several instances when she had almost got up to go to his aid, but he proved time and again that he was comfortable in his surroundings.

Her only problem was going to be how to prevent herself from developing a crush on him. Presley's sexual experience was non-existent, she did read erotic romance and watch late night Cinemax. Apparently her libido was healthy and intact, for she kept having these erotic visions of the two of them wrapped in one another's arms. It was strange, she had never been this ultra-aware of a man before. Right now, she was picturing herself on her knees in front of him, her fingers tugging at the zipper of his pants. Presley licked her lips.

Zane walked around the desk and sat down in front of her. She loved how his pants molded to the muscles in his thighs – Lord, he was sexy. He handed her his small recorder and she forced herself to pay attention to business.

"Here are some notes I made. I'd appreciate you taking care of these things for me. If you don't come across related items in Chloe's files, feel free to ask me anything. Okay?"

"I'll be glad to, Zane."

A slight tap at the door drew their attention. "Hello, I've come by to meet the new temporary employee."

"Come in Renee," Zane stood. Presley could tell that he was, inherently, a gentleman. The woman approaching them was older, but elegant and sophisticated – beautiful. When she got close enough to look Presley in the face, Renee got an odd, sour expression. "Oh, my," she didn't even try and hide her reaction. "What happened to your . . ." The other woman caught herself, cutting the question off in midstream. "I mean, I'm Renee Wallace. I am Mr. Barclay's secretary."

Presley stood out of respect. She held out her hand, but the other woman was staring at Presley's face so intently that she missed the gesture of greeting, forcing Presley to slowly drop her arm.

"It is a pleasure to meet you, Ms. Wallace. I'm sure I'll enjoy working with you." It was a shame that she doubted her own words, but she had seen that expression before – it was distaste.

As the stately lady turned to talk to Zane, Presley touched her lip. The lower one was full and normal, but the top one was cleft. There was a vertical mark that ran from the center of her lip up towards her nose. It wasn't as bad as it used to be, she had received corrective surgery when she was young, but medical procedures today were much more successful at eradicating a cleft than they were when she had the operation. Someday maybe, she could have plastic surgery. But until then, she just had to live with it.

"Is this a party?"

"Adam, join us. Presley, this is my partner, Adam Barclay. Adam this is Chloe's choice of who will be taking care of me, Miss Presley Love."

Meeting new people was never fun for Presley, and she met Adam's eyes, hesitantly. But all she saw was a warm smile on a handsome, friendly face.

"Miss Love, welcome. How pretty you look in that yellow. You're like a ray of sunshine this morning."

Presley flushed, Renee frowned and Zane chuckled. "And they say I'm a smooth talker."

"Can I talk to you a minute about the Taylor case?" Adam addressed Zane.

"Yes, I have a few ideas to pass by you."

"Great, hold on a second, I'll be right with you."

Adam spoke quietly with Renee about another case and she left the room before he began to confer with Saucier. Presley took a deep breath and sat back down. As the men spoke quietly, she listened to Zane's notes on the recorder. His deep sexy voice sent shivers of goosebumps over her arms. Shaking off her response to him, she concentrated and jotted down a few reminders.

The conference at Eagle Canyon was familiar. Chloe had left extensive notes on what needed to be done. Apparently, Zane was the main speaker. Quickly, she called up the resort's website and was captivated by the beautiful photos. When she went to their calendar page, Zane's photo was there and a blurb about the conference. God, he was so photogenic! She couldn't help but glance over to where the two lawyers were intently discussing the sad case of the missing woman, Laney Taylor.

"The more I find out about what happened to Laney, the madder I get." Adam paced in front of Zane. "She was tiny and sweet. Someone should have been watching over her. Hell, I would give anything if I had met her nine months ago."

Zane heard the pain in his partner's voice. He was serious. "Maybe you shouldn't be the one to work on this case. It sounds like you've let your emotions get involved."

"No, I'm exactly who should be working on this case – I care."

"You know what the DA said, and he's right, without a body, we're going to have our work cut out for us. It will be up to us to prove she's dead."

Adam closed his eyes, pained at the thought of that son of a bitch maybe beating Laney to death. "Let's start with what we know; it's true that we don't have a case for murder, but we might have a case for abuse. When the sister returned from Mainland China, she was shocked at what the neighbors said who had lived around her sister. Kendall had kept Laney isolated. He had spread the word that she was ill and mentally unstable. Shelly categorically denies this. Laney had married this man without Shelly ever having met him and all communication with her had ceased months ago. She's convinced her sister was abused and most likely murdered and is willing to file a civil suit in order to gain access to what may very well be the crime site. I think the best place to start is with the evidence the police already have."

"What do you mean?"

"I've done some research. Laney came to the police for help not too long ago and Sergeant Rodriguez took pictures and an in-depth video statement. Laney gave her dates and a plethora of details. I'm sad to say that the police did nothing, Kendall had laid the groundwork for just such a time and had told the police that Laney was incompetent and schizophrenic and if she were ever to come in with a wild tale of abuse, they needed to call him immediately and he would take her and return her to safety. Kendall had friends in high places. The whole thing makes me sick.

After they turned Laney back over to Kendall – and they did so with her begging and crying for help – she was never seen again. Now, according to Kendall she has escaped again and no one knows where she has gone. But Shelly is adamant that if Laney were alive, she would contact her. The approach we are going to use is some deeds and coin collections that Laney was holding for Shelly. She wants them back, but that's not all she wants. We need evidence of what happened to Laney Taylor. Kendall needs to be brought to justice, one way or the other."

"Presley!" Zane called out. "Call the Private Investigator, Marcus O'Neil, and tell him we need a meeting with him ASAP, around two p.m., if possible. Did you already call the D. A.?"

"Yes sir, I did." Presley assured him.

"Good. Marcus needs to question the neighbors and we need to find out everything we can on Kendall." Looking at Adam sadly, he added. "We also need to hear the story in Laney's own words, so call the police chief."

Presley scrolled through the online rolodex and found the PI's phone number and quickly placed the call, confirming Zane's choice of time. Neither Adam nor Zane were hiding their concern and all Presley could think about was the poor girl and what she must have suffered. It made the verbal bullying and discrimination she had received to be of little to no consequence.

"They think you're dead, bitch." Raymond, or Rayford as he was known now, chunked two bottled waters down the hole.

Laney dodged them. "Let me out, please Ray? I won't tell anyone. Please?" she begged.

"Nope," the big burly man was adamant. "You sealed your fate the date you went to the police. Now you're gonna die in this little grave I've fixed for you. How long have you been down there?"

She didn't bother to answer him. All she could do was stare at the small circle of light and fresh air above. "Please don't close the hole, no one can hear me. I can't stand to be buried alive!" Panic made her whole body shake. Kendall had made her life a living hell for almost nine months. She should have run away when she had the chance instead of going to the police. What must Shelly be thinking?

"Oh, I'm taking no chances on you getting out slut." He poked a couple of twinkies and some cheese crackers in the hole. "Good nutrition isn't that important to you now, is it?" A snort of laughter echoed down to where she sat in the darkness. The creak of heavy earth on top of her made her want to scream and never quit screaming. Was this how she was going to die?

The last thing she remembered was being chained to the kitchen table. Her life had grown so small, living had become a burden. All she could do was creep as far as her chain would allow, praying to be invisible. As she had sat and eaten a piece of white bread and ketchup, Laney had felt a pinprick on her neck. Kendall had drugged her, knocked her out and when she had come to, she had found herself in this hell-hole.

Laney's skin crawled, there were things in here with her – earthworms and other unspeakable horrors. Her tormentor had pushed her into an old tank that someone had planted in the back yard to serve as a survival bunker. There was no floor and no seats, she was sitting on bare earth with nowhere to use the bathroom but over in the corner near the back. With her bare hands, she had dug holes to hold her waste, but the smell was being to permeate her tiny cage. Claustrophobia was also beginning to set in. Laney had screamed and cried, but no one came. "Why don't you just kill me, please? Just shoot me. Wouldn't that be more merciful?"

She looked up, Kendall's face almost blocked all light. "I'm not interested in mercy, Laney. Letting you die will be much more fun. You aren't the first you know, I've done this before. I know just how long you can stay down there before you go mad."

"Oh, God," she prayed. "Have mercy, O God."

Laney prayed for a miracle.

The day passed quickly. Presley ate lunch at her desk and made herself at home with the work. Periodically Zane would make a comment or ask a question. Whatever he asked for, she was able to provide. A couple of times Presley wanted to give him more than he asked for – to put her education to good use – but she didn't feel that comfortable, yet.

She had been bad during lunch. He had gone out with Rex, presumably to the kitchen area while she ate the peanut butter and jelly sandwich she had slipped into her desk drawer. Work Force temp jobs didn't give her enough money for much more than the bare necessities.

The lunch hour was only half over when Zane had come back in and told her he was going to take a power nap in the side room. As he walked by her with his coat off, she was treated to a view of his tight rear end and the most muscled-up biceps she had ever seen. Presley's imagination went into overdrive. After a few moments, she couldn't resist – she followed him, slipping to the back, tiptoeing ever so quietly – just to watch him sleep.

Maybe it was because she had never been privileged to date, or maybe it was because Zane had such a knight-in-shining-armor reputation, or maybe it was because he looked like a bulked up Christian Bale – whatever the reason - all Presley could do was fantasize what it would be like to touch him. Before she could stop it, her hand reached out and if he hadn't shifted and turned over, she would have caressed his hair. Taking a deep breath and closing her eyes, she drew her hand back and stood as still as a deer hiding in the woods. He had loosened his tie and crossed his arms. The muscles of his arms were so big that they were clearly outlined and visible through the crisp cotton. Her mouth watered.

Presley pressed her knees together, recognizing the not-so-familiar ache that gazing at him was having on her pussy. What she wouldn't give to feel the rough five o'clock shadow of his beard rasp over her skin. She absolutely shivered with delight. Letting her eyes rove down his body, she took all of him in. His legs were long and well-developed and – oh my goodness! -if she wasn't mistaken, there was a definite bulge in his pants. Leaning over, she got a better look. Yea, he was hard. And as she stared at it, his cock seemed to grow even larger.

Damn! Zane didn't need sight to know Presley Love was standing over him, watching him sleep – supposedly. He wanted to smile. She seemed so cute. If he didn't find out what she looked like soon, he was going to go mad. He wondered if she tasted as sweet as she smelled. Her perfume had been making him hard all day. It was sweet and innocent and reminded him of sunshine and spring rain.

She was still there – watching. He didn't feel creeped out in the least, because over the lilting scent of her perfume, he could smell her arousal. Well, well. Little Miss Presley Love was warm for his form!

She moved! He could hear the faint rustle of her clothes and the air near his cheek vibrated. It seemed as if the very cells of his body reached out to her – but she drew her hand back with a tiny, sexy gasp.

And that was when he started to get hard. Hey – he was a guy. What did you expect? To give his Little Miss a thrill, he stretched and turned on his back so she could get an eyeful.

Oh my goodness! He was huge! Presley's jaw dropped as she gazed at the ridge of his erection under the tailored slacks. A sizzle arced its way through her girl parts and Presley wheeled on her heels and escaped before she revealed herself. Settling herself at her desk, she pressed her palms to her cheeks and smiled. This was one job perk she had never anticipated.

Despite his nap-time visitor, he had dropped off to sleep and he felt damn good. Back at his desk, Zane sat and listened to Presley talk on the phone. Her voice was perfect. It was part soft/part husky and when she got excited there was the slightest hint of a lisp with her s's. It wasn't annoying at all – it was sexy as hell. Now was the time to find out what she looked like – his curiosity was getting the best of him. Of course the easiest thing would be to ask someone like Sherwood or Adam, but he decided to ask her. It was always interesting to know what a person thought of themselves. "Presley, I need some help."

"Sure, of course." He heard her get up and walk across the room toward him. "What can I do for you?"

"I want you to tell me what you look like. I need an image in my head."

Presley froze. Oh, no. Crap. Just the thought of telling Zane what she looked like sent her into a tailspin. "There's not much to tell." Yeah, like that was going to satisfy him.

"I lost my sight in 2007, do you look like any movie star or singer that I would know?"

"No, not hardly," that was easy. Presley was glad he couldn't see her because she was tensed up like a mouse hiding from a hawk. He, on the other hand, was sitting with his feet propped up on his desk looking like a sexy sultan on a harem holiday.

"I have good height and depth perception, so from the sound of your voice, you can't be over five-foot-five."

"I'm five-four and I weigh about a hundred twelve pounds." Perhaps if she volunteered some information, he would be satisfied and let it go.

"What color is your hair?"

"Brown."

"Like a fawn or like rich dark chocolate?"

"Brown like dirt."

Zane laughed. "You aren't being very cooperative."

"Okay, potting soil."

"I bet its beautiful potting soil. How long?" Zane could hear the soles of her shoes squeak as she moved. "You are looking over your shoulder, aren't you?"

Presley got amused. "Yeah, I wanted to be accurate. It comes to the top of my bottom."

Zane loved it. "The top of your bottom? Can I feel?"

"Sure."

Zane held out his hand, hoping to be met with the curvature of a firm female tush, only to grasp a long silky lock as she laid it in his palm. "Hmmm, nice – not what I was expecting, but nice."

"What were you expecting?"

"Nevermind. I like long hair. What color are your eyes?"

"Green."

"Grass or moss?"

"Forest."

"Okay." He wanted to ask for more detail, but he didn't want to push it. "Thank you, Presley. I'll fill in the other details with my imagination."

"That's good." His imagination would beat her reality any day.

"What did you find out about the conference?" Zane knew he should have given her more specifics about what he needed to know, but that was his fault. Any additional information he required, they could get later.

"Quite a bit, actually; they have over two hundred attendees pre-registered. And I'm sure you realize the predominant theme is 'green issues'. There are four other speakers, but you are the main attraction," a teasing tone entered her voice. It wasn't lost on Zane.

"Who is my opening act? Do you know?"

"Honey Ross, the District Attorney. She is doing a presentation on tort reform."

"Boring," he gave his verdict.

"That might be, but her picture was on the site and you would think she's hot."

Zane laughed out loud. "Really?"

"Yea, she's blonde and tall and stacked," Presley knew what the ideal woman looked like, and it wasn't her by any stretch of the imagination.

"Hmmm, I hate to tell you this, but I prefer pintsize brunettes with big green eyes."

His response made Presley smile. He couldn't see it, but he had made her happy. She didn't comment, but it was hard not to. "I also checked on their facilities for the conference. If we do PowerPoint presentations, they can handle those and there is an onsite printing service for any last minute changes we might have to the handouts or brochures."

"I'm impressed," he said, and he was.

"Also, I have asked for an itinerary and recommendations for side trips and things to do, especially for any spouses that might be coming to the conference."

Damn – she was going to work out perfectly. The only problem was, Zane could feel an attraction to her growing quickly. He wondered how she felt about office romances? "I hope you realize that I'll need you to go with me."

"Yes, Mr. Saucier," he swore he could hear her smile.

"The car is ready, Mr. Zane." Sherwood stood at the office door, fully expecting to be told to come back later.

"Come in, Sherwood. I won't be but a few more minutes." He turned to Presley. "Do you need a ride home?"

"No, I came on the bus. It goes right by my apartment, but thank you."

"If you're sure," he'd like to insist they take her home, but he didn't. "I think today went well and as far as I'm concerned – you're hired. I'll call the Temp agency tomorrow and book you for a month. At the end of that time, if we're both still satisfied, perhaps you'd like to join the family."

Presley tried not to stare at her handsome boss in front of his chauffeur. His words were normal, but they seemed to have a double meaning. 'Both still satisfied' and 'join the family' were odd ways of saying he might want to hire her full time, but she got his gist. Zane Saucier was undeniably attractive – big, strong, gorgeous and, most importantly, sweet. "I think I will be very happy here."

"Good, it's settled." He walked her to the door.

Presley gave Rex a pat in passing, wishing she could touch Zane instead. His driver gave her a kind smile, and Presley's own smile dipped. Zane couldn't see her – but he could.

"Goodnight, I'll see all of you tomorrow."

When her footfalls had faded, Zane turned to Sherwood. "So, what do you think, Sherwood? I always value your opinion."

Sherwood hesitated. "About what, Sir?"

"About my new employee. What does she look like?"

Sherwood didn't say anything, at first. He started to speak, "Well," then stopped. Something told him that Miss Presley was a special lady. He had seen the way she looked at Mr. Zane and Sherwood had hopes that someone would come into his life and love him like he needed to be loved. "I think she's lovely, Mr. Zane. Just lovely. But you knew that, for you do not see as I see. While I am lured into judging only from outward appearances, you have a unique perspective. By listening to her words, knowing how she reacts to people and situations, you are privileged indeed. You are privileged to look upon her heart."

Chapter Two

Sherwood's answer wasn't exactly what he wanted to hear. Yes, he had good instincts about people, but that didn't make up for not being able to look upon their face or their body. 'Just lovely.' That wasn't much of an answer. Zane wanted to know more, but he didn't ask. Nobody would give the blind guy a break. That was fine – he was used to making his own breaks, or taking advantage of those that came his way.

The two men and the black lab made their way to the car that was housed in the parking garage adjacent to the Littlefield Building. Saucier and Barclay was fortunate to be located in the heart of downtown Austin at the corner of Congress and Sixth Street in the very building where former President Lyndon Baines Johnson had his offices when he was state director of the National Youth Administration. LBJ had only been twenty six years old, but he had impressed the first lady herself. Eleanor Roosevelt had visited Johnson to tell him what an effective job he was doing.

"How's the deck coming along?" Zane knew Sherwood was adding on to his house and he knew why. One of these days, he'd get either Sherwood or Rachel to admit their courtship, but until then he would pretend he was in the dark. The thought made him smile. He might be blind, but he was never in the dark.

"Just fine, sir, the contractor is using redwood. I'm thinking of getting me one of those hot tubs." Sherwood's home was located on Whispering Pines land and Zane enjoyed having him close.

"Nice. I wouldn't mind having one of those myself."

"I think you ought to, Mr. Zane. They come in handy when you're trying to impress the ladies." Sherwood cleared his throat as if expecting an argument.

"Is that right? I thought maybe you were getting one because of your arthritis." He enjoyed sparring with Sherwood, but he needed to find a way to let them know he approved of their relationship. Losing Chloe was enough, he didn't intend for Sherwood and Rachel to leave him. They could marry if they wanted to, but there was no reason they couldn't stay and take care of him.

The drive from Austin to Bastrop was never very long. Zane enjoyed the time in the car. He enjoyed listening to Sherwood's choice of music – Lyle Lovett, Willie Nelson and Waylon Jennings were usually featured. All of them spent a lot of time in Austin, which is considered to be the live music capital of the world.

He could tell when they turned off I35. Laying his head back on the seat, he wondered about Presley. She said she wasn't married, and didn't think she ever would. What did that mean? Marriage wasn't necessary for a relationship. Did she have a man? Did she like to dance? She was smart, that intrigued him. There were many things he wanted to know about her, and tomorrow seemed like a good day to start.

"Looks like Frank is waiting to talk to you."

"Yes, he's here to update me on the preparations for the auction. Since this is the first one Whispering Pines has hosted, I want it to be successful." Zane raised registered Beefmaster cattle and ranchers from all over the world were interested in the Warrior's bloodline. He and the McCoys had worked hard to develop a reputation for championship quality breeders. "Come on, Rex." Man and dog made their way up to the porch. Both were glad to be home. The night air was crisp and Zane could smell hay and a leftover waft of smoke. Frank indulged in an occasional cigar.

"Evening, Zane."

"Frank, it's a pleasure. Have you been waiting long?"

"Just a bit, but I've been enjoying sitting on your front porch with my feet propped up on the railings. That mama cat of yours has had her kittens up here and they've been practicing war games. I was part of their obstacle course."

"Sorry about that. They tend to take a person in. Are they gone?"

"Yea, she led them back to the barn a while ago. It looked like a parade."

"Let's go in and have a drink. I want to hear all the details about tomorrow." Zane held the door open for his foreman. "How's Shalimar?"

"She's been waiting for you. I'll swear she can tell time. About six o'clock she starts staring down the road where your car will come from and she doesn't move until she sees it. Right now, she's looking up here at us. You have spoiled that animal."

"That's the plan. She knows the routine. I spend time with her every night." As their boots echoed on the hard wood floor, Frank pulled off his coat and hung it on the hall tree. The tip-tap of Rachel's heels announced her presence.

"Good evening, Mr. Saucier, Mr. Frank. May I get you a drink? I also have some fresh apple cake right from the oven."

"Sounds wonderful, Rachel. I'll take some cognac. How about you Frank?"

"I'd rather have a Shiner beer, boss. But I'll take some cake."

"Plebian. But that does sound good. Make it two beers Rachel, and three pieces of cake. Rex likes cake."

They made their way to the big leather couch in front of the fireplace. A warm inviting wave of heat greeted them. Zane could hear the crackle and hiss of flames eating the oak. "Sit down, Frank. Are we all set for this weekend?"

"Yes sir, we are. With the McCoy's offerings, we have thirty bulls and forty cows and plenty of embryo flushes and straws of semen. It's going to be quite an event. The invitations you sent out garnered about a hundred RSVP's "

"Excellent, and is the meal coming together?"

"Well, the McCoy's women commandeered that. You know how they love to cook and party. Your sister-in-law is in the middle of it, too. She's representing your interest quite well. If you ever bring a wife home, she'll probably step back, but I think she enjoys being the lady of the manor."

"Lilibet is a great organizer. And there's no wife on the horizon. I'm a confirmed bachelor and loving it."

"I don't blame you a bit."

Zane heard Rachel set down a tray on the marble coffee table. "Here you go, if you need anything else just call me. I'm giving Rex his cake on a paper plate on the floor."

"Thank you, Rachel." In a few seconds, he could hear Rex enjoying his treat. Carefully, he found one of the cold cans of beer and popped the top. Taking a sip, he found the plate with the cake. Eating in front of people didn't bother him anymore, he just enjoyed his food. "This is good."

"Shore is. I've got some extra hands coming in Friday to handle the heli-pad traffic and the parking lot. And as Aron suggested, I'll have a welcome area set up at the gate to greet the ones who drive in for the auction. The first thing they'll be met with when they enter Whispering Pines will be their choice of a cocktail."

Zane laughed. "I thought that was a little over the top, but he says that's the way it's done at these blue-blood cattle auctions."

"Should be some shin-dig, that's for sure."

"Is the pavilion all set up?" Whispering Pines was a beautiful ranch with rolling green hills dotted with big oaks and stately pines. A stone pavilion sat behind the main barn alongside one of the three ponds that decorated the landscape. Big pecan trees spread their branches and Zane could remember how proud he would be to see the big bulls lounging underneath them like kings surveying their domain.

"We don't like much, there won't be any problems finishing by Thursday night. Henry said it beat all he'd ever seen. He's been to cattle auctions all of his life, but this one was the first where the cattle would enter the arena walking on a damned red carpet."

Zane heard Frank drain the last drop from his can. "Want another beer?"

"No, I'm good."

"These cattle aren't like the ones destined for the meat market. Some of those bulls will sell for over a hundred thousand dollars each."

"I can understand that, look at how much each straw of semen sells for. And when you buy the bull – you buy the whole load, so to speak."

"May I get you gentlemen anything else?" It was Rachel. Zane was sure it was time for her to go home – to Sherwood.

"No, thank you, Rachel. You have a good evening. I'll put the tray up." He heard her retreat to the kitchen and knew she'd let herself out the back.

They were quiet for a few moments, enjoying their beer and cake. Then Frank cleared his throat. "Boss, I hate to tell you this, but I'm worried about something."

"What about?" Immediately Zane was concerned.

"Yesterday, one of the younger hands found two cows had miscarried."

Hell. "Miscarried? Which ones?"

"They weren't in the registered herd, it was the Holsteins."

The big black and white breed was usually kept as dairy cattle, but Zane used the females as surrogate mothers for the registered Beefmaster embryos. "Tell me exactly what happened." Losing a calf was always something to be dreaded, but a miscarriage could mean several things – several bad things."

"He said they were moving them up to the north pasture. We plan on planting some alfalfa in the section next to the woods and two of them lagged behind and when he went to check, he found the dead calves. They were nowhere near term."

"Damn. Did you notice any other symptoms? Were their joints swollen? How about the bulls? Did you get a look at their testicles? Sometimes they swell." Zane was talking fast. If his herd was infected with brucellosis, they would all have to be destroyed – and it was a determination that would have to be made fast. Their purebred herd was in danger of exposure, and McCoy cattle was scheduled to be brought over the day after tomorrow for the auction. There was no way he could let his neighbor's purebred stock be exposed to Brucellosis.

"I wish you'd come see for yourself. . . "Frank's voice trailed off.

Zane couldn't come see.

"Boss, I'm sorry . . . "

"Don't be. I wish I could look for myself." He pulled his cell out of his pocket and dialed a number. Frank waited patiently. "Casey, I know it's late, and I hate like the devil to bother you. But I have an emergency. Two cows have dropped calves prematurely, and I have to rule out brucellosis – pronto." He paused while Casey spoke. "Great. I appreciate it. Frank will meet you down by the barn." Zane closed the cell, put it back in his pocket and sighed. "Quarantine the herd and get the two mama cows tied up. The vet will be here within the hour. He has a lab in his office, so he can tell us something pretty quick. I'll change clothes and be out there in a bit. I think I'll call the McCoy's. They deserve to know. "

"We've already separated them, and got the two females culled out to one side." Frank stood up. "I just didn't know who you'd want me to call. You know how these things can set off a panic in the community. Bruscellosis is highly contagious. I've known of whole counties losing their herds."

"Casey, won't set off any alarms prematurely. He'll find something out quickly." Standing, he dry-scrubbed his face, clearly worried. "I'll walk out with you. I want to check on the horses."

"You want me to do it? You're all dressed up in your suit."

"No, suits can be cleaned." Zane accompanied his foreman to the truck and stood as he listened to it drive away crunching gravel as it left. "Shit, what a mess. Come on Rex, let's go." As he made his way to the barn, he called Jacob. The second eldest McCoy was levelheaded and had been through too much upheaval in his life to get panicked over something like this. As he shared the concern, he wasn't surprised that Jacob took it in stride. "Let's hope this is something else that's easily fixed."

The McCoys were good neighbors and clients. Six brothers who had lost their parents too early, they had banded together and made Tebow ranch a force to be reckoned with. Just like any other family, they had their ups and downs, but they stuck together and Zane was proud to call them friends.

Tonight he needed to be with the horses, he needed the calming effect they had on him. Maybe it was time to try and brush Shalimar. Zane wondered if she would be able to stand still for it. Rachel kept him a sack of carrots and apples hanging on the tack room door and when he would delve into it, there would be whinnies and nickers echoing up and down the stable. Filling his pockets with crunchy snacks, he got the curry comb from the shelf and put it in his back pocket.

Zane made his rounds speaking to Onyx and Cheyenne, telling the big appaloosa they would greet the dawn together tomorrow. Two golden Palominos, Sundance and Starbuck were eager to have their turn at some petting; so he spent a few minutes rubbing noses and scratching ears. He couldn't see, of course, but he knew Shalimar stood at the end, watching him – and waiting. Zane didn't keep her waiting long. He could feel her bulk and warmth before he drew near. Even though they had shared many hours together, she still shivered when he touched her. He kept his hand on her jaw while she took an apple from his fingers. "Will you let me comb you girl?" After she had consumed the fruit, he took the comb out and unlocked the stall door, entering the small space with the large horse.

Zane knew he was at a disadvantage, he had to rely on his sense of hearing and perception of her mood and movements to keep from being stepped on, but the progress he had made was too important to let fear hamper him. Placing a hand on her shoulder, he whispered to her and began brushing her coat lightly, taking the scarred ridges into consideration. "Does that feel good? Do you itch?"

To his surprise, she answered him with a low satisfied neigh. Trust. She was rewarding him with her trust. He smiled. There was no better feeling in the world than knowing you had made a difference for good in the life of another. Gradually as he soothed the horse, Zane let his worries slip away, too. Everything would be all right, he just had to have faith.

Presley undressed, it would feel good to get on some comfortable clothes. She could stand in one spot in her bathroom and literally reach anything. Her apartment was small, but her bathroom was tiny. Scrimping every nickel, she had decorated it with garage sale finds and thrift store merchandise. Still, it felt like home and she was grateful for what she had.

Face it – she was in a good mood. Today had been a good day. All of a sudden the future seemed like a brighter place. Practicing law had seemed so out of reach, but now she could sense that Zane would let her spread her wings – maybe not as a full-fledged lawyer, but he would listen to her suggestions. It would be a unique experience to be able to put her knowledge of the law to work.

Stripping her plain white cotton underwear off, she placed them in the dirty clothes hamper. Tonight, a bath sounded heavenly. She turned on the water and dumped a couple of tablespoons of salts under the tap. Suds and bubbles began to grow in the water. Presley walked to the sink and brushed her teeth while the tub filled. Smiling around her toothbrush, she thought about Zane. Now she had something to look forward to – or someone. Nothing could come of it, but there was no harm in enjoying herself where she could. Thoughts of how he looked spread out on the couch for his nap filled her mind. Now, that was fantasy material.

Pinning her hair on top of her head before she got in the tub, she looked at the top of her head in the mirror. It was very rare that she looked directly at her reflection; it was something she just didn't do. Presley knew how she looked and reminding herself daily of the reality was something she chose to avoid. In college she had taken a psychology course that had dealt with people like her. She knew it wasn't uncommon for women, especially, to have a mental image of themselves that had little to do with how the rest of the world perceived them.

In Presley's heart, she was pretty. In Presley's heart, her mouth was normal and her upper lip was as smooth and perfect as the bottom one. When Presley thought of herself, she was a perfect match for Zane. It was all in her mind, but if she didn't look in the mirror – she could prolong the charade just a little longer. And when she lay down at night, in the dark, she dreamed of a man who would look at her and see Presley as she saw herself, not as the mirror reflected.

So she turned from the telling glass, and stepped into the tub. The warm silky water felt good against her skin. Sinking down, she rested her head against the porcelain. "Would you like to come in for coffee, Zane?" she spoke out loud in an inviting, seductive (maybe) voice. Did people actually drink coffee this late at night? Or did coffee stand for something else entirely? Probably, or it would in her book. Squeezing a little bath gel on her fingers, she coated her arms and massaged the aching muscles. She didn't know why she was so sore, unless it was because she had been so tense all day.

"Kiss you? Yes, please I'd love a kiss." She puckered her lips and kissed the air. Countless times she had fantasized about kissing a special man. It must be heavenly. Presley had never been kissed; she didn't expect she ever would be. A few times men had approached her because they liked the way she looked from the back or the side, but when they got a good look at her face, they always made some excuse and told her they had thought she was someone else or they said something inane like asking her for the time.

None of that stopped her from wishing and dreaming, however. With automatic thoroughness, she washed herself. Maybe warm milk would help her relax - -or an orgasm. Presley didn't often gift herself with self-induced pleasure. Somehow it just made her loneliness more pronounced. But she had never had Zane to fantasize about before. He was so Greek-god handsome. She closed her eyes and pictured him – when he threw back his head and laughed he was cum-worthy. His smile was contagious and his physique was straight out of a magazine.

Running her hands over her body, she imagined what Zane would look like naked. "Is it warm in here? Can I help you off with your shirt?" Giggling, Presley had to admit that sounded dumb. Surely if she ever got a chance with a guy like Zane she could think of something better to say than that.

Cupping her breasts, she squeezed the round globes, rubbing her thumbs over the nipples. Her breasts weren't very big, just a B cup, but they were very sensitive. What would it feel like if he touched them – or kissed them? Just the thought of Zane's mouth on her breasts made her shiver with pleasure. He would lick the nipple, running his tongue around it. And she would hold his head to her breast and rub his wide shoulders while he sucked. "Oh, that feels so good," she moaned.

Easing down in the tub, Presley spread her legs and let her fingers slide down her stomach and over her mound. Little dollops of sudsy bubbles decorated her skin. With a tentative touch, she rubbed her clit. How incredible it would be for Zane to make her feel this way. But as much as she longed for him to make love to her, what she dreamed of most was being allowed to touch him. Even fully clothed, she could tell his body would be incredible. Twice, she had bought a magazine with naked guys in it. Her curiosity just got the better of her. In fact she still had them hidden in her closet. But as far as she could tell, none of the men even came close to being as handsome as Zane.

With fast movements of her fingers, Presley petted her pussy. Arching her hips, she groaned out loud. "Zane!" If he were here, she'd climb in his lap and run her palms over his shoulders and chest. His back would be strong and he'd pick her up and let her wrap her legs around his waist.

Yea, she had fantasies. What would his manhood look like? His cock. The thought made her smile. "Cock," she said the word out loud. It sounded wonderfully naughty. What would he look like? She had some idea of its size by what she had seen today, but what would the head look like? How would he taste? "Hmmmm," she pushed her finger into her sheathe as she imagined Zane – thick and hard and long – pushing up deep inside of her. "Yes! Zane!" she panted as her hips jerked and she splashed water over the side of the tub.

As she came down from the orgasmic high, Presley smiled, knowing that it would be hard to look at Zane tomorrow without blushing. Then she remembered he was blind – God, she had forgotten! He was so self-assured and so sexy that he seemed perfect to her. And he was perfect – if God would give her a chance with a man like Zane, she would make him feel like the most loved man in the history of the world.

Despite her doubts, Presley prayed for a miracle.

Who knows? It could happen.

Thank God! The vet was almost sure the culprit was contaminated feed instead of brucellosis. A shipment of bad range cubes was most likely to blame, and only the Holsteins had eaten any. Losing a few calves was bad enough, but at least he wouldn't lose his whole operation or pass on the unfortunate circumstances to anybody else's cattle. Casey was still waiting on the test results, but there had been other reports of the same symptoms from other ranchers who had purchased the same defective product.

Zane could breathe easier now. But still – he hated the helpless feeling of trying to analyze the situation based on someone else's description. Kneeling down he unfastened Rex's halter. "Let's go to the kitchen and I'll get you a snack. This has been a rough day." Carefully, he felt on the coffee table for the tray. He liked to leave the house fairly straight for Rachel. Picking it up, he moved through his familiar home with slow, even steps. He could hear Rex's toenails clicking on the tile floor behind him.

With practiced moves, he counted the steps into his kitchen. Funny – he couldn't be sure of what it really looked like. He had it redecorated along with everything else when Margaret had walked out of his life. Oh, he knew there was Mexican tile on the floor and the cabinets were made of oak – but the vision of the room he had in his mind might not be close to the reality. What difference did it make?

Lowering the tray to the counter, he felt around and cleared an area for it, scooting over what felt like a loaf of bread and a roll of paper towels. Next, he opened a drawer and located the can opener and moved over to the pantry and found what he hoped was a can of dog food. As long as Rachel put the items in their designated places, he was okay. "I hope this is your food and not a can of baked beans," he teased the hungry animal. Finding Rex's bowl with his foot, he picked it up and dumped the contents of the can in it. "Stinks about right." Setting it down, he patted the big Lab. "You eat; I'm going to take a shower. You can join me in the bedroom when you're through."

Living in a world of perpetual night, he constantly relied on his other senses to make up the difference. Right now, he could feel the downward draft of the air-conditioner; he could smell fresh grapefruit on the counter. Their odor vied with the aroma of Rex's pungent meal. Standing still, he listened for sounds beyond the kitchen. A faint low of a cow and a bark of a coyote was all he could discern. Zane knew he was fortunate in many things, but sometimes he was so lonely, it was almost unbearable. What he wouldn't give for someone to just be with him – to share, to back him up. Fuck! He needed someone to hold tight.

With sure movements, he left the kitchen and let his hand slide down the hall wall. How much different it would be if a woman waited for him in his bed. He could imagine her lying there, anxious. "I'm coming, honey. Warm up my side of the bed and I'll warm you up as soon as I get there," he spoke to no one. What he wanted and what he felt he should have were two different things. The truth was he was hesitant to ask a woman to share his life. But the image of Miss Presley was haunting his thoughts. Chuckling, he remembered she has said her hair was the color of dirt. Now what other woman would give an answer like that? She was sweet and unassuming and he bet she was as pretty as a picture.

Long silky hair, green eyes – his mind couldn't help but strive for an image to go with that husky little voice with the tiny hint of a lisp. Most seeing people didn't realize that blind people who had their sight at one time can still see – in a way. They hear a sound first, like the rush of the water as he turned on the shower faucet. The haunting vision will come from the side and then quickly rush into the mind's eye. Scientific studies have suggested that the brain rewires itself to create visions from sound rather than sight. So, he couldn't help but begin imagining how Presley Love looked. As he featured a curvy body, long legs, a face looking up at him with lust glazed eyes, Zane got hard.

Stripping off his clothes, he ran a hand down his abdomen and over his cock to cup his balls. "Miss Presley, I bet you're fine." Just the thought of tangling his hand in those long strands of hair, wrapping it around his fist and anchoring her still for a kiss had his flaccid cock stiffening with lust. How long had it been? Too long.

With practiced strokes he massaged his cock, using a little soap as a lubricant, he worked it till it was hard and throbbing. "God, I'm so fuckin' hard," he moaned as he rubbed the tender skin up and over the head of his prick in a smooth circular motion. His cock knew what was coming – it was heat, erotic expectation at its best. Zane enjoyed his body, and he had no qualms about giving himself pleasure.

Wrapping his hand around his cock, he slowly jerked it – long smooth strokes, sometimes over the head and sometimes stopping at the base. What would Presley's breasts look like? He had no way of knowing, unless he asked. She could be flat-chested for all he knew – but probably not. With a sexy name like Presley coupled with a bedroom voice like she had, Zane suspected she had a rack to match. As he conjured up images of round, firm, soft tits he felt the pleasure begin rising from the base of his dick. God, how he'd like to suck on her tits, there was nothing like taking a woman's nipple in his mouth and nursing. As he fantasized, he could feel his shaft thicken and the head swell. Damn, it felt good. He could have cum right then – but he wanted the feeling to last – so he backed off, tracing the veins and wondering what color Presley's nipples were. How would they be shaped?

Women's breasts fascinated him. Now that he couldn't see – touch would be paramount. What he would like to do was pull the woman back against him and run his hands up from her waist to cup her tits. He would weigh them in his palms – run his hands over and around them – lifting them, cupping them, learning their shape. Just the thought of fondling Presley's tits, taking her nipples in his fingers and pulling them, tweaking them – milking them – "GOD!" had him back to full strokes. With his other hand he rubbed on his balls, letting his hips pump, feeling his ass tighten. Lord, he needed a woman. He loved to sink his cock into warm, wet pussy – feeling her tight little sheathe stretch to accommodate him.

Zane needed that sensation – that gliding of his glans into a hot, grasping haven. Making a small ring with his thumb and forefinger, he pushed it over the head of his cock, massaging the tip end. "Hmmmm," he gasped, that felt good. He wondered if she liked sex, some women didn't. But when a man found a woman that loved to be loved – God, he had found a treasure.

Presley would lay down for him – offer herself – open her legs and let him see the place that would take him to paradise. His daydream made him smile – yeah, he still thought of himself as 'seeing'. He'd rub the head of his cock up and down her slit, make her moan and beg to be taken. Using both hands, he doubled his pleasure, let the water sluice over his back and shoulders. Still, he toyed with the head, giving himself the illusion of fucking in and out of a snug little pussy and upped the ante by pumping himself, furiously, letting his hips roll with the rhythm. His climax hit him hard – the pleasure and the cum jetting out in long, creamy sprays. Zane groaned, still fisting his cock as it pumped endlessly.

"Presley," he whispered.

Nights spent in total blackness were endless. Even though he kept his curtains open, he never saw a shaft of light. If he slept in, he would feel the change in the temperature as the sun rose, but most of the time he had to rely on an alarm clock. This morning, however, he just couldn't stay in the bed. He had a clock that announced the time at the touch of a button – "five-twelve a.m." Ignoring his morning wood, he promised his Johnson a repeat of last night's performance later, jerked on a pair of jeans and a shirt and went out to greet the day.

Rex didn't need any encouragement, he loved these pre-dawn jaunts. Cheyenne knew what was up too, as Zane entered the barn, he was met with several greetings, but his appaloosa had a distinctive, rumbly neigh. It was a welcoming sound. "You ready to go?" With practiced moves, he put on a saddle and bridle, grabbed his whip and led the animal out into the misty morning.

Not many blind men rode horses by themselves, but not many blind men had a horse like Cheyenne. Cheyenne was a seeing-eye horse. Oh, Zane had bought him and rode him before the accident. And he had given a lot of things up, but not his horse. Kane had found a place in South Carolina that trained horses for the blind. True enough, they usually worked with miniature horses or Shetlands, but Kane and Zane had met with them and shown them how special Cheyenne was and just like they had anticipated, the appaloosa had taken to the life-style like a duck to water.

Horses can see phenomenally well in almost total darkness and Cheyenne's memory was incredible. He already loved Zane and being trained to be on the look-out for danger and avoid obstacles was not a giant leap. At the ranch, Zane had no qualms about taking off with Cheyenne and Rex – he knew he was safe in their hands. Four eyes out of six weren't bad odds. "Let's head down toward the creek," Zane led Cheyenne past the gates, shut them behind him and climbed on. With a gentle pull to the reins they were off. He tipped his hat back, and took a deep breath, enjoying being in the saddle again.

"Woof!" Rex raced ahead, knowing that he was free to be adventurous while the service horse was on the job. A cool north breeze hit Zane in the face and he could smell wood smoke from a nearby chimney. His body moved naturally with the horse, the dip and sways as much a part of him as the rhythm of lovemaking. From the left he could hear the lowing and shuffling of the royalty that awaited the registered auction that would commence at the end of the week. "Narrow miss," he grinned, relieved that none of his animals were infectious with the dreaded disease.

Leaving the pavilion area, he could tell the ground dipped down. He was headed downhill through a thick growth of white clover. The smell was sweet, but the memory it invoked was bitter. The last time he had made love to Margaret was in this field of clover. A choking sensation of wasted dreams clogged his throat. Five years had passed, five years – by this time he had planned on having children. A harsh laugh erupted from his throat and the horse raised his head as if asking for directions. "Easy, boy, everything's okay." Everything was okay. He had a good life. It wasn't a perfect life, but it was all he had.

The lapping and trickling of water told him they were nearing Piney Creek. Cheyenne's hooves clopped over the small rocks that littered the ground on the bank incline. He was just about to get down and stretch his legs and let the horse drink when he heard Rex growl. It wasn't a playful growl. Cheyenne stopped dead still. Even when Zane nudged his knee to move him forward, the Appaloosa stalled. And then he knew why – an eerie, unearthly scream shattered the night. Every hair on Zane's neck stood up. For a split second, he thought he had run into a banshee – but then he heard the snarling, guttural growl of a large pissed-off feline.

Cougar.

Hell! He heard Rex lunge. He heard a splash. The horse reared, but he managed to hang on. "Rex! Rex!" Cheyenne backed up. The big horse was shivering, frantically trying to do what he was trained to do when every reflex he had was telling him to flee. "Rex!" Without hesitation he unwound the whip from where it was attached to the saddle. "Heel, Rex! Come!"

Zane pulled back on the reins, but Cheyenne was adamant. He didn't turn. The service animal could see what the man could not. With powerful moves of his hind legs, the animal lunged backwards. "Rex!" Zane could hear the bodies of the canine colliding with the cougar.

Sounds bombarded his mind – the hard panting of the horse, the frenzied barking and growling of his dog and the hissing, spitting angry snarls of the cougar. "Rex – here!" Cheyenne whirled and almost unseated Zane. Zane pulled him back. "Rex!" A wounded yelp from the dog made cold chills run up and down his spine. Damn! He had done this. He had put them all in danger. How utterly stupid – what was he doing? Two animals who would die for him were the only thing between him and a killer cat. And one of his animals might die. "Rex!" he cried one more time. And then he heard him – an answering bark.

"Heel!" He demanded. Finally, he heard the breathing of the dog near the dancing hooves of the horse. Focusing with everything in him, he listened for any evidence of where the big predator was crouching. It seemed as if an eternity past – and then a sound – a snarl. He drew back his arm, flashed the whip in the air and let it go. "Raarrrr!" The sharp, slash of the leather had connected with cat hide. Immediately he repeated his motion, moving the black snake a few feet to the right and he heard the same zing and the same snarl, and then – silence.

Climbing down from off the horse, he searched for his dog. After a few seconds, Zane found Rex laying a few feet away. "Oh God boy, are you hurt?" Feeling over the lab's body, he felt the slick wetness of blood. There were deep scratches and several bite marks. "Damn" Picking the heavy dog up, he managed to get him across the saddle and climb up with him. "Let's go, Cheyenne."

Cheyenne set off at a lope and Zane prayed that Rex would be all right. Every step of the way, he half expected shredding claws and piercing teeth to tear into his flesh. But it didn't. In a few minutes, he was back at the gate. Cheyenne slowed to a walk and Zane reined him in. "Frank! Frank! Anybody! My dog is hurt!" Rex was more than his eyes, Rex was his friend.

"Boss!" Running footsteps announced that several of his employees had heard him. "What happened?"

"Cougar. Call the vet."

Zane sighed. He'd be going to the office without his companion today. He'd be lost.

Presley dressed for Zane. She knew it didn't make any sense, but she did. Today, she wore her version of a power suit she had purchased at a second-hand store. It was appropriate office attire, but she felt comfortable in it. The pants were linen and the top was silk. Presley preferred feminine clothes with soft lines and softer fabrics. With her coloring, she usually chose jewel tones. A short jacket completed her deep blue ensemble. As usual, she avoided looking in the mirror. Even when she put on make-up, she glanced up or concentrated on just one feature at a time. Pink lip gloss was her only choice of make-up for her mouth, anything that would draw attention to her problem was avoided – so no bright colors, just the barest hint of pink.

What would today bring? She had spent a couple of hours the night before reading everything she could find about Zane online; about his family, about the firm and the cases they had handled. She had felt respect for the man, before – but now she felt awe. Time after time he had taken on people's problems, represented the underdog, stood between hopeless situations and lost causes. She knew there were some people who practiced law to make money – and apparently he did, but he had high standards and a big heart and Presley wanted to be a part of his life so bad she could taste it.

But she also saw photo after photo of him with beautiful women hanging on his arm. Just this past weekend he had been a part of the McCoy wedding held at Tebow Ranch. Everyone knew who the McCoys were – and everyone was beginning to know the Saucier brothers. Zane wasn't married, but it was obvious he could have any woman he wanted. So what would he want with her?

Zane would never want her for her looks or be attracted to her – but he could need her. So as Presley prepared for her second day of work at Saucier and Barclay, she prepared to make herself indispensable to one handsome lawyer with a heart of gold.

When she arrived at the office, it was a little different than the day before. Presley didn't wait to be shown in, nor did she linger at the front desk, rather she went right into the big bosses inner sanctum – just like she belonged. Without hesitation, she threw herself into the task. Glancing through his calendar, she got everything ready.

Looking around the office, she checked everything out. His computer was on. His water pitcher was full. The blinds were cracked at just the angle she had noticed they were at yesterday. What else? Presley's eyes roved the room – ah, the ivy! Yesterday she had noticed it and wondered whose responsibility it was to keep it watered. As no one had – she supposed it might be hers. It was a beautiful display and very real as she could tell from the one or two partially yellowed leaves. Finding a watering can, she pulled a chair over near the window. A shelf over the top held the spreading green vine. But it was high – and she had on high heels. So she had to be careful.

Stretching up, she almost had it. Dang! If she were only a little taller, biting her lip, Presley gave it everything she had – and slipped. "Ratz!" she squealed and tumbled backwards – right into Zane Saucier's arms.

"Gotcha!" He had walked in and after listening for a few seconds, he had known exactly what she was doing. But instead of scaring her, he had placed himself near in case she fell. Talk about something being in the right place at the right time! Now, he didn't have to wonder what kind of body Miss Presley had, because he held it to his own – intimately. Not being able to see, he had grasped her wherever he could to ensure she hadn't slipped to the hard floor. One hand splayed over her lower abdomen, her hips ground back into his groin. The other hand cupped one luscious breast like it was made for it – and perhaps it had been – because Zane had never known anything that had felt so right. She was soft, curvy, rounded in all the right places – Miss Presley Grace Love was the perfect armful. "Are you all right?"

"Yes," Presley managed to whisper. "I'm sorry, I landed on you."

"I'm not, I'm glad I was here to catch you." And he wasn't letting her go very fast. Her breathing was fast and shallow. Zane did move his hands to slightly less conspicuous spots; he had no intention of embarrassing her. But he did enjoy the feel of her in his arms. "You shouldn't have climbed up there like that, it's dangerous. We have people to water the plants with long wands and proper tools."

"Sorry," she managed to apologize. "I thought I was helping."

"It's okay, no harm done. I'm just glad I walked in at just the right moment." He had to smile, she just made him happy. And he needed that. The last twenty-four hours had been full of nothing but worry. First the brucellosis scare had thrown him for a loop and then had come the run-in with the cougar. Rex was going to be okay, but the vet had insisted on keeping him for a day for stitches and antibiotics, and then he would probably need some recuperation time. There had been no life-threatening injuries, but the lab had come away with some deep scratches and a few bite marks. So for the first time in a long time, Zane was having to get around on his own with one of the despicable canes that Margaret had hated so.

"Me, too," she conceded. Letting out a deep breath, it occurred to her that she hadn't moved. She was still lounging in his arms like she was at home, there. Good grief! What he must be thinking! "Sorry," she managed to begin pulling her body away from his. It was hard. She felt entirely too comfortable there. "I need to move."

"Quit apologizing. Holding you wasn't a hardship."

Presley blushed. Zane couldn't see, thank goodness.

Stepping back, she noticed Zane's tie was crooked. "May I?" she touched his chest. "Your tie needs straightening."

"Okay," he readily agreed. "I thought I was all spiffed up."

He held up his head and stood still while she rearranged and tightened it a bit. Being this close to him made her quiver. There was no doubt in her mind that her head would rest naturally against his chest. At this angle, Presley could gaze at his face – the strong jaw, the kissable cleft in his chin. "Smile for me," she requested before thinking.

"Why?" he asked but he smiled and she had to laugh a bit.

"I knew it, you have dimples," and she touched the one on the right side with her index finger.

"Turn about's fair play, let me touch your face so I can 'see' you."

He lifted his hands and Presley panicked. "No!" she almost shouted and backed up, catching her heel on the leg of a chair and this time she sat down hard.

"Presley!" Zane bent over and held out his hand, feeling for her. "Are you all right?"

"Yes," she said with a resigned embarrassed tone. "I just landed hard on my bottom. I'm fine."

"I didn't mean to frighten you; I wouldn't hurt you for the world."

He sounded so contrite that Presley felt ashamed. "It wasn't you, I'm . . ." The phone rang and she breathed a sigh of relief – saved by the bell. "Let me get that, excuse me." She jumped up and went for the phone.

"Hello?" she asked breathlessly.

Zane was a bit confused. Her reaction to his request to touch her had been so unexpected.

"That was Mr. McCoy, Jacob. He needs to see you about firming up some plans to adopt his wife's baby." Presley's voice sounded a bit unsure, as if she was speaking of something that should be kept secret.

"Did you tell him to come in?"

"He asked for an appointment on Friday. I checked your calendar and made it for that day at two unless you have plans I don't know about."

"No, that's good. I was with him last night, he didn't mention it – of course we were preoccupied with sick cattle at the time."

"I hope everything's okay." Zane could hear her get up. "Let me make your coffee today. Where's Rex?"

"Thanks," he heard the coffee machine make its comforting brewing noise. "He's at the vets. We went for a morning ride this morning and met up with a cougar."

Bang! "Dang! I spilled the coffee," he heard her grumbling and shuffling around. "Did you say a cougar? My God, are you okay?"

"Rex defended me; he got a little ripped up."

She brought a cup to him and sat it by his hand, touching it in the process so he'd know where she placed the warm mug. "You had an active evening, sick cattle and getting attacked."

"The cattle problem turned out to be bad feed, I was proud of that. At first they were showing symptoms of a disease that would have forced me to put them all down. And the cougar episode was a freak thing. I had my whip with me, and I got in a couple of licks before I was through."

Presley was impressed. "I'm not surprised, I'm sure you can do anything you set your mind to. But I'm so glad you weren't hurt. And I'm so sorry about your dog. He's so sweet. Don't you think you ought to have someone close by who cares about you when you ride? It worries me to think of you going about by yourself. I know Rex is trained well, but you need a companion."

For a moment, Zane thought she was about to volunteer and he found himself thinking how it would be to have her 'close by'. But her next comment put that notion to rest. Presley pulled out a chair and sat down across from him.

"I know I can't help you at home, but is there anything I can do for you here? Help you in any way?" Presley wanted to do something for him to make up for acting like a fool when he wanted to touch her face. Many sight impaired people used that technique so they could have a mental image of the person they were with.

Zane sipped his coffee, trying to get his thoughts together. She meant she wanted to be with him and help him at work. Damn! He needed to get his out of control libido in check. "We'll need to get forms listed in the Uniform Parentage Act and follow the Artificial Insemination Statues for Jacob's request. His Jesse was a surrogate mother. It was her egg, but a sperm donor was used. Jesse is keeping the baby and Jacob wants to make sure he is listed as the father."

"I'll pull a copy of the Domestic Relations law, just in case he has any questions."

Once again, her knowledge was above and beyond a legal secretary. He was about to ask her what law courses she'd taken when something else occurred to him. "Presley, I spoke with a woman yesterday, a Laura Bettes. Would you look up her address in Chloe's rolodex and send her some flowers. I won't be able to make the date she suggested."

"All right. Any particular message?" His question sorta took the wind out of Presley's sails. Thinking of Zane with a woman wasn't a thought she wanted to dwell on.

"No, just tell her that I appreciate her thinking of me and we'll get together another time."

"Very well," Presley got up and made herself a note. "How about the Taylor case, is there anything I can help with there? I know you met with the PI yesterday." She hadn't been in the room when that happened, Building Security had required her to go and have a photo badge made. All in all, it had been an uncomfortable chore.

"Adam is heading that one up, but I know we'd both appreciate it if you would just familiarize yourself with the whole thing. That way – if we need something or something comes up, you'll be up to speed."

"Good, I will." Presley went right to it, reading everything she could find. And what she discovered made her heart ache. Justice for Laney Taylor was something she would help win, any way she could. While she worked, she kept an eye out for Zane. It made her nervous that he didn't have his dog with him.

"I'm not dead, I'm not dead, I'm not dead." Laney rocked herself as she sat in a small knot. She wasn't dead yet, but she soon would be. Kendall fed her only sparingly now, he was gradually cutting her rations down, it was a form of torture, wondering if she had tasted her last bite of food or drank the last bit of water.

How had her life come to this? Ray had seemed like such a nice guy. She had only gone out with him a couple of times before he had swept her off her feet, promising to build a life and a home with her. Laney had been studious, small and plain. Her experience level with men was negligible, and with her sister out of the country, she was lonely. From the moment he married her – that very night – he began to show himself. Soon she realized she had married a monster. He had not even pretended but told her what he needed from her and what he expected. Some people kept a pet, he kept at toy. He had begun by locking her in a room, but she'd find a way out. Kendall had told her he'd kill her, he confessed that he had killed before, even showing her pictures.

People began to ask where she was – neighbors, the postman. Sometimes she could hear their conversations out in their front yard. But he told them all she was sick, not right – a paranoid schizophrenic. His games were varied and destructive Laney was beaten, water-boarded, burned, tortured in unspeakable ways. Not long ago she had escaped and gone to the police, but he came after her. And when he got her back, he told her that was her fatal mistake. Laney had fallen into the hands of a serial killer and she knew survival was unlikely.

Time ceased to have meaning; there was no difference in night or day. Laney didn't know when hours or days passed. The only thing she could do try and keep her sanity was fantasize. Laney escaped her prison and dreamed of a hero who would rescue her from this nightmare. She saw him, she talked to him, she begged him to come and rescue her. And even though it seemed impossible, Laney had to believe that someone, somewhere had heard her prayer.

Adam tossed and turned in his bed. He couldn't get Laney Taylor out of his mind. It was absurd. She was dead. But he dreamed about her. He dreamed she called out to him, he dreamed that she held her hands out and begged him to help her and the idea that he couldn't do anything for her ate at his very soul.

For the past several years, Adam had played the field. He had dated all kinds of women, but none of them had captured his interest or his heart – until he had opened a file and looked into sweetest face he had ever seen. His heart had thudded, hunting her name until he had read enough to realize it was too late. Adam had missed her. She was missing, presumed dead. But even the knowledge that he had no hope of ever holding her, he couldn't turn it loose. If he couldn't speak to her or touch her, get to know her, he would give her the only gift he could. Adam would give her peace.

Over the next few days, Presley began to feel at home with her duties and with Zane. Whatever she could do for him to make his day go smoother, she did. She tried to anticipate his needs and make sure everything he needed was in its proper place. If he had a meeting, she made sure he was prepared. Whatever case he was working, she did her own research so she could save him time and trouble. Not surprisingly, she enjoyed it all and every word of praise he gave her was worth more than diamonds to her attention starved soul.

None of this escaped Zane's notice either. Very quickly Presley was making herself indispensable to him. She was also becoming important to him in other ways. He liked her. He was also attracted to her – big time. In all of his adult life and experience with women, he had never met someone so unselfish and giving. If she ever thought he wanted something, it wouldn't be long before he had it. Every morning, she met him with coffee; several times he found delectable pastries on his desk that he finally got her to admit she made herself. One thing that amused him and touched him was her preoccupation with the window blinds. He knew she was concerned that the bright shafts of sunlight would bother him. He wished that were true. Oh, he felt the warmth of the rays of the sun, but he saw nothing. But it was the warmth of Presley's spirit and her capacity for caring that touched Zane.

Cloe, God forgive him, was a mediocre employee compared to Presley Love. She did all the leg work for him. When he introduced a new case or task, she went the extra mile to gather all the information he would need to make a decision or plan a strategy. No associate could have done a better job.

All she did for him was only the beginning of what Presley managed to do around the firm. As she moved through the building taking care of her and Zane's workload, if she saw someone needing a hand, Presley pitched in. At least a dozen times this week different employees had told him how considerate she was. Larry Gephardt had mentioned that she helped him at the copy machine, Felicia Richard called him and thanked him for allowing Presley to help her with the United Way drive, and even prissy Melody had commented that Miss Love had impressed her when she had helped a client who was in a wheelchair maneuver through the building. Presley never told him any of these things, nor did she let any work he gave her go undone. As far as he could tell, she asked for no special favors nor did she do anything to draw attention to herself at all. A very rare woman indeed; and what she did this morning – just capped it off for him. "Zane, if it would be okay with you, I'd like to take on some probono work. I know I can only go so far with it, but I could do the prep work on wills, custody cases, divorces, adoptions – lots of things – and then it would take a quick review and some signatures for one of the partners for it to go forward. Would that be possible?"

"I'd love that, Presley. I'm a firm believer in pro-bono. If you can take some on, I'd be thrilled."

A sweet giggle met his ears. "What's so funny?"

"It's Rex," she giggled again. "He's dreaming. He's lying on his side and his legs are moving and he even raised his lips and snarled." To Zane's delight, she giggled again – a deep, husky, serious giggle. Then he heard her moving around.

"What are you doing now?"

"I'm getting Rex sugar," he heard her kissing the dog and the damn dog sighed. More than anything he wanted to ask her to come get some Zane sugar.

Around noon, he got up and excused himself. She had brought a salad from home and her tummy was grumbling a bit. For the past few days she had made it a habit to slip into the kitchen, retrieve her lunch and come back to eat at her desk and read. Presley was addicted to romance novels, but she limited her reading time to lunch and right before she went to sleep. Romance novels gave her the opportunity to escape into a world that she probably would never get to experience in real life.

Presley stepped out in the hall and saw that Zane and Rex were walking down the corridor toward the kitchen ahead of her. But what they were not aware of was another employee pushing a box up on top of a file cabinet. The backs of the file cabinets formed the wall that was to Zane's right and the tops of those storage bins were filled with all matter of things. It all happened in a split second, the heavy box was pushed into place dislodging a big, old paper cutter that had probably been gathering dust there for a long while. The cutter had a big arm with a heavy sharp blade and as it began to tumble over the side, swinging open right over man and dog – Presley moved quicker than she ever had before. "Zane!" she called, but he couldn't react quickly enough, so she put herself in between him and the object that could so easily hurt him.

"Hell!" Zane felt the impact of the heavy object against her small body. Several people had called out, but no one had reacted as quickly as she had. Presley made a small sound of pain, but she didn't cry out. Whatever had fallen had just plowed into her and pushed her against him. "Presley!?! Are you okay, little love? What the hell? Why did you do that?"

"It was about to hit you, and you couldn't see it coming."

Her voice was soft and measured, she was in pain. The realization of what she had done for him slowly sank in. It was an act of pure unselfishness and it floored Zane to the bottom of his soul. "Let's get you to a doctor."

"No – no need, I just had the wind knocked out of me. There are no broken bones or blood or anything, I'll just have a little bruise where it hit my back."

"Damn, I wish I could see. Come back into the office with and let me check you out, at least I can make sure you don't have any scrapes or broken ribs." He led her back to the office and before she knew it, he had her shirt pulled out of her pants and his hands were all over her back. Presley was shaking, but not with pain.

"I'm all right – promise." She wasn't lying, but it wasn't the whole truth either. There probably would be a huge bruise on her back, but the main sensation she was feeling right now was her body reacting to his touch – her nipples were peaking and she wanted to turn in his arms so bad she could cry. When he was satisfied she was going to live he pulled her clothes back into place.

"Why don't you come into the kitchen with me and rest? Did you bring a sandwich?"

"I have a salad in the refrigerator."

He took her by the arm and they and Rex led one another back to the break room.

"I'll get it," he said as he led her to the first table. "Where is it placed, on what shelf?"

"The second shelf, it's the only round container there."

Several people came over to ask about her. She didn't like the attention. Zane retrieved both of their lunches, and she couldn't help but notice how very self-assured and independent he was. She hoped she hadn't embarrassed him, but the thought of that heavy piece of office equipment hitting him in the head had horrified her. "Thank you," she took the salad from his hand and he sat down by her.

"What do you have?"

"Rachel made me bacon wrapped stuffed jalapenos," he answered with gusto as he bit into one.

Presley didn't want to know who Rachel was, but she was glad he had someone to feed him. She was sure Zane had ample women eager to take care of him. "Those things look spicy. Let me get you some water."

She was up and away from the table before he could stop her. "I could have gotten it, you're the injured party."

"That was nothing, I've been knocked on my rear before," she handed him a glass of ice water. As she sat down, Renee and two other women joined them, sitting at an adjacent table. "Hello," she spoke politely.

"Hi, Zane," one of them spoke and giggled. They ignored Presley.

"Hello, ladies," Zane spoke in between bites. "Presley, did you have a good evening last night?"

She was a bit self-conscious in front of the other women, but she tried to just forget about them. "I did. I went to one of my favorite places, the pediatric unit at Breckenridge. I do a story-time there twice a week. Sometimes it's heartbreaking to see the sick children, but I love to spend time with them all. Their indomitable spirits are inspirational."

"I bet they are. That's sweet of you, I'm impressed. Do you want to try one of these?" He offered her a pepper.

"Okay, thanks." She bit into it and found it to her liking.

"Mr. Saucier, you have a phone call from the DA," Darla stuck her head around the door. "Can I transfer it to your cell phone?"

"Yea," he stood up. "Excuse me Presley; let me see what Honey wants, the reception isn't very good in here." He stepped out and she focused on her meal.

"Excuse me, Presley?" It was Renee. Presley turned to face her and the two other women. Both were tall, fashionable and dressed to the nines.

"Yes?"

"We were wondering if you wouldn't mind eating at your desk from now on. When we have to look at you while we eat, it turns our stomachs and we lose our appetite."

It took two or three seconds for Presley to realize what they were saying. The blatant, heartless insult stole her breath. Immediately tears sprang in her eyes – but she forced them back. They would not see her cry. "Okay," was all she could think to say. Quickly she gathered her things, keeping her eyes cast down. But she didn't get very far.

"Wait," Zane growled. Oh my word! Had he heard? "I might be blind, but there's not a damn thing wrong with my hearing." He moved to where she stood, as if he could see where she was. "Renee, Lisa, Margo – I don't know what to say. I can't believe you could treat someone like that. This is a place of business, not a school yard. Bullying will not go on here. Do you understand?"

"Zane," Renee began, her voice shaking.

"It's okay, let it go," Presley whispered to him.

"What they said didn't even make sense," he directed that comment to Presley. "But it's certainly not the kind of attitude I want at Saucier and Barclay."

"Let's go," she tugged on his arm. Two of the three women weren't even attempting to hide the darts of dislike flashing from their eyes, but one looked sheepish.

"We're sorry, Zane. It was a joke," Margo whispered. She wasn't willing to lose her job over Renee's jealousy.

"Please," Presley begged – the word just a mere breath by his ear.

"We'll discuss this during your evaluations."

Zane led her out and Presley knew she owed him an explanation. Honesty was called for, but everything within her rebelled at the idea of laying herself bare to his scrutiny. "We didn't pick up our food."

"I have people for that," he stated simply. Zane wanted to ask her what happened, but he felt it was one of those mystical female one-upmanship games that men never understood. Of all the predatory creatures in the world, women could be crueler to their own kind than any other – cannibalistic, even.

When they were back within the safety of his office, Presley knew the time had come. "I have something to tell you. Something I've been hiding from you. It's about the way I look."

Zane stilled. She sounded so defeated. "Presley, you don't have to . . ."

He stood there, so handsome in black slacks, a crisp white shirt with the sleeves rolled up over his strong forearms – his tie, endearingly askew, as usual. His hair was more unruly than usual and he had the sexiest dark scruff on his face that she had ever seen. She looked him in the face - those beautiful brown eyes of his were unfocused but saw more than most. Presley closed her own eyes and gathered strength. It was probably wrong, but she had enjoyed him thinking she was normal, pretty. "I was born with a cleft lip. When I was eight I had surgery, but there is this scar that goes up from the center of my lip."

"Presley, it's . . ."

"No, I want you to see it." First, she closed the door, then she stepped up to him and took his hands. "Look at my face. I want you to know me."

Zane's hands shook. "Are you sure?" He had no desire to make her uncomfortable.

"If you don't mind, I want you to. I mean you don't have to, if you think it would be icky." God, she wasn't making much sense. She was so confused. Before he had wanted to touch her, and she wouldn't let him. Now if he didn't touch her, she'd be hurt. God, there was no pleasing her, was there?

"Come here," he put his hands on her shoulders and stepped closer. "I've been wanting to get my hands on you since the day you walked in. Of course, I want to touch you." Her whole little body shook. "Easy, I'm not going to hurt you."

"I know," Presley sighed. "I'm just ashamed."

"Shhhh," he crooned. "Don't be silly, you have a little scar – that's all. Now, let me feel how pretty you are."

Presley stopped breathing as he framed her face. His thumbs began moving over her cheeks.

"Your skin is so soft, like silk. High cheekbones, wide set eyes – long, long lashes," he touched her closed eyes, "you're so pretty. Smooth forehead, wispy bangs, small shell-ears – now let me feel your nose. Do you have a big nose?"

He was teasing her and she laughed a little, "no – not huge. It's turned up a little bit." He skated a finger down her forehead and traced her nose.

"Feels kissable to me," he teased. Presley held her breath - - oh, God. But he skipped the dreaded area and cupped her chin. "You have a sweet little heart shaped face."

"Touch my mouth," she directed, needing to get the ordeal over with. Presley was wound tighter than a drum, her whole being felt like she could just spin out of control at any moment.

He did.

Zane passed his fingertips over her lips. His thumb touched her bottom lip. "Beautiful mouth – pouty and full." Then, his thumb moved over her poor upper lip. Presley stiffened and would have jerked back, but he began to talk. "Now, what's the big deal? I feel a tiny mark right here." Zane rubbed the reddened ridge that divided her upper lip. She knew he could feel how it was misshaped, the way it was curved upward in the middle. "Kitten," he whispered.

"What?" Presley didn't know what he meant.

"You have a kitten mouth," Zane explained. "It's precious."

And then he bent close, one hand leaving her face, his arm curling around her, his palm on the small of her back. Presley's sexual experience was nil – but the touch that drew her near him sent a jolt of excitement through her whole body. Unless she was badly mistake – Presley Grace Love was about to be kissed.

Chapter Three

Yes, Presley was about to be kissed. She didn't close her eyes; she didn't want to miss a thing. Zane's eyes weren't closed either, and it was as if he looked at her – as if he could see her, the real her. And he wasn't repelled.

"Can I taste you? Please?" he whispered.

"Oh, yes. I want that very much." Slowly he urged her forward, and his body came to meet hers. The first part of her to touch him was her nipples – they were distended and hard and the heat that flashed over her when their bodies pressed together was like a supernova.

She bit her lip to hold back a gasp – and she couldn't help it, she stood on tiptoe to meet him. He smelled just like a man should – like the clean fresh outdoors, a hint of musk – all male.

"I've thought about kissing you, what it would be like."

"You have?" that was totally amazing. Presley didn't want to rush him, but this was something she had dreamed of for her whole life and the anticipation was killing her. It might be a pity kiss, but she wanted it desperately. Zane pushed his body flush up against hers, and if she wasn't badly mistaken, he was aroused. The headiness of the possibility made her head spin.

Zane was enjoying himself. He pulled her even tighter against him. Every curve of her body fitted to every plane of his perfectly. His whole body tensed and tightened with arousal. Perfect, soft pillowy tits rested on his chest and he could feel diamond hard nipples even through her clothes and his. God, he wanted to suck on them! They must be incredible! What he wouldn't give to reach down and cup her ass – but that would come. The few moments the other morning when he had felt it nestled against his groin had burned the memory into his brain and he knew exactly how it looked – it was lush, squeezable – spankable.

"I've thought about kissing you, too, Zane," she confessed – hoping against hope he wouldn't change his mind. What was he doing? He wasn't kissing her that was for sure. But he was close, inhaling her scent. Then he began to rub his cheek against hers, brushing his lips over her hair – God, her neck. She was being seduced. Didn't he realize it wasn't necessary? But, Lord help her, it was fun. But what if someone came in and spoiled it? What if someone interrupted them and she never knew the thrill of her first kiss? "Any time now, would be good," the words slipped out before she could stop them and she felt him chuckle, a rumble vibrating against her chest.

"Oh, the kitten wants to be petted, doesn't she? If I stroke you, will you purr for me?"

Presley almost came right then – right there – just from his suggestive teasing. God, what could this man do to her if he really tried? They were standing just inside the door and Zane reached over, ran his hand down the wooden surface and turned the lock.

Presley gulped, this could be good.

Zane was fascinated. Something about this woman turned him on beyond anything he'd ever known. Desire welled upside him, surging toward the surface. It wasn't the place – or the time, but he wanted to strip her naked, lick every inch of her body and place his mark all over her. Possessing Presley was becoming necessary, but he didn't just want to make love to her, he wanted to learn everything about her. God, he wanted her to know him, too and that was an emotion he hadn't felt in a long, long time. The moment he'd took her in his arms, traced her beautiful features – he'd been shook – but then, the feelings had crystalized and he'd known that she was different, she might be exactly what his soul had been longing for.

"Zane," she whimpered.

"Coming." Almost.

He touched his lips to her – just rested them there, letting the reality of the joining wash over him. But Presley was impatient; she feathered her lips over his – grabbing his shoulders and rising even higher on her tiptoes. He opened his lips and took her top one between his own, tracing the little imperfection with his tongue, showing her that it mattered not a whit to him. She moaned and he swallowed the sound with a deeper kiss.

At last.

Presley blossomed under his attention as Zane took control and unleashed the full measure of his passion on her. His tongue tangled with hers in a sensuous chase. She didn't protest – whatever he demanded – she gave, freely. With a bold possession, Zane consumed her mouth, sucking on that pouty lower lip, demanding a response. Rubbing his hands up her arms, he rejoiced when she joined in the chase, her tongue flitting and flirting with his like a tiny butterfly. God, he wanted her! He was hard as a rock! With a grunt, he bucked his erection directly against her pussy mound and she almost collapsed in his embrace, moaning. God, she was responsive.

Unwilling to end the kiss, Zane nipped at her lips, licking the corners, making her come to him and ask for more. Taking her wrists, he put them together and held them immobile with one hand right at the top of her hips. He spread his legs, enclosing her lower body and pressed her backwards until she was braced against the door. Damn, his control was slipping; he could feel himself trembling with the need to possess her utterly.

But voices outside the door brought him to his senses and he eased his grip, and began kissing her face, bringing her down. "That's my girl, my sweet girl."

"Thank you," she said as she laid her head on his shoulder.

He rested his weight on his forearms, still bracketing her against the solid surface and announced the obvious – or at least to him. "Well, this changes everything, don't you think?"

"Zane!" A knock on the door right behind Presley's head made her jump. Zane leaned into her a bit more and grinned.

"They can't come in unless we want them to, can they?" he whispered.

"Zane!" It was Melody, the receptionist. "Mr. McCoy is here – a bit early, but he's here." She sounded a little exasperated. Jacob McCoy could be overwhelming.

"I think we'd better move," Presley suggested reluctantly. She would rather stay right where she was. All she wanted to know was how things had changed? What had he meant? She was afraid to hope. But she knew what had changed for her – everything.

Zane had just turned her world upside down.

Propelling himself gracefully off of her and back a step or two, Zane stood before her. She had yet to move. Her gaze slid helplessly down his body till she could see the visual evidence of his attraction for her – for her! The bulge in his pants looked as good as it had felt pressed to her mound. Presley felt her cheeks blaze. Out of pure instinct, she covered her cheeks at the thought of him catching her looking at him. But he couldn't see – and, if she wasn't badly mistaken – she had caused that swelling, so she owned up to it. "You might want to sit behind your desk, Zane."

He flashed her a cocky grin. "I look excited to see you, don't I?"

She realized he was playing with her. "Yes you do, and if you don't sit down, Jacob is going to think you're excited to see him too."

"Ha!" he laughed. "You're adorable."

He made it behind the desk a millisecond before the door swung open and Jacob McCoy strode in. "Zane, thanks for seeing me, I'm sorry about being early. We came in for Jessie's last ultrasound and she's tired. I hated to make her wait any longer than she had to."

Presley couldn't help but be impressed. She had heard about the McCoy men of Tebow Ranch and the talk hadn't been exaggerated. Any other time, Presley would have been drawn to the bigger-than-life cowboy who was every woman's definition of sexy. But not now. She had eyes for only one man – Zane Saucier.

"No problem, Jacob," Zane motioned for him to sit. "We were just discussing things – that uh, contribute to the rise in inflation rates." He said the comment with a straight face, but Presley choked and started coughing. "The beautiful woman whose breath I've seemed to manage to steal is Presley Love. Presley, this barbarian is one of my best friends, Jacob McCoy."

Presley walked over and greeted Jacob. "It's very nice to meet you. Congratulations on your baby, I wish you all the luck in the world."

Jacob got to his feet. She saw him look at her lip and that made her tense up, but he gave her a big smile and his eyes were friendly, so she relaxed.

"It's a pleasure, Miss Presley. How do you stand working with this rascal?"

Jacob winked at her as if he were asking her to play along. So she did. "It's hard."

"Yes, it is." Zane broke out in laughter and then Presley realized she had walked right into his erotic by-play. Good gracious. Time to think about something else. "Did you say your wife is here? Would you mind if I went out and asked her if she'd like something to drink? I'll be right back. I have all the packets for you to take with you and the forms ready for you to sign."

"That's very sweet of you, Presley," Jacob thanked her. "I appreciate that. I escorted her into the coffee shop next door, but I bet she'd like some company if Zane can spare you."

"She's already got most of the forms ready for us to sign, so no – I have no problem with you checking on Jessie. I'm sure you two will get along well." With a smile at Jacob, Presley grabbed her purse and took off to go check on their pregnant guest.

"I can't believe you let Jessie out of your sight."

"My wife likes to think she's independent, but I slipped the barista my card before I left – just in case."

"Have you heard from Aron and Libby? I guess they're having a good time on their honeymoon."

"Yea, we heard from them last night. They're having a big time. Libby has even talked him into going in the water – and that's a big thing for that huge ole' landlubber. They're going snorkeling today." Jacob leaned back and stared at his lawyer friend. "You do realize you're grinning like an idiot, don't you Zane? You've got it bad for your cute little secretary, don't you?"

"She is cute, isn't she?" She was goddamn adorable was what she was. Zane couldn't get the kiss out of his mind.

"I'm a married man, but – yeah – she's a little hottie."

"She different, Jacob," Zane became more serious. "I've never met a woman like her."

"About damned time, you need a woman."

Zane knew Jacob spoke the truth.

Presley moved down the busy sidewalk, out of habit she didn't meet people's eyes. The wind was whipping hard down the street and she held herself tight to stay warm. Pushing into the coffee shop, she sighed with relief at the warmth. The small shop was almost deserted, but she saw a woman over in the corner with her back to the door. What was odd was the man standing just behind her – quietly watching – with a strange grin on his face. Presley noticed the shopkeeper watching, too.

As Presley moved closer, she realized that Jessie was reading out loud, but it was slow and halting. Presley had no idea what was going on, maybe she didn't glasses – and it was surely none of her business. But the man that was leering at her made Presley's blood run cold. And then he said something - - "Hey, retard! You must be real dumb. You can't even read a kid's book."

Presley saw Jessie jump, clearly startled. The man didn't even give her time to respond. Instead, he moved closer. "Read me a story, you fat little moron!"

Enough! "You stop that, you asshole!" Presley ran right up and grabbed the man by the arm, afraid he was going to try and touch Jessie. The man's wasn't huge – not by Zane or Jacob standards, but he was a lot bigger than she was.

"Get your hands off of me!" The tall, wiry man turned and Presley got her first really good look at him. He was pale, blonde and well dressed – perhaps even a professional. What did he think harassing someone as helpless as Jessie?

"You leave her alone!" She got right in his face. His breath was atrocious.

"Back off you ugly little hare-lip!" He actually pushed Presley hard enough that she fell.

"Ow!" She landed on a sore spot. Dang, she had been knocked down a lot, lately – but she didn't stay down. Getting back up, she grabbed the man by the shoulder just as he started to grab for Jessie. "Stop it!"

Jessie wasn't quiet either. She didn't know who Presley was, but she didn't mind coming to her defense. "You leave her alone! Are you crazy? Or drunk? My husband is Jacob McCoy and he's gonna make mincemeat out of you!"

"Who'd marry a fat cow like you? The two of you deserve a lesson in more than just how to read."

Okay – that was it. Presley looked around for something to brain the guy with. The woman behind the counter was gone – great! There! She saw a good-size sugar dispense, that would put a knot upside his head. Grabbing it, she turned to defend Jacob's wife. "Let her go!" she exclaimed, seeing that the man had Jessie by the arm as if he were going to pull her from the shop.

"I said back off hare-lip!" The ugly name was one she had heard a thousand times before, but it always hurt. But the man backhanded her – literally took his big fist and struck her in the mouth with the back of his hand. Presley felt her lips gash against her teeth and she tasted blood. It also knocked her sprawling – but this time she didn't hit the ground. Strong arms caught her – familiar strong arms.

Zane kissed her on the side of the head and sat her aside and – unbelievably – he hit the crazy man a stunning blow right to his chin – flattening him. How did he do that?

"Get up, you bastard! Pick on someone your own size!" Zane was a formidable figure.

"Why you blind idiot!" the man snarled as he got up. "I'll take you apart!"

Before he could do anything, Zane threw two blows – a martial arts chop to his shoulder and a kick that knocked his legs out from under him. And the man went down – again.

"He may be blind, but he's a black belt," Jacob stated as he pulled the man to his feet. "And you're going to jail. You don't assault women in our neck of the woods – especially not our women." He pulled one of the man's arms behind his back and up a bit causing him to wince. It was clear that the big McCoy wished the dolt would give him reason to deliver his own punch.

Jessie looked a bit embarrassed, but pacified and Presley was just confused to be included under Jacob's umbrella of protection. In a few seconds a policeman met Jacob at the door and he returned to gather Jessie up in his arms. Presley stepped to one side. She didn't know what to think.

"Are you all right?" Zane reached out for her and she went to him, thankful to have a place to go. He held her to him, cradling her next to his chest.

"Yes, I'm fine." She had grabbed a napkin off of a nearby table and dabbed at the blood.

"Your voice is shaking. I don't think you are all right at all."

"I'm sorry."

"What are you sorry for?"

"That Jessie was insulted, that you were disturbed. . ." she trailed off, then finished. "That you had to hear what he said to me."

Zane kissed her forehead – the second time in just a few minutes. "Who better to hear than one who will fight your battles for you?"

Presley didn't know what to say.

"Thank you for helping me," Jessie pulled Presley down to sit next to her on the couch. Presley was in awe of the beautiful woman. There was a glow about her that came not from pregnancy alone. Jessie McCoy was loved and she knew it.

"You are welcome. Do you think the man was on drugs?"

"He had to be, surely a man can't be that mean of his own volition."

"I'm not retarded, I have dyslexia. I can't read worth beans." Jessie looked down as if confessing a huge sin. "It's my greatest desire to be able to read to our baby."

"I understand," Presley patted Jessie's hand. "I am sure you will find a way." Wanting to make Jessie smile, she turned to self-deprecation. "You may not be retarded but I do have a cleft lip." She couldn't' bring herself to use the other term.

Jessie touched Presley's mouth. "You have a mouth that's been well kissed if you ask me."

Presley blushed and touched her mouth. "How did you know?"

"Ah-ha!" Jessie laughed. "I knew because your lip gloss is smeared and you have scruff-burn on your chin and neck. Zane, I presume?"

"It didn't mean anything. It was a pity kiss. It had to be. Look at me!" Her voice had risen a little and she glanced over to see what the men were doing. She let out a breath, they were bent over Zane's desk and Jacob was studying paperwork. "He can't see me." She looked at Jessie imploringly. "If he could, he wouldn't have wanted to kiss me."

"Presley, look at me," Jessie waved her hands over her body. "I was chubby before I became pregnant and now," she giggled, "I am chubbier! Jacob McCoy thinks I am the most beautiful woman in the world. He adores me. What he sees in me, I don't know, but I thank the Lord every day that he looks at me with eyes of love."

"You are gorgeous," Presley argued.

"And so are you," Jessie looked Presley up and down. "That little scar on your lip does not detract from who you are. Zane is very much like Jacob, he is a hero. Your boss may be blind but he sees the world much clearer than most people do."

What Jessie was saying was just too wonderful for words, too wonderful to contemplate. "When are you due?" She needed to think about something else.

"A few weeks at most, although it looks like I should have delivered yesterday!" Jessie did look a bit miserable. "The doctor has said that if I don't go into labor by the middle of November, he'll induce."

"Are you ready to go treasure?" Jacob stood close. "The papers are in the works. This baby will be mine in every way possible. I've also took care of my will and made provisions to ensure that my neighbor Henry gets some of the proceeds from the gas well. With his criminal nephew in jail, the old man is going to need some help."

Presley didn't know what Jacob was talking about, but she was sure Zane would explain.

"Your heart is the biggest thing about you," Jessie kissed him on the cheek. "And that's saying a lot," she whispered and much to Presley's delight – he blushed. Seeing the big man respond to his wife's affection just made her want to cry. Presley looked at Zane. How she wished the things Jessie had said were true. She wanted to be loved more than anything in the world.

"Are you coming to the auction tonight?" Jessie asked touching Presley's arm.

Presley knew what she was talking about, Zane had spoken of the event several times. "No," she began, but Zane interrupted her.

"That's the best idea I've heard in a long time." He slid a hand down her arm. "I'll do my best to talk her into accompanying me, Jessie. I need her with me tonight. What do you say, Presley? Do you want to come home with me?"

She was going home with Zane! What a prospect! In what capacity, she wasn't sure, but the idea almost made her giddy. It was necessary that she go home to change, but Zane had his driver take her by her apartment and they had waited for to go up and get some more clothes. What did one wear to a cattle auction? She didn't have a huge wardrobe so she did the best she could. Last year she had purchased a denim blue dress with turquoise bead insets in a cutout pattern on the bodice. But she did have a pair of boots to wear. Hopefully she wouldn't embarrass him.

Racing around her apartment, she changed purses and put the hamburger back in the freezer that she had set out for dinner. Taking a last look at her hair in the mirror, she turned to go - no, she stopped and faced her reflection. It was time she looked herself in the face. Raising her eyes, she stared. Her hair was okay; she pushed a lock of it over her shoulder. The eye shadow went well with her dress. Letting her gaze drift down, she steeled herself to look at her mouth. Crooked. Her mouth was crooked.

Yet, he had kissed her. And he seemed to enjoy it.

She had turned him on.

But would he have felt the same way if he wasn't blind – if he could see her with clear vision, would he still want her?

"Are you ready, Presley?" It was him! He had come to fetch her.

"Yes, I'm ready." She opened the door and he offered his arm. Rex led them out and she felt like she was stepping out into a brand new world.

The drive to the ranch was exciting. She had never been chauffeured before, much less in a Mercedes. She had been to Bastrop before, but never out to where his ranch was located. Sitting up straight in the seat, she tried to take it all in.

"Come sit next to me," he held out his hand.

Presley's heart jumped and she started to move over, but Rex jumped up between them. "Hey!" she huffed in disappointment. "Share him with me, Rex!"

Zane laughed. "Hold on, I'll fix this problem." He stood up and scooted Rex over and got in between them. "Now, I can sit by both of you. We can't have any jealousy."

From the front Sherwood cleared his throat. "Oh my goodness," Presley exclaimed. She had almost forgotten about his driver.

"Eyes on the road, Sherwood," Zane said good-naturedly. Angling his body toward her, he put his hand on her neck and captured her mouth.

Presley just melted. She gave herself up to his kiss, enjoying the soft smooches and the rubbing of their tongues together, but then she began to feel self-conscious. They weren't alone. Letting her lips slide from his, she whispered. "I'm shy. Will you kiss me later?"

"You got it," he kissed both eyelids. "Thank you for everything you've done for me, Presley. You put yourself between me and danger, you stuck up for Jessie, you have gone out of your way to make my life easier at work – don't think I don't notice and I'm grateful."

Great. He was grateful.

Of course. That was why she was here, he was paying her back. "You're welcome." She eased away from him and ever so slightly she put just a little bit of distance between them.

Gratitude was not what she had wanted from him.

"Come on Sweet Cheeks, let's get our feet wet," Aron held out his hand for Libby and led her down to the waves. He had rented all of their gear and even went through a safety demonstration. Anything his baby wanted was what he tried to do.

"I'm so excited!" she literally was pulling him toward the water. "I've wanted to do this forever!"

Together they sank beneath the waves and Libby was mesmerized. She saw fish of every conceivable color. Constantly she was touching Aron and pointing. He swam by her side enjoying her excitement.

Libby spotted a yellow angel fish and took off after it. Aron's attention was caught by a shiny object in the mouth of a cave. It wouldn't hurt to investigate. He swam up to get a breath then dove back down to see what treasure he had spotted. If he found a gold doubloon, Noah would shit all over himself. Bubbles obscured his vision as he made his way to the outcropping of rocks surrounded by Seagrass. Glancing over his shoulder, he made sure Libby was okay. She was high-tailing it after a brightly colored fish like the little mermaid.

Grabbing onto a rock, he came in closer . . . Hell!

Presley didn't know where to look first or where to look longest. When he had said they were going to a cattle auction, she had envisioned one like a friend's dad had taken her to in Liberty. It had been held in a rustic auction barn, with dirt floors and smelly goats and cowboys running around with prods and clipboards. The smell had been distinctive eau de manure and people had been dressed in regular western attire.

This production was nothing like what she had thought it would be.

And she was woefully underdressed.

Her first indication was when they came to the front gate of Whispering Pines. Oh, she knew Zane had money, but she hadn't realized he had MONEY. This wasn't a small time ranching operation, this was serious business. The stone pillars that Sherwood drove through and the ornate sign was intimidating, but the guard house they passed by and the welcoming committee of two elegant women passing out drinks shocked her. "What would you like to drink, Presley? We might as well indulge," Zane urged.

"Uh – a margarita?"

"Good choice and I'll have a Miller light."

Thank God, he had ordered a beer. If he had asked for a martini, she might would have got out and hitched a ride back to Austin. "Thank you," she muttered when he handed her the glass – and it was glass, probably crystal. No paper cups for this cattle auction. She settled back for the drive because from where they had entered, she didn't see a house or a barn or anything. The winding road led by picturesque lakes and a rushing stream. There were large pecan groves and herds of contented looking cows grazing on pastures planted with thick winter grass. Large well-kept barns and corrals were on one side and she saw beautiful horses running through the field with their manes blowing in the breeze. On one hand, she was thrilled that they were able to get out here early enough that she could see all of this splendor before the sun had begun to go down – but on the other – she was struck by one very obvious fact.

Presley Grace Love did not fit into this world – at all.

Sherwood let them out near the pavilion; a couple of men came up to talk to Zane. She presumed they were employees. He ably answered their questions and gave them directions. What he did next surprised her. He put his arm around her. "Frank, Henry – this is Presley Love. Presley, these two keep everything going around here."

"Mam," they tipped their hats and Presley greeted them.

He put a hand at the small of her back. "Let's go over to the grandstand. We can play host and hostess." That comment made a sparkle of hope dance in her heart. He was almost talking like this was a date or they were a couple.

"You have a beautiful ranch," she had to comment. "This is like nothing I was expecting." And it wasn't. People were arriving in everything from King Ranch pickups to limousines. Helicopters were landing and the people milling around looked like they had stepped off the set of the television show Dallas. All of them made their way to speak to Zane and he always introduced her, in fact he rarely took his hand off of her. He caressed her back, her shoulder – he fit his palm to the back of her neck and caressed her. Every so often, he'd kiss the side of her face. Zane had her so turned on that if they weren't in the middle of a crowd she'd have tackled him to the ground and had her wicked way with him. Well – probably not – but it was a nice thought.

People stared at them, there were some curious glances – lots of smiles, but a few skeptical looks. For the longest, Presley kept a couple of fingers over her lips, but it was hard to talk and respond when your mouth is covered up. Finally she relaxed and just went with it.

Libby surfaced. She couldn't believe Aron had went off and left her in the water. One minute he had been right behind her, the next – he was gone. Pulling the mask off her face, she looked around. Hmmmm. Odd. He wasn't on the beach. A splash behind her made her turn with a happy squeal. "Aron! How could you do that?" She laughed with relief, but the laugh died. He wasn't there.

Scanning the beach one more time, she looked from right to left, as far as she could see.

"Dang it! This isn't funny, Aron." She pulled her mask down and put her head back in the water, sinking down. He had to still be down here. Was he playing a trick on her? She wouldn't put it past him, he had been so happy and playful since the wedding. But she wasn't enjoying herself now, she wanted Aron.

With jerky, frenetic moves, Libby swam around – looking. She couldn't see him. She couldn't see anything but fish. Where was he? Frantically, she turned left – right, spun around and looked again. A horrible uneasy feeling washed over her. No, no, no, no. Rising to the surface, Libby began to swim for shore. He had to be here somewhere – somehow they had just got separated in the water. Padding through the serf, she stripped off the gear and adjusted her bathing suit.

"Aron!" she called. A few people stopped to look at her, maybe to see if she needed any help. "Aron!" Libby knew she was making a spectacle of herself, but she didn't care. "Aron!" she screamed louder. Stopping, she looked out over the expanse of blue water dappled by sunlight. Tears began to flow. Libby was scared.

"Aron! Aron! Aron!"

"Presley!" A happy voice drew her attention. It was Jessie! She was trying to hurry across the floor toward her and Jacob was busy trying to make her slow down. They were so cute. "Where are you sitting? I want to stay with you. Jacob is going to go baby-sit the cows."

"We'll have to behave," Zane whispered in her ear – "Till later."

Shiver. 'Later' sounded good to her. He might be grateful, but he was showing his gratitude in a way she couldn't resist.

"Come on up here, Miss Jessie." Zane held out his hand. It always amazed Presley that he seemed to have no trouble knowing where people were or even who they were. She was impressed.

Jessie plopped down beside her and threw a kiss to Jacob who stood there as if he was reluctant to leave her. "Go, darling. I'm in good hands. But if you see Cady or Avery or Skye tell them there is someone here I want them to meet."

"Or Lilibet," Zane added for good measure.

"I'll never remember all of that," Jacob grumbled as he went off, then stopped in his tracks and came back to get a kiss. "You're making me forget what's important giving me all this stuff to do."

"Oh, poor baby," she kissed him tenderly.

Presley was just flat-out jealous. She wanted what they had – she wanted it with Zane.

"The sale's starting," Zane rubbed his hand up and down her back.

"I'm not going to ask how you can tell. You are aware of everything, aren't you?"

"I'm sure as hell aware of you," he chuckled and scratched a line down her spine that made her actually wiggle in his arms. "Like that?"

"You know I do."

"WELCOME!" the announced shouted. "We are proud to announce the opening of the bidding for some of the best registered Beefmasters in the country. The McCoys of Tebow Ranch and Zane Saucier of Whispering Pines want me to tell you how glad they are to have you here and they hope you have a good time. Waitresses will be checking with you often for drink orders, which are on the house by the way, and as soon as we find these babies some new homes, you are all invited down to the pavilion for BBQ and dancing. You won't believe it – but Willie Nelson is here with us today. The hometown Austin boy is back for a visit, he's a good friend to Joseph McCoy and Jo talked him into singing us a few songs. So – we'll dance, drink, gossip and buy some mighty fine cattle."

"Willie Nelson?" Presley nudged Jessie. "Did you know that?"

"I did, he was over at the house last night for supper." At Presley's wide-eyed stare, she grinned. "Joseph knows a lot of celebrities from his extreme sports days. Why, Zane used to compete with him, before . . ." Jessie paused, aware where she had let the conversation go.

"It's okay, Jess," Zane assured her. "She knows I'm blind," he teased his friend. But he went on to explain to Presley. "The accident that took my sight was only five years ago. I was spraying some insecticide and it blew back in my face."

"I'm so, so sorry," she hugged his arm. "I didn't know how it happened, but if it were in my power to trade places with you, I would."

What she said amazed Zane. "Why would you say that?"

Jessie turned away, at least pretending not to listen. Presley had spoken without thinking, but she went ahead with her explanation. "It would be better if I were blind; I don't have as much to offer the world as you do."

The announcer interrupted their thought process. "FIRST UP is Offer #3706. We call this young man Crimson Warrior. He's out of Buttercup by Red Warrior. His pedigree is better than Prince William's. The bidding starts at fifty thousand dollars."

But Zane was still 'looking' at her, he didn't say anything, but he took her chin in his hand and held her still while he gently kissed her lips. "Are you for real?" he whispered.

She didn't answer because the bidding started and his attention turned to the action between the buyers and the auctioneer. Truly, Presley had never seen anything like it. The cattle weren't pushed or panicking. They weren't prodded or rushed. These registered cows and bulls marched out on a red carpet with no fear that they would be mistreated or end up between two hamburger buns.

Having forgotten she had it, Presley picked up the brochure and was impressed – it looked like a glossy magazine. Each animal was photographed in a pose. She smiled; it was like looking at a fashion rag for cows except they weren't dressed up in clothes. The backgrounds were green pastures and well-kept fences and in the text below their picture, their height and weight and pedigrees were laid out like beauty queen statistics.

"SOLD to Harbison Farms for seventy-two thousand dollars!" And so it went. Presley was amazed at how much money changed hands. And the people that were there to buy these show animals were wealthy and coiffed and fully comfortable in their own skin.

After all the cattle, embryo flushes and straws of semen had been sold, everyone retired to the pavilion for food and music. Presley stayed right with Zane, he made sure of that. But he did introduce her Joseph's and Isaac's fiancés. Presley was surprised to say the least, they weren't anything like she had envisioned them to be. Libby she had never met, but if she were anything like the other three, she would be exceptional. Cady, Joseph's love, came to meet her first. She wondered why they were making such a big deal about her presence. She soon found out. "Excuse us, Zane. Avery and Jessie and I need to borrow Presley for a bit. Lilibet is getting us some hot apple cider. Let's go sit by the fire place."

She only hesitated a second, but his, "Go on, I'll wait for you right here," made her feel better. He sat down with Jacob and Joseph and Presley let herself be led over to the big outdoor fireplace that stood like a mammoth monument on one end of the pavilion. It was nippy and the fire was welcome. Cady led her by the hand and Presley couldn't help but notice she was an uncommon beauty. "I've known Zane for years. We were friends in New Orleans," Cady offered. Presley realized then that she was Creole, her skin was the shade of Dulce de leche ice cream. And her eyes were the color of amber jewels. "We are so happy you are here."

"Thank you," she wasn't sure why Cady would say that.

The group of women sitting around the fireplace was having a good time. One girl with corkscrew curls was telling an animated story, waving her hands around and laughing.

"Girls, this is Presley Love."

Immediately all talk stopped and Presley felt awkward until they all got up and came forward. "I'm Avery," announced the one who had been speaking.

"I'm Lilibet," said another who didn't hold back, but stepped right up and hugged her. Presley didn't know what to think, but she patted the other girl's back. "I belong to Kane."

She knew Kane was Zane's twin brother. "I'm so glad to meet you." She looked at the rest. "I'm glad to meet all of you." They invited her to sit and gave her something warm to drink.

"I guess you're wondering why we're so ecstatic to meet you." Avery with the bouncy hair asked.

"Yes, I am." Presley answered slowly.

Lilibet clapped her hands together. "Kane says you're the first girl that Zane has brought around any of his friends or family since the accident. Oh, he's taken dates to public social events – but this is different. And I'm so glad!" She hugged Presley again.

"Don't scare her," Jessie warned. "She'll think we're already planning the bridal shower."

"That would definitely be premature," Presley tried for a voice of reason. "Zane is my employer." She hesitated to go even one step farther than that. His words of gratitude kept ringing in her ears.

"Perhaps," Cady smiled mysteriously. "I'd offer to read your palm or look at the tarot cards, but since I got pregnant, my powers seem to be waning. Nana Fontenot told me this would happen. It seems to be a family trait."

When Presley's eyes widened, Jessie laughed. "Yes, Presley, our Cady is a tad magical."

"How wonderful, I've always wanted to believe that something more than chance is involved in how our lives unfold." She didn't bother to explain that she knew there was no hope for a happily ever after in her life.

"We're giving Libby a surprise baby shower when she gets back from the honeymoon. We'd like it if you could come." Jesse's invitation surprised Presley.

"Thank you," there was no way Presley couldn't be gracious, but she also couldn't prevent the question from slipping out. "May I ask why you all are being so nice to me? I have to remind you that this thing with Zane is not anything for you to get excited about. There's no way he is actually interested in me." What made her bare her soul like that, Presley didn't know. The whole thing was making her a bit nervous.

"Why would you say that?" Avery asked with an innocent expression on her face.

For an answer, Presley didn't use words, she just passed her hand over her mouth.

"Balderdash!" Jessie said. "There's nothing wrong with the way you look. I told you that the other day."

"None of us are perfect," Avery offered.

"You're close," Cady patted Avery on her knee. "My mirror tells me I'm plain, but Joseph sees me through the eyes of love – so to him, I'm beautiful."

"And we've already talked about my body image issues," Jessie offered.

"Look," Lilibet lifted her skirt and showed Presley that one of her shoes was built up. "I'm a gimp." At her self-deprecating comment, the other girls just lost it. Presley tried not to laugh, but she finally gave in.

"Does Kane treat you like a cripple?" Cady raised her majestic head and looked Lilibet directly in the eye, like she was daring her to answer the question incorrectly.

"No," Lilibet confessed. "He treats me like I'm his most precious possession."

"We saw Zane, Presley," Jessie propped her hands on her protruding little tummy. "He couldn't keep his hands off you."

"Well – well," she had no come back. He had been very attentive. "But why would you want me to be friends with me? Zane and I may see one another again and we may not. I have no idea what's going to happen. I may not even be his employer much longer – I'm just a temp."

"There are other reasons – like you being a wonderful person that we'd love to get to know. Zane has been talking about you to the boys. We know about helpful you are, we know about the volunteer work you do at the hospital. We even know you cook like an angel. But the clincher for me was how you stood up for me when that idiot in the coffee shop was giving me a hard time."

Presley sipped her drink, needing the warmth and needing the time to process what the women were trying to tell her. Jessie was sincere, and so were the others. "Okay. I would love to be your friend," she looked at them one by one. "I'd be honored to come to Libby's party."

"Can I have my secretary back now?"

Zane slipped up on them and Presley jumped a little when he touched her. His secretary - as a temporary employee that should have been music to her ears, but somehow the words made her sad. She wanted to be more. The girls didn't react to his words other than to smile, but she knew they knew what was going through her mind and it embarrassed her. "Sure, is there something I can do for you?" She stood up and as she did, Willie Nelson broke into song and sporadic applause sounded around the pavilion.

"Yea, you can dance with me." Zane took her by the hand and pulled her body up close to his.

Dance? "I don't know how," she whispered.

"We're in trouble, then," he chuckled. "Because I'm counting on you to lead."

"Blue Eyes Crying in the Rain" was one of her favorite songs, but Presley paid little attention to it or to the singer. She was being held close to a man on the dance floor for the very first time. It was hard to breathe.

"See, we are doing just fine," Zane bent his head and spoke only for her. They weren't really dancing, but rather swaying to the music. "I just wanted an excuse to get my hands on you."

Presley chewed on her bottom lip. She wanted nothing more than to stay right where she was, because being cradled in Zane's arms was heaven. He held her right hand, but his left was resting right at the base of her spine, and he was drawing the most incredible circles on that sensitive spot. But she had to ask – she needed to know. "Are you being nice to me because you feel sorry for me? Or because you're grateful that I helped Jessie?"

The music hadn't stopped, but Zane went still. "What the hell?" He let go of her hand and surprised her by cupping her bottom and picking her up, sliding her up his body far enough till she was pressed right against him, her mound nestled in the cradle of his pelvis and what she felt there was hard and long and thick. "Does that feel like I'm sorry for you or that I'm just grateful? Don't you remember what shape your kiss had me in right before Jacob came for his meeting?"

Presley's feet weren't touching the ground. She knew she ought to be feeling self-conscious, but a glance around showed that no one was watching them. They were on the far side in a pool of shadows. "I remember," she whispered. "I can't believe it, but I remember. You did hear me tell you that my mouth is messed up?"

"Yes, and I ran my fingers and my tongue over your mouth to show you how I felt about it, didn't I?"

She was looking into his eyes and it was as if he were looking back at her. To stabilize herself she had been holding to his shoulders, but now seemed like a good time for a hug. Wrapping her arms around his neck, she kissed his cheek. "Yes, you did. I don't understand it, but I believe you."

"I want more of your kisses," Zane slid his lips over the exposed skin of her shoulder. "Will you stay with me tonight?"

"What?"

Zane grinned. "I want to have a sleep over with you." She looked surprised, but she wasn't the only one. He was surprised at himself. What had changed? With Presley he had no real fear of rejection. She wasn't like that. In some ways, she was as vulnerable as he was and maybe that made all the difference. But the main reason was that his body was in sexual overdrive. Years of near-celibacy had ramped up his need to the point that he was literally starved for the touch of a woman. Zane craved sex. He wanted to bury his cock as deep into Presley's heat as he could.

"I'm so happy. I never thought I would find someone like you," she buried her head in his neck and let her body relax into his.

A niggle of doubt attempted to break through the haze of lust that blanketed every molecule of Zane's being. Part of him realized that Presley was reading more into this than he intended. But he didn't have the strength or the ability to deny his body the delights of partaking of the sensual offering of Presley's sweet embrace. Zane needed the touch of another human being – desperately.

"Let's get something to eat and get through this evening as quickly as we can. I can't wait to get my hands on you."

Wow. "Okay," one small word, but to Presley the short expression of agreement was momentous. She was relinquishing her doubts, her insecurities and her innocence into Zane's hands.

Presley Grace Love was a virgin.

Rex wove his way through the people and Presley held his hand and went with them. The crowd parted, everyone knew their host couldn't see to find his way, but they also had been around him enough not to be surprised that he moved with a high degree of certainty and assurance.

When Zane held out her chair, Presley wasn't surprised. Two plates of BBQ were set before them and Zane leaned over, "what's on my plate and where is it – clock wise."

She hesitated a second, then comprehension dawned. "Baked beans are at two o'clock, potato salad is at six and brisket is at ten. A roll is sitting at high noon."

"Perfect, gorgeous," he placed a hand on her knee and caressed the soft skin. She jumped. "It's okay, I'm just getting you used to my touch."

Becoming accustomed to his touch sounded like an impossible dream – but one she would love to have come true. He slid his hand up a little farther, Presley closed her eyes and waited to see what he'd do.

"Zane, aren't you going to introduce me to this pretty lady?"

Heck.

It was Kane.

"Hello, brother," Zane smiled, "meet Presley Love Grace, she's helping me in the office and keeping me company. Presley, this is my twin Sheriff Kane Saucier."

"Very nice to meet you," she smiled a greeting.

"I can't tell you how glad I am to meet you."

Zane cleared his throat as if he were giving Kane a warning and Kane laughed. "Maybe you two could come over for supper one night." Presley started to answer with a noncommittal nicety but Zane beat her to it.

"Lilibet's cooking is always a treat," was all he said before he moved on to another topic. "I wanted to let you know that the grand jury will convene on Hanks next week and Lilibet needs to get ready to testify."

Kane let out a long sigh. "I knew it was coming and I know it's necessary, but I dread it for her. It's going to drag up so many unpleasant memories."

"You'll be there with her, she'll be fine," Zane assured him. "I'll take care of all the details, we're gonna put that bastard away for a long, long time."

Turning to her, he explained. "A thug with a grudge against Kane kidnapped Lilibet a while back in an attempt to extort money from our family." They continued the conversion while Presley tried to listen, but it was hard because Zane was still stroking her leg just above the knee.

"Oh, I forgot to tell you," Kane left one subject for another. "I know you've been handling Noah's case against that shithead Ajax. I thought you ought to know that Harper has just up and disappeared. She and Noah weren't seeing eye-to-eye and after the bad experience she had and the beating Noah took for her, I guess she couldn't handle it. Coincidentally, I just got a call today from a fellow over in Louisiana looking for Harper. I thought you ought to know."

"What was his name?" Zane asked quizzically. "Does he have anything to do with Ajax? Could he be part of the BDSM world?"

Presley's ears perked up, the conversation was taking an odd turn.

"I don't think so, he sounded legitimate. His name was Revel Lee Jones. He said he was an old friend of Harper's and was just trying to locate her. I didn't tell him much, but I did say that when or if we saw her again that I would pass the word along."

"Hmmm," Zane mused. "I might ought to check up on him, just in case he's one of Ajax's thugs trying to cause more trouble."

"Good deal," Kane doffed his hat at Presley. "If you need me for the next couple of days, I'm headed to New Orleans."

"What's going on? Were you summoned?" Being called home by the family wasn't always a good thing.

"I'm not sure, but I'll let you know,"

Zane thought his twin was being unnecessarily mysterious, but he let it drop. Right now, he had more pleasant things to think about. "All right, be careful on your trip."

"I'll do it, brother. I hope to see you again, Miss Love. And don't let this conniving legal eagle take advantage of you – he bears watching."

"Thank you, Sheriff," Presley nodded her head and smiled shyly.

Willie sang on, people danced and they ate their fill. Several others came up and introduced themselves to her and she knew she'd never keep all the names and faces straight. It amazed her that Zane always knew exactly who was speaking to them. "You have a fantastic memory," she complimented him.

"Thanks," he brushed off the compliment. "People are leaving; soon we can head up to the house. If you'll sit here for just a few minutes, I'll go to the barn and make sure all of the arrangements have been made to ship these babies to their new homes." Standing up, he leaned over and kissed her on the temple before he and Rex strode confidently off. Presley couldn't help but notice the looks she was getting from the remaining few who were still lingering at their tables or on the dance floor. She could read their expressions clearly – some seemed approving, but there were a few who gave her odd glances and knowing smiles. Her imagination might be running away with her, but it was almost as if she could hear them thinking that Zane wouldn't be showering her with attention and kisses if he could see her face.

A waiter brought her coffee and she took a few sips. Her hand was shaking so much she put the other one up to steady the cup. Gracious! She needed to calm down. Thoughts were rushing through her head like white rapids. She was nervous. Being intimate with Zane was mind-blowing. She wanted it. She wanted him. Desire for the handsome lawyer was cascading through her body like lava.

Presley didn't know for sure what he had in mind for the evening, but she didn't think it was a late-night work session. Could she do it? For so long she had just accepted the fact that a relationship was not in the cards for her. And now, this incredible man had noticed her. Honestly, she didn't have a clue what he saw in her. Lord, the irony of that thought wasn't lost on her. And God help her, she would give Zane back his sight if she could, but right now she was grateful that he couldn't see her – because if he could, he wouldn't want her. No one realized that truth more than she did.

Chapter Four

"Well, I'm glad that's over with," Zane spoke right behind her causing her to jump the tiniest bit.

"You say that a lot, don't you?"

"Kane always said it was my mantra. I said it after finishing every project, after every distasteful chore, even after every tedious date that didn't work out like I planned." He picked up her hair and kissed it. "Are you ready to go inside?"

"Yes," she stood up, her knees were weak.

They didn't have to walk, Sherwood stood ready to drive them further into the property. "Did the sale go well?"

"It did," he allowed her to enter first. "Thank you, Sherwood," he acknowledged his driver's help. Rex settled at their feet with a flop and a huff. He was tired too.

"Where to, Sir? Am I taking the lady home?"

"No, we're going to the house, please."

Presley was embarrassed, but Zane covered her hand with his.

"Very good, sir."

She couldn't tell what Sherwood was thinking, hopefully it wasn't bad thoughts about her. When the car pulled up in front of the house, Presley was in awe. It was so beautiful! But it fit Zane so well, "I love your home," she told him as they exited the vehicle.

"Thank you, Presley." Zane unleashed Rex and he ran happily around the yard. "He needs to do his business." Sherwood left them after a brief exchange with Zane.

"Will he come back when he's through?"

"Yes, Rex is impeccably trained." A whinny from the barn drew Zane's attention. "The horses are accustomed to me spending some time with them every night."

"Go, if you need to, I don't mind," it would give her time to settle her nerves – before – before – whatever was to come.

"No," he stepped right up against her, his body heat encompassing her and making her shiver. "I'm right where I want to be."

He took her face in his hands and caressed it tenderly, pushing her hair back behind her ears. As he had earlier, he ran his finger over her face, lightly, but this time he retraced the path with his lips. By the time he was finished, Presley was wet and wanting.

Rex bounded up and Zane got them in the house. He refused to turn her loose. But it was dark. "Can I turn on a light?"

Zane laughed. "There's not one on?" At her groan of embarrassment, he chuckled. "It's okay, I'm teasing. Please, turn on the light. If I remember correctly, it's to the right side of the front door. Rachel had the evening off and she didn't know I'd be having company."

She found the light and flipped it on, instantly the darkness was illuminated by recessed lighting built into the wood ceiling. Presley took the room in – it was beautiful.

"Did you find it? Can you see now?"

She touched his shoulder, "Yes, you have a beautiful house."

For a moment her tone reminded him of Margaret's. The memory gave him an uneasy feeling. "What appeals to you?" He knew what the answer would be: the expensive Persian rugs, the original art work on the walls and the sumptuous leather furniture. All women were impressed by fine things.

He heard her walk away from him and if he wasn't mistake, she twirled around – he could hear the tap of her feet dancing on the floor. "I can just see Christmas stockings hanging from this amazing stone fireplace and the hearth is wide enough to sit on and pop popcorn." He heard her skitter over to toward the dining room. "And the staircase is perfect for sliding down the banister!" Again she had surprised him. Presley saw the world through different eyes than most people.

Presley ran her hand over the rich wood of the walls and admired the fresh flowers that sat on the sofa table and the dining table. "If you could see where I grew up, and where I live, you'd know why I think this place feels like home."

"Come to me," he directed her with a seductive tone. "I want you right by my side tonight."

Presley felt a bit playful, in fact she felt better than she had in a long time. "So, this isn't overtime? I thought maybe you brought me here to take notes on some briefs, or something."

"Ha! The only briefs I want you concentrating on tonight are mine, and I mean how to get them off of me."

She nestled up close to him, confidently and he wrapped his arms around her.

"Sounds like you are going to be playing hard to get."

This time he threw his head back and laughed hard. "No, I don't think you'll find me holding back. I'm ready to give you everything I've got." He pressed his hardness against her and made her gasp, which reminded him that he needed to take it slow. "Tell me about where you grew up."

A bit embarrassed, she hung her head – which he couldn't see, so she lifted it and just spoke the truth. This man was so far out of her league that there was no use pretending they had anything in common but the law – and hopefully friendship. To hope for more than that was just almost impossible to even conceive the possibility. "I lived with my grandmother in a trailer park on the south side of Beaumont. It was clean, but really small and the neighbors made me a little nervous. I've only seen my mother a few times and the last time was when I was six years old. And I have no idea who my dad is."

She had let her voice trail off and he knew sharing that information with him had been hard. "Don't you dare be ashamed of who you are – you are beautiful and smart and have one of the sweetest spirits I have ever encountered." With that declaration, he covered her mouth with his and took her breath away.

A pitiful whine and clicking toenails reminded Zane that somebody needed to be fed. "Heck, let's take care of Rex, then we'll take a shower."

Shower? "Together?"

"You'd better believe together." Zane took her by the hand. "Come on," he led her through the dining room – in the dark – to the kitchen.

She felt on the interior wall where the light switch would normally be and found it. "Wow, what a kitchen!"

She pulled away from him and began to make little oohing and ahhing noises.

Zane loved to listen to her. He could imagine her making those same noises when she touched his body. "What are you finding to get so excited about?"

"A lot of things - like refrigerated cooling drawers, a marble slab and a convection oven. This kitchen is a bakers dream. I can't imagine having all of this space and wonderful equipment to use." She didn't sound jealous, instead she giggled – the sweetest little sound of total contentment. "You are very fortunate."

"I suppose so," he agreed as he opened the cabinet to find Rex's meal.

Presley thought about what she had said, "I didn't mean to downplay what has happened to you with your eyesight, but I forget. To me, you are strong and brilliant and perfect."

Zane felt like a boulder had been lifted from his shoulders. "You don't think of me as less than a man?" He filled Rex's dish and sat it down in its standard place.

Her footsteps fell softly as she moved toward him, the faint scent of her perfume and another clean, sweet scent that he was coming to associate just with her fell on his senses. "Zane, you are more of a man than anyone I've ever met."

She drew near to him; he could feel her heat before she touched him. Seemingly, without a qualm, she molded her body to his, pressing the pillows of her breast into his chest. Zane felt his cock jump. Holding his face steady with one hand, she kissed him gently on the lips.

"I need you, Presley," he groaned.

"I need you, too," she confessed as she continued to steal kisses from the corners of his lips. For the first time, Presley felt a heady type of feminine power. Zane wanted her and she was allowed to touch and kiss and enjoy his body. Oh, she knew that she was basically unschooled and probably not the kind of woman he was used to, but she had her hands on him now and this chance may not come again.

Sliding her lips down his neck, she kissed a path and started to pull his shirt from his pants with the other.

"Wait," he stilled her hand.

His one word was like pouring cold water all over her, she stilled, moved her hands and stepped back, never saying a word. Presley had made a practice of never venturing where she wasn't wanted – it just made things easier. "Sorry," she said simply.

Zane heard the hurt in her voice. He knew she thought she had overstepped her bounds. "No, hell no," he grasped her arms. "I loved what you were doing, but it's been a long time. I want to pleasure you; I don't want to cum prematurely like some untried school boy."

What he said made her like she could breathe again. "I don't think you could do anything wrong with me," she said softly. "I just love to be close to you."

"Damn, you make me feel like a fuckin' king," he felt for her hand, spun her around and began walking. "Rex, I'm closing the door, buddy – you're on your own."

Presley had to take double steps to keep up with him. "I'm nervous," she announced, just because she thought he ought to know.

"Why?" He was a little nervous too, but he had already expressed enough sexual trepidation to have his man-card revoked. What man told a woman that he hadn't fucked in so long that he had little to no control? Well he hadn't, in so many words, but he had been damn close.

Presley could tell they were in his bedroom, she could see the shape of a massive king-size bed, but – as usual – it was dark. Now if he could see her, she would opt for the light being off – but since he couldn't, she wasn't going to miss the chance to look at his beautiful body, no sirree. "Where's the light, Zane?"

He veered to the left and stubbed his toe on something – "Ow, here," and light flooded the room. "Come on to the bathroom," he flipped that light on too.

With sureness born of familiarity, Zane turned on the water in a huge tiled shower. Presley looked around in awe. "This bathroom looks like a Roman spa, Zane."

"Does it?" right now he didn't care if they were in one of those outdoor stalls at a state park – if he didn't get his hands and mouth on her sweet little body soon he was going to go mad. "Let's get nekkid," he quipped as he turned around and made a grab for her.

Presley didn't try to elude him, she wasn't stupid.

"Okay," immediately her hands went to her own clothes. "I'll undress."

"Let me," Zane had gone dead serious. "The only way I can see you is to touch you and I want to see you more than I want to see tomorrow."

"Just as much as I want to look at you," Presley couldn't be quiet. She was determined.

"Okay, okay," he had to smile. "Let me pull off my stuff and then we can get to the important part."

"Speak for yourself," she was grumbling just a bit and helping him undo his shirt all at the same time. "I love your body, you are so damn fine."

Zane chuckled – he was having such a good time. How long had it been since he had experienced such joy just being with another person, especially a woman. What he had missed out on! It was unbelievable! "I am speaking for myself." Together they got the buttons undone and he began to shrug it off his shoulders – and

Holy God – he could feel feather light little kisses dusting across his chest. "Fuck!" The little vixen giggled.

"Pants, Presley," was all he could say. She hopped right to it, he couldn't fault her level of enthusiasm, they did have trouble with the hardware, though. Finally she just swatted his hands away, "Let me!"

"Yes, mam, Miss Patience," he stood still while she unbuttoned and unzipped. But when it came time to push them down, she relented.

"I guess you better do that, this is outside my area of expertise."

"No problem." If he weren't so damn horny, he might pursue that line of questioning, but he was in too big of a hurry to think. Skimming off his pants, he pushed them aside with his foot and jerked down his shorts and kicked them aside.

"Oh my Lord," Presley muttered under her breath.

"Do you like what you see?" God, he hoped so. He held his breath and he knew her answer when he felt the slightest brush of her fingertips down his shaft.

Zane's whole body jerked and Presley was amazed at the response she could draw from this big, sexy guy. "Yes, I think you're big and beautiful." With a little more self-confidence, she wrapped her hand around the thick stalk and marveled at how hard and warm it was. As she caressed him softly, she let the fingers of the other hand trail up and down his hard, hair roughened thigh. God, he was all man! Especially the part she held in her hand. And this was supposed to fit inside of her? That might be a problem.

All right, enough. He wasn't made of steel. "Hell, I can't wait, baby. I've got to touch you." He slid his hands up her arms and held her head, kissing her hard. "Damn, I'm trembling."

"It's okay – it's just me, I'm nobody special."

Zane supposed her humble comment was meant to be comforting, but it just succeeded in making him crazy. "Hell yes, you're special. Don't you know what this means to me? You have no idea how lonely I've been." He began mapping her face with kisses as he ran his hands over her shoulders, skimming down over her breasts. "Are there buttons, a zipper or over the head?"

It was hard to formulate words – a man was touching her body. She stifled a giggle, he had found the turquoise bead insets and were rubbing them between his fingers – and then – oh God! "That's my nipples."

"I'm blind, Presley Love – but I remember basic anatomy." It was through her dress and her bra, but he was rubbing the little nubbins and the spark he was igniting between her legs was about to catch ablaze. "Turn around," she did as he bid. Moving her hair aside, he slowly lowered the zipper. "God, you smell good, fresh and sweet as summer rain." Zane parted the material and pressed a kiss right at the nape of her neck while he undid her bra. "Can I touch you?"

He was asking permission? Presley thought that was a given. "Yes," her answer came out sounding like a croaky little frog's voice.

"Good," he slid his hands inside her dress, and around to cup her breasts, pushing her bra up and out of the way. "Oh God, yeah – you feel so good." Her soft, luscious tits were more than a handful; they were round, firm globes that were smooth as silk with big puffy areolas and hard suckable nipples. He spread his legs and widened his stance so his cock could rub against her ass. "Presley – hell, Presley – I want you so much," he nuzzled her neck as his hips involuntarily bucked forward, his hardness nudging her softness.

"I – uh – I, oh God, Zane – I want," the last word rose in pitch and intensity, and it said it all – she wanted. Presley wanted Zane. New feelings and intense longings were swamping her senses. She laid her head back on his chest and just luxuriated in the wonder of his hands on her breasts.

Zane was in heaven. Why had he waited so long to experience pleasure such as this? As the sweet woman in his arms pushed back against him and whimpered, he knew why – he needed someone who would accept him just the way he was. And she did. "I need more." More. He needed more of her. "Hold up your arms," he directed. She did and he lifted the dress over her head. "Now turn around, Baby – I want to see you."

She knew what he meant and her whole body quivered at the thought. "I hope you like me. And before the night is over, I want equal time."

"I'll give you all the time you want." He rubbed his palms over the slope of her shoulders. "You are so dainty. Your skin is like silk."

She eased a little closer to him, there was no way she could stay away. "Thank you, I love your chest."

Presley leaned over and nipped him and Zane growled his approval as his hands returned to her breasts again, as if he couldn't stay away. "Perfect. I love your tits."

"Touch me, please."

"Where, Presley?" Her desperation just fueled his passion. Being desired and needed was incredibly addictive.

"My breasts," she whispered.

"I am touching you," he crooned to her, suspecting what she was really asking.

"With your lips," she said so softly he almost couldn't hear. "If you don't mind – that is."

Sinking to his knees, he pushed her tits together and molded them in his hands, caressing and shaping them – rubbing his thumbs over the nipples. "You want me, don't you?"

"Please," she begged. He didn't make her wait any longer. Zane wrapped his arms around her waist and took a nipple in his mouth and began to suck. Presley couldn't help but watch his face, his lips as they worked at her nipple. The sensation was exquisite. She clasped his head and stroked his hair as he nursed at her breast. "That feels so wonderful, Zane," she praised him.

He switched to the other breast to suck and let his hands explore. Her waist was small, and her hips flared just right. He traced her curves and the image in his mind of her gorgeous body made his lust rise even higher. He opened his mouth wider and drew hard on her breast and exulted in the moan that escaped her lips.

Presley pressed her thighs together, she was so very wet. Hunger for him consumed her. More than anything she wanted to ask him to touch her between the legs but she couldn't bring herself to ask. What she was receiving from him was more than she had ever expected. He was licking all around her nipple, nipping and nuzzling and his hands were now moving lower, skimming over her thighs and down her legs. Zane was learning her body.

Pulling back, Zane sought for control. "You're beautiful. Your body is perfect. I can't believe how fuckin' perfect you are. Presley Love, you have long, smooth, supple legs that I can't wait to feel wrapped around my waist, a spankable lush little bottom, a tiny waist and tits that a pin-up girl would die for."

Zane thought she was beautiful. To Presley, his words were a miracle. Of course, he couldn't see her face, but right now – that wasn't important. She caressed his shoulders, loving how his powerful biceps flexed. He was holding back. "What's wrong?"

"I want you so much," he ground out the words. Standing up, he took her by the hand. "Let's get in the shower, I want to kiss you."

Presley didn't want to complain, but a kiss was a bit anticlimactic. But she went, simply put – she'd follow him anywhere. The shower was huge, at least eight foot by five foot. And she counted an incredible fourteen sprayer heads. "This is more like a spa. I've never seen a shower like this." The tile was cream colored with ornate accent tiles and a see-through glass door gave the illusion of privacy. She didn't get any more time to examine her surroundings, because Zane pulled her against him and began kissing her voraciously - deep drugging kisses. Pushing her against the wall, he rubbed his cock back forth against her front, letting her know how aroused he was.

"Are you wet for me?" he fingertips danced over her lower belly, delving between her legs.

"Yes, I've been wet for you for days," she admitted her weakness.

"Good, because you know I've been hard for you. Even when you slipped up to the couch to watch me sleep, I got hard for you."

His revelation made her gasp and squirm. "How did you know?" God, she was embarrassed.

"I could hear you, I heard soft, little footsteps and shallow breaths that caught with excitement." He trailed his lips over her shoulder and took the cord of her neck in his mouth and bit it gently. "And I could smell you, not only your natural sweet scent and perfume, I could smell your arousal."

"Oh, God," Presley wasn't sure how to feel. Truthfully, she could only feel. He had stolen her ability to think.

"Oh yeah," he growled. "You're wet. And I fuckin' love the way your pussy feels. I like it that you're not bare, but you're soft and downy, trimmed short. I'm gonna love moving my lips back and forth over your treasure."

Presley's womb contracted with need as he made a come hither motion with his fingers, spreading her juices from back to front. Her clit throbbed with anticipation and she was so overwhelmed with arousal that her whole body jerked in response.

"Lean back, I'm going to pick you up."

"What?" The next thing she knew, Zane had placed both hands under her bottom and lifted her up – and up.

"Put your legs around my neck."

"Oh my God!" she grasped the ledge at the very top of the shower and held on for dear life. Her legs were splayed open and her pussy was right in his face. "I'm too heavy, what are . . ." And then he transported her to paradise as he began licking and kissing her slit, his tongue rasping over the tender flesh, singing it with each touch.

"Zane!" Presley cried out as she arched her back and pressed her shoulders against the wall, pushing her pelvis more fully in his face. "I need you, please," she moaned. This was pure heaven. It was unadulterated ecstasy. "More, more," she pleaded. What Zane was doing to her was the most pleasurable thing she had ever known in her whole life.

Lord help, she tasted good. Zane flicked his tongue around the perfect berry of her clit and reveled in the honey he lapped up with his tongue. Presley wanted him. She wanted him – the blind man. He was pleasing her; he was making her pulse with joy. "Cum for me, doll. Let me know how much you want me." He closed his lips over her clit and began to suck and hum and she went wild. Tightening his grip on her waist, he held her steady while she bucked and jerked in his arms.

"God! Yesssss! Zane! Please!" Sweeping, sweet arcs of pleasure whipped through her body as she panted and strained to get closer to him. Even in the dampness of the shower, perspiration beaded up on her body and it was because she was on fire – literally on fire for a man for the first time in her existence. "I don't think I can stand it," she whimpered.

Oh, yes she could. He was going to give her everything he had and then he was going to take all she would give him. Zane ached. His very soul hungered to become one with this woman. His cock was so swollen and distended that precum was leaking from the tip. If he didn't get some relief soon, he would explode involuntarily just from giving this incredible woman sweet pleasure.

Moving one shoulder farther under her, he freed one hand to play with. Flicking his tongue on her clit as he suckled, he pushed two fingers inside her tight little canal and eased them in and out – in and out and when he did she screamed – she literally screamed and it was the sweetest sound he had ever heard. Zane Saucier had brought a woman to a raging orgasm and he felt like a fuckin' king.

Stars exploded and galaxies collided as Presley felt for the first time an orgasm she didn't give to herself. He held her while she quivered, letting her down slowly, her body sliding against his. "Thank you, Zane. I loved it, thank you so much." Her adoration and gratitude couldn't be contained.

"It was my pleasure, Presley," and that was no lie. Cradling her next to him, he loved how her body molded to his. When her little hands edged between their bodies and found his cock he almost went to his knees. "God, yes," he groaned.

Presley sank down, unsure of what she was doing, but determined to do it anyway. She held his member and caressed it, rubbing her cheek against it. This was part of him and therefore it was beautiful. She held it upright and licked it from bottom to top. Every little move and touch she gave him, he rewarded her with a moan or gasp. Clearly, Zane was not unmoved by her attention. With a tiny smile, she studied the head of his cock. "Can I taste you?"

"Yea," he growled, the only word he could manage to say.

Presley was desperate for him, her lips trembled as she licked them. Could she do it? He was big and hard, heavy in her hand, the base so thick that her thumb and second finger wouldn't meet. The huge mushroom head was dark red and throbbing and she couldn't resist swiping her tongue across it. The drop of clear liquid at the tip was salty and tangy and she wanted more. Fitting her lips tightly to the top, she slipped them down and over, sucking the end of his cock into her mouth and swirling her tongue around it.

"Ah, damn," he groaned as he held her head, tangling his fingers in the air. "That's so good. Suck me, baby."

Ecstasy made Zane's toes curl. The muscles of his legs became like stone. All of his concentration was on his cock as it was enveloped in the wet, hot haven of Presley's mouth.

BAM! BAM! BAM!

What the hell?

Presley, bless her heart, was so into sucking him, she couldn't hear whoever was beating down his front door. Hell! God, he was close. This little angel was sipping at his cock like it was the finest wine and if he had to. . . .

BAM! BAM! BAM!

"FUCK!" he bellowed and Presley jumped.

"What's wrong?"

BAM! BAM! BAM! BAM!

"There's somebody at the damn door and they're not going to go away." Shit! "I'm sorry, Baby." He stepped out, grabbed a towel and stalked out of the bathroom. "Somebody better goddam be dying."

Presley stood up and stepped out of the spacious shower. She took a towel and dried off and slipped back into her clothes. What had happened? She heard voices.

"Who is it?" Zane asked gruffly as he swung the door open. "This better damn well be something important." He had just walked away from a beautiful woman and a blow-job and he was not happy.

"Zane, God, Zane, we need you. Why didn't you answer your damn cell phone?"

It was Noah.

"I was busy," he expected Noah to realize he was standing here in a damn towel and get the idea that he might possibly have feminine company.

But he didn't. Instead Zane heard him hit the door facing with his fist.

"Get in here. What's wrong?"

"He's missing, Zane."

"Who's missing?"

"Aron. Aron's missing."

"What? How?" Zane felt a horrible feeling in his gut.

"He and Libby went snorkeling and when she came up – he didn't."

"God, are you sure?"

Noah's voice cracked. "Yea, I'm sure. Zane, can you come help?"

"Let me get my pants on, we'll be right behind you."

"Are you dressed?" Zane came back and he seemed disturbed. She hoped he wasn't regretting what had happened.

"Yes, I didn't know what was going on." What they had shared had been more than wonderful, but something had happened to dampen his mood. "What's wrong?"

"I need to go to Tebow Ranch, Aron's missing."

"Missing? My God! How?"

"I don't know very many details, only that he and Libby went snorkeling and Aron didn't surface."

"He drowned?"

"Hell. God, I hope not." All the time he was talking, Zane was dressing.

"Did they find a body?"

Zane felt for her and pulled her close. "Noah didn't say so," he squeezed her tight. "We have to go, but I just need to hold you for a minute."

She let him hold her, taking what comfort she could give. Aron McCoy was his friend.

"Hold me as long as you want, I like to be close to you."

When he finally let her go, she knew it was time to go. "Do you want me to call a cab?"

"No," he tucked her hand in his arm. "I need you with me. And not just for work reasons, although we're going to have work to do too. Do you mind?" He stopped in his tracks. "It is after midnight, am I asking too much?"

"No!" she petted his arm with her free hand, "I want to help you and the McCoys if I can." All she could process was that he wanted her with him and 'not just for work reasons', whatever that meant."

Zane smiled. "That's all I needed to hear. Let's go." He hooked Rex up with his halter and hesitated. "Do you drive?"

"Yes," she answered slowly. For a moment she didn't understand what he was getting at. "Oh sure, you don't have to wake Sherwood. If there is a vehicle you don't mind risking with me, I'll be glad to drive us."

"Good, I have a pickup."

Presley followed his directions to Tebow Ranch. Along the way, Zane told her a little bit about the family. "I've only been their lawyer a little over two years. Kane and I knew Joseph in college, we knew all the boys, but we were closer to Joseph. Before I lost my sight, Kane and I rocked climbed and rode dirt bikes with him. Something most people don't know about Joseph is that he can sing. He doesn't do it often, but when he gets a guitar in his hand, I swear the boy can charm the birds from the trees. That's how he met Willie Nelson. Willie sang at one of the clubs on Sixth Street and Joseph was there. One of his band members recognized him from college and remembered how he used to perform at Austin City Limits with some of the local boys. Willie knew Joseph by reputation and drug him up on stage – and the rest they say, is history. They ended up singing a duet, got drunk and both got arrested. Of course by the time the boys in blue realized who they had, it turned into a celebration that rocked city hall – in a good way.

"I remember seeing Joseph play in college, wasn't he called 'The Stallion' at UT?"

Zane snorted, "Yea, he was. I guess all the girls fell for Joseph. He sure has settled down. Did you know he was paralyzed earlier this year, it's a miracle that he's walking today."

"No, I didn't know that, I'm glad everything is okay. His fiancé is nice. She said that you knew each other back in New Orleans." She was holding up her end of the conversation, but the night was dark so Presley was being careful on the unfamiliar stretch of road.

"Yes, I took care of her families legal affairs for a while. I'll have to share with you about them someday. You won't believe the stories I could tell you."

She glanced over at his profile in the dark. "They believe in magic, don't they?" she had picked up on that much from the earlier conversation with the women. With all her heart, Presley longed for a little magic in her life, magic that would make her beautiful enough for a man like Zane.

"Yes, they do." Zane didn't elaborate. "I believe the McCoy family is going to need some magic or a miracle or both." He looked out the window as if watching the countryside go by. "Aron was married before to a woman named Sabrina. It didn't work out and she has caused problems for the family every way she can since then."

"That's awful," Presley saw the FM sign she had been looking for and turned right. The big pickup was easier to handle than she had anticipated. "How did he meet Libby?

"Bess, their housekeeper had to take care of a sick relative and brought in Libby to pinch hit for her. It was the damn luckiest day of Aron's life, I'll tell you that. He was so hurt by Sabrina's antics that he had practically given up on women. Aron's a sculptor, I have several of his pieces in my front lobby. You'll have to check them out."

"I've seen them, they're beautiful, but I didn't know they were Aron's. I pray that he's okay," Presley could see the Tebow sign straight ahead. "I think we're getting close, Zane."

"Good, I'm worried. Libby is in remission from leukemia and she deserves happiness in her life, not heartache."

Presley's heart ached for Libby and Aron. "We'll do all we can, Zane. I know she's pregnant and vulnerable and scared to death. I'll pray for her."

"Prayer sure couldn't hurt."

As Presley pulled up to the ranch house she saw that all the lights were blazing and cars were parked everywhere. They parked, got out and she and Rex walked with him to the door. "Zane, I'm glad you're here," a voice spoke from the shadows on the porch.

"Lance," Zane recognized the Tebow foreman's voice. "How are they?"

"It's bad," Lance sighed. "I won't lie to you. But I'm here and I'll keep everything going. This is a damn shame and a hard shock. I don't know what we'll do without Aron."

Zane stopped near the front door. "Don't give up on him yet. Aron's a tough ole' cuss. Lance, this is Presley Love. Presley, this is Lance Rogers, the foreman of Tebow."

"Miss Love," Lance tipped his hat.

"Where's Jacob?"

"He's gone," Lance explained. "As soon as Libby called, he was out of here. He's probably down there by now."

The door opened and Cady stood there, her face tear-streaked. "I thought I heard voices. Why don't the two of you come in? Lance, you too, I've made a pot of coffee."

Presley stepped in behind Zane, but before Lance, and she quickly took in the huge warm room that had surely seen so many family celebrations, but now looked like it housed a wake. The girls who lived at Tebow had made themselves known, fall decorations and wreaths were in abundance. Love was displayed everywhere. One of the focal points of the room was the fireplace, but instead of a painting or a wreath, there were photographs of the family. Presley strained to see, because the room was dim but she could make out all the brothers and their women. A distinct family resemblance prevailed, only one brother stood out with his lighter hair and she wasn't sure which one he was. And there was a young one too, he looked sweet. But another resemblance was evident; all of them looked happy and loved.

Presley was jealous.

Zane was immediately surrounded by big McCoy men, their faces somber and drawn. "God, we're glad you're here."

All of them started talking at once and Zane held up his hand. "Let's go to kitchen table and I want you to tell me everything. But first – let me introduce you to Presley." Zane moved Rex to one side so he could draw her closer. He made her feel so special, it was such an alien feeling.

Graciously, the men turned to her and introduced themselves one by one.

"Hey, Presley, I'm Joseph."

"Hello, I wish we were meeting under better circumstance." Now that she had seen his face up close, Presley realized she recognized him from magazine covers. Later she would tell him how much she admired him, but now wasn't the time.

"Me, too." He put a hand on each of his brother's shoulders. "And these are my little brothers, Isaac and Noah."

So, Noah was the blonde. They both greeted her, but there was only politeness – it was more than obvious they were scared to death for their brother. As they moved through the living room, Presley looked at the others. Jessie smiled at her weakly, she had her arms around a young teenage boy whose head was buried against her baby bump. Avery and Cady were in the kitchen and one solitary man sat at the dining table staring down at a cup of coffee. "Presley, meet Bowie Travis." The man named Bowie stood up and held out a chair for her.

"Hello, Presley. Jacob and Jessie speak very highly of you."

"I'm glad," she met his warm gaze. There was something about his eyes that looked familiar. He was haunted about something; Presley felt he was a kindred spirit.

Cady didn't even ask but began setting warm muffins and hot coffee on the table. Zane found a chair, released Rex and patted the one next to him. The others joined them, it pained Presley to see the looks of despair on their faces. "All right tell me what we know. When's the last time anyone talked with Libby?"

"We spoke to her the last time about fifteen minutes before you arrived." It was Isaac speaking. "Hell, Zane," he ruffled his hair and banged his fist on the table, "when Libby first called it took me five minutes to get her to quit screaming and crying enough to calm down and tell me what was wrong. I have to tell you that was the most awful thing I had ever heard in my life. Libby's in agony. We all are."

Presley knew Zane was here, not only to help, but also to be the voice of reason. "I know you are and we're going to do everything humanly possible to find Aron and bring him home. Now, tell me what you've done as far as making sure the search and rescue operations are in full swing."

Noah stood up to look out the window, but he proceeded to give details of what had transpired. "Jacob should be there by now; we're waiting to hear from him. I've already spoken to the Chief Inspector and he assures me that they are doing everything they can to find Aron."

Zane touched Presley's arm. "We need to get on top of this." Facing the brothers, he asked, "Do you have a laptop we could use?" Joseph got up and stepped out of the room as he continued to give her instructions. "Find out what you can about their procedure on how to handle missing person cases and get me contacts for helicopters, boats, k-9 units and any volunteer rescue teams that may be available. I want every bit of manpower we muster on the case."

Joseph returned and presented her with a computer. Immediately, she logged in and began her search. An undeniable sense of urgency permeated the room.

"Are you going with us?" Joseph asked out of the blue. "I have a plane gassed up and waiting, I want to get in the sky as soon as possible. It just seems like if I could get there, I could do something about this nightmare."

As Presley located the numbers and information that Zane had requested, she saved them into a file. Glancing around the table, she couldn't help but feel sorry for the family for their loss. Aron McCoy was loved, that much was for certain. Bowie Travis rose and came to kneel at her side. "I do search and rescue, I'm a tracker. Mostly, I work in the high country, but I do have contacts around the world. There's a group down there that I'm familiar with called Blue Hope. If you'll call them and mention me, I know they'll help and I'll be there to do what I can, too."

"Thank you," she smiled at him and turned back to see if she could find Blue Hope. Under the table, Zane cupped her knee. She cut her eyes at him, he was still talking to the McCoy brothers. There was no indication that he had heard Bowie speaking to her, but his act of possessiveness made her feel good.

"I want Presley to go too," Zane's mention of her brought her out of the mental fog she had slipped into. We? She had expected to help him prepare, but she had not anticipated going along.

But she did.

Zane had not given her any time to go back to her apartment and pack. He told her that they could find anything they needed at the hotel or the nearby resort. That made Presley nervous because she had very little money. Oh well, she'd just have to rinse her clothes out at night and wear them again. Noah had seen to the reservations and now they were winging their way south in a private plane. Zane was on the phone making arrangements for a suite of rooms to serve as a headquarters for their operation near the area where Aron had last been seen.

"You're what!?" he voice exploded through the dimly lit cabin. Others turned around to see what the raucous was all about. "I'll be there in a little over an hour and I dare you to ask her one more question. Libby Fontaine McCoy worships the ground that man walks on and to treat her any other way is an insult. Have you looked at her? She's pint-sized and pregnant." He paused and listened. "I don't give a damn about protocol. She's been through enough. I'm her attorney and I said no more questions until I arrive. Is that clear?" He slammed his phone shut and cursed.

Presley laid her hand on his arm. "Is everything all right?" Even Rex moved uneasily in his window seat. No pet carrier or cargo ride for this privileged character.

Zane put his arm around her shoulders. "Come here, I need to hold you." At the first nudge, she melted into his arms. It was like coming home. "That's better," he kissed her temple. "It's been a wild twenty-four hours, hasn't it?"

"Yes, it has. I'm so sorry; I know you and Aron are close."

Zane peppered kisses on the top of her head. "I know you are, and I'll be honest with you, what's happened with Aron makes me want to grab onto life with both hands and not let go. You never know if a day will bring sunshine or rain into your life."

"I want lots of sunshine," she yawned against his chest.

His chest vibrated with near silent laughter. "Well, we'll see what we can do about that." He rubbed her arm, then leaned in to whisper. "Are you on birth control?"

Presley tensed up in his arms which made him hold her tighter. "Yes, but not because I was sleeping around," the way she had phrased her comment made Presley cringe. She had meant that the pills were to regulate her cycle.

"I didn't think you had been bed-hopping, Presley," Zane whispered with a tinge of humor in his voice. In the back of his mind there was a warning bell going off. He couldn't afford to fall for her, it wouldn't be fair. There was no way he could ask a woman to tie herself to his imperfect life, not even sweet giving Presley. Still, he couldn't deprive himself of a few nights in her arms, it was unthinkable. He was torn – she was a heck of an employee. Could their professional life survive an affair?

"I'm not that experienced, though." She felt guilty for the understatement – okay, okay – outright lie. Having a cleft lip was bad enough, but if he knew she was a virgin, he might not want her at all.

Chapter Five

Sobs could be heard all the way down the hall. "God, just listen to her," Isaac sighed as he held Avery's hand. "She's going to make herself sick."

"She can't help it," Avery shuddered at the thought of being in the same position as Libby. "Put yourself in her place."

Isaac pulled her close for a kiss. "Perish the thought."

Joseph opened the door and all of them stepped in. Presley could see a young woman sitting all alone on a large sectional sofa. She was curled into a ball and her hands covered her eyes. Jacob rose from a chair nearby to come greet them. "Damn, I'm glad to see all of you." At his voice, Libby looked up and sprung to her feet and flew right into Joseph's arms. He hugged her, whispering words of comfort in her ear. She went to Isaac next, then Noah, working her way down the line.

"It's my fault," she wailed. The reality of seeing his brothers and the sadness in their eyes was almost more than she could bear. "It's all my fault!"

"Nonsense," Jacob interjected as he stood up and walked toward his family. "You've got to stop saying that."

"It's true," she was hugging Avery now and together they walked back to the couch. Sitting down, Avery held Libby's hand as she explained. "He did it for me. He always did things for me. I was so stupid and so selfish. It was like the time I had to go to the bar or ride the motorcycle, he let me do it because he knew it would make me happy."

"He loves you, Libby." Noah spoke with a shaky voice.

"Yes, he does," Libby said almost defiantly, "and I pushed him to do something he didn't really want to do. Aron didn't care a thing about going in the water, but I just kept on about it – and now he's gone!" Despair rung out loudly with every syllable.

Isaac went to her and knelt down at her feet. "Libby, Aron is strong. Don't you dare give up. He'll come back to you."

Libby set up, her eyes wide and her body tense. "I didn't say he was dead, he's not dead. I'd know it if he was. Something's happened to him, but he's not dead."

All in the room were quiet, no one was unaffected. Joseph eased over to Presley and Zane where they were setting up at a conference table. "We need to get a physician to see Libby, she needs something to help her relax. This can't be good for the baby."

"I'll go speak to the concierge," Presley rose to take care of the matter.

"I asked the Chief Inspector to meet with us, he should be here any moment," Jacob pulled out a chair by Zane. "The police questioned her," Jacob murmured close to Zane's shoulder. "But they agreed with me that she had nothing to do with whatever happened."

"Of course not." Zane moved over slightly when someone bumped him on the shoulder. A waiter excused himself and explained that he had placed a tray of water and coffee in front of him. Carefully, he located a bottle of water and a cup and poured it for his dog, holding it down and letting him drink. "What has the Inspector told you?"

As Jacob updated Zane on what he knew, Presley returned with the hotel doctor in tow. He took Libby into an adjoining room to check her out. When she returned to where her boss sat she heard them discussing how many search and rescue boats had been deployed and the range that the helicopters would search. As soon as Zane had called from Texas, things had been put into motion. Presley sat down and contacted Blue Hope via email and left her cell phone number. Soon she and Zane and the McCoys had contacted every avenue of aid that was at their disposal. If Aron McCoy could be found, they would find him.

After several hours, Presley was beginning to feel in need of freshening up. They had been without sleep, food and the last shower she had enjoyed hadn't been exactly geared toward getting clean. Thoughts of that amazing erotic event made her turn to gaze upon the object of her desire. As always, watching Zane was a pleasure. He was so invested in helping Aron that he had rolled up his sleeves, undone the top three buttons of his shirt and beads of perspiration had formed over his upper lip. Presley wanted to kiss him so bad she ached. Landsakes! She needed a break, just for a few minutes. Not knowing where she could go, or what room they had put her in, she leaned forward to ask. "Zane, would it be possible if I went up to my room for just a minute. I need to splash some water on my face."

"Damn, baby," he almost looked guilty. "I'm sorry. Of course, let me get you a key. Noah!"

"Yea, Zane."

"Could you give Presley a key to our room?"

Our room? Oh my goodness! For a second, all eyes in the room were on her, but there wasn't a condemning look among them, they were just seeing what Zane was carrying on about. "Sure, here you go, Presley."

"You go up and rest. We're going to have to break here soon, we all need to catch our breath. Why don't we make a schedule and take turns checking on all of the different efforts, dividing our responsibilities might be more efficient and productive. Some of us need to be down at the beach."

"Isaac and Joseph are down there now," Jacob reported.

"How's Libby?" Presley wanted to know before she went upstairs.

Avery answered. "She's asleep on a couch in the next room. We can't get her to return to the honeymoon suite, she just can't stand it. Later, I'll try to get her up to my room. She needs to be in a real bed."

"Okay," she touched Zane on the shoulder. "I'll be back in a few minutes."

"No, I'll be up in a few minutes. I need to feed Rex." He patted her hand. "There should be some things up there you need. I hope I didn't forget anything."

What was he talking about? "You didn't need to do . . ."

"Oh yes, I did." Zane 'looked' up at her, his beautiful brown eyes were tired but so kind. "And it was a pleasure."

She couldn't resist, but pushed a lock of his hair off his forehead. "Don't be long. You'll be more good to Aron if you get some rest." When he angled his head and kissed the inside of her wrist, her heart began to hammer in her chest. "I'll be upstairs." Presley rushed off, she didn't trust herself to stay any longer, if she had – she would have kissed him right there in front of everyone.

Making her way to the elevator, she looked out at the window and saw the crowd at the beach, the boats on the horizon and even a couple of helicopters flying overhead. How devastating to Libby and their family. She felt so sorry for them.

"Are you getting on, miss?" A man's gruff voice brought her out of her fog.

"Yes, thank you." She stepped in and walked to the far corner. As normal for her, she kept her eyes on the floor.

"That was bad about that fella from Texas, wasn't it?"

The man had a thick accent that she couldn't place. "Yes, it was. Hopefully, we'll find him, he's a good man." Presley looked up and him and smiled, thinking how nice it was that he had mentioned Aron with concern.

"Damn Girly, you ought to get something done about your mouth. You'd be okay looking if you'd get it fixed."

With a quick, but jerky, movement she covered her mouth. How stupid! For a while, she had forgotten how different she was. Her critic was still looking at her, so she tried to think of something to say. "I know, when I get a job with insurance, maybe I can get another operation."

He snorted, "I doubt that. Surgery like you need is usually classified as cosmetic, and that's a shame because I'm sure looking at yourself makes you sick."

The elevator door opened and the man exited giving her a half, dismissive wave. Presley's confidence plummeted, for a few hours she had let herself forget her reality. Sometimes she thought it would be easier if she wore a bag over her head or a hockey mask like one of those creepy Halloween movie characters. A veil might be an alternative, and at least that would look halfway normal. When she arrived at her floor, Presley exited and walked down the corridor still covering her mouth. As soon as she was able to punch the card in the door and hear the click of release, she pushed in, pulled it to and leaned against the door feeling dejected.

Crossing her arms under her breasts, she tried to squeeze herself hard enough to squish the bad feelings out. It just wasn't fair! More than anything, Presley wanted to be just a normal woman. Wiping the tears from her eyes before they splashed on her cheeks, she tried to settle her nerves. Zane would be up soon.

As soon as she thought of Zane, Presley groaned. How stupid could she be? She didn't have a problem. Libby and the

McCoys had a problem. They had, conceivably, lost a loved one and she just had a cleft lip. Shame made her grow hot. Pushing away from the door, she stepped into the beautiful hotel room. One huge king-size bed drew her attention. She couldn't believe she was sharing a room with Zane!

Images of how he had lifted her up on his shoulders and kissed her in her most private place made her skin flush hotter than her shame had only moments before. Would he want to make love to her again? He had said, yes. But – he might change his mind, or someone might enlighten him about what she really looked like. What had he called her? Kitten. Hope made her want to believe that Zane was genuinely attracted to her. But how could he be? He was attracted to whatever mental image of her he had conjured up by touching her face. Wishful thinking was what he was, he just wished she was pretty, and since he couldn't dispute that fact with his own eyes, she was pretty or at least she was in his mind.

What to do first? A shower would be so nice. Dang! She had forgotten to stop by the hotel gift or dress shop and pick up something to sleep in. This dress was much worse for wear. It was going to have to be rinsed and re-ironed. Oh well – not now. She'd just have to make do. Zane might need her later on. Walking into the dressing room, she stopped in shock.

What in the world?

Hanging in the closet was an array of clothes. Women's clothes. And there was a note lying on the dressing table.

Ms. Love

These clothes were delivered by request of Mr. Zane Saucier. If you need a different size or if there is any other problems, feel free to call ext. 2524. All charges have been taken care of.

Sincerely

Island Fashions

Presley didn't know what to think. She began to examine garment after garment. What was here amazed her! There was some of everything – dresses, slacks, jacket, blouses, shorts – there was even a bathing suit. Some of the items were dressy and some were casual. "Oh my goodness!" There was even nightwear – sexy nightwear! Her jaw dropped – literally. What was she going to do? She couldn't accept all of this!

As soon as Zane arrived, she would have a talk with him. Somehow she knew that he didn't anticipate her paying for the items, he would know she couldn't. And that made it a little worse. Why was he giving her these things? Maybe she was just supposed to choose one or two outfits. Yea, that made more sense. Perhaps she could afford that much.

The suite was amazing. Presley looked around and took note of all the amenities, but what she didn't see was anything for Rex. Knowing how quickly they had departed, she called room service and had a couple of hamburger patties with cheese sent up and she also got a couple of sandwiches. Zane might be hungry. While she waited on the delivery, Presley made notes of everything they had accomplished today and some things that she thought Zane might need her to do later.

A knock on the door alerted her that their food had arrived. Digging in her purse for a tip, she dealt with the server.

"Now, I'll take a quick shower." Grabbing the pretty robe she had seen in the closet, Presley took off for the bath to quickly wash off. When Zane came up, she wanted to be ready.

What a day! Zane should have been tired, but what waited for him in his hotel room gave him an untapped source of energy he hadn't known he had. God, he was hard already! Remembering the taste of Presley's sweet pussy, her whimpers of delight and the feel of her warm silky mouth caressing his cock had him ravenous with need. Damn, he couldn't wait to touch her again! Opening the door to their room, he called out her name, "Presley, we're here!" he had no desire to scare her.

The water in the sink was running, his first thought was to join her in the bathroom, but he had to see to about getting Rex some food first. "Hell!" He ran into something! Feeling around, he tried to visualize the room. Normally, he didn't have problems. On each door, the room number was in Braille and the concierge had taken time to go over the lay-out with him, but apparently he had been confused of his suite location because nothing was where it was supposed to be. It wasn't a tragedy, it would just take him a few minutes to acclimate himself.

"Zane?" A waft of sweet smelling woman and a blast of warmer air from the bathroom swept over his skin. "Are you all right?"

"Yea, I just whacked my shin on the credenza or some such piece of furniture. I was briefed on the suite, but I think they confused my directions." For some reason, he was a bit embarrassed. Huffing out a breath and ruffling his hair, he admitted that wasn't true. He knew exactly why he was embarrassed, he wanted her to see him as an attractive, capable man – not a damn invalid. With regret, he felt the erection he had been sporting begin to dwindle.

"I'm wondering around in the dark myself," she flipped on a light. "From where you're standing the bed is to your right, the dresser and TV is behind you, the bathroom is to your left and if you walk past the dresser, there is a sitting room and small kitchen father down where the couch is to your right and the wet bar is to your left." A small delicate hand touched his arm. "You must be tired. Sit on the bed, its five feet ahead of you and I'll get you a drink and take care of Rex. There's a nightstand right by the bed."

Her matter of fact analysis and concern for him and his dog, touched Zane.

"I took the liberty of ordering room service for you and Rex. If it's okay, I'll serve both of you. Babies, first," her voice changed when she talked to the dog. Zane loved how she was with his lab.

"Thanks, I appreciate what you're doing." He found the table, took off his watch and laid it and his wallet on it.

"It's my job."

"No, its not," he countered. "Are you being nice to me because you think it's your duty?"

To his surprise, she laughed. "Now, you sound like me. I'm being nice to you because I like you. How could a sexy hunk like yourself doubt his own appeal?"

Zane perked up, "You think I'm a sexy hunk?"

She didn't say anything for a moment and he could hear her putting ice in a glass and pouring something that bubbled and fizzed. When she walked up to him, he was super aware of her every movement. "You know I do. Didn't I prove that yesterday? Hold out your hand."

Presley was sort of taken aback by her own brazenness, but she was so hoping they could pick up where they left off. When he carefully took the glass of soda from her and sat it on the table with one hand, he used the other to quickly capture her wrist. "Yesterday was amazing and while I am worried for my friend, I need to celebrate the fact that I'm alive with you."

Gently he pulled her between his legs. His plan was to kiss her right on the heart or as close as he could manage without seeing his target. But to his delight, his lips found warm, bare, soft woman. My God! He had just buried his face in Presley's luscious cleavage. "Fuck," he whispered. "You're naked."

"I have on my robe, it's just undone." Ah! She closed her eyes and bit her lips as he licked a path between her breasts. "I didn't think you'd notice."

Zane chuckled. "I noticed."

His legs tightened around hers, effectively trapping her between his thighs. Zane pushed her robe off her shoulders and she helped him drag it down her arms. All of that effort, and his lips never left her flesh. When his disrobing task was complete, he plumped both of her tits and pushed them together and he made himself at home kissing the valley and the upper swells. His thumbs were driving her mad, rubbing her nipples and all she could do was cradle his head and kiss his hair. "That feels so good, it makes me weak-kneed."

"God, I love kissing you. It's like being sat down to a feast after years of fasting." Zane was lost in the pleasure, his face – lips, nose, cheeks – rubbed against the silk of her skin. And the pleasure of touching her body was overwhelming, he knew how she looked now as well as if he could see her with his eyes. Presley Love was beautiful and for now – she was all his.

She wanted him. Presley wanted Zane to make love to her more than anything. Surely, he knew. Should she say something? "If you want to," oh, lord – she was nervous. She tried again. "If it's not too much trouble," darn, her tongue was tied in a knot.

Zane had never been more turned on. He ran his hands all over her body, memorizing its contours and tracing her curves.

There were so many places he wanted to lick and learn – "What do you want, Doll?" He knew what he wanted. God, her back was smooth and her ass was divine. Gliding his hands over the soft swell of her hips, he felt his cock rising to the occasion. What if she wanted him to stop? God! There was no way he would survive that. "Don't you like my touch?" The wait was killing him, but he wanted to make sure she was aroused. He dipped two fingers between her thighs and she bucked against him. God, she was wet. He spread the slick cream all around her soft pussy. "Do you want me to lick this little clit again?"

"I love your touch." She kneaded his shoulders, aware of his strength and power. Gathering her courage, she just said it. "I want you to make love to me so much. Will you do that? I mean not just kissing, would you. . ." that was as far as she could go.

With utter joy, Zane laughed. "You are so precious. I was trying to take it slow and woo you."

"Consider me wooed." Presley squealed with delight when he picked her up by the waist and flipped her over on the bed.

"Take your robe off," he tore his clothes off, popping a couple of buttons in the process. "Damn, I ordered you clothes and forgot mine." He'd have to remedy that – later.

"We've got to talk about that when I can think straight," she panted, entranced by his ripped body and – oh, lord – engorged cock. Should she tell him she was a virgin? Surely, he realized that no man had ever - - - - umph!

"There you are!" he had bounced up in the bed next to her. Presley smiled; he acted like he was so happy to be with her. His boyish excitement thrilled her. In a way, she was making him happy.

"You are the sexiest man I've ever met," she blurted out as he moved over her. She felt so small and delicate and feminine next to him.

Zane dipped his head and ate at her lips, she framed his face and opened her mouth to his tongue. She loved how it felt to have him half on top of her. He had reclined beside her, one arm up by her pillow, his body halfway covering her. "You are exquisite," he groaned as he massaged her left breast.

"Don't say that," she admonished, not being able to handle the irony.

"I'll say it till you believe it."

She arched toward him as he soothed her belly, rubbing over the top of her mound, pushing her legs apart.

"Oh, Jesus!" she gasped as he two fingers inside of her. Presley felt herself clamp down on him. "It feels so good." Lifting her hips, she spread her legs farther and pushed up against his hand.

She was more than ready and his control was nonexistent. Zane shook with desire, it had been a damn eternity since he had really made love with a woman. He didn't count those two cold, clinical encounters. Going to his knees, he moved between her legs, making sure her knees were bent. "Since you're on the pill, do you want me to use a condom?" He didn't want to, but it was lady's choice.

"No," she wanted him, as close as she could get him. "I'd rather feel you, if that's okay."

"Damn, yes," he ran his hands down her thighs – smooth, creamy, lovely woman – ever inch of her. Placing one hand on her mound, he moved in close and taking his cock, he rubbed the head through her dainty slit. "Velvet, softest velvet."

Presley watched his long, dark lashes drift down over his eyes. His jaw tightened, and he hissed his pleasure.

"You don't have to wait," she coaxed him.

"Patience," he whispered. "I have fantasies, you know."

"Oh, my God," Presley gasped. Zane smiled. She liked that. He was tapping the head of his cock on her clit – and she liked it. The woman didn't realize that a lot of the pleasure he derived was in giving her pleasure. More than anything, he wanted her lost in the pleasure of his loving, craving his touch and the release only he could give her.

Every part of Presley ached. For the first time in her life, Presley felt wanton and sexy. "Don't make me wait anymore, please?" She couldn't take her eyes off of him. He was so sexy – his shoulders were massive, his pecs were mouthwatering and his abs were pure corrugated muscle. A flush of heat had reddened his cheeks and when he licked his lower lip, she trembled. "Zane!" she moaned.

"You want me don't you?" he drug that luscious cock head up and down her slit. His eyes were glazed with lust. Presley wished he could feel more for her than lust, but she knew she had no right to want more, but it didn't keep her from dreaming about it.

"Yes," she managed to answer. "I've never. . ." she started to warn him, but she didn't get the chance.

He put the wide head of his cock into her tender opening and pushed.

Sweet Mother of God! The wet, hot haven of her body welcomed him, it enveloped him in the sweetest of embraces. God, she was tight. He had to work his way in, sharp little jabs – drilling – a sweet fight for the tiniest distance. Zane leaned over her, letting his hips do the work as he took his pleasure. A white heat of ecstasy swept up his body from his grateful cock and he pushed a little deeper, needing to seat himself completely within her.

Presley grabbed his wrists, she couldn't help but let her fingernails sink in the tiniest bit. She was so full! And she wanted it – but God, it hurt! But she didn't want him to know because he might stop. And if he stopped, he might never start again.

Zane thrilled at the bite of her nails. "Are you going to be a little wild-cat, Presley?"

She heard his voice, but despite every good intention- Presley winced, pulling back.

Through the haze of bliss, Zane felt two things – a barrier give away and the woman whose body he was enjoying flinch. "Hell! I'm, sorry." He froze and began to pull out.

"No!" Presley exclaimed. "Don't. Keep going."

Shit! Why hadn't she said something? And then he realized she had, the whole time. She had told him over and over again that she was innocent – untouched – unsure. "I'm so sorry, Baby." He bent to kiss her tenderly. "I'll make it good for you."

"It is good." She kissed his neck. "I'll be okay, now. You're just so big." The last two words were enunciated very carefully, making Zane chuckle.

For a few moments, he kept still, letting her body adjust to his. Then slowly, he began undulating his hips, moving a little inside of her, but also putting pressure on her clit. To his relief, he felt when her body began to welcome him. It wasn't that she relaxed, it was that she strained toward him and locked her beautiful legs around his waist. 'That's it, show me what you need, Baby. I'll give it to you."

"You, I need you." Presley kissed his shoulders and he wanted to weep with relief. He needed her more than she would ever know.

Covering her mouth, he drank from her lips and eased all the way in. Buried to the hilt, he was seated fully – she was stretched tight, but moving with him and it felt absolutely incredible. Nothing in his life had ever felt so good.

The pleasure moved up Presley's body, radiating out from her vagina. She felt tingles all over her body, her nipples were swollen and every thrust of Zane's body moved his chest over the tips of her breast. More, she wanted more. Arching, she pushed her chest up, pressing her tits harder into his chest. "This is wonderful," she moaned. Returning to his mouth, she nipped at his lips, needing his kiss more than any woman ever had needed her lover's touch. There was a storm rising within her, a force that she really didn't understand.

Zane could feel her hunger and it fed his own. Sliding his arms under her back, he gathered her close as he thrust into her sweet body. She entwined her arms around his neck and writhed beneath him, seeming desperate to be one with him. How had he lived without this? How could he return to a life of sexual starvation after sampling heaven?

It was hard to breathe with so much pleasure pulsating through her body. Presley felt the electric arc of orgasm begin in her pussy and she was helpless to stop it. "No, I don't want it to be over," she scraped her teeth on the cords of her neck.

"Let go, Baby – I'll love you all night long. It's not over, this is only the beginning."

Presley listened as best she could – and she let go. Spasms of rapture shook her to the core, deep convulsive shudders of delight had her screaming his name. "Zane! Yes! God, yes!"

"You're so perfect. A treasure!" Zane praised her as the flutters of her orgasm milked his cock. There was no way he could hold on to the thin threads of control that had held his release at bay. His balls tightened and Zane felt the incredible rush of pleasure boil upward and out. Closing his eyes, he let loose all control and felt himself splinter into a million shards of perfect light. As his seed pulsed out, he kept moving, relishing the sensation of his cock being bathed in their passion. Was anything ever this good? Gently he let his weight settle on her, using his forearms to keep the pressure from being too much. "Thank you, thank you, thank you," he breathed into the softness of her hair next to her face.

Emotion overtook her normal composure and she hugged him tight. "No, thank you. That was incredible. I never expected to feel anything like that in my lifetime. Your loving me was a magnificent gift." His body trembled in her arms. He had enjoyed her, but what she felt was indescribable. Presley felt whole and vindicated and accepted. As she gazed into the room over his shoulder, not really seeing – only feeling – she knew she would never forget this feeling as long as she lived.

Zane didn't sleep very much. It wasn't the fact that he was unused to sharing his bed, the sensation of Presley curled into his body was a feeling he wouldn't trade for anything. She made no noise as she slept, and she rarely moved. As far as bedfellows go, she was just about perfect, and from the moment they had finished making love, she had placed one hand on his body and no matter which way they turned, she had kept contact with him all night. It was as if she were afraid he'd get away from her. And he loved it. Zane lay on his back and she lay half on top of him, her head on his chest and one of her legs thrown over his. She had him trapped. He had to smile. Absently, he stroked her back – her bare back. She sighed and snuggled even closer. His baby liked to be petted.

Words she had said earlier stuck with him. In the immediate aftermath of their lovemaking she had said that his loving her was a magnificent gift. What was he going to do? Could they continue on down this incredible path without hurting one another? He had no answer; all he knew was that he couldn't go backwards – not now. Being with Presley and enjoying her was too important. And it wasn't just the sex, he almost moaned out loud at the memory of the utter pleasure she had given him, no - it was all of her – the complete package. She was smart, sweet, kind and he craved her body like a drug.

As he caressed her, his hunger grew. God, loving her had felt so good. Her pussy had been blistering hot – tight, holding onto him like a velvet vise. And he wanted her now, more than he wanted his next breath. Zane was determined to create in her an equal addiction to him. Gently, he pushed her onto her back, and he felt her stretch and yawn like a sleepy kitten. He waited to see if she would awaken, but she didn't. Her body settled back down. Zane smiled. Now, for the good part, he was going to wake her his way.

They had slept naked and during the night he had explored her body, especially her sweet little face. His kitten was so self-conscious and had so little reason to be so. Now as morning light was breaking, even though he couldn't see the sun – he was gonna make his baby rise and shine. Carefully, he coaxed her legs apart and rising over her, with a hand on either side of her hips, he leaned over and pressed a light gentle kiss over her heart and then another every inch or so, until he arrived at his chosen destination.

Deep in his heart, Zane felt tenderness. He wasn't taking, he was giving. Oh, he loved it – he fuckin' loved it! But this was for her. Presley hadn't known much male attention in her life, and he wanted her to know what it was like to be desired. And it was no hardship, because he desired her more than he had thought possible.

God, she was soft. He rubbed his nose and lips through the down on her pubis. Opening her up with his thumbs, he licked her sweetness with a light stroke of his tongue. He little body pushed down into the mattress in reaction to his caress. Zane repeated – lots of times. Little rivulets of cream began to flow and he lapped them up – Presley was exquisite. A whimper from her lips let him know he was doing something right, even if she thought it was a dream.

Zane nuzzled her pussy, pushing his tongue up in her tight channel. Again she writhed, he placed a steadying hand above her mound, but he didn't stop. He kissed her outer lips, pushed two fingers deep inside of her and set up a rhythm deliberately designed to make her crazy. Damn, he loved this.

"Oh, oh, oh," she moaned. His little dove was waking up. Now for the piece-de-resistance, Zane took her clit in his mouth and he began to suck. "Zane!"

Sweet merciful God! Presley almost levitated off the bed. Zane was eating her out! What a way to wake up? Every nerve ending in her body tingled and sizzled. God, she had never felt anything so luscious in all her born days. He was driving her insane! Undulating her hips, Presley sought more – she pushed her pussy against his face and tangled her fingers in his hair, just daring him to try and get away. "More, please more, don't stop – God, don't ever stop!" she pleaded, almost weeping.

How long had it been since a woman had begged for his touch? So, he gave her what she needed – he licked her, laved her, sucked and kissed, reached up and tugged on her sweet nipples till she flew apart in his arms and sobbed her release. And then she surprised him, she pushed up and into his arms. "I need you, Zane."

Realizing what she wanted he pulled her into his lap and eased her down onto his cock. "Fuck, yeah!" he moaned. Being inside of her was like coming home. Damn, he didn't even have to move.

Her little pussy was still quivering and she held him so tight, pressing her whole body into his. "I can't believe you did that for me," she whispered in amazement. "You make me so hot, I could eat you up with a spoon!"

Even in the throes of extreme lust, Zane had to chuckle. "I loved doing that to you, the way you respond to me just blows my mind." He stroked her back. "Now, move for me – not your body, move those talented little pussy muscles. Do you know how?"

"I think so, it's like those exercises women do, huh?" She proceeded to tighten on him – over and over – massaging his cock with a glove of hot, wet velvet.

"I think you've got it," he held her tight and let her have her delicious way with him.

Presley moved her hips back and forth and every movement made her clit tingle for more. "I'm gonna cum again, I can't help it," she bit his shoulder and wished there was some way she could meld herself with him for eternity. Noting in her life had ever prepared her for the way he made her feel, she hadn't even known it was possible.

"Lay down and let me do it right," he eased her back, pulled her thighs over his and proceeded to thrust and pump into her until they were crying their release.

"Hold me, hold me," she begged. Zane pulled her back up and did just that and marveled as she trembled in his arms. It just went on and on and he kissed her temple and cradled her to him. "I've got you," he crooned.

"Is it always like this?" she managed to ask.

"No, it's not," Zane admitted. But he was beginning to wonder if it might always be like that with her.

Libby stood looking out the window at the calm water. It was hard for her to realize that something so beautiful could have stolen everything she had. She had cried enough tears to rival the ocean, and now she just existed. Placing a protective hand over her baby bulge she wondered how in the world she was ever going to be able to go on without him. Before daylight she had slipped out of the room away from Isaac and Avery's watchful eyes and wandered along the beach. A new group called Blue Hope had arrived and they were making a last ditch effort to find any type of evidence at all. Bowie was with them and she knew he, and everyone else, was doing the very best that they could.

Her every instinct had been to run into the tide as hard as she could. It just seemed to her that if she could sink beneath the waves that she would find him. Wrapping her arms around her desolate self, she tried to consider what the next few days would bring. She wasn't giving up – she couldn't give up. But she had no answers either.

As she stared at the scene before her, she saw one of the divers come from the ocean waving his hand. Others ran toward him. Libby's heart leaped within her chest. They had found something.

"I appreciate the clothes, Zane. But I can't accept them. Let me wear this pretty green silk dress today; I'll pay for it and you can get your money back for the rest." As she explained, she picked up Rex's dish and rinsed it out. The black Lab was smiling at her and she couldn't help but smile back.

Her tone was adamant. Zane hadn't seen this side of her before. "Don't you think all of your efforts and overtime are worth a bonus?"

"This isn't a bonus," even though he couldn't see, Presley pointed toward the clothes. "This is half a year's salary for me."

Zane was taken aback for two reasons. First, he was stunned at her reluctance to take from him. Women weren't usually like that. They tended to take every gift from a man that they could get. But not Presley.

Second, he hated to be reminded how little she had. While she was a temp, he paid Workforce an hourly rate and they paid her much less, so he didn't like to think about what she tried to live on. At the time, he hadn't paid much attention, but he knew she made pastries for Chloe's fiancé's club. As soon as he got back to the office, he intended to rectify the situation and make her an offer to work with him permanently. Right now, he needed for her to feel appreciated so he walked right into her space and kissed on her face till he made contact with her lips. "Sweetheart, I didn't mean it as an insult; I just wanted you to be comfortable." Surely, she couldn't stay mad at him after he smooched on her.

His tone – and kisses - mollified her, she wasn't really upset, she just didn't want their relationship to be about money or paybacks, - she wanted it to be about . . . . Heck! He was her employer, even though right now, he wasn't acting like it. "I know, and I'm not insulted." She twined her arms around his neck and rested against him for a minute.

"Good." Zane returned her embrace.

His actions made her hope. But Presley knew she needed to get her feet back on solid ground and quit traipsing around in the clouds. They had made love – he hadn't proposed. "I know, and I'm not insulted. It's important to me to pay my own way, so I'll pay you for this dress. Okay?"

"Pay?" For the first time Zane raised his voice, but a knock on the door interrupted his rebuttal.

"I'll get it." She skittered away from him, and the vacancy she left in his arms was telling.

"Hello, Jacob," Presley greeted the big McCoy.

"Presley," he tipped his hat. "Zane we need you down in conference room, Bowie and Blue Hope found something. I don't know what it is, but we're about to find out."

"Let's go," Zane snapped his finger for Rex and held out his hand for Presley. She grabbed it with one hand and her laptop with the other and they left the room.

"How is Libby?" Presley asked as they headed down the long corridor toward the elevator.

"She's about the same." Aron's brother's voice sounded tired and she knew the strain the family was under had to be incredible. "Beau LeBlanc and Harley got here a while ago and they're with her now."

"Zane! Jacob!" A voice behind them called. They turned, as did Presley, and a woman she didn't recognize came hurrying toward them. She was beautiful.

"Shit," Jacob muttered under his breath. 'It's the shark."

The shark? Presley though she looked more like a swan. The woman was tall, blonde, long legs and wore four inch heels. She made Presley feel like a little brown wren. "She's official legal counsel for the Foundation set up by Jacob and the other boys mother. Aron is the trustee. Listen to this."

"I'm glad I caught the both of you. I just heard that Aron is dead. My condolences," she paused a micro-second. "Now, moving on. I need decisions and signature. Jacob will you take his place?"

Presley watched. Zane stepped back. He knew Jacob and he didn't have to say a word. "Excuse me, Ms. Fuller, but you need to understand something. No one has said that Aron is dead. We're not moving on. And I can't take his place – anywhere. He is irreplaceable. Now if you need signatures, speak to my attorney, he'll know exactly what we need to do." And Jacob stepped into the elevator and held the door.

Ms. Fuller was silent. But Zane wasn't. "Presley, get Ms. Fuller's number and tell her we'll get with her as soon as we get back to the states and some decisions are made. I'm sorry you made this trip for naught, Ms. Fuller. Right now, finding Aron is more important than writing him off. You won't go lacking for signatures or decisions, I promise you that. Good day."

Presley smiled, knowing they had her number. This was obviously a power play on Zane's part. As Ms. Fuller handed her a business card, she tried to cut Presley in half with a poisonous glare. It didn't work, the new clothes and Zane's attention made Presley stand up tall, she felt worthy for the first time.

"Come on, love."

Love smiled and stepped into the elevator with Jacob and Zane.

Bowie was waiting on them and so was Libby with a stunning looking couple that Presley assumed were Beau and Harley. The man was big with shoulder length hair and shadowed his woman like a mighty oak sheltering a tender flower. This morning, before their discussion of her new wardrobe, Zane had told her about Joseph's Cajun friend, Beau, a weapons designer and dealer, and owner of a wildlife preserve who wrangles alligators regularly. His petite, gorgeous wife Harley was also outstanding in her field – one of the top bomb techs in the nation, an EOD expert. Today however, they were here in the more important role of friends.

Something had happened and all that were gathered – waited. Libby was small and fragile looking, yet her eyes were filled with hope. They all stood, no one sat.

Bowie Travis Malone, who had been working with Blue Hope, a group of divers who specialized in underwater investigations, stepped forward. He looked at each brother, then lastly, he looked at Libby.

Presley held her breath. Had they found a body? That thought had to be going through the mind of every person in the room. It was obvious Aron hadn't been found alive, or he would be here. Tension built. Bowie Travis reached into his back pocket and removed something small, holding it in his fist. He stepped forward to Libby and she held out her hand and he placed within it a band of gold. Aron's wedding ring.

"Oh, no!" Libby crumpled. She sank to her knees, holding the hand that clasped the ring to her heart.

"What does this mean?" Joseph demanded.

"Could it have slipped off in the current?" Avery asked as she joined Libby, taking her into her arms and holding the poor girl as she shook with fear.

"No," Libby spoke softly and haltingly, "it wouldn't have come off that easily, I had to push it on, it was a little too tight."

"Do you think a shark. . . ." one of the nameless volunteer divers interjected and he was immediately shushed by another volunteer.

The McCoy brothers closed in around Libby and Zane requested for Presley to tell Bowie to clear the room except for family and friends.

"What does this mean?" Libby cried. "Does this mean he's dead? I can't believe he would have pulled his ring off."

Beau came and knelt by Libby. "Sweet girl, would you let my Harley hold Aron's ring and see if she can sense anything? She's like Cady, she was born with the power to know things the rest of us don't and I trust her with my life."

"Please," Libby looked hopeful and held out the ring to Harley.

Presley was mesmerized as the beautiful Hispanic woman took the band and held it to her heart, bowing her head.

Harley understood that she held a family's dreams in her hand.

Concentrating, she let herself be immersed in the energy surrounding the ring. Flashes of a wedding came into view, and she could see Libby's face, radiant and happy. Passion from the honeymoon made her cheeks pinken, but the strongest impressions she had were filtered through a haze of blue water. "I see clouds of bubbles, a opening like a crevice, he sees something on the floor of the ocean that draws his attention, it's shiny. But there is movement – a rush . . ." as Harley spoke everyone tensed and there was nervous shuffling.

"Something happened to cause debris or rocks to fall," Harley shook her head trying to see more. "Blackness," was all she said.

"Is there a cave down there? Did we find one? Did we check it out?" Jacob started to run from the room.

"Aron!" Libby sobbed in heart-rending despair sinking to her knees. Avery went to her and held her as she rocked with grief.

"Wait!" Harley stopped them. "There was an accident, but I did not sense an ending. There was no break in the life force. Whatever happened during the dive, Aron didn't perish."

"You don't believe he's dead?" Libby exclaimed.

As everyone held their breath, Harley stated softly. "No, I feel that Aron survived."

After Harley's revelation, things moved quickly. Blue Hope returned to the waters to check out the cave and the McCoy brothers and Zane decided to call in Vance and Roscoe, the private investigators that the McCoy's kept on retainer.

It was a consensus among the family and close friends that the focus of the search should move from water to land. Harley's reading gave them purpose, but Presley didn't know what to think. She sat on her legs in the conference chair and watched Zane confer with Jacob. He had worked for hours coordinating tactics to move the effort to a wide-spread search that would include the surrounding islands and to inland Mexico. And even though she listened carefully, she didn't hear any opinions voiced about possible scenarios of why or how Aron could have left the water without Libby seeing him or why or how he left the area. Another thing that surprised her was Zane's seeming acceptance of Harley's psychic impressions.

"Are you getting tired?" He rubbed her leg, his familiarity was welcome. She had been busy making contacts with him for search teams, some equine and some k-9. Rex had required attention and she and Avery had also gotten lunch for everyone.

"I'm okay. How about you?" she wound her fingers with his. Even though the situation was serious, she couldn't prevent her body from responding to him. Her nipples peaked and her clit tingled. Getting back in his bed and his arms was never far from her mind.

"I'm gonna need a break soon. We've done what we can to turn this from a water rescue to a missing person's investigation. What I'm going to concentrate on now is getting Libby to go home. I don't feel it's good for her and the baby to continue to stay here."

His handsome face was full of concern. Presley wanted to caress the stubble of his beard that made him look like a sexy rake. "I think Libby needs to go home. This can't be good for her pregnancy. What do you think?"

"I think you're right." He picked up her hand and kissed it. "Wait here." He took Rex and went where some of the family sat in a side room. When he returned, he told her. "Get your stuff, let's give them a little privacy." She picked up her things and they made their way back to the room.

"What's going on?"

"I made the suggestion and Jacob had come to the same conclusion. I think they're all going home except for Noah. Aron wouldn't want everything in their lives to come to a grinding halt. The McCoy's won't give up and they'll hire the very best help that can be had. We're going to get a good night's sleep and head back to Texas. How does that sound?"

Her heart skipped a beat. "Can we do more than sleep?" Presley had never dreamed she could be so forward.

Zane just groaned. His erection was already pounding between his legs. "There are a thousand things I want to do to your lovely body, and I will – one erotic thing at a time."

Presley glanced around to see who might be in listening range, but they were alone, so she joined in the game. "Would you let me finish what I started in the shower the other day? I have been thinking about how good it felt to kiss you - down there."

A laugh of pure delight escaped Zane's lips. When she had said 'down there' her voice had dropped both in loudness and in tone. "You are precious!" He heard the elevator ding. "Are we alone?"

"Yes," she said – hesitantly. What did he have in mind? "I don't want to get arrested," she assured him.

"Oh we won't – maybe."

As soon as the doors closed, he backed her against the wall. Presley glanced at Rex, poor thing, at least he had the good grace to turn his head. That was the last thing she saw because Zane covered her, blocking the light.

Placing a hand on both sides of her head, he devoured her lips, making her mewl with delight. He kissed all over her face like he was mapping uncharted territory. "It's only fifteen floors," she gasped.

"Hit the stop button," he growled.

Pulling herself from his grasp, she pressed the button, hoping against hope an alarm didn't go off. It didn't. He felt down the front of her dress and began lifting her hem. "Don't you want me to . . .?" she cupped the front of his crotch feeling the large bulge that made her mouth water.

"Yes, I do – later – now it's my turn. Ladies first is my motto." He ran a greedy hand between her thighs. "Spread your legs, I just wanna pet you, Kitten."

As he slipped his fingers under the leg of her panties and tugged them to one side, she went on tiptoe, seeking more. "Ummmm," she couldn't help but moan. Wrapping her arms around his neck, she held on. God, his shoulders were broad – his arms were huge and right now he was working to pleasure her. There was a God!

Zane let himself play between her slick folds. Damn, she was sweet! Every part of her was just what a woman should be. "Describe the color of your pussy for me. And this little down, I feel – is it dark brown or lighter?"

"Uh – lordy," she tried to think. It was hard. He was rubbing her slit, spreading her juices around. Any other time she would have been embarrassed to be so wet, but she knew he would take it as a compliment. "My nipples and vagina are a dark pink, sorta mauve, I guess."

"Mauve, my new favorite color," he growled, scraping his teeth over the soft skin of her neck.

With a sure, firm touch Zane massaged Presley's pussy, working it with a come hither motion. Sweet-thing rode his hand and bucked her little hips toward him. With his longer middle finger he fucked her tight little hole, making her whimper and cling to him as she begged for more. "I love this, Zane. Don't stop, Baby, please!"

"Are you ready to cum for me, Presley?" When she nodded her assent, her face pressed tight on his neck, he gave her what she needed. Taking her clit between his thumb and first finger, he rubbed the small, engorged knot of nerves until he felt her break –

shuddering and quivering against him. He held her while her whole little body pulsed. No woman had ever reacted to his touch like this one. Presley was more than special. "God, you make me want you so much."

Leaning into him, she lay quiet as he brought her down with long strokes to her back. He had pulled her panties in place and soothed down her skirt. Presley was so happy. "I didn't know pleasure like this existed. Touching myself feels nothing like what you do to me. Do you ever masturbate?"

Her candid question stunned him, but he answered. "Yes, my right hand has been my prime source of sex for years."

"Why? You're so good at it."

"I guess I was waiting for you," he admitted. "Jacking off is pale pleasure compared to fucking you, Presley." He bared his teeth and Presley almost went to her knees in front of him. He was so primal male and she was willing female. "Do you know what I'm going to do when I get you to the room?"

"What?" she was breathless with anticipation.

"I'm going to fill your hot little pussy up and hear you scream and beg for more."

His erotic words reignited the embers. Presley could die now and be happy that she had experienced true pleasure in her life. She was almost at the point of melting at his feet when the phone inside the elevator rang causing her to jump. Zane chuckled as he reached for it. "I think they've made us."

"Oh, no!"

"Hello?" He listened. "No, thank you, we're fine." He pressed the button. "Oh, look! It's started up again."

Presley muffled a laugh. It was only a few seconds later and they were scrambling off the elevator like kids. Only Rex seemed to have any adult decorum. Presley had never laughed so much in her life. Being with Zane was so much fun – pleasurable, toe-curling, amazing fun! They made their way to the room and opened the door. This time, Presley released Rex. She had left his food out and he made his way over to it. The Lab was hungry and so was she. Zane was still between her and the door and now it was her turn to pounce. She walked right up to him, put her hands on his chest and pushed.

"Hey baby, what are you doing?"

"Ravishing you."

"Okay," he was up for that. He went where she guided and found himself flat up against the door. Wow, this was a first, he smirked to himself. "Are you gonna respect me in the morning?"

"I guess that depends on if you earn it or not," she whispered as she unbuckled, unzipped and unleashed the object of her desire. "I love the way you're made," she sank to her knees so she could get up close and personal with his cock.

"Take what you want, Presley Baby." He could feel her warm breath fanning his swollen flesh and he needed more.

"Do you want it too, Zane? Do you want me?" She voiced the question, but she couldn't quite believe he could want her. But to encourage him, she caressed his manhood, luxuriously, rubbing it between her palms.

"Hell yes." Cupping her head, he tangled his hand in her hair. "I want your lips on my cock. I want you anyway I can get you."

Presley realized what she possessed was the ability to give Zane a gift, a gift of pleasure. He had given to her, now she wanted to give back. With great care, she set out to make him insane. She tantalized the tip of his cock with flicks of her tongue as she pumped his organ slowly, rubbing his balls tenderly with her other hand. Zane groaned. Excited by his reaction to her attention she only tried harder to make him happy.

Zane thought he might die of a stroke. Presley wasn't experience, but what she was lacking in expertise, she made up for in enthusiasm and – God – thoroughness. "Suck me, Baby – suck it deep." Opening her mouth wider, she took more of him in, laving and sucking on the engorged head. Stroking his shaft, she massaged his balls until his whole body tensed over her. "More," he demanded, so she opened her throat and let him take over.

Zane let himself loose, giving her what she craved – what he craved – over and over he pushed in and pulled between her soft, sweet lips. Her hands moved to grasp his thighs, like she was anchoring herself to him, lest she fly away midst the wild winds of passion. God, he was going to come. "Let go, Doll, I'm about to explode."

Quickly she let him know how she felt, "Uh-uh," and held on tighter. Presley wanted him to cum in her mouth. She wanted to taste him. She wanted him – all of him.

Her willingness and desire to accept him frayed the last bit of control he had. Zane immersed himself in the heaven of the moment, her name was a whisper on his lips. He felt his semen flood her mouth and he felt her throat work accepting his seed. At that moment something changed for Zane. He felt acceptance – period. The doubts he had kept alive in his soul were set free and the pain of the past rolled from his shoulders. And unbelievable he was still hard as a rock. His desire for Presley Love was off the charts and as she sucked at his release, humming her enjoyment he knew he had to be inside of her – now. "Stand up, Baby. Come to me."

Hands under her arms lifted her and Presley reluctantly let go. She wasn't ready to stop, her whole body was quaking with need. "Okay." But to her surprise, Zane picked her up from the floor.

Need throbbed within him. "Put your legs around my waist, I need to be inside of you." Ah, Jesus – she was so wet. "Guide me in, kitten. Then put your hands on my shoulders."

Presley shook in her excitement. She needed Zane so much. Kissing his cock had made her ache to be taken. Taking hold of his penis she didn't understand. "I know you came. Why are you still so hard?"

Zane snorted and teased. "'Cause I'm a virile stud. Are you complaining?"

"God, no," she moaned as she placed the swollen, leaking tip just inside her. "I'm grateful. I'm so hungry for you I could die."

"Fuck!" Her admission set his blood to boiling. Taking her by the waist, he began to move her up and down on his cock. He was strong and she was small, he could control their movements with ease. "Just enjoy, Baby, let me do the work."

Presley threw back her head and just felt – the stretch and burn as he moved in and out of her was exquisite. She had no fear of being dropped; Zane was massive and held her with great care. And when he bent his head to suck at her breast, she swooned. How her existence had changed? Dreams that she had held close in the dark of the night had come true. Presley now knew what it was like to be desired.

Zane buried himself deep inside of her, over and over. The only regret he had was not being able to see her. He had no doubt she was beautiful and to see her in the throes of delight – to see his cock pulling in and out of her, covered with her cream would be a sight to behold. But in his heart, he could see her clearly and she was breathtaking.

Presley raised her head and watched him. Honestly, he was so beautiful she almost forgot to breathe. How had it happened? How did she find herself in this glorious predicament? His mouth was perfect – kissable, so she kissed him, nibbling at the upper lip and he kissed her back. She rubbed her face on the scruff of his beard and tingles caused goosebumps to rise all over her skin. She gazed into his eyes and wished he could see the love reflected in her own – but that emotion probably would be best kept secret. Presley's waxing eloquent in her mind was cut short when he turned and backed her against the door and began thrusting and pumping in earnest. The grunts and growls he emitted just upped her blood pressure a thousand percent. Zane was pure sex and she met every plunge into her body with an inner caress that she hoped made him as crazy as she was.

Tension built in Zane's body. After the powerful orgasm he had enjoyed in Presley's mouth, the flesh of his dick was so sensitive that he gasped at the excruciating pleasure he was feeling. Every cell of his body bellowed out in demanding lust as he worked his cock in and out of her. He was also not unaware of her excitement and enjoyment for she made it completely evident with her little grunts and whimpers and the honey that flowed so freely over his cock allowed him to glide in and out of the snuggest little pussy he could have dreamed of.

"Harder, Baby, please. I need harder."

Presley's request almost set off his eruption, but he fought to maintain control in order to give her maximum satisfaction. Bracing her more securely against the solid surface, he gave himself over to rapture. She was tiny, but she was perfect for him. Incredibly, she was able to accept everything he dished out and beg for more. A woman had no idea at the turn-on a man felt when she showed him, unreservedly, that she wanted him, needed him. Perspiration ran from his body in rivulets as his little doll pressed her heels into his hips and canted her pelvis to accept and parry every thrust. Lord Have Mercy! Grasping her hips, he surged deep within her, pounding her with desperate strokes. With a scream of pure delight that was probably heard clear down the hall, Presley came – squeezing and milking his cock and he joined her. "God, Baby – I want this so much. I love your body."

Presley felt him buck – jerk – she heard him cry out his ecstasy and she felt even more of his essence pump into her channel and then spill out to run down her thighs. Zane was pleased, and she reveled in her ability to please him. The only thing she wished was that it could last beyond these unusual circumstances. Presley wanted it to last forever.

Chapter Six

Curled up beside him in bed, she slowly and softly stroked his chest. It wasn't smooth; instead it was rippled with muscle and covered with a light furring of dark hair. He was magnetically beautiful and kind, he had been good to her. "Thank you for this, Zane. I know it was in the midst of unfortunate circumstances, but I have enjoyed myself so much. It's going to be hard to return to normalcy."

Normalcy? Zane didn't know what to say. He didn't want to return to normalcy. Presley was fast becoming necessary to him. But what could he offer her? Would she want more with him than the here and now? And what would that do to their working relationship? Because she was an excellent employee and he intended to offer her a full-time job as soon as he got back to Austin and consulted with Human Resources. "I enjoyed every moment with you, Presley." And then – dammit, he just said what was in his heart. "Does it have to be over?"

Presley raised up so she could see his face in the moonlight. "No, it doesn't."

She was afraid to say more because she didn't want to make any assumptions.

"Good."

He was afraid to say more because he didn't want to scare her off.

So they slept in one another's arms all night long, content to just be together.

"Thank you, Zane."

"You are welcome and thank you for going with me. Your help was invaluable." He couldn't convince her to keep any of the clothes so he fully intended to make sure she was compensated monetarily.

Sherwood had met them at the airport and Zane had insisted he stay in the car when they got to her apartment. It touched Presley's heart that he carried her suitcase up. "Point me to your bedroom and I'll put this case on your bed."

"Uh," Presley was embarrassed. She didn't have a bedroom. "You don't need to go to that much trouble." Quickly, she took the case from him and set it aside.

It wasn't any trouble, Zane had to bite his tongue. He wanted to just carry her home with him – permanently. But he had some thinking to do, some decisions to make. "Presley?"

"Yes?" she stepped a little closer to him, she couldn't help it. More than anything she just wanted to go with him, to stay with him. Being alone again was not appealing at all. But it was late and tomorrow was a work day and she knew that there were cases that needed attention – they both needed their rest.

Zane hesitated. Hell. He reached out for her and drew her close, seeking her mouth. He was certain that he meant it to be a quick one, but once he tasted her – he lingered, sipping at her lips, stroking her tongue with his. When he pulled away, it was with great reluctance. "I'll see you in the morning. Take care and sleep well."

"You, too," she stood at the door and watched till he made it to the elevator and when Sherwood and Rex stepped from the shadows and greeted him, she was relieved. Presley would gladly take care of Zane if he would let her.

Adam had read and reread the evidence and files concerning Laney Taylor. Countless times he had watched the video as she explained to Lieutenant Rodriguez what she had been through and why she thought she was in danger. "Why have you come to the station?" the Lieutenant asked.

"I'm afraid." Laney spoke quietly, a blackened bruise on her cheek did nothing to mar her fragile beauty in Adam's eyes. God! Why hadn't he had the good fortune to cross paths with her when she was alive?

All of his life, Adam had expected to find that one woman who was meant for him. All of the dating he had done, all of the women he had met – no one had ever touched him like this one small woman. To think that he might have missed his chance and she was gone from his world was gut wrenching.

He turned his attention back to the screen.

"If you're afraid, why don't you leave?"

"He won't leave me. He keeps me prisoner."

"Really. What makes you think you're a prisoner? You have to give me some evidence. Mr. Kendall is a respectable member of the community."

Laney let out a sigh. The woman didn't believe her. "Because he keeps me chained to the bed or the dining table."

Adam believed in proper interrogation techniques, but it infuriated him that the Lieutenant was more interested in protocol than protecting Laney.

"Have you been taking your meds? We're going to have to call your husband. You do realize that, don't you?"

Laney sat up and looked wide-eyed and afraid. "If I'm turned back over to him, especially after he finds out that I've come to you, he'll kill me. Please don't make go back. Couldn't I go into witness protection or something? Or could I at least just spend the night in the jail? I'd be safe there."

"You're tying our hands, Miss Taylor."

"You're going to send me back, aren't you?" she bowed her head and faced away from the camera. Adam could see odd shaped burn marks at her nape. He leaned forward. What was that shape? Was it a star? He made a note of the abnormality for future reference trying to keep his rage down at how the burns might have got there in the first place.

"Give me some specific things you are going through, help me compile evidence." Rodriguez's voice was clinically withdrawn, funny – he had always thought a more compassionate tone would encourage confession.

A nervous laugh bubbled up from Laney's graceful throat. "Oh my, where do I start?"

"Does he hit you?"

"Yes," she admitted.

"When? How often?"

"Every day, it depends on how often I'm bad."

"Bad? How are you bad?"

"I don't do things fast enough or perfect enough. I talk back sometimes." Adam's heart lurched to think this small woman was treated so abominably.

"What type of injuries have you had?"

"Broken bones, eight of them," Laney's voice dropped to a whisper. "He makes me sleep on the floor, but that's not that bad. It's better than sleeping with him."

Rodriguez seemed to ignore that part. Adam drew closer to the monitor and let his eyes rove over her gentle features. She was so pretty, he wanted to take her in his arms and protect her – but it was too late.

"Anything else?"

"He burns me sometimes in places you can't see and he ties me up to a hook on a door jamb and whips me with a quirt till I bleed."

"What else?"

"He waterboards me or holds me under the bath water till I fear drowning."

It tore Adam up that she recounted these horrors so matter-of-factly.

"Do you have a piece of peppermint or something I could chew on?" Laney looked at Rodriguez hopefully.

"Is your breath bad?" the Lieutenant snorted.

Laney looked sad. "No, I was hungry."

The subject was dropped and it plagued Adam that she might have never had anything to eat. For Laney had gone missing the night this video was made. The PI the firm had contacted a few days ago was due to report in today. But it had been ten days since anyone had seen the young woman and there were few who think she had just walked off. Somewhere in all of this was an answer, but he couldn't see it. "Damn!" Before giving it much thought, he hit Print and a capture of her face fed out from his copier. He picked it up, gazed at it and imagined how different it all could have been.

Presley fell into a pattern at work. The cases that Zane gave her to work on were increasingly more complex and requited more usage of her legal skills. Daily she took on more pro bono work and daily she tried not to think about the fact that he hadn't asked her out nor made any move to renew their 'relationship' or whatever they had shared.

Of course, it had only been a few days – and he had been busy. Monday, the conference would be upon them and she was waiting for him to mention for sure whether or not she would be going with him. There was also a lot of talk in the office about the upcoming world premiere of Vision Star Studio's production of "Burning Love" which was this weekend. Saucier and Barclay represented Vision Star and the law firm partners and a few other select employees were attending the opening and the swank party that would follow. She couldn't even imagine what it would be like to attend an event of such magnitude.

"Presley, may I talk to you a moment?"

Zane's voice sounded – different. Was she in trouble? Had she done something wrong? "Yes sir." She moved over to his desk and sat, waiting to see what he would say.

Zane had been busier than he wanted to be ever since he returned from the Caymans. Matters with Aron's search hadn't improved. There was still no sign of him, although the family had not and would not give up until something concrete was discovered. Libby had returned home ill. She had hope but her pregnancy and the stress and strain had taken its told and the doctor had put her to bed for an indefinite period. Noah had remained in Mexico along with Roscoe and Vance and they were intending to increase the range of their search.

Other things were crowding into his time – Laney Taylor's civil action, several anti-trust suits and even a murder trial that was proving to be big news all over the state – the Lavonne case where a husband and father was accused of killing his whole family. The police had focused in on him and Zane believed he was innocent, only time would tell what would happen. And while all of these things were important, overtime and business trips had kept him from taking care of what mattered to him the most – Presley. As soon as he could, he sat down with human resources to work up a package to offer her a permanent job as his personal assistant. When he had requested her file from Work Force and HR began collecting her records, he was shocked at what he found. Presley Grace Love was licensed to practice law in the state of Texas. Her bar exam grades were exemplary and her GPA from the University of Texas was as high as his had been. Even though he knew the answer – he just had to ask.

"So, when were you going to tell me that you are an attorney?"

He couldn't see it, but Presley's face paled. "I don't know," was all she could think to say. Zane just sat there with one leg propped over the other with no expression on his face at all. Was she about to be fired?

"Don't you think that was pertinent information?"

"No," she felt a little bit of her stubborn streak emerging. "Why not?"

He didn't seem to be giving an inch. "Because I don't practice law, my education only helps me do jobs like this more efficiently."

Zane wanted to smile. He bet her stubborn little chin had raised an inch. "Why don't you practice law? You have one of the sharpest legal minds I've ever seen." And she did.

Silence.

"Presley?" He pressed her.

"You know why."

"No, I don't – explain."

Presley wanted to be anywhere but where she was. Having to admit her failure was so hard. "No one would hire me."

"How many firms did you interview with?"

"Only five," she whispered. "But after I got the same answer from all of them, I quit trying."

"What was their reason for not giving you a job?"

She couldn't be still instead she got up and paced the room. All of the anger she had felt for the people who had rejected her just boiled out. "What does it matter?" she spoke in a strained whisper. "No one would give me a chance. They didn't say it was because of my face, but it was. Just like the woman at Work Force told you, I'm not front office material."

"You knew she said that?" Zane was stunned – and very angry.

"Sure, I heard her say it to several people, and it was true."

"You seem to be working out well here."

Presley lost it. "Because you can't see me!" she gritted through her teeth. She wasn't a fit-thrower, but sometimes you needed to throw something. She looked at her desk for something appropriate, picked up a good sized law journal and just flung it across the room – not at Zane – but toward the couch. Rex jumped, hopped up and went to see if it were something to fetch.

All right. Enough. Zane got up and walked right to her. "Stop it." He managed to capture both her hands and hold them in one of his. She was about three feet from the door and he felt over and locked it. "That's stupid."

"But it's true." She didn't struggle with him, but allowed him to keep her stationary.

"They didn't tell you that," surely they didn't tell her something so cruel.

"No, they told me I wasn't a good fit for their firm," she overemphasized the word 'fit'.

"Ridiculous." He pulled her up against him. It was unprofessional of him, he knew that, but he couldn't help it. What he felt for Miss Presley Love was very close to 'possessive'.

His adamancy in her favor made her feel better, it didn't make him right – but it did her heart good. "I think I could have done research for them, worked behind the scenes to do research on cases, but I could never argue a case in court because of my lisp." Presley cringed when the word 'lisp' came out with a lisp.

Zane kissed her sweet lips – lisp and all. "You sound adorable and its only when you get nervous, I'm sure with practice you could deliver arguments without doing it at all."

She had no answer for that – too many disappointments had dulled her expectations. But when he kissed her again, she leaned into him and let the hope rise within her.

"I have a proposition for you."

Relief swept through her, he still wanted her in his bed. "You do? What?"

"I want to offer you a position with the firm as a first year associate." He proceeded to tell her the amount of salary and benefits and Presley lost all ability to speak. He had pulled her hands up between them and they now rested on his chest and he was stroking her small closed fists. "How about it?"

Tugging hard, Presley pulled away and walked off.

"What's wrong?"

Tears weren't far away. She didn't know whether to cry because she was happy or cry because she was sad. What was he doing? "Are you offering me a job because we slept together? Because you feel sorry for me?"

Damn. "Come back here to me," he ordered. Now, **he** was a little mad. "I'm offering you a job because you're brilliant, you're compassionate and I think you would make a damn good lawyer for this firm." He heard her footsteps coming back to his side. Good. "As for our sleeping together, I'm not willing to give that up. Are you?" It may not be right, but he couldn't fathom depriving himself of the haven he had found in her arms. Where they were headed – he didn't know.

"No, I love to be with you. Before I met you, practicing law was the ultimate dream of my life. I want the chance, but I don't want things to change between us, either."

"It's doesn't have to," Zane assured her. "I want you to start your practice working with me. I'll begin to put out feelers for another assistant, but until I find someone suitable, I want you to stay where you are, I'll just increase your level of responsibility and we'll get you a secretary to help with the clerical work. How does that sound?"

"Incredible." Presley launched herself in his arms. She caught him by surprise, but he still managed to catch her close. "Thank you, Zane. You have changed my life in more ways than I can count.

During the night, Zane had been carefully considering his choices. More and more, he was beginning to think that Presley might be the one woman he could trust to bring into his life. She didn't see him as half a man, she found him desirable. They could talk about anything and he found her wit and intelligence to be almost as intoxicating as he found her body. In fact, he was very tempted to ask her to move in with him, but he wanted to be sure because her feelings were just as fragile as his, of that he was sure. "Get your coat, let's go out to celebrate."

Go out? "On a date?" she said the phrase then wished she could call it back.

Zane didn't let a second go by. "Yes, a date."

Presley's head spun. This would be her 'first' date. She had always envisioned getting ready for the auspicious occasion and spending hours in front of the mirror and closet, preparing herself – just so. With Zane, nothing was going as she had always dreamed, but it was equally amazing. "Let's don't go anywhere fancy, I'm looking very ordinary today." Okay, she looked ordinary, at best, everyday.

"You are beautiful, as always. I see you quite clearly, Presley. No eye can see as clearly as the heart. Don't you know that?"

Presley stared at the broad-shouldered, absolutely scrumptious man who still had his arms wrapped around her. Sometimes he said the most amazing things. "Thank you, Zane. I'm grateful you feel that way." What else could she say? He let her go and she grabbed her purse and coat. Rex was ready, he loved to go.

They unlocked the door and left the office, as they were making their way through the lobby, Adam stopped them. "Zane, what do you think about getting a search warrant to check out Kendall's house."

"On what grounds?"

"Shelly thinks her possessions are in there, that will be our excuse to search. What we find might indicate if she Laney actually left or not."

"You don't think he might have rid the home of her stuff, anticipating this very action on our part?"

"I'm hoping he isn't that smart or else he's cocky enough to have kept trophies. While we're in there I also want to look for evidence of waterboarding and for that quirt she talks about being whipped with. If it has blood on it, that good be construed as grounds for assault charges."

"I don't know," Presley spoke up. "So many people are in the BDSM lifestyle, Kendall might propose that Presley wanted to be tied up and whipped – some women enjoy that."

Despite the seriousness of the conversation, Zane laughed. "Why, Miss Priss, what do you know about BDSM?"

Adam laughed too, because she blushed. "I read."

All Zane could think about was tying her to the head of the bed and making her beg for whatever he wanted to give her. Dang!

He was getting hard, time to make an exit. "Let's do it." Placing one hand at Presley's back, he started to propel her forward.

"One more thing, Zane. I just got off the phone with Ralph Dyess, he's invited us all to his place after the party for breakfast."

"I don't know, Adam, I may have other plans." His other plans were standing very close to him and she smelled heavenly.

"Talk to Renee when you get a chance, she said something about Alicia Fields making a request of you."

Zane's hackles rose. He didn't have time to cater to a celebrity, no matter how beautiful people said she was. "We'll see. Hold down the fort, Presley and I are leaving a little early. We're celebrating her coming on board as a first year associate."

"I heard," Adam beamed at her. "Congratulations. I should have said something to you right off the bat," he apologized. "But Laney's case has been consuming my thoughts. You were hiding your light under a bushel weren't you?"

"Not really," Presley protested. "I'm grateful for the opportunity, working with you and Zane will be a privilege."

"I think we're the lucky ones. Everyone has been talking about how helpful and intelligent you are. Hardly anyone was surprised to find out you are an attorney."

Hardly anyone, Presley noticed his clarification. There were those in the firm who did not approve of her, Presley had enough sense to realize that fact. Still, people like Adam and Zane and a few others made the prospect of being a part of Saucier and Barclay an irresistible proposition.

Finally they were able to depart. Austin was sparkling in the fall evening. The traffic was light and a faint drizzle of rain was falling. A distinct chill filled the air, the holidays would be on them before they knew it. "Do you enjoy Christmas?" she couldn't resist asking. One day she hoped to build traditions of her own.

"I do," he led her to where Sherwood was waiting for them in his normal parking spot. "Rachel goes all out decorating and Kane comes for dinner. Since he has Lilibet this year, our routine might change."

"How about your parents?" She knew a little bit about his family. At first she hadn't known he was of one THOSE Sauciers, because Zane managed to act completely unassuming and not like a member of Louisiana's royal family.

"I visit with them during Mardi Gras season, usually. They are so busy during the holidays that I don't think I'm missed."

"That's a shame," she nestled down into the back of the car. The heater felt good. Rex had found a place next to the door and this time she was sitting between Zane and his lab. "I always watch Christmas movies and I fix one of those small game hens for dinner."

"Do you have a tree?" Zane loved the smell of Christmas trees and he missed seeing the magical twinkling lights most of all.

"No, I don't put up a tree. I'm alone and it doesn't seem necessary."

"You should have a tree," Zane insisted. "Everybody should have a tree."

"Maybe I will this year," she agreed with him, not seeing the use of debating the issue.

"Where to, Mr. Saucier?"

Zane named a restaurant a few blocks away and Presley considered how things would change at work. "What case will you let me help with first?"

"What case would you rather work on?" he countered.

"I promise to keep everything else going if you'll let me help Adam with the Taylor case." Laney Taylor's sad story weighed heavily on her mind. It just seemed if she spent more time on it, she could help.

"Done," he agreed. In a few moments they were at Ches Nous, a French restaurant that Presley had only heard about. "I hope you like French food."

"I like gumbo," she laughed, knowing that French Cajun cuisine and real French food weren't the same thing. "I'm easily pleased."

Zane and Rex exited and Sherwood informed them that he would be waiting, it seems he had brought his eReader along.

"I feel bad about leaving Sherwood out here. Wouldn't he like to eat with us?" Presley was unused to the ways of chauffeurs.

"Don't worry about him, I know for a fact that my housekeeper is meeting him a few blocks down for a meal. He will be just fine."

Zane offered her his arm and they made their way into the restaurant. Their entrance was not unnoticed and it was hard for Presley to tell what garnered the most interest – Zane's good looks, Rex or the fact that she was his escort. She found herself covering her mouth again, and she had been trying so hard to be more self-confident.

Apparently Zane had made reservations because they were escorted to a table in a secluded corner. Rex was brought something that smelled really good and a bowl where the waiter poured Perrier water. Presley had to laugh. She was glad he was being taken care of. A menu was brought to Presley and while she read the selection, he ordered a bottle of wine. "See anything you'd like?"

"I think I'll have the veal scallopini."

"Good choice, I'll have the duck. And we'd like some chocolate mousse for dessert." In a moment, they were alone. Starched white tablecloths hang elegantly to the floor and Presley soon became appreciative of them when Zane edged his chair closer to her and found her leg under the table. "I've been here many times, but this is the first time I've wanted to play footsie under the table."

Her dress was a modest length, coming just above her knee, but his curious hand worked the material up until he had it where he wanted it. When his hand glided over her stockings, he groaned when he encountered bare flesh next to the garter belt. Presley hadn't known what possessed her to buy such adventurous underwear, but since being with Zane, she had become preoccupied with erotic fancies such as sexy underwear and toys and sexual positions. Thank God for the internet. She had found countless sites where she could learn things and buy them without encountering embarrassing situations. "That's not my foot you're playing with."

"You're right," he growled as his finger went farther up her leg and she spread her thighs wide to give him easier access. Her fingers curled over the side of the chair as Zane grazed the silk of her panties, teasing Presley with the possibility that he was about to move them over and touch her while they sat in full view of a dozen people.

"Zane," she whispered in a tone that was both a warning and an invitation.

"Zane Saucier, is that you?"

Dammit.

Zane recognized the voice and it was the wrong place and the wrong time to deal with Honey Ross. "Yes, indeed, Miss. Ross. How are you?" A caress on his neck was meant to entice, instead it served to cement Zane's intent to distance himself from local politics and this piranha. The District Attorney was trying to twist his arm to serve on a committee for the current mayor's reelection and it just wasn't happening. Plus, she was trying to get in his pants, and the likelihood of that happening was even less.

"Have you considered our offer to head up the reelection campaign? We could sure use your unique brand of charm."

The whole time Miss Ross was speaking, she never acknowledged Presley's presence at the table. She didn't know where to look, so she just looked down.

"Miss Ross, may I introduce to my newest first year associate, Presley Love." Zane squeezed her leg. "And my date."

His explanation floored Presley. He had acknowledged her, not only as an employee, but also as a romantic interest. Surprise made her jerk her head up and she knew without a doubt that the shock was evident on her face. But the stunned look on Honey Ross's face was greater than her own. If she hadn't been struggling to comprehend his words, she would have thought it was funny.

"Your date?" Disbelief and disapproval rang as clearly as a bell.

Zane picked up Presley's hand and kissed it. "Yes, and the answer to your question is 'no'. We have several important pending cases and my personal life is about to require more attention than usual.

"I hope you don't come to regret your decision."

The coldness in Honey's tone was hard to miss. But she left, nearly colliding with the waiter as she did so. Neither spoke until they were alone again. "I'm sorry about that," Zane apologized.

"She's not one of my favorite people. I just hate we'll be sharing a podium at the conference."

"I think she wanted to be one of your favorite people," Presley teased. "Women must make themselves available to you all the time." Before he could answer, she touched his arm. "The duck legs are at six, the potatoes are at ten and the grilled vegetables are three."

Again he was touched by her automatic, but matter-of-fact aid. She didn't make a big deal of it, but she did look out for him. Her gentle concern touched him more than all the fawning in the world would have. "Since I became blind, I have made a habit of closing myself off to women." Without warning, he found himself opening up to her. "At the time of my accident, I was engaged."

Presley put her fork down. This was important, she could tell. "What happened?" It was probably an insane thought, an improbable scenario – but if she were to have any chance with this man, she needed to understand him, because Presley was falling in love with him. No, that wasn't true – she was already in love with him. She loved his intelligence, his big heart, beautiful body, but what she loved most was how he treated her. Zane treated her like she had value, and that was something Presley had not known before. Even with her grandmother, she had been an obligation, a responsibility that did not necessarily have feelings or purpose. In a move that broke her heart, he tried to meet her gaze. She looked at him with all the love in the world and wished that he could perceive how she was feeling. If he only knew that she could see her unborn children in his eyes.

"She, uh, couldn't stay with me. Her closing argument summed up the fact that I'm now only half a man, not a suitable companion for a woman like herself."

"Well, that bitch."

Presley's vehement words expressed in her soft feminine voice shook him out of his melancholy mood and caused him to laugh out loud. "Thank you, I don't think I've ever heard a more eloquent defense."

"You're welcome, she was shallow and short-sighted. You, Zane Saucier are a catch. Any woman in the world would be lucky to have you notice them."

Unaware that her words sounded like a magical incantation to his ears, she went back to eating and changed the topic. "This is very good food, thank you for bringing me. I'm going to enjoy practicing law. I didn't think I'd ever get the chance."

Over the course of the next few minutes, they consumed their food and laughed over chocolate mousse. It didn't surprise them that they both loved it and Presley dared to feed him a few spoonful's and then stole his good sense when she kissed a tiny spot of the creamy dessert from the corner of his mouth. It might have seemed that he was trying to end their date early, but what he was really aiming for was to get her somewhere private. "Are you ready? I have some things I need to take care of."

"Sure," she wasn't ready to go, but what could she say? Perhaps, he had a late meeting. After he paid the bill, he offered her his arm and they made their way back out into the night. Sherwood was waiting for them in his appointed place. "I rode the bus today, and I don't need to go back to the office. There's a bus stop right down the street, I can walk."

"Not so fast," he covered her fingers with his and squeezed. "Do you think I would make you take a bus home from our date? What I need to take care of - is you." Leaning over, he whispered in her ear, "I need to be alone with you and I don't think I can wait to drive back to Bastrop. Can I come home with you?"

Home with her? Landsakes! He knew how little her apartment was. How could she entertain a man of his caliber in her dinky little rundown digs. But it was obvious he had more on his mind than the ambiance of her dwelling place and she wholeheartedly approved. "Yes, if you don't mind crashing on the couch."

Not exactly what he had in mind. "I was hoping to sleep in your bed, with you." Sherwood held the door open for them and Presley blushed when he winked at her.

Fine – two could play that game. "The couch is my bed." She winked back at Sherwood. He smiled. She could tell he enjoyed Zane playfully sparring with someone.

"You sleep on a couch?".

"Yea, I have student loans to repay, I live in a one room apartment," that was all the explanation he was getting. "The couch is comfortable, though and I like it because I can snuggle up the back of it – it makes me feel like I'm sleeping with someone." Lord that sounded pitiful. "But just for you, I'll make it down into a bed. It is a sleeper sofa."

"Sounds perfect to me." Right now he'd take her on the dining room table if that were the only available surface. But a couch? She didn't have a bed to sleep in? Zane didn't like the idea, not at all. "Sherwood, take us to Miss Love's apartment."

It wasn't a far drive, she lived just south of the Congress Street Bridge, a few blocks off of South First Street. "Can you pick us up in the morning early and bring me a change of clothes?"

Presley looked for a rock to crawl under, but Sherwood's happy agreement eased some of her dismay. "Take Rex home with you, Sherwood. I think he needs a little vacation. Let him run in your fenced backyard if you don't mind." Zane rubbed Rex's head and told him he would see him in the morning. "Presley will take good care of me."

He had no idea how much she wanted to take care of him. Sherwood looked bemused and relieved and she wasn't sure exactly why, but she wasn't about to look a gift horse in the mouth. Zane was spending the night with her and she intended to take full advantage – of him.

They held hands as they made their way into the building and up the elevator. After a couple of tries, she had the door open. "Come in. Can I get you anything?"

"Yea, you," he swung her right up against him, not touching her wasn't an option. "I am so hungry for your kiss." But he made himself wait as he feathered his fingertips over her face, relearning its features, everyone of them becoming so dear to him. "Your face is so beautiful." At her groan of protest, he insisted. "Yes, it is. I love everything about it – your smooth brow, long eyelashes, high cheekbones and this extremely kissable mouth." With tender licks and nibbles, he drew her into his web. She'd never know how much she made him feel. Presley brought out new emotions in him, she made him warm and wishful – she made him want things he had thought he would never deserve.

With longing she touched his face, pushed his hair out of his eyes and caressed the ever-present stubble on his cheeks. Opening her mouth for his kiss, she welcomed his tongue and let her own rub against his – a mutual taking and giving. God, she'd swear that magic was in the air. Miracles were afoot. The pleasure he was giving her was the fulfillment of every dream she'd ever had – the granting of every wish she'd ever whispered in the dark of night when she was all alone and convinced it was her destiny.

Zane was her grace, a gift of unmerited favor. For some unfathomable reason, he had welcomed her into his world. Desire ripped through her system, making her arch into his body and offer herself to him, the only reward she had to offer.

Zane's hands moved under her coat, clasped her hips and pulled her against him so he could grind his cock against her softness. God, he'd never get enough of her kiss! She was becoming as necessary as oxygen to him. "My sweet baby," he groaned as he let his lips slide over her jaw and down her neck. "I need you so much."

Presley couldn't help but read more into his words than he probably intended. Hope blossomed in her heart like a flower facing the sun. As his hands pushed at her clothes, she helped him, holding up her hair as he reached around her to undo the zipper of her dress. "I always need you, I'm shaking with it, Zane."

"Lift up your arms," he instructed and then he made her giggle as they struggled to get her naked. At odd purposes, she worked on his clothes while he kissed her breasts through the lace of her bra. "I swear, I've never missed my eyesight as much as I do at this moment. What I wouldn't give to see how you look. I bet you're all flushed with desire. Are your eyes glazed over with passion? Do you want me?"

"I wouldn't have you blind for anything in the world, but if you could see me, I wouldn't be here." Truth tumbled from her lips before she could call them back.

Zane stilled. "Do you mean that, Presley?" He grasped her by the shoulders.

She didn't answer.

"Do you?"

"Yes," she didn't know what else to say.

"Who is it that you doubt, Presley? You or me? Do you think you are lacking in looks or am I lacking in character?"

"No, no, no" she wound her arms around his neck. "The fault is mine, I'm just insecure."

"Have I done or said anything to make you insecure?"

"No," she had to admit. "You've been perfect."

"I know what's perfect," he found her breasts, pushing up her bra, seeking out her nipples and licking them, sucking – determined to take her mind off her perceived shortcomings. Once his mouth was occupied, he went to work down below, pulling up her skirt and pulling down her panties. God, her thighs were so smooth and soft. The heat of her pussy almost brought him to his knees.

"Pull your shirt off, please," she was having a hard time getting where she wanted to be.

"Damn, tie," he fumbled and unbuttoned as fast as he could, needing her breast back in his mouth. But Presley had other ideas. She stroked the hard expanse of his chest and he stood still, enjoying the passion in her touch. But what surprised him was when her delicate little tongue curled around his nipple and she began to suck. "Christ!" he wound his fingers in her hair and pulled, testing her reaction. A moan of erotic excitement was all he needed to know. His baby liked to play. God, he was a lucky man!

Picking her straight up in the air, he found her nipple and began to suck ravenously. Presley linked her legs around his waist and just held on while he made love to her tits. "Will you make love to me please? Now? I can't wait another moment," she was breathless with need.

Zane could hear her, barely. His heart was pounding so hard that the blood was roaring through his ears. "Sweet baby," he let her body slide down his. The heat of her skin was like a magnet, he wanted to get closer and closer.

"My nipples feel so good against you." She loved how they caught and drug on the fur of his chest. "You are so sexy."

"Lean over the arm of the couch, someplace that you can hold on. This is going to be all you can handle." He kept a connection as she turned around. "Let me feel you." He ran his hands over her smooth back, narrow waist and that incredible ass of hers. "Tilt it up to me, Presley. Spread your legs."

She braced herself on her arms, she felt feminine and powerful. Her breasts hung down, the nipples were tight and swollen. Glancing over her shoulder, she looked at him – tall, in control with a look on his face that made the cream flow from her pussy. She felt her very core ache for him. "I can't wait to feel you push inside of me, that's my very favorite part." Her eyes followed the luscious line of his body till she saw his cock standing up, firm and proud. "I'm so wet for you. Put him in," she demanded.

"All in good time," he molded her ass in his hands. It was heart-shaped, firm, rounded – "Damn." He popped her once and laughed when she squealed. And then pure eroticism took over as he slapped her bottom with his cock.

"Watch me," his request drew her eyes. God, he was stroking himself, his hand moving up and down the thick, long shaft.

Presley pushed her ass higher, "Touch me, please." He did, taking his cock and nudging her between her legs, running the head up and down her slit. Every pass he made, her clit got bigger and more needy. "Zane, it's hungry. My pussy is starving for you."

Shit, her words drove him crazy. Reaching between her legs, he pushed his finger up into her vagina, it was wet with sweetness. As he worked in and out of her, striving to find that sweet spot that would make her scream, she bucked with pleasure. "Do you like that?" He added a second finger and thrilled when she clamped down on him.

"Yes," she panted, "but I want YOU!" she almost yelled at him. Her desperation made his throbbing cock rock-hard.

He couldn't wait another moment, placing one palm on her back, he steadied her and took his cock in the other hand and eased it inside of her. There was one thing about being blind – all of his other senses were stronger, including his sense of touch. He allowed his whole soul and body to concentrate on what it felt like to join himself to her. Warm, wet, satin – damn, it was a tease. With every fiber of his being he wanted to just plunge in and take her hard and fast and deep.

"Please, Zane, I need you, Baby." She pushed backwards, trying to impale herself farther on his cock. His fingertips tightened on her hips and with tantalizing slowness, he let himself sink deeper. Little by little he plumbed her depths and she quivered as the electric sparks of sensation danced from her vagina to her clit, all the way up to her nipples. Presley clawed at the couch, seeking to find a hand-holt as he began to thrust inside of her. "Oh, my God!" she moaned. "It's so good."

It was good, it was always good with Presley. His hips pumped, his muscles bunched and he drove into her over and over. Euphoric pleasure made his blood sing, his toes curl and his balls tighten. Needing more of her, he bent over and covered her, grasping her tits and taking the nipples between his fingers. As he hammered into her, he milked her tits and took the flesh of her neck between his teeth.

Zane's lovemaking had always been more than she had ever imagined, but this was different – this was primal. He was the ultimate alpha male and he was marking her, branding her, claiming her and she surrendered to him unequivocally. The pleasure was so intense that she couldn't comprehend it – it was the perfect burn, the irresistible force.

Hard, heavy – powerful strokes, Zane fucked Presley and felt like he owned the world. She was loving it, she wasn't pretending – she wasn't tolerating – she was luxuriating in his possession. For days he had imagined this moment, relived their previous encounters and thought there was no way it could get any better.

He was wrong.

"Zane! Hold me, hold me, please." she writhed beneath him, her pussy pulsating on his cock as she came hard. He held her tight, absorbing the vibrations as she whimpered his name and squeezed him so hard that he felt his own release barrel through him like a steam engine. Flesh slapped against flesh and he jettisoned his seed into her in one hot wave after another.

Explosions of light and sparkles of rapture lit up her world as tremors shook every part of her body. Zane enveloped her, his hips still pumping slowly as his cock pulsed inside of her. It touched her to feel the big man shudder and know she played a part in making him feel so good. She felt fulfilled, she felt wrapped in warmth and safe from anything that could threaten her. In Zane's arms, she felt whole. He might not realize it, but he held her heart in the palm of his hand. She was totally at his mercy.

Presley woke up early. They had slept in her make-shift bed, him wrapped around her, his legs encasing hers, her head pillowed on his chest. She knew her apartment would never feel the same again. The small room could barely hold the power of his presence. She'd never be able to look around and not see him here. As the sun came up, she stared at him, grateful for the opportunity. Very lightly, she caressed his face, tenderness overwhelming her senses. He was so beautiful and she loved him so much.

"Morning, Kitten," he kissed her palm.

"I woke you, I'm sorry."

"Don't be," he tightened his arms around her. Actually, he loved to cuddle a woman in bed. It was something he had missed. Zane didn't really like to sleep alone. "Is the sun up yet? What time is it?"

Presley looked over his shoulder, "the sun is coming up right now. The sky is bursting with pink and orange clouds. It's beautiful." She kissed his chest. "The time is almost six-thirty."

"Tell me a secret," he smiled around the words, enjoying their pillow talk.

"Hmmmm," Presley mused, wondering what about her dull life he would find interesting. "Well, I love to watch cartoons on Saturday mornings while I eat cereal and my second toe is a little bit longer than my big toe."

"Really? Let me see." With a strong, sure move he reversed their positions until he was on top, caught her leg and lifted it – kissing his way down from knee to ankle. When he came to her toes, he rubbed his lips over them and nipped her on that second toe.

"Ow!" She kicked playfully and he spread her legs out and lay between them. "I love being here with you like this."

Presley caressed his hair, wishing she could stay like this forever. "I love to be here with you, too."

"There's a movie premier and party tomorrow night. Would you like to go with me?" As he waited for her answer, he weaved his fingers through hers, caressing her empty ring finger. Zane smiled to himself, the thoughts running through his head were alien to him.

"Yes," Presley answered slowly and hesitantly. Yes, she wanted to go. But what she would wear – that was the million dollar question. Heck! She had just gotten a new job, what better way to spend her money than on a dress to make herself fit better into Zane's life. "I would love to go with you."

"Great,"

At first she thought he was about to give her an intimate kiss and it excited her, instead he kissed her tummy, rubbed his face on her flesh and laid his head there and just settled down like he belonged.

And you know what?

He did.

"You have no idea how proud we are of you," Chloe hugged Presley. "I had no doubt that you would prove yourself."

"I'm proud too, little girl." Fraser held the warm apple dumplings that she had baked hours before sunrise. "Zane is a lucky man. You'll do good work for him."

"I plan to work hard." Presley glanced at the clock on the wall. She only had a few minutes before she had to be at work. Today would be a red banner day – Presley Love was attending one of the big social events of the year.

"Hey, I have a big catered event tomorrow and I know you just got a brand new important job, but I'll pay you triple for some of those pecan sticky buns you do so well."

Presley could feel the heat rise on her face. "I wish I could, I really do – but I have a date with Zane. He's taking me to the premier of Burning Love."

"Whoop!" Fraser clapped his hands and Chloe hugged her again. "I'll gladly do without the sticky buns! That's wonderful news!" She celebrated with them a few minutes before she hurried on to work. It took her two trips from her car because she had brought all of her clothes to wear to the opening. The executive dressing room behind Zane's desk came in handy, she hung her new dress up and admired it. Picking up the silky blue material, she held it to her face and imagined dancing in Zane's arms again. When she had tried it on at the store it had fit like a dream. Princess cut seams and a swirly skirt made her figure look pretty good and in her mind she had been beautiful – that is until you looked up at her face. Nevertheless, Presley was determined to go on the date with Zane and enjoy herself, because he wanted her with him, of that she had no doubt.

For some reason, she had beat Zane to work and that was unusual. She hadn't seen him since they had come to work, the morning after he had spent the night at her apartment. He and his brother had made an unexpected trip to see their folks, she had no idea what about, but it had seemed to be important. While he was in New Orleans, he had called her and that had meant more to her than a bouquet of roses. The phone call hadn't been about business either, he had whispered sweet nothings in her ear and she had whispered them right back.

Presley couldn't deny that she was excited about how her relationship with Zane seemed to be developing. He was already the most important thing in her world. Sometimes she just sat and stared at him and thanked God he had come into her life. And today was going to be another milestone, she was stepping farther and farther out of her comfort zone and it was because of him. He was her rock. As long as he wanted her around, it didn't really matter to her what anyone else thought.

Tackling everything with renewed zest, she threw herself into her work. The next looming deadline was the conference and she had prepared PowerPoint presentations to backup his talk on renewable energy. This was something she enjoyed doing. As she automated the slides, Presley added audio.

"Did you miss me?" Zane spoke at the same time as he kissed her neck. Presley jumped and squealed and Zane gathered her close and chuckled.

"Yes, I missed you – so much!" she kissed his lips over and over again in her exuberance. "How was your trip?"

"It was good," Zane didn't want to talk about the trip – not yet. He had been shocked by the information his family had presented to him, but he needed to process it and check it out before he got his hopes up – or Presley's.

"God, you look good." And he did. Zane was dressed in tight jeans and a black western shirt, boots and a hat. He looked good enough to eat.

She was so sweet. Zane touched her face. What if he could see again? Lord, the very thought of being able to see the world again, to see this incredible woman was thrilling – but he had gotten his hopes up once before and had been disappointed. Willow said this time would be different and he wanted to believer her more than anyone could imagine. "You know what I did this morning?" Sitting on the edge of her desk, he pulled her between his legs.

"What did you do? You and Rex look like you've been up to something." The dog did appear happy to see her. She held out her hand and the lab licked her fingers.

"I had a foal born this morning to a golden palamino that we rescued from the slaughter pen."

"Oh, no! We don't slaughter horses here in the states, do we?"

"No," Zane rubbed her up and down her back. "But buyers come here and ship them to Canada and Mexico. This little beauty was sold because her owner was having financial difficulties. When she went to the auction office to find out where to send the breed certificates, they told her that where the horse would be going, she wouldn't need them. The owner was horrified and contacted me and we found her just in time. I just wish we could rescue all the others." He let her take his hat off and was as still as he could be as she ran her fingers through his hair. Never had he thought he could be so comfortable in a woman's arms. Presley felt like home to him.

"I'm so glad. I bet she's cute."

"The foal? It was a boy. Hey would you like to . . ."

Presley tensed at the question. Was he about to invite her over? At the mere thought of spending more time with him her nipples peaked and she shivered a bit. But before he could voice his thought, Renee burst in. Zane couldn't see her look of approval at their closeness, but Presley could.

"Excuse me, Zane. But I have to talk to you. It's important."

Presley stepped back and Zane stood up. "What's wrong?"

"It's about Vision Star. Ralph just called and Angela Fields is in town and her escort has come down with the flu. She is requesting that you take his place."

Presley stiffened, waiting to see what Zane would do.

His reaction was calm, but adamant. "Tell him that will not be possible, I have already made plans with a young lady for this evening."

Rene cut her eyes at Presley and sliced her in several pieces with her narrow sharp gaze. "Sir, with all due respect," Renee could be charming when she needed to be, "their contract is up for renewal and Miss Fields is considering relocating here for a mini-series. If we land her as a client, it would open up doors to broaden our media accounts."

"I admit that this is an opportunity, but I don't see why I have to be the sacrificial lamb. Why can't Adam do it?"

"Adam's mother fell and is in the hospital, he's with her. All of this happened while you were in New Orleans. In fact, I spoke with him a few minutes ago and he has been on the phone with Ralph this morning. Adam thinks that if you charm Alicia Fields we might could be in the running for other studios that she works with. Miss Fields is a big star and one of the most beautiful women in Hollywood, I don't think escorting her would be that great of a sacrifice." Even though her voice was saccharine sweet, Renee's eyes sent a private message of dislike to Presley. "I'm sure your date would understand that this is all business."

His date understood. "Renee, if you would excuse us, I need to tell Mr. Saucier something important." Presley was standing behind Zane and she placed a hand on his back and pressed slightly, letting him know all was well. Renee gave her a smug look and left, closing the door behind her.

Zane turned. "We had plans, and I'm not letting some selfish diva disrupt them."

God, forgive her. She was about to lie. "I didn't get a chance to tell you. My plans were changed. I can't go. Fraiser needs me to help with a catering job and I could use the money. One of my student loan payments is due." All of that was basically true, but she could scrimp by until her first official paycheck came from Saucier and Barclay, but she had no desire to be instrumental in depriving Zane of a business opportunity, either.

"Presley, dammit," he said the words softly like he was in pain. "Are you sure? I wanted to be with you."

"It's just one night." In a move she used to wouldn't have made in a thousand years, she cuddled up against him and laid her head on his chest. His arms came around her. "Let's both take care of our obligations and tomorrow I'll cook dinner for you. How does that sound?"

"It sounds good," he rubbed his face on her hair. "Not long ago, I would have jumped at the chance to expand the firm with the film set. Only Hollywood outranks Austin in the movie industry, but my priorities have changed."

"I'm not going anywhere," she assured him. "You take care of your business and I will always be here when you have time for me."

"You're amazing, did you know that?" Zane framed her face and rested his forehead against her own. "How did I ever get so lucky?"

As the day wore on, Zane's words were never far from Presley's thoughts. She concentrated on tying up loose ends so she could begin her associate's work. The Taylor case was where she wanted to place her focus, so she needed the files. That meant facing Renee again, but it had to be done. At least she had the memo from Zane authorizing her to be a part of the process. He had been busy – meeting after meeting. From what she gathered, there were no advances in the search for Aron and that was not good news. At the moment, he was working on his notes for the conference. Presley looked forward to getting away with him to Lake Buchanan and the Canyon of the Eagles resort. Monday couldn't come fast enough for her.

Rising from her desk, she took the memo from Zane and went to Adam's office to get the files she needed. To her relief, Renee was gone and Adam's file clerk gave her what she needed with a smile. She was anxious to delve into the facts and see if she could help. When she stepped back into the reception area, it was obvious something was going on. A crowd of gawkers stood back and watched one particular woman as she studied the photographs of Zane on the wall.

"Now that's what I call a man!"

Presley's teeth went on edge as she heard the sultry, sexy voice comment on the man that Presley was fast coming to consider her personal possession. She stepped closer. The woman was an absolute vision. Alicia Fields was recognizable, but watching her on television was nothing like seeing her up close and personal. This was no mere mortal, but an ethereal being from another realm. Her designer gown shimmered with jewels and it flowed over her perfect body with a sensual and elegant flair. Presley recalled the off-the-rack garment hanging in Zane's dressing room and was grateful that she, and it, would be staying home tonight.

Ducking her head, Presley rushed back to the sanctuary of her office. Zane was not there, but she could hear noises coming from the dressing room and knew he was getting ready. Laying the files on the desk, she fixed herself a cup of coffee, hoping the caffeine would settle her nerves. When Zane emerged, he was wearing a black tux and she almost groaned at the sight. "Don't you look good," she couldn't help but compliment him.

"Do I?" He walked closer to her. Rex stood, he knew something was up.

"You know you do. Come here and let me fix your tie." She tried to make light of the situation, but her heart was aching a bit. It hadn't bothered her a great deal until she laid eyes on the woman who would be on his arm tonight. If Alicia Fields set her eye on Zane, Presley didn't know how she could compete. "Maybe we should have gotten Rex a formal vest to wear. He needs to dress up, too."

"That's an idea." Zane stood still while Presley tended to him.

"Your date is here, you'd better get going. I have to go run an errand." God, how dear he was to her. She brushed off imaginary lint and patted his chest; this was going to be harder than she thought. "I hope you have a good time." Actually, she couldn't stand to see him leave.

"Be safe going home, I'll see you in the morning." She tip-toed up and gave him a kiss on the cheek and walked quickly away.

Zane listened to her retreating footsteps and he felt bereft. "Stay, Rex," he instructed the lab which was completely unnecessary. Rex was as faithful as the day was long. Making his way back into the dressing room to brush his teeth, he wondered at the dissatisfaction he felt in his gut. Once upon a time he would have considered his life to be full to the brim, now he was longing for things he thought were forever out of his grasp. Rinsing his hands, he felt for the towel dispenser and his hand brushed something silky hanging on the wall. He moved closer and examined it. A dress! He smelled of it, knowing the scent he'd detect – Presley.

Sadness washed over him. She had intended to go with him. She had brought clothes to wear. There was no doubt in his mind that she fabricated that excuse of helping Fraiser and Chloe just to give him the freedom to do what he needed to do without a guilty conscience. Damn! He hit the wall. Nothing was worth hurting Presley. He was going to talk to her, but when he came out, she wasn't in the office. Renee and Alicia were and they were waiting on him. "Do you know where Presley is?" he asked Renee.

"No, but I'll give her a message if you'd like. Do you need her to work overtime?"

Zane got his dog by the harness and offered his arm to the woman he could sense standing by his side. "No, I don't expect her to work overtime." He almost growled in frustration. "Tell her that I'm sorry and I will make it up to her." There was a very light harrumph behind him and he knew – good and well – that his message would not be delivered.

Presley stood in the conference room window and watched until Zane and Alicia emerged and Sherwood opened the door to let them into the car. As they drove away, she stared through a blur of tears until they were out of sight.

Chapter Seven

"May I pour you a drink?" Zane released the lever that opened the mini-bar.

"No, thank you."

From the moment he had greeted the movie star, Zane had a funny feeling that something had changed. By all accounts she had been anxious to spend the evening with him, but her tone was frosty and sharp. "Is something wrong? I'm sure Burning Love is going to be a huge success."

"That's not it," he heard the woman huff as she rearranged her skirt. "I've heard of you, Mr. Saucier. I know you are a good lawyer, and Ralph had shown me photographs of you. But when I requested that you be my escort, I had no idea you were – handicapped." Contempt rolled off her tongue and Zane couldn't help but be shocked. Even though he had spent years attempting to avoid situations like this, he had not really encountered venom like this since Margaret.

"Miss Fields, the limp's not that bad. I get around okay." His off-hand comment hid his true feelings quite well.

"I have an image to maintain and you are attached to a dog."

"Ah, but he is a handsome dog so I'm told, and he has impeccable manners." 'Unlike you' went unsaid. Zane was torn. He could either schmooze the woman and court her business interests or cut her to shreds with his rapier tongue for being a total bitch.

"When we get to the theatre, I think I can manage quite well on my own. I won't be needing your services."

Hell. "Miss Fields, you are a marvelous actress and I am honored to see after the interests of Vision Star. If and when you need legal representation, I think you'll find that my firm should be your first choice. But having said that, let me assure you that I have no emotion involved in this evening. My being blind hampers me very little." Zane was laying it on thick, but he couldn't help it. "Tonight, I'll be glad to step aside. I have no wish to embarrass you, but I will stay near in case you have need of my protection."

Silence.

"Pardon me, I did not mean to insult you."

"Yes, you did." A bit of honesty slipped it. "But, that's okay. I used to think that all women felt like you, but they don't. And for that I'm grateful."

The evening went by with excruciating slowness. He was at home in the beautiful restored Paramount Theatre on Congress, he remembered it well - a blind man at a movie premier might be an oddity, but Zane supported his community in every way possible. Afterwards, the party was held in the grand Driscoll hotel and Zane made some valuable contacts. Alicia wasn't entirely rude, but he kept trying to read more into what people said to him than they probably intended. It was hard to think they might be smiling at one another or sharing a private joke at his expense. Damn! He hadn't been this paranoid in years. But, he did his best to take care of business. By the end of the evening, he had sewn up Vision Star's contract and passed his card to several big names who had heard good things about Saucier and Barclay. Now, all he wanted to do was go home. No, that wasn't true – he wanted to go to Presley.

Pushing her hair back, Presley breathed a sigh of relief as she took the last tray of sticky buns from the oven. Fraiser had been glad to hear he was getting them, but he had also asked what had happened with the date. She had tried to explain, but the words had just sounded hollow to her own ears. All she could dwell on was what a good time Zane must be having with Alicia. She could just imagine the woman's lilting laughter and how she would place her small white hand on his arm and how he probably held her close while they danced. In truth, Presley was just torturing herself.

Something good had come out of the night, however. The odd feeling she had experienced when reading up on the Taylor case had finally come to the forefront of her memory. And she couldn't wait to talk to Adam, in fact – she planned on doing it as soon as Frasier picked up the pecan buns. Presley couldn't shake the idea that Laney might still be alive.

She had papers scattered all over the kitchen table and every chance she got, she settled back and rifled through them again. Yes, there it was. She didn't think she was wrong. All evening she had researched sites on the internet pertaining to a Houston cold case from six years earlier. A woman's body had been found in a storm cellar in the back yard of an older home in an upscale neighborhood. The man's name had been Raymond Kershaw. Their situation had been very similar to Kendall and Laney's. According to testimonies obtained after the fact, Mr. Kershaw had been a total jerk who preyed upon women and once he got his clutches on one, they had a hard time extricating themselves. Apparently he was a smooth talker that poured on the charm. Neighbors had testified that he had been seen acting so normal, playing ball in his front yard with a small dog. The woman who had been murdered had been there too, laughing and playing. They had seemed like a normal couple.

But when Chelsea Norieaga had gone missing, the police had bought into Kershaw's explanation and by the time they had gone full circle and finally searched in his own home, it had been too late for Chelsea. The forewarning he had received had resulted in her death and his complete disappearance. The city had been horrified to find that she had been caged in that underground coffin for several weeks. Presley tried to imagine the despair and terror the woman must have felt at being buried alive.

One more time, Presley compared the notes on the burn marks on Chelsea's body and compared them with what she had seen in the stills of Laney's interview. Yes, it was stars. When Kershaw's house had been searched, they had found a set of art metal punch stamps that he had used in making belts and billfolds. Presley's skin had crawled when she had thought of him holding the metal star to a flame and then pressing it on their tender flesh. How they must have screamed! But the marks and the circumstances were too similar to ignore. What if Kershaw had just reinvented himself and was going by an alias? What if Kershaw and Kendall was the same person and Laney Taylor was still alive? She had to get hold of Adam before the search warrant was approved. If what she suspected was true, the police wouldn't get a second chance to find Laney. At the first hint of danger, he'd kill her and be gone like before.

Fraiser came and left. He was so sweet, but what she had found concerning Laney had taken her mind off of Zane and Alicia – for a little bit, anyway. Her heart felt tender and there was a knot in her middle the size of a baseball, but there wasn't anything she could do about it. She wished she were sure of Zane, but her own insecurities prevented her from being so.

From what Renee had said, Adam was not at the function. She hated to bother him while he was with his mother, but this couldn't wait. Dialing his cell, she sat at the table tense, but excited.

"Hello?" It was Adam's voice.

"Adam, this is Presley. I hate to disturb you, but I think I've found something on the Taylor case that you should know."

"Tell me, I welcome any information you have." Adam's voice immediately sounded with the concern he had developed for a woman he believed to be beyond help.

In a few minutes she had outlined her suspicions and was gratified that he took her seriously. "So you think these two cases might be related?" His voice was full of hope.

"I don't know, Adam, but I think it's worth checking out."

Adam grew quite for a second, then let out a harsh breath. "I won't waste a minute; if there's a chance Laney could still be alive, I'll move heaven and earth to find her." Presley smiled. Adam was a knight in shining armor, no doubt about it.

Having done what she had set out to do, Presley went and took a bath. It was nearing eleven o'clock and she wondered how Zane's evening had turned out. Dressing in a pair of panties and a t-shirt, she settled down on the couch to read a few pages before she turned in. Glancing around, she remembered how amazing it had been to have him here with her. Of course, his size had made the small room seem even smaller, but never had it felt more like a home than when he was there.

Lying back on her pillow, she pulled the comforter up over her and picked up a thick romance novel. One day she would get an e-reader, but right now an old fashioned book was a comfort. She had only read two pages before a knock sounded at the door. Presley jumped. She never had visitors. Who could it be? Scrambling around to find her robe, she padded barefoot to the door and rose up on tip-toe to look through the peep-hole. Zane! Throwing open the door, she didn't even consider holding back but launched herself at him, almost knocking him over. "I am so glad to see you!"

Zane let out a long sigh. What a difference between the woman he held in his arms and the one he had walked to her penthouse suite. The ironic thing had been that she had attempted to seduce him – after insulting him, ignoring him and treating him like an underling, she had come on to him like a two-bit whore. Zane had not had any trouble resisting the temptation. "Can I come in?"

"Yes, of course," she attempted to back up, but he just picked her up. "Nope, you aren't getting out of my arms. I've missed you so much tonight." Her little body was soft and sweet and fit so well up against his. Just like the romantics of old, Zane was beginning to believe he had found a woman whose worth was far more than rubies.

"I will need to make the couch into a bed; I had already turned in for the night."

"Hmmmm, I have an idea." He carried her, loving when she nestled against him, arms around his neck and head buried against his shoulder. A raging arousal filled him and the only thing that could appease his appetite was Presley. How he had missed her! When he had been in New Orleans listening to Willow's proposal, all he could think about was getting back home and back in her arms. Putting her down gently, he said just one word. "Strip."

Zane could hear her following his order and he made quick work of his own clothes. The tux might not survive the rough handling, but it didn't matter.

"I'm naked."

God, he'd give ten years of his life to look his fill at her body. "I'm dying to touch you. For days, I've dreamed of taking you again."

"I can't believe you came to me, tonight, Zane. I'd rather be with you than anyone else on earth."

Kneeling beside the couch, he placed his head in her lap. All of the wealth his parents possessed, all of the power and acclaim he had garnered and worked so hard for – all of his friends that stood by his side - - none of it meant as much to him as she did. Nothing in his life was as important as this one beautiful woman who accepted him so readily and asked for so little in return. Oh he had given her a job, but he knew full well that wasn't the reason she was willing to hold him close when the night threatened to close in on him. She was his lifeline, she was his anchor in the storm that raged in his soul.

"Stand up and then you lay down on top of me," they changed places and when he was stretched out, he pulled her body down on top of his. Jesus! He just wanted to moan in relief; there was no sweeter thing in the world than having a woman's body on top of his own. It ought to be a law. "Stretch out now and just let me feel you." She did and it was a sensual experience unlike any he had known. "I need you, Presley." How long had it been since he said those words? Had he ever said them? Searching his memory he couldn't recall a time when he had told Margaret that he needed her. The emotional bond he had with his former fiancé paled beside the one he had with Presley Love. Slowly and sensually, he rubbed her back and hips, enjoying the silk of her skin and the suppleness of her muscles. Hard little nipples poked him in the chest and she repaid his caresses with kisses and butterfly touches of her own. "You belong to me. Do you want to belong to me?" Even as he made a sure, authoritative statement, he questioned if he overstepped his bounds.

"I want to belong to you more than anything." Tears of absolute joy dripped down her face and splashed on his skin.

"Don't you dare cry. Do you want to break my heart?"

"They are happy tears. I feel freer with you than I ever have with anyone, yet you make me feel safe and grounded all at the same time."

"Oh, Baby," he whispered as he kissed her tears away. "You make me feel exactly the same way. Do you know how I broke my neck to get back to you tonight? I couldn't wait."

Joy coursed through her veins. "Really? You'd rather be with me that those Hollywood types? Alicia Fields was really, really pretty. I don't know if anyone told you, but you were out with the perfect woman."

He pushed her hair over her shoulder. Here she was, in his arms, trying to convince him that some other woman was perfect for him. "She was dowdy by the side of you – no personality, and she didn't smell good like you, either." Conspiratorially, Zane pulled her down to whisper, "and when I danced with her, I couldn't help but notice that she didn't have magnificent boobs like you do."

Presley giggled, "You sure were dancing close – maybe a little too close." But his affirmations made her happy and she settled down on top of him.

"Not as close as I want to be with you." His hand smoothed down her side until he was molding her hip, loving the shape of her and wishing he could look into her eyes. Maybe. Someday.

Presley felt her pussy dew. The thick hard ridge of his erection was right at her mound. She held herself up over him and drug her pussy up and down over it and loved it when he stiffened and groaned.

"My God, woman!"

"I need you, you belong to me. Do you want to belong to me?" she whispered his words back to him and Zane thought his heart would pound so hard they could hear it in the next county.

"I don't think I have a choice."

"You always have a choice," she spoke in a tone that could have been used by a courtesan. Presley was in full seductress mode, and she had no clue that he was already putty in her hands. Sitting up, she scooted back and sat on his legs, taking the heavy weight of his erection in one of her small delicate hands. Zane lay there – completely at her mercy – as she began to stroke that silken little fist up and down his cock, pumping him with a sure, firm motion designed to drive him fuckin' crazy.

"I do belong to you. You're all I can think about," his voice cracked as he felt one small lick of a velvety tongue. "I think about kissing you, rubbing these round, luscious tits, sucking those puffy nipples and sinking my cock into a pussy that has to be the snuggest, tightest, wettest little piece of paradise in the world."

God, she was wet. "I think about you, too, Zane." Before she said more, she leaned over and placed her lips right on the tip of his cock and slid them down, but kept her mouth tight – one, long sucking kiss that had him bucking his lower body off the couch. She had to hold on or she would have fallen off of him.

"Christ!"

Pulling her lips from him in a slow sucking motion that ended with a little pop, she told him more. "I love to recall how you make me feel when you press deep inside me – how good it feels when you stretch me and your cock drags over that one spot that makes me want to scream your name to the rooftops!" Beneath her his big body shuddered. Presley felt powerful. "I think about how it feels when you hammer into me, how I love for you to lose control and feel all the power in your thrusts. I love how your hips pump and how I can feel you all the way to my womb. And when you cum and all of that rich cream shoots up inside of me, I just melt."

God, he was horny! His little angel was becoming a vixen. "Tell me more." He loved it.

"My nipples ache so much. They want to be sucked." She moved over him, dragging her tits over his chest, the nipples dragging in the light dusting of hair. He charted every move and when he knew she was near his face, he opened his mouth. "Do you want to suck my tits?" She drug one nipple over his lips and he lapped up at it like a hungry tom-cat. "Oh, that feels good. Now this one," and she drug the other tit across his face. Zane had had all he could take. He stopped her movements with a firm clasp of his hands and opened his mouth wide, capturing the entire areola and nipple in his lips. And he inhaled them, ate at them, sucked and licked and kissed until she was humping his stomach and groin, spreading Presley honey all over him. "God! Yes! More! More!" she demanded as she came hard, her nails biting into his shoulders. The frantic movements she made as she scrubbed her wet pussy over the length of his massively aroused cock, alone, were almost enough to make him cum.

"Damn! You came just from my lips on your tits. If you aren't the sweetest, sexiest woman in the world, I don't know who is." Zane lifted her and held his cock up and – thank God – she eased herself down onto it – slowly. They both exhaled sighs of utter ecstasy and relief. "Shit, yeah. You are heaven to fuck."

They were crude words but he said them like a prayer and the sentiment warmed her heart. "Hold my hands," she wove her fingers with his as she began raising and lowering herself on his rock-hard shaft. With every stroke she became more delirious with pleasure, it felt so good! Her pussy began to contract, she felt voracious for him. Where once she would have been embarrassed;

now she was proud that she was wet. Her cream ran thick enough to coat his cock and flow down to dampen where they were joined.

"Ride me, Presley Love."

He raised his hips, adding to their pleasure, urging her to move. She followed his lead and moved back and forth on top of him, her too-sensitive folds dragging over his groin. Oh God – she was losing her grip on reality. The look on his face was worth everything to her, he was lost in the throes of pleasure – they both were. Pulling from her grasp, his hands bit into her hips – molding – clutching – controlling her movements as her clit drug back and forth across his pelvis. "Spank me," she invited, surprising herself. God, she was becoming a wanton!

"My pleasure," he almost snarled at her, but he wasn't mad, far from it. The spanking began with heavy pats, rubs and caresses, but she wanted more.

"Spank me," she reiterated.

Okay, little girl, he thought. Using one hand to warm the soft flesh of her behind, he brought the other one around to tickle her clit. Two could play at this game. Gradually, slowly – the little slaps became more erotically heated, not burning her flesh, but setting off a wildfire that raged through her veins. It was too much! She tried to hold back, she wanted it to last, but it was impossible. "Zane!" she screamed as her pussy began to vibrate and spasm.

"That's my baby, cum for me!" he commanded. One slap to the side of her ass caused her to cry out again.

"Zane!" He felt her pussy clutch his cock like a tight little fist, milking him into ecstatic oblivion.

"You're mine, Presley," Zane vowed. "You're mine. No one else's." Holding her steady, he thrust upward impaling her over and over, a powerful pounding that prolonged her orgasm and shot his climb to ecstasy rocketing out of control. With mindless thrusts he let it happen, the white-hot blaze of glory that shot his cum deep up inside of her, exploding bursts of rapture that had him bellowing incoherent words of possession and intent. "Never – gonna – let you go. Mine. Mine. Mine!"

Presley took it all in, every bit, tucking the words in her heart where they belonged.

Easing her off of him, he stood. "Rest, my love. Tell me how many steps to the bathroom and what's in my way."

"Let me help you."

"Just tell me."

"It's one room, sugar. And there's nothing ahead of you but a couch to your right. Walk straight ahead ten steps and touch the screen, the tub, sink and potty are right there. The tub is in the corner, the commode is between the tub and the sink."

"Where are the wash cloths?"

Damn, he looked good striding across her room. His ass was tight and that instrument of pleasure that hung between his legs was still large enough to make her pussy tingle at the sight. "They're under the sink on the left. You need to let the water run for a few seconds, it's slow to warm up." She'd get up and shower with him, but she didn't have that much energy. Heck! She needed to make out the bed; they couldn't sleep on the couch all night. Was he staying the night? Might as well ask.

"Are you staying with me tonight?" she called out.

Zane was warming two wash cloths. With one he cleaned himself and the other one was to clean up his little kitten. "I'm staying if it's okay with you," he answered.

"Good. I want to keep you."

Her lilting voice answered any question he might have had that he was welcome. Welcome – what a wondrous concept. "Here I come," Zane announced, stepping slowly, trying to ascertain how the layout had changed since she had pulled the sofa apart. "Am I clear?"

"Dang, baby," she reached out for him. "I forget, I'm sorry."

"Really? You forget I'm blind?"

Presley clasped a pillow to her front, afraid that she had offended him. "Yes, I'm sorry. I'll be more conscientious."

"No," Zane shook his head. "That pleases me more than you'll ever know." How could he make her understand that her forgetting he was different, handicapped, or less than other men – meant everything to him. He longed to be normal. Zane longed to be just a man. Presley's man. "Lay down and let me clean you up."

"What?" she didn't understand.

"I am taking care of you. Don't you remember me saying that you were 'mine'?" There was humor in his voice, but he was as serious as a heart attack.

"You don't have to," she began, but she was getting into position as quickly as she could. Presley wouldn't miss this for the world.

Zane crawled in beside her, throwing a towel at the end of the bed, his left hand raised with the warm cloth spread over it. Reaching out, locating her body, he smiled. She had readied herself for him, spreading her thighs, splaying all that lush womanhood out for his delectation. "There you are," he placed an anchoring palm on her thigh and took the washcloth and gently wiped her pussy. As he did so, he kissed her all over – neck, breast, arm, stomach. Then he dried her. Wrapping the wet cloth up in the towel, he tossed them to one side. "Scoot over, make room for me."

"Gladly," she pulled back the covers and held them up for him to get in beside her. He might not realize it, but she would make as much room for him in her life as he wanted.

Adam Barclay stood on Kendall's porch with the police. Everything Presley had told him had been true. He had conferred with the PI, the chief investigator and the DA. And it had all been done under wraps. Hopefully their suspect had no idea they were coming, and thus no chance to cover his tracks or hurt Laney, if she was still alive.

Instead of banging on the door and yelling 'Police!' like in the movies, all of them stepped back and one knocked politely on the door. Adam held his breath. For weeks he had stared at Laney's face and watched that damned video and mourned the fact that he had come into her life too late to save her. And now – miracle of miracles – there was the slightest chance she could still be alive. It was a long-shot, but Presley had given him enough reason to hope. So here they were. His whole body was taut with adrenaline. The police were on their mission to gather evidence, but he was headed to the backyard to look for any clue that Laney might be somewhere on the property – alive. Criminals usually did not change their modus operandi, they tended to keep their techniques and habits intact and work only to perfect them.

Hell, he hadn't even taken time to call Zane. Hopefully, Presley would clue him in. Or maybe he would be the one to call with good news.

"I don't have any Cocoa Puffs," Presley explained slowly. "I have Raisin Bran."

"Rachel is a good cook, but she doesn't approve of cereals with high sugar content. I like Cocoa Puffs."

Presley began to giggle. She was so happy. Sitting at her breakfast table was the sexiest man in the world and if he wanted a kid's chocolaty cereal, that's what he would get. "I tell you what, there's a store just down the street, you sit tight and I'll be right back." She was already dressed, so Presley grabbed her purse and stood, about to take off on a mission of mercy.

"Not so fast," he pulled her back into his lap. "I think I can get my sugar fix right here," he kissed her soundly on the lips. "How about you and I pick up a selection of good cereals on the way to my house tonight? I want you to spend the weekend with me."

"Really?" she pushed a lock of beautiful dark hair off his forehead. "I would like that very much."

"Let's go on to work and stop at a donut shop and get the biggest, sugariest cinnamon rolls they have!" His gleeful expression reminded her of what she had in the oven.

"Let me up," she wiggled. "I have something you want."

"Damn straight," he popped her on the butt.

"No, silly," she pulled out the sticky buns. "Let me microwave this and you can tell me how talented I am." With a few economical movements, it was a small kitchen, after all – she placed her offering before him.

Zane sank his teeth into the luscious pastry. "You are a goddess," he proclaimed. "I am in love."

The words hung between them. She said nothing, and he didn't seem to realize he had said the magic phrase. Oh, they were spoken in jest – she realized that. But still her heart quaked with excitement. She searched for something to say to fill the silence while he enjoyed the sweet treat. "I called Adam last night, I think I might have found a connection between the Laney Taylor and a cold case."

Mid-bite, Zane stopped. "What did you say?"

Presley explained more in depth. "Right after you hired me, you let me look at the Taylor file, including the video Laney made with Lieutenant Rodriguez. Something about it bothered me, but I couldn't put my finger on what it was. It took me awhile, but I finally figured out that I had seen the star pattern burn marks on her neck before. After a few searches, I found some old articles on another case where a woman had been abused and tortured and buried alive in a storm cellar in their backyard. The man responsible was not caught, he disappeared. Unfortunately, the woman didn't survive – but it was estimated that Chelsea had been kept in her underground prison for almost two weeks. I may be totally wrong, but if Kendall and Kershaw are the same man – Laney might still be alive."

Carefully, he laid the uneaten bite down on the plate. His mind raced with the possibilities. Finding her hand on the table next to him, he picked it up and kissed it. "You are amazing." If she was correct, Presley had just saved a woman's life. Pulling his cell-phone from his pocket, he dialed Adam. After six rings, his partner finally answered.

"Barclay."

Whatever was going on, the man was out of breath. "Where are you?"

"I'm standing by a stretcher. We found Laney Taylor and she's alive. When you see Presley, kiss her for me. She solved the case."

"Hot Damn!"

There was a festive atmosphere at Saucier and Barclay the next day and Miss Presley Love was the star. Zane was so proud of her, but she refused to take the compliment. Her position was that it had all been pure coincidence, not talent. If she hadn't been living in southeast Texas at the time of the first crime, and just hadn't happened to follow the case closely because she was interested in the legal system – she would never have put two and two together.

Zane and Adam did not agree.

After lunch, Zane insisted that they take a half day off. He said he wanted her to see the new colt and spend the weekend with him. They also needed to firm up their plans for the conference that started bright and early on Monday morning. In fact, they'd be traveling to the Canyon of the Eagles resort after lunch on Sunday. Presley had gone shopping for a few more appropriate clothes and a few items that she didn't usually splurge on like a new purse and some new make-up.

"Are you ready to go?" Zane stuck his head in the door, a big smile on his face. Rex stood by him and bounced once on his front feet. Their good mood was contagious.

"I sure am," she grabbed her laptop and a brand new brief case she had acquired for just such an occasion. "This is going to be like a slumber party, isn't it?" She was kidding, teasing Zane was fun. She so enjoyed playing with him.

"Hahaha," he retorted in his own teasing tone. "I don't think we're gonna do much slumbering, you sexy thang." He popped her on the rear when she got close.

"How do you do that?" she laughed.

"I got your cute little ass on my radar, baby." As they made their way out to Sherwood, Presley couldn't help but notice the envious glances she was receiving from other women in the office. And as Zane stopped to talk to a client who called his name, she couldn't help but overhear a conversation behind her.

"Poor Zane, I can't believe he's taken up with that pitiful creature."

"Yea, if he could see her, he wouldn't touch her with a ten foot pole."

"Well, you know what they say . . ."

"What do they say?"

"There is none so blind as those who cannot see."

The two women cracked up and Presley drew into herself, trying to be just as small as possible. She didn't turn around, but the gossipy women had to have known she could hear them. They just didn't care.

When Zane was ready to continue on, Presley was much more subdued. He didn't seem to notice but kept up a running commentary with Sherwood on the weather, local politics and the price of gasoline. She occupied herself by petting Rex and watching the scenery go by. A gentle buzzing noise brought her out of her reverie, "Hello."

"I have a transfer call for you, Miss Love. Jessie McCoy would like to speak to you." It was Melody, the receptionist.

"Hello?"

"Presley, hey!" Jessie's voice sounded fairly happy. Even though they all still were tore up over Aron's disappearance, it was good to know they were able to go on with their lives.

"Hi, Jessie. How are you?"

"We're coping. It's not the same, but we haven't given up."

"Of course not, how's Libby?"

"She's fragile, but very brave. Actually, that's what I'm calling about."

Presley put her hand on Zane's knee. He and Sherwood had stopped speaking and she knew he was aware she was on the phone with one of his friends. "Is there something we can do to help?"

When she said 'we', Zane covered her hand with his in support.

"Do you remember us mentioning a baby shower for Libby? And that we wanted you to come?"

"Yes, I do." Presley had just assumed the shower would be cancelled. She hadn't heard any more about it.

"We debated even having it, but I think Libby needs a show of support. And gifts for her baby boys would make her happy. She needs to know she has friends and that we love her."

"When will Libby's shower be?" Presley knew she and Zane had plans. They were going out of town on Sunday, but there was no doubt in her mind that he would want her to go to the shower, if possible. She leaned in to him so he could hear the conversation and got amused when he used it as an excuse to cuddle.

"Tomorrow night, I know that's quick and it's only going to be close family and friends. But we sure would appreciate if you'd try to be here."

"Tell her yes," Zane whispered in her ear.

"What can I bring? Would you like for me to make a cake?"

"No, you don't need to do that," Jessie laughed. "Although, I have heard amazing stories about your baking skills. All I need you to bring is yourself and a gift if you'd like to. Either way, we just want you to be here."

"I wouldn't miss it. What time?" Jessie told her the rest of the details and hung up.

"Sherwood, we need to make a stop at the mall, if you don't mind." Zane requested.

A trip to the mall with Zane was a blast. She never laughed so much in her life. He told one funny story after another. As they made their way from the ground floor to the third where the baby boutique was, he kept her in stitches.

"You'll have to meet one of my cousins – the good one, I have two other that aren't so hot. She's a hoot! Her name is Willow and she's a doctor in New Orleans." She was also the one who had shaken the foundations of his world a few days ago. Zane was still trying to process what she had told him. "Willow has never married. She's two years younger than Kane and I, and as pretty as a picture, but she's more confident in her ability as a doctor than she in is her worth as a woman."

His voice trailed off as if he were remembering something that bothered him. Presley didn't interrupt and in a moment he continued with his story. "Anyway, let me tell you what happened to her just recently. Willow has a dog that she thinks the world of. That dog is more important to her than any family member could ever be. He's a fat wiener dog named Oscar. Anyway a few weeks ago, Willow decided to dye her hair. She has long dark hair, but occasionally she'll get a wild idea and decide she wants to go auburn or streak it or something. And Willow is too tight to go to the hair salon to have it done correctly."

"I thought your family was well-off." Oops, she probably shouldn't have said that, but Zane didn't act like it mattered.

"Willow has enough money to do anything she wants to, but she still pinches every penny till it screams. Well, the other day she went out on the porch to dye her hair and she's not the most coordinated of women. By the time she got through, she had dye on the porch and on the dog and on five of her seven cats."

"Did they appreciate their new look?"

"No," he snorted, "but they are used to it. The dog, however, is central to the story. Oscar was ambling about the yard while Willow applied the dye. He's so fat, he doesn't go far, but there's always a chance he might wander off so Willow watches him like a hawk. She lives out in the country between New Orleans and Madisonville and she's always afraid an alligator is going to eat him or he's gong to get picked up by dognappers or some such nonsense. In other words, she's a worrier."

"Did you inherit that quality?"

"No, baby-cakes, I'm perfect," he said with a straight face.

Now it was her turn to laugh. "What happened next?"

"When she finished dyeing her hair, she and Oscar went back in the house and Oscar piled up on the couch and went to sleep. Willow piddled around and did some chores, careful not to get the dye on anything in the house. After forty-five minutes, she got into the shower and rinsed off the hair dye. Now here's the kicker – Willow never forgets anything. Her memory skills were legendary at Tulane, it was purported that she had a photographic memory." Zane laughed again, he was enjoying telling his own story. Presley clung to his arm and stared up at his face, loving everything about him. "Well, that day was the day her photographic memory card filled up, because as she was drying off – it hit her – she had left Oscar outside. She panicked."

"But, I thought . . ." Zane held a finger up.

"Willow panicked – big time. She got to thinking about big owls swooping down and taking Oscar, or voodoo priestesses nabbing him for sacrifice. In her distress, Willow dropped the towel and took off outside screaming "Oscar! Oscar! Oscar!""

"Was she naked?" Presley gasped, giggling.

"Stark," Zane laughed. "Oscar! Oscar! Oscar! Neighbors came running, other dogs started barking, it was chaos. And when she realized she was naked, Willow nearly died!" They were at the baby boutique store by now, but Zane was still gesturing and laughing.

"Did someone call the cops on her?

"No, no cops. I think her fit was overlooked, except by one. Willow has a neighbor that has asked her out faithfully once a week for three years and she never says yes."

"Oh, that's sad. She doesn't like him?"

"I think she likes him too much, but that's my theory. Later, someone found a bouquet of flowers on the porch and the note on them said, 'don't you be embarrassed, all I saw was a glimpse of heaven. She knew the handwriting, it was her neighbor's."

"Awwww, that's sweet, how do you know what the note said?"

"Because Kane and I are the ones that found the flowers."

"I can't believe you two read her note!"

"Hey, we're her cousins. We've spent a life-time tormenting one another. What do you expect?"

They wandered into the baby store and were immediately met by a clerk who had to stop and take time to pet Rex. "What can I help you with? Are you two expecting?"

Oh, my goodness! Presley blushed. "No, we're looking for a shower gift for a friend who is having twin baby boys." She hadn't spent a lot of time in store of this nature, so Presley was fascinated. There were baby clothes of every description – designer names, sailor suits, onesies – even cowboy clothes which immediately drew her eye. "Oh, Zane! Look at these!" Ratz, her tongue had slipped. "I didn't mean . . ."

His hand rubbed a gentle pattern in the small of her back, "It's okay, Honey. Let me see them through your eyes."

"Okay," she picked up one item after another. "There's the cutest little denim jeans, you've ever seen. And cowboy boots! And the sweetest little snap western shirts and teeny-tiny belts with Texas buckles. Oh!" She squealed. "I love these little University of Texas t-shirts, they say "Little Longhorn!"

"I bet they're cute. Let's get them all."

Presley was excited, then she had a sad thought. "Aron's gone, wouldn't these clothes just make the pain worse?"

"Libby doesn't want to forget Aron, Honey. She's not going to give up until all hope is gone. Let's buy these for the boys."

"Okay, I'll get the jeans and the boots and you can get the shirts and belt." She set about making piles.

"Let's make the present from both of us and you pay me back with kisses."

Presley stiffened the least bit, "I have money."

Zane realized he was walking on eggshells. "Of course you do, but you have something else, too."

"What's that?" She wasn't following.

"Me."

Presley couldn't argue with that and she didn't want to.

As they were leaving the mall, Zane couldn't help but ask. "Would you like a baby, Presley?" At one time, having a family was something Zane had longed for.

Her answer made his heart sing. "Oh yes, if anyone ever loves me enough to give me one I'll cherish him and his father everyday of my life."

"It's too dark in here, I'm sure. Let me turn on the light." He knew right where it was, "Watch your step, too. I have on shit-kicker boots, but I bet you've got on a pair of those dainty heels and you don't want to step in horse hockey."

Presley inspected the hay strew path. "I don't see any anywhere; I think your employees keep the place immaculate." A chorus of whinnies greeted them. With uncanny knowledge of where he was, Zane led her to the first stall. Inside there was an Appaloosa, a snow-white thin horse, with a smattering of fawn colored spots on her rump. "Meet Shawnee and her little man."

"What a little living doll! Can I go in?"

Zane opened the stall door. "Sure, she's as gentle as a lamb."

"I can't believe someone sent her to slaughter." Going to her knees she embraced the wobbly, leggy colt whose coat was the reverse of his mothers. He was tawny brown with white spots. "You are so good to rescue these horses, Zane. I admire you so much."

Her words were a balm to his soul. The sound of her affection did something to his breathing. She giggled and cooed to the small animal, the noise of tiny kisses made him want to jerk her up and ravish her right here in the barn. "What do you think we ought to name him?"

"His mother has an Indian name. If you don't mind, I'd like to call him Comanche. I bet he'll grow up to be a beautiful boy." Presley stroked the little beast, feeling the tiny animal tremble beneath her hand. He was nervous.

"Comanche is a good name; it's the name of an American Calvary horse that survived Custer's Last Stand. Perhaps this mite will be as brave."

Zane leaned over the stall door, his head resting on his strong forearms. She wondered if he knew how sexy he looked. Just to make sure he realized it, she stood and kissed his cheek – one sweet kiss. "Thank you for letting me name him."

More than anything, Zane wanted to tell her that the horse was hers. She could raise him and ride him and call him her own. There was no question about it, he was falling in love with Presley and if he dared hope Willow was right, he'd ask her to move in with him today. "I wouldn't have it any other way, Sugar. Let's go meet the rest of the family." He led her through the stable to where one horse was leaning over his door and watching them approach. The big animal let out a rumbled greeting. "Hello, Onyx. Meet Presley."

With hesitant fingers, she stroked the muzzle of the black horse. Not even the dimming light could hide the fact that the horse had been abused. Scars covered his coat, even his face. She was sure in time he'd heal, but right now the evidence of his maltreatment could not be hidden. Except from Zane. "He's been hurt."

"Yes, he has. But he's getting better every day. Aren't you boy?" Zane went on to explain what they were doing to restore the horse's faith in mankind. He worked with them as often as he could, and after he got them to the point where they could trust again, he had another trainer come in and give them even more positive reinforcement.

Next, Zane led her to Shalimar, and watching him with the skittish mare, Presley lost the rest of her heart. When Zane put his face against Shalimar's and began to talk to her, it was like seeing the photograph hanging in the office come to life. "Aren't you my pretty girl? You belong to Zane, don't you?" He stroked her face and the horse nudged closer to the big man. Presley was entranced. "Isn't she beautiful Presley?"

She wasn't. Shalimar had suffered under the whip. She was battered and ravaged, but if anyone could heal her spirit and body, it was Zane. "Yes, she's beautiful." What else could she say? The truly beautiful thing, though, was seeing him love her unconditionally. To Zane she was beautiful. With a thud of her heart, Presley realized he did the same thing with her. Zane looked at her through the eyes of love.

Presley was silent as they walked up to the main house. Rex was romping around and several of the men came over to speak to Zane. When they entered his home, she couldn't help but remember the last time they were here and the shock of finding out that Aron was missing. That sad/happy day seemed like a lifetime, ago. "Is this Presley?" From the kitchen a happy voice greeted her. "Bring her to me, Zane. I'm trying to get a cake in the oven."

Zane led Presley by the hand and introduced her to his housekeeper. From what Zane had told her, Sherwood was sweet on Rachel and Presley could see why. Even though she had a touch of grey, her dark hair hung lush and lustrous to her shoulders and her eyes shone like blackberries in the sun. "Hello, Rachel." Presley watched the woman's face carefully to see how she would react to someone so imperfect being with her Zane, but she saw only happiness and welcome in her eyes.

Rachel put an arm around Presley and whispered in her ear, "You'll never know how happy I am for you to be here. He has needed someone like you for so long." If Zane heard, he was too polite to say so, but Presley knew how well he could hear, and she was embarrassed.

"Something smells good," she tried to maneuver the conversation back to safer ground.

"Rachel spoils me." With sure moves, he found the cookie jar with no problem.

Rachel swatted him with a dish towel. "You do not need to fill up with sugary sweets. Next you'll be wanting to have Cocoa Puffs for breakfast!"

At that Presley laughed at loud. "He asked for them this morning."

"Did you give him any?" Rachel looked at Presley with mock disapproval.

"No, she gave me a sticky bun, instead." As they laughed and picked at one another, Presley realized how much she had missed in her life. The cold home she had grown up in and the absence of a mother had taken their toll on her perception of family.

"Come on, let me get you settled where you'll be sleeping – with me." He pretended to lower his voice from Rachel, but she heard the older woman laugh. She knew exactly what was going on.

This was the first time she had seen his room in the light of day and she was fascinated to see how it was decorated. Dark, masculine Spanish furniture dominated the room and the colors were vibrant blues and greens. Desert scenes and paintings of the Texas Hill Country graced the walls and a beautiful sculpture sat on the dresser. "This bronze looks so lifelike, is it a Remington?"

Zane walked up to her, "No, its one of Aron's." Presley ran her hand over the cold metal and prayed for the family. She was dreading going out to Tebow, if the truth be known. Seeing the family trying to cope with the separation and continue living their lives was going to be hard. A movement and rustle behind her caused Presley to turn and her mouth flew open when she found Zane naked, aroused and laying on the bed. He held his hand out, "I need you." It was as simple as that. Presley disrobed in great haste and joined him.

He couldn't see her, so she told him what she was doing. Presley longed for him to be as happy and fulfilled with her as he could possibly be. "Seeing you, all naked and hard makes me wet, Baby." Presley had never spoke this way before, but she read enough romance novels to have some idea what men liked to hear.

"Come up here, little girl. I'll lick those titties and suck those sweet nipples for you." With satisfaction, she saw his cock swell a little bigger, the head bobbing as it pulsated with lust.

"There's just so much of you to look at – and love – and kiss." She leaned over and kissed the top of his foot, nibbling her way up to nip the tops of his toes.

"Shit!"

"Did that hurt," she asked coquettishly.

"Made me harder, why are you dilly-dallying? Am I going to have to come down there and get you?" Zane was having a ball. Presley was so much fun to play with. Light kisses began to trail their way up his leg and Zane had to grab onto the pillow to keep from cutting her play-time short.

"Just give me a minute, I'm fulfilling a fantasy."

Holy hell. She was nuzzling his cock, licking his balls, massaging his thighs – just giving to him as unselfishly as she knew how. His whole body jerked with a jolt of pleasure as her little tongue began to lap at the head, paying special attention to the sensitive glans underneath. Zane felt that same rush of satisfaction he always felt any time she touched him. "I need you up here," he cajoled. "Tonight I want to do the giving."

"Sounds good to me," she gave his cock one more sweet kiss and began moving sensuously up his body, rubbing herself on him like a contented cat. There was no area of his abs or pecs that went unadored. Zane's whole being was aroused almost beyond enduring. Presley straddled him at the waist, leaned down and began kissing him tenderly. "Do you know how sexy you are? Do you have any idea?" she purred.

"I feel sexy with you," he admitted. "Now feed me those succulent little nipples." To his delight, he could feel her coming closer, and in a moment warm mounds of tit flesh were dangling in his face. Zane could feel pre-cum dripping from his cock. Gathering her breasts in his hand, he pushed them together and just rubbed his face all over them. God, he loved a woman's breasts.

"Oh, my Lord," Presley sighed, loving the rub of his whiskers on her skin. "Bite me a little," she suggested needing all he could give her.

Zane molded and massaged her tits, sucking voraciously. He took one nipple in his mouth and sucked on it, tonguing the tip and nipping it just enough to make her jump. The other nipple was not ignored, he tweaked and pulled on it, milking it with his fingers. Spreading kisses down her cleavage, he went back and forth suckling and licking until he could feel her tremble in his arms. "Move up," he instructed. He needed to taste more of her.

"What?" Presley didn't understand.

"Sit on my face. I want to lap at that tender little pussy."

"I don't know how," she began, but he took over and she gladly let him. Taking her by the waist, he lifted her and she held on to the headboard not wanting to settle herself completely over his mouth and nose.

"Lower, Sugar." He took her by the waist and brought her right where he wanted her.

Presley almost swooned as he tickled her clit, licked her slit, and speared up inside – fucking her with his tongue. That a man would do this for her just overwhelmed her heart with gratitude. Soon, being grateful was the farthest thing from her mind as he sucked at her clit and massaged her nipples with his strong fingers. Without conscious thought she rode Zane's face, lifting and settling in rhythmic erotic undulations. "Yes, oh yeesssss!" she wailed as an avalanche of rapture took her breath away.

Pride and satisfaction fueled Zane's own desire as he lapped at the cream that spurted out when she came. There was no doubt in his mind that he had satisfied his woman. What a huge fuckin' turn-on that was. He kissed all up and down her pussy, bringing her gently back to earth. But his own need soon won out, "I'm turning you around, Doll." He helped her, she was so pliable and willing – his to play with – his to enjoy – his to love. When he had her facing his feet, she showed her appreciation by bending over to kiss his cock again, but that wasn't what he needed right now, he needed to be inside of her – desperately. "Mount me, sweetheart. Sit on my dick."

"Facing this way? Aren't I backwards?"

Bless her heart, she was in many ways still innocent. He was a damned lucky bastard! "This is called reverse cowgirl, but I want to do it my way." She followed his guiding hand and eased herself down on his turgid, swollen cock. "Damn, that's good," he sighed as she enveloped him in her wet warmth. "Now, lay back," she leaned toward his voice. "No, all the way back," he laughed at her trepidations. "You won't break me, it points naturally that way."

"I like this," she sighed as he cupped her breasts in his hands and began to plump them between his fingers. "You can touch me all you want."

"That's right, and I want to touch you all the time." In this position, Kane had total control of her, and he loved it. He kissed her neck, fondled her tits and bucked his hips hard, pounding her pussy with sharp jabs that drug the head of his cock over her sweet spot over and over.

Zane was in heaven. Letting go of one breast, he cupped her mound and began to swirl her clit. Presley arched and writhed, and he held her tight and continued to give her every bit of pleasure she could handle. But whatever she was experiencing was nothing to the bliss that he was feeling. Driving his cock in and out of her depths, he held her tight, scoring her collarbone with his teeth. Over and over – in and out – he possessed her, he marked her, he laid claim to her body, her heart and her soul.

With unerring mastery, Zane brought her to an earth-shattering climax. Crashing waves of ecstasy rolled over her body, her whole being awash in pleasure. If he hadn't held her tight to him as she shook, Presley felt she could have broken the bonds of earth and flown beyond the stars. Every inch of her skin tingled with sensation. "Hold me, hold me, please. Never let me go," she begged.

"I've got you, Baby." As her tight sheathe clamped down on him repeatedly, Zane allowed himself to take his pleasure, erupting in intense spasms, filling her with his life-giving essence. For the first time, he felt himself become one with a woman. There was no separation between them, she accepted what he gave and returned to him in full measure. Zane felt complete.

For long minutes, she lay on top of him, her body dewed with passion's dampness. He rubbed his palms over her skin, letting the vision of her beauty permeate his soul. Presley. His Presley. Since going to the mall together and hearing her exclaim over the tiny clothes, he couldn't get the idea of giving her a child out of his mind. What had she said? 'When someone loved her enough to give her a baby', had been her immediate, sincere response. Well, here he was, and he couldn't think of a better man for the job than Zane Saucier. Willow had given him hope that a radical new treatment existed that could restore his sight. But even if that didn't pan out - Presley's loving, unassuming, sweet nature had convinced him that he wasn't a lost cause. For the first time in a long time, Zane felt worthy to be loved.

Pressing kisses to her temple, he wrapped both arms across her chest. "Thank you, that was out of this world."

Wiggling around, Presley managed to turn over on top of him and snuggle down. "It just keeps getting better, doesn't it?"

A confession of love was on the tip of his tongue when voices from the front alerted them to the fact that they had company. Jumping up, Presley redressed in record time and Zane pulled on his pants and shirt with more leisure. "You know, this is getting to be a habit. I hope to high heaven there's nothing else gone wrong."

A male voice called out. "Zane, did you know it's the middle of the afternoon? What are you doing in your room?"

"Who's that?" Presley whispered as she attempted to straighten her hair.

"That's my brother, and he knows exactly what I'm doing. Ass."

Feeling shy, Presley followed Zane into the living room where his twin and Lilibet were waiting. Both seemed pleased as punch to see her and nothing would do Zane but his brother go with him and check out the new foal and a new bull he had acquired recently. Their departure left Presley to play hostess to Lilibet since Rachel had already departed. "Would you like some coffee and cake?" She hoped she didn't offend the sheriff's wife by playing hostess. Presley had heard it was a role that Lilibet had assumed in this house before.

"I'd love some."

Presley sat out the cake and some plates and gave her visitor access to the variety of one-cup coffee flavors she could choose from. Lilibet's friendly demeanor and infectious smile put Presley at ease.

"Are you going to the shower tomorrow night for Libby?"

"Yes, I am. We bought the cutest outfits you've ever seen," she proceeded to share the purchases she and Zane had made for Libby's coming twins.

"Jessie called me this morning and the doctor has pushed her due date out, she's not happy."

"I bet she isn't," Presley commiserated. "She is definitely ready to bring that baby into the world." As they fixed their coffee and cut their cake, the women discussed the McCoy family and how they were sticking together and keeping hope alive that Aron would be found.

"Well, I believe in miracles," Lilibet smiled. "I've had them in my own life. I survived being kidnapped by a mad man. My brother has turned his life around, I have found the man of my dreams and we've been blessed with one little boy and have another one on the way." Some of this was news to Presley, she hadn't heard about Kane's ex-wife trying to cause trouble for him and her role in kidnapping Lilibet. After explaining what she went through and the other woman's tragic death, she summed up with "Dwayne has brought joy into our lives, we wouldn't trade him for anything." Presley had so few memories of her own mother and those weren't good ones. The idea that Kane and Lilibet had welcomed someone else's child into their lives with open arms almost made her want to cry.

"He is a very lucky child to have you."

"Speaking of miracles, aren't you excited that Zane might be able to get his sight back?"

Chapter Eight

"What did you say?"

The blank look on Presley's face prompted Lilibet to repeat herself. "Don't you think it's wonderful that Zane may get his sight back? I'm sure you are almost as thrilled about it as he is."

"I'm speechless," was all she managed to say and it was true.

Luckily, Lilibet began to expound. "His cousin is a doctor, you know. Willow is one of the premier neurological surgeons in the south. She's so sweet and pretty. You'll love her."

Presley was trying to follow the conversation, but her world had just been turned inside out. Why hadn't he told her? Did he not want her to know? Was she not important enough to him that he'd want to share this huge piece of news? "I'm sure I would love Willow."

It was a good thing that Lilibet was so caught up in the conversation or she would have realized that all the blood had drained from Presley's face. She felt weak and faint.

"Willow called a family meeting and we all went. Kane and Zane's parents are powerhouses, you know. They intimidate the heck out of me, but they were willing to pay my ransom when I was kidnapped, so I have learned to respect them and maybe someday I'll be able to string a complete sentence together in front of them."

Presley could hear Lilibet speaking but she only comprehended part of it. That didn't deter Kane's wife's enthusiasm. "The family is ecstatic. You'll have to get Zane to explain the procedure to you, but from what I understand, it's almost guaranteed to give him back his sight. It's understandable he was skeptical and wanted to know more, a previous operation failed, I'm sure he told you."

Presley realized there was a lot that Zane hadn't told her. "No, I didn't know."

Her denial went unheard, Lilibet continued, "I don't really understand it all, but Kane donated some T-cells and Willow is growing Zane new corneas. It sounds like science fiction, but it is a procedure that has helped others and if anyone can make this happen for Zane, it's Willow." The lovely young woman clasped her hands together as if in prayer. "Just think, in a few weeks, Zane might be not be blind any longer."

"Excuse me." Presley was mortified, but she had to run to the bathroom. Barely making it there, she sank to the floor as the contents of her stomach came spilling out into the bowl. God, she felt sick. She felt sick and ashamed and devastated and scared absolutely out of her mind.

"Are you okay?" Lilibet hovered behind her.

"Yes," Presley lied. "I must be coming down with something."

"Oh, you poor thing." She wet a washcloth and handed it to her.

"I'll be okay, now." Forcing herself to her feet, she followed Lilibet back to the kitchen and while Lilibet discussed remedies and family news and local happenings, Presley said the right things at the right times and tried to pull herself together.

Zane was going to regain his sight. The very thought of it was like an answer to prayer. She loved Zane. She really, truly, completely worshiped the ground upon which he stood. There was nothing in the world Presley wouldn't do for him. If one of them were called upon to die for the other, she would face death a thousand times to preserve his. But he was regaining his sight! Everything within Presley made her want to get up and run and run and never quit running. Because the sad, horrible truth was – if Zane regained his sight, he would see her. There would be no hiding behind imagination or wishful thinking. Zane would see her as she was, and Presley knew she was not at all what he envisioned her to be. In Zane's mind, in his private daydreams, she was beautiful. But when the harsh light of day shone on her, he would see her exactly as she was – no rose colored glasses or filter of affection would hide the truth.

In a few minutes, Kane and Zane returned and before she was ready, she and the man she loved more than life were alone. It was all she could to act normal. Should she ask him about the operation or wait until he was ready to tell her? Presley held herself tight around the middle, she was literally shaking.

He was happy, there was no doubt about it. And she would have it no other way. Standing near to her, he 'looked' into her face. "Would you do me the honor of going out on the town with me tonight? I have some good news I want to share with you."

Oh, Lord – here it was. "Yes, I would love to." She made damn sure her voice conveyed all the excitement and gratitude and love he deserved.

"Good, go get pretty."

"I wasn't expecting this," Presley could barely contain her surprise. She had followed his directions and dressed a bit casual, but she had figured they were going out to a regular restaurant or perhaps a club. Oh no, when Zane wanted to impress a girl, he didn't hold back. She was amazed and delighted when Sherwood drove them up to The Vineyard at Florence. Presley had heard of the luxury resort and had always wanted to visit, but had never hoped too. They were escorted to a private villa where a five star chef had left them every conceivable delicacy. A fire burned in the fire place and the solid glass wall by their king-size bed looked out on the picturesque vineyard just down from the rolling hills that separated the mansion from the panoramic hill-country view. "This is magnificent." She leaned back into his strong chest and just thanked the Lord she had been blessed with this time to share her life with him – no matter how long or short or what the future held; it had been more than worth it.

"Come on; let's get a glass of wine. I want to talk with you." She helped him with the glasses and to pour the wine. Presley wasn't much of a drinker, so she had no real appreciation for the vintage and bouquet and all the things that Zane shared with her about the wine. It tickled her nose and made her smile and that was good enough for her.

"Thank you for bringing me here, I appreciate it so much."

She was always thankful; never demanding – never presumptuous – Presley was a breath of fresh air in his world. While Kane had been at Whispering Pines and while Presley had been in the house visiting with Lilibet, he had spoken to his cousin and she had confirmed that Kane's cells had responded and she had viable corneal material to use in the transplant. And now, he had to tell the most important person in the world to him that their lives were about to change. For the better. "Let's sit on the rug by the fire. I want to cuddle with you."

She joined him by the hearth. "Help me, darling." She did, and they sat their glasses of wine on the hearth where both could reach them easily. "Now give me your hands." She did, but her hands shook in his. "What's the matter?" he raised her fingers to his lips. "I have good news, nothing for you to tremble over."

"I'm just excited," she lied.

"I want you to know what you have come to mean to me," Zane spoke low as he turned her hand over and kissed the palm. "The day you walked into my office was the best day of my life. Not only have you saved a woman's life, you have become someone upon whom I can rely. I have no doubt you will make partner someday." Yea, and the firm's name would be Saucier, Barclay and Saucier, if he had any say in the matter. But today wasn't the day to propose, that day may very well come soon, but he didn't want anything to overshadow the importance of his asking her to become his wife. He had a plan. There was a method to his madness. "More important than work, though, is how you've stepped into my life and heart and restored my faith in humanity. It has taken five years – and you – but you have given me back my confidence. You have given me back my sexuality. You have given me a reason to get up in the morning that has nothing to do with a job or a case or an obligation."

Presley couldn't hold back the tears if she tried. Zane heard her little gasp and he pulled her close and kissed the dampness from her cheeks. "Don't you dare cry, I owe everything to you and now I want to tell you the most amazing news."

Should she tell him that Lilibet had already told her? No, she decided, he needed to do this. No use spoiling this for him. "Tell me, my love."

She did love him, Zane could feel the love with every fiber of his being. "My cousin is a very good surgeon, and she has convinced me to have surgery on my eyes, again. We tried a transplant once before, but it wasn't successful. It's almost guaranteed to work, and the details just amaze me. It involved harvesting my twin's stem cells and culturing them on an ordinary pair of contact lenses." He went on to explain how the lens would be placed on his own damaged corneas for several days and that, at the end, his sight could possibly be restored. "Isn't that amazing, Presley?"

He pulled her into his lap and she wound herself around him. "It's the best news in the whole world, Zane. I am so, so happy for you." She kissed him all over his face. The tears she was shedding were tears of joy. No matter what happened between them, she could never regret that his vision could be restored.

"Just think," he whispered as he buried his face in her neck. "It won't be long till I get to see your face for the first time."

Every moment was precious. Presley intended to love him within an inch of his life. As he undressed, she stared, memorizing every detail. Massive shoulders shrugged as he took off his shirt. Lord, she loved to see the man without a shirt, his wide chest rippling and that dark band of hair across it that arrowed down below his belt buckle. When he pulled off his pants, she couldn't have looked away if her life depended on it. Long muscled legs, tanned from the sun, strong as tree trunks made her want to go up and wrap one of her legs around his and rub herself against him till she came. Zane was her weakness.

He moved onto the big bed, pulling back the sheets and invited her to join him. "Come to me, Presley. You are the only one I want to celebrate with." She drew nearer, already weak with want. His arm came around her waist and he pulled her on top of him, then rolled them over, bracing his body above hers. Presley caressed his chest, curling her fingers through his chest hair. "Just think, soon I'll be able to see this beautiful body, not just touch it."

Zane pushed his cock into her thigh and Presley felt the soft flesh between her legs begin to melt. She didn't want to think about him seeing her, but she couldn't deny that she wanted him. "Kiss me, Zane. Kiss me so deep and hard that I'll never be able to forget you."

"I won't give you a chance to forget me," His mouth covered hers, slanting against it, Zane's tongue stroking and pushing against her lips, licking the seam till she let him in. Presley wrapped her arms around his shoulders, one leg over his, just like she had envisioned. A wild and desperate hunger rose within her as she kissed him back, pushing her tits up against his chest. He rose up over her, and the way he looked down at her made her wonder if he could already see. "If the operation works, our first night together, we're going to sleep with the lights on, just so I can look my fill at you." He cupped the mounds of her breasts. "I can't wait to see the color of your nipples, to see how my hands look when they are full of your tits." Presley trembled at his words, as much from the excitement as from the thought of being vulnerable to his gaze. "I want to see this precious mouth," he lowered himself to kiss her again, and this time she took control, sucking and nipping, pushing her hand down between their bodies to stroke his cock.

"You are like no other man in the whole world, there is none like you. I'm the luckiest woman in the world to be able to touch you like this." A groan of appreciation slipped from his lips, as he was drawn to her breasts, nuzzling and licking at her nipples. Presley watched him, fascinated by the way he worked the sensitive tip. When he opened his mouth wide and sucked hard, she felt herself grow wet and achy. "Take me, Zane. Take me hard and fast and deep."

Her need just multiplied his. Rolling her to her side, he spooned her, enveloping her body in his, one arm under her, her legs resting on top of one of his. "You like this don't you, baby. You like me to dominate you, take control."

"God, yes," she couldn't deny him anything. He nipped her neck, licking a hot patch to the sensitive place behind her ear.

"Let me in," he spread her legs, bringing the top one to rest up on his, opening her wide, splaying her so he could reach between her legs from the back, testing her readiness. Taking his cock in his hand, he drug it in the honey, pressing right at the place he wanted to be the most. "How much do you want me, Presley? Beg me for it."

Oh, she could beg, but there would be repercussions. Pushing her ass back into him, she wound an arm around his neck and thrust her tits out. "Do you ache for me, Zane? Does your cock want to push inside of me? Do you want me to squeeze you, milk you?" As she pumped her hips back against him, his cock was nestled between her legs, lodged in the valley of her slit, she was riding the ridge of his cock, slowly – driving them both into a frenzy.

"You're playing with fire, Sunshine," he growled in her ear as he pushed hard into her with one mighty thrust. She arched her back and he held her steady by cupping her breasts, holding on to them as he pumped. "Feel us together, close your eyes and know who you belong to. It's me who's stretching you, filling you." Presley tightened around him. "That's right baby, hold me tight, milk me," he crooned.

"Don't stop, please," she finally begged as he had asked her to. She loved how he felt inside of her, thick and hard, blistering and burning her from the inside out.

"I can't stop, Witch," he pulled her head back so he could kiss her. "You love it as much as I do, don't you?"

"More," she conceded, wishing she could hold him to her forever, wishing she could be just what he wanted, just what he needed. With every bit of control she had, she tightened around him, holding on to the tip end as he pulled out and pushed back inside of her in the erotic dance of love. "Love me, Zane," she demanded, wishing with all her heart that she could be as beautiful as he thought she was.

"I do, I do," he pulled out just long enough to push her to her stomach.

She went to all fours, knowing exactly what he wanted. Zane's hands were constantly touching, soothing and rubbing her body. She knew it was his way of 'seeing' her. "You love me?" she sought clarification.

"Damn right," he pressed into her again, wrapping her hair around his fist and pulling on it, exerting a measure of control as he thrust and pumped in and out of her. Zane was lost in Presley, completely lost, "I love making love with you."

Ah, a clarification – no matter. It was true, no matter the emotions involved, she was his to do with as he pleased, there was no way she could deny him anything. Pleasure pulsed through her body with his every stroke, his every caress. He buried himself as deep in her body as she held him in her heart. The flames of orgasm flashed over her and she shattered, clawing at the sheet trying to hold on, biting her lip in an effort to keep from screaming out her feelings. She felt like a rag-doll, helpless as his arms tightened around her. And then it was over – Zane shouted her name as his cum jetted into her, their essences mingling even as she could feel a disturbing premonition that their lives would soon separate.

Afterwards she lay in his arms, just watching the shadows dance across the wall as the curtain moved in the slight breeze from the window Zane had cracked open. He loved fresh air and was always opening doors and windows. She knew that his blindness made him slightly claustrophobic. She smiled. There was no way she could resent the opportunity that he had to regain his sight. It was an amazing turn of events.

Several sounds vied for Presley's attention as she lay in Zane's arms. A night bird called out for its mate, she didn't know what kind it was, but it sounded peaceful. In the living room, the chime of the grandfather clock announced that it was four in the morning and all was well. But the sound that gave her the most comfort was the strong, solid beat of his heart beneath her cheek. She was trying to decide what to do. What would be best for them both? Should she walk away now? Should she stay and let him be the one to tell her to go? Covering her eyes with her hand, she struggled to decide.

"We'll be back to get you in two hours," Zane had walked her to the door of the McCoy home. "I'm going to go back and pack for the trip tomorrow." He kissed her on the cheek. "And thank you for going with me to The Vineyard; I am so grateful I have you to share good news with."

"You are welcome. I had a wonderful time." They had just arrived back at the ranch in time for her to get ready for the shower. She hadn't made any concrete decisions about their situation. Maybe their time at the conference would give her some insight in what she should do. Hurting him was not an option, but putting him in an impossible situation wasn't what she desired either. Last night, after she had finally drifted off to sleep, she had awakened crying with tears streaming down her cheeks. Zane had sat up and held her, asking her what was wrong, but she couldn't tell him. Trembling in a cold sweat, she tried to remind herself that it hadn't happened, it was just a nightmare. She had dreamed that Zane had gone through the operation and she had remained with him, but one day she had overheard him telling one of the McCoy brothers that he could barely stand to look at her face.

Standing on the porch, Presley watched the taillights until they were out of sight. What a bittersweet weekend this had turned out to be. Zane had made love to her twice more and she, greedily had cherished every moment. He was such an unexpected gift. Love, for her, had always been a scarce commodity. For years, she had longed to reconnect with her mother, but that didn't look like it was ever going to happen.

Before Zane, she had been relatively satisfied with her solitary existence. Now that she had tasted paradise in his arms, how would she survive when it was over?

"Aren't you going to come it?"

Presley turned and was surprised to find Libby standing there.

"Hello, Libby. It's so good to see you. Am I late?" She hugged the woman who, unabashedly, hugged her right back.

"No, I ruined their surprise," Libby ushered her into the warmth of the house. Baby decorations were everywhere and the sounds of women whispering and laughing drifted from the kitchen region. "Avery thought I was napping and I caught her and Jessie and Cady as they were blowing up balloons and hanging streamers. Just look at all of this blue."

Presley held out her gift. "Zane and I got this for your boys. We hope you like it."

Libby took the package and glanced up at Presley. Her eyes were brimming with tears. "I know I have to go on, but it's hard. It's so hard." She lowered her voice to barely above a whisper. "The family has been amazing, so I put on a brave face, but I'm dying inside."

There was no use saying she understood, because she didn't. Even her turmoil over Zane's eyesight and what that might mean to their relationship was nothing compared to what Libby was going through. "I'm so sorry," she took Libby in her arms. "Zane checked with Vance and Roscoe today, they are still looking."

"I'm not giving up," Libby said almost ferociously. "Aron will come back to me, I have no doubt about that. And when he does, I'm going to kick his ass for putting me through this."

Presley hadn't meant to, but she couldn't hold back a smile. When Aron did return, he might find more than he bargained for.

Despite the expected sadness, the shower was a success. Libby loved the presents and held everything up so all the girls could ooh and aah over it. Jessie lay on the couch, so near to giving birth that everyone waited on her hand and foot. She had to take Presley up to see the nursery that Noah and Jacob had prepared for her, it was a cowboy theme. "When we move into the new house, I am going to have the nursery just off of our bedroom. This one is a little far away for my taste." She pointed at a suite just across the hall, but Presley understood. As they returned to the first floor, Presley let her mind wander. When she and Zane had their . . . She caught herself mid-thought. Oh, lord. If, she corrected herself, if she and Zane were to ever have a child, she would want to keep it close by, also.

Cady, who was also pregnant made copious notes of all the gifts and who had given them. She looked a little pale to Presley. "Do you feel okay?"

"Yes," Cady assured her, "I feel fine. I'm just tired. The past few weeks have taken a toll on all of us."

"Where are the men?" she asked, glancing at the clock. Zane would be here in a few minutes.

"Scattered," Cady shared. "Noah is still gone. He has followed every lead that the investigators have unearthed," she leaned close and dropped the level of her voice, "he even had to view some bodies, but thank God none of them was Aron. Does Zane know anything we don't?" she looked at Presley with hope.

"He talks to someone every day – Noah, the authorities, the private investigators. Zane won't give up as long as there is a shred of hope." What she said was true; she had all the faith in the world in Zane. And as she sat and watched the McCoy women and their friends rally around Libby, strengthening her with their love and their laughter – Presley knew, she knew that she would stay with Zane as long as she could, until it was time for her to go.

Canyon of the Eagles was located in the high country on beautiful Lake Buchanan. As they drove up the winding road to the entrance of the resort, Presley did see an eagle and before she thought, she exclaimed, "Look!"

Zane, always the tease, glanced out the window – on the wrong side – and said, slowly, "Wow."

"Stop it," she laughed. Presley caught Sherwood's eye in the rearview mirror, he was smiling. "I saw an eagle."

"Soon, I'll be the birdwatcher in the family," he stated matter-of-factly.

"I hope so," she was sincere. As they drove through the gates, she began to tell Zane everything she had learned and describe to him all she was seeing. "Lake Buchanan is beautiful; it's so blue and much bigger than I thought it would be. The resort itself is a nine hundred forty acre nature park. All of the facilities are green; in fact the owner is very involved in alternative energy. That's one reason he is one of the sponsors. Oddly enough, the family's name is McCoy. They are from Montana and moved into the area earlier in the year. Heath McCoy is the owner of the resort and his brother Jaxson owns a massive ranch that surrounds the resort and lake called Highlands."

"More McCoys?" Zane scoffed. "I don't think the world can handle anymore of those arrogant rascals."

"All of the buildings are patterned after Hill-Country homes with big porches. They are made from native stone and batten-board siding," sidling up to him, she added with a giggle – "whatever that is, I've never heard of batten-board siding." Unable to help herself, she curled into his side. "There are no televisions in the guest rooms."

"Oh, no!" Zane exclaimed. "Whatever shall we do for entertainment?!"

At his outburst, Sherwood laughed out loud.

For the moment, life was very, very good.

Honey Ross was the first person that Presley saw and she stiffened. "Hello, Miss Ross."

"Do I know you?"

"I'm with Saucier and Barclay," Presley explained evenly.

"Really," she drawled.

A bark from Rex caused her to turn. "I'm over here," she spoke loud enough for Zane to hear her, "Sweetheart," she added taking just a bit of devilish satisfaction in Honey's furious stare.

"Good thing he's blind – isn't it?"

Well, she guessed she deserved that, so Presley let Honey's remark roll off her back.

Zane joined her. "I want you to come to the registration desk. The owner and his brothers are over there and I want you to tell me what they look like."

"Why?" Presley was mystified.

"Because there's something about their voices that is very familiar," as they walked he went on to explain. "Genes influence the way our vocal folds work, which is what gives a voice its timbre and its tone. In other words, families share similar voices." As they neared the front of the luxurious lobby, Presley could see three big men in cowboy attire looking at something on the desk.

"You know you're the Daredevil, don't you?" She compared him to the Superhero blind lawyer who lost his sight in a radioactive accident while his other senses were increased beyond normal human ability.

"I'll show you my superpowers when we get to the bedroom," he promised. "Now, get a good look at them and tell me what you see."

Trying not to stare, she checked out the men in question. They were big, broad-shouldered with dark hair. The one behind the desk stood with hands on his hips and looked at the other two with a tolerant, bemused expression. "What am I going to do with you two?" he asked. "Jaxson, I don't care what Philip told you, there's no gold in that mine."

Philip crossed his arms over his chest and stared at what had to be his brother. From the side, their faces looked almost identical. "You are an eternal pessimist, Heath. Why don't you loosen up? Jaxson and I came to show you what I found. Do you want to see it?"

"No one said anything about gold, brother. What Philip found was the biggest vein of silver ever discovered in the great state of Texas." He laid a big nugget of silver on the counter.

As the third one entered the conversation, it hit Presley what she was seeing. McCoys. These men looked enough like Jacob, Joseph and Isaac to be their brothers.

"Well?" Zane prompted.

"If they aren't related to our McCoy's, I'll eat Rex's harness," Presley whispered. "The resemblance is uncanny."

Zane turned her around, "I knew it. And the funny thing is, our McCoys don't have any relatives, at least none they know about."

A scuffle at the desk had them turning back to see what was going on. A uniformed man had arrived. "Philip McCoy?"

"I'm Philip."

"What's going on?" Zane asked. Other people were milling about and she was doing her best to look like they were checking out a pamphlet she had found on Vanishing Texas River Tours.

"A policeman of some kind has arrived. He's pulling out a pair of handcuffs."

"Philip McCoy, you are under arrest."

"What the hell?" Heath came around the desk, ready to defend his brother.

"There must be some mistake." Philip protested as the cop proceeded to put him in the cuffs.

"Damn, where's a lawyer when you need one?" Jaxson fumed.

"We have a house full of them, find one!" Heath instructed as he attempted to delay the arresting officer.

Zane didn't even hesitate; he stepped up. "My name is Zane Saucier and I'm a lawyer. What are the charges?"

"Murder, he's under arrest for the murder of Dalton Smith?"

"Who?" Heath asked. "Do you know anyone named Dalton Smith?"

"Don't speak to anyone until we've talked," Zane instructed.

Heath laid a hand on his arm. "Are you a good attorney?"

"He's the best in the state," Presley assured him. "Bar-none."

Murder has a tendency to throw a wet blanket on the best laid plans, but the conference did go on. Zane met with the McCoy's and after checking out his reputation, they were grateful to retain his services. Because of his involvement in the arrest of Philip McCoy, more of the work fell on Presley, but she was up to the task. Checking her watch, she saw that only a half hour remained before Zane's first presentation. Honey Ross had already led the first session and according to several of the attendees, she had done a pretty good job. But to her dismay, the minutes ticked by and there was no Zane to be seen.

A full house had gathered in the conference room and conversation was abuzz. Zane's topic was water management and it had sparked quite a bit of interest. She paced at the side of the room, knowing there was only one solution and it wasn't going to be an easy one. The conference director was headed her way so she took a deep breath and readied herself.

"Where is Mr. Saucier?" the woman's high-pitched voice was strained.

"He has been delayed with a client on an important case. I'll cover for him." Actually, Presley couldn't believe she was doing this. Just months before, she would have rather bungee jumped off the Empire State Building rather than stand before a group of people and speak, especially others more experienced in the law than she could ever think about being. But in the last few days, she had realized what was important in life and a little discomfort didn't amount to a hill of beans. She was doing this to help Zane and that was all that mattered.

As she stepped up to the podium, there was a lot of whispering. Many of the attendants had come specifically because Zane Saucier had been advertised as the key speaker. They deserved to get what they had paid for, but until he arrived, she had no choice. Luckily, she knew the topic backwards and forwards. All of his notes and slides were familiar to her; she had put them together herself. Taking a deep breath, she let her eyes rove the crowd. Some of the faces were familiar, big names in the world of law. And here she stood, a newly-hired first year associate, a veritable babe in the woods. Her clothes were decent, but inexpensive. Her hair was loose and casual, hanging below her waist. Her hands trembled as she brought the microphone closer to her lips. "Good afternoon ladies and gentleman. I bring you greetings on behalf of Zane Saucier. He will be here at any moment, but until he comes, please allow me to introduce the topic of water management. Water is the new gold. Wars of the future will be fought over water. Our western states are on the verge of controversy over water reallocation. Cities like Las Vegas are clamoring to find alternative sources of water. Climate change has escalated a problem that has been growing for a hundred years. As population increases, the idea of water as an inalienable human right comes into sharp focus. We, as members of the justice community will be called upon to help make decisions on who will live and who will die."

Zane stood at the back of the room. He knew he was running late, the meeting with his new client had gone on longer than he had planned. Zane had placed calls to Adam and to his regular PI to get the ball rolling on building a defense for Philip McCoy. From what he had learned so far, it was clear this would be one for the record books. A lost mine, Indian lore, an old feud and a jealous woman were just a few of the factors he had already uncovered. It was clear to him that McCoy was being framed, but now he had to prove it. Even more intriguing to him was the fact that the McCoy family he had just met could be related to his McCoys – and neither band of brothers was even aware of the possibility. All of that was interesting, but nothing he had learned in a long time was as amazing as listening to his Presley woo a roomful of stuffed shirts with her husky little voice and endearing lisp. As she took his thoughts and put her on unique spin on them, she held the entire room in the palm of her hand, because you could have heard a pin drop. He only wished he could see her in action.

"In the last six months, legal action has been taken against a man whose only crime was to dig ponds on his own property. Water management will be a critical factor in politics, in financial communities and civil rights." Presley looked up from her notes and a movement from the far corner of the room caught her eye. "He's here. Thank you for putting up with me, but the man you've come to hear has arrived – Zane Saucier." The crowd clapped, not only for Zane, but for the woman who had so ably filled his shoes.

"Thank you, Miss Love. I'm certainly glad you're on my team." Giving up the limelight was a relief to Presley, but it hadn't been nearly as bad as she had feared. Standing to the side and watching the master at work, she realized why he was a legend in the courtroom. Zane knew how to work a crowd. His voice resonated, his body language was precise and the fact that he was a commanding presence only served to increase the impact of his message.

"Presley Love?"

A somewhat familiar voice broke into her thoughts. Turning, she looked into a face she hadn't seen in three years. "Professor Maddow." She couldn't help but smile. "How are you?"

"No longer a professor, I started my own firm the year after you graduated. How are you?" To keep from disturbing Zane's presentation, they stepped out into the hall.

"I'm well; it's so good to see you. You were my favorite student, you know."

Professor Charles Maddow was one of the bright spots in Presley's law school experience. He had believed in her when very few others gave her any encouragement at all. "Thank you, and you were my favorite teacher." She couldn't believe he was here. During his stint at UT, he had broken more hearts than a rock star. All of the female students had crushed on him. Presley hadn't suffered from the malady; however, she had been too busy with her grandmother.

"So, you're working with Zane Saucier?" As people passed by, Charles got plenty of attention. He looked nothing like Zane; instead, he was good looking in an iconic blonde surfer way.

"Yes," she smiled. "He has given me a marvelous opportunity." He had given her many things, but that was no one's business but theirs. "I'm so glad to see you, how is your wife?" She remembered he had a wife and a small child.

"She's great, and the kids are growing like weeds," he said with a smile on his face as he stepped aside for a woman with three children to pass by.

"I'm so glad."

"Would you join me for a cup of coffee? I think Saucier will be lecturing for a few more minutes."

"Of course," she followed him into the restaurant. The hostess seated them next to the glass wall that showcased a spectacular view of the lake. Presley couldn't wait to tell Zane about the sailboat whose white sails shown like diamonds in the setting sun. Charles ordered for them and soon they were sipping at the coffee. He stared at her, making Presley the slightest bit uncomfortable. "You were such a good teacher, do you miss it?"

"In some ways I do, teaching students like you made the lower salary and long hours worthwhile. It always bothered me that you weren't offered a job right out of law school."

"It bothered me, too," she admitted with a sigh. "But things happen for a reason." Truthfully, she wouldn't trade having met Zane for ten jobs.

"I agree, perhaps our running into one another today is a sign."

"Do you think so?" she didn't understand.

"Presley, I have put together some of the brightest and best minds in the state, and I would love to talk to you seriously about joining Maddow and Lawton if you would consider moving to Dallas."

"I'm flattered, thank you." She didn't know what else to say, the future was so uncertain at this point.

"Here's my card. You call me night or day and I'll get you moved – all expenses paid. Are you married?"

A deep growling sound behind her caused her to glance back. It was Zane clearing his throat – sort of. "No, she's not married – yet."

"Zane, I'm so glad you're here. Charles this is Zane Saucier, my boss. Zane, this is Charles Maddow, he was one of my law professors at UT."

"I graduated UT and I don't remember you."

"You probably graduated right before I came."

Why was Zane scowling so? "Charles was a wonderful teacher, but he has his own firm in Dallas now."

"Yea, I just offered Presley a job."

Zane moved in behind her and placed his hands on her shoulders. Charles looked from him to her and back again.

"Presley has a job," Zane ground out. "Are you ready to go up to **our** room, Baby?"

Charles raised his eyebrows and Presley suppressed a smile. Zane was jealous! He was also about as subtle as an earthquake. "Yes, I'm ready." Holding out her hand, she said goodbye to Charles. "I'm so glad to have seen you. Perhaps we'll see one another again before the conference is over. And thanks for the job offer, I am honored that you would consider me."

"The offer is still open; let me know if you change your mind." The last two or three words were said as Zane propelled her out of the restaurant and toward their suite. "Are we in a hurry?"

"Rex is hungry." They moved outdoors and around by the pool.

"Do we know where we're going?" She trusted both man and dog, but it didn't look like they were headed toward the cabins.

"Yes, I got directions and Rex and I checked in earlier. I cancelled that extra room. Now, we're in the honeymoon suite close to the water." Zane knew he was being surly, but he was so jealous he couldn't see straight.

All right, she was a woman. And women were supposed to be able to calm the savage beast. "I want you, Zane."

"You have me." With minimum effort, he opened the door. "We need to talk – soon, but first things first." Releasing the dog into the room, he shut the door and immediately pinned her to the wall. "You won't be accepting any other offers, but mine." Without waiting for permission, he took both of her wrists and held them over her head.

"Zane," she whimpered, repeating herself, "I want you."

For an answer, he nipped her upper lip, then soothed the spot with his tongue. "Open for me," he directed, his heavy thighs pushing between her own. With forearms resting on either side of her head, he held his body away from hers just enough to allow her to breathe. Presley was painfully aroused, her nipples and clit swollen and aching for his touch. She could feel his long, thick cock pressing against her pelvis and all she wanted was to wrap her legs around him and beg him to take her.

Zane's lips rubbed against her cheek, a hot velvet caress. She turned her head and joined her lips to his. God, she was so hungry for him!

When he heard her breath hitch in her throat, he knew she was as turned on as he was. "You're gonna spread those pretty thighs for me, aren't you, Baby? Are you gonna give me what I want?"

"Yes," she whimpered. He ran one big hand between her legs and curled his fingers around the crotch of the tiny lace panties she wore and tore them like tissue paper. "Oh, God," she sighed.

Zane could feel her juices begin to flow and he rubbed her slit, massaging it, teasing her clit.

"Take your cock out."

Zane couldn't see her, but he knew exactly how she looked. Presley was flushed, her eyes were glazed with passion and her lips were trembling with pure desire. Granting her request, he unzipped his pants and pulled his dick out and she stood on tiptoe to give him better access.

"Touch me."

Zane chuckled, his baby knew what she wanted and wasn't afraid to ask for it. With cock in hand, he drug the wide mushroom head through the cream in her slit causing her to gasp and groan. When he pushed it over the little speed-bump of her clit, she jerked and pushed toward him.

"Please."

"Your pussy's as hot as a firecracker, Angel. How much do you want me?" he asked as he repeated the intimate caress.

"Bad," was all she could mutter.

"Do you want me to slide in slow? Could I make you scream?"

Pulling one wrist from his grasp, she wrapped her arm around her neck and one leg around his knee. "I'm desperate, please. Fuck me!" she wailed.

Not wanting to disappoint his lady, he fit himself to her small entrance and rocked his hips forward, impaling her. "Mercy!" She was so tight, tunneling into her heat was the closest thing to heaven he'd ever know.

"Oh, Zane," she laid her head on his shoulder. They were both still dressed and she thought it was sexy as hell. As always, the pleasure was too much. Presley's senses were swamped with his scent, his sexiness, his extreme maleness. With sure, deep thrusts he took her. She could feel her sheathe contract and ripple, accepting him.

"Look down, tell me how we look joined." Zane was hungry for more of her, he didn't want to miss a thing.

Presley gazed down to see them together. "It's beautiful, we're beautiful." He didn't stop, but continued to pull out and push in. "You are so thick, and I'm stretched open and when you pull out, your cock is shiny wet. I love how it sounds." When she added that dimension, he pumped harder and focused on the slap of their bodies together, the suction of their union. "More! Harder! It's just too good!"

She didn't have to beg, but he loved to hear it. His hunger was overpowering, yet he relished every stroke, every moment inside her tender wet heat. She arched her back and he felt her tits – the tip ends hard. Bending his head, he covered the whole areola with his mouth, sucking at her through the thin layers of material.

"I'm fixing to cum." She could feel herself losing it, her pussy began to spasm, closing around the hard length of his erection. God, she could feel it all. When he was connected to her in this erotic dance, she felt whole. He was the missing piece of her world.

Zane pounded inside of her, so hard they were jarring the damn door. Good thing there was no one on the other side. "Do . . .You . . .Love . . .Me?" He bit the words out, almost tortured as if her response was the key to everything.

Sometimes there is no room for anything but truth, so as her climax raged out of control, she clung to him and gave him all she had – her love. "Yes, God yes. I love you, Zane." A rough, low groan erupted from his chest as tremors began to shake his body. Presley just held him tighter as his semen shot up inside of her body. "I love you, always and forever." She cupped his head and kissed him, hoping for the impossible.

Zane had slept the sleep of the satiated and happy. Holding Presley next to him, he wondered what time it was. The alarm hadn't gone off, so he knew it was still early. He rubbed his face against her hair, she was cuddled up next to him like a kitten. Presley loved him. She loved him. What an amazing gift that was. A low buzz from the nightstand alerted him that he had a call.

Reaching for the phone, he pressed the button and whispered. "Saucier."

"Zane, it's Willow. I have made arrangements with the hospital there in Austin to perform the procedure as soon as your conference is over. Does that suit you?"

His cousin's tone was professional, but he could hear the underlying excitement. "Willow, this is a miracle. How can I ever thank you?"

"By being happy," she told him. "I've worried about you for so long. Brace yourself, the whole family's coming."

"Teresa, too?"

"I think so."

"Well, I'm not going to complain. I'm too blessed to complain." He kissed Presley on the cheek.

"Will Presley be there?"

"She's in my arms right now, of course she'll be there."

"Good. I'll talk to you between now and then. Okay?"

"Anything I need to do to get ready?" He didn't know if there was a drug he needed to take or something.

"Don't eat twelve hours before the operation, that's all."

"Have you talked to your neighbor again?"

"Yes."

"And?"

"I gotta go, Zane. I'll see you in a few days, and hopefully you'll see me too," she rang off with a giggle before he could question her further.

"The operation's been scheduled?" Presley shifted in his arms.

"Yea, I don't know what to think." He was very still as she caressed his face.

"I think you should be thrilled."

"I'm scared," he confessed.

Presley turned in his arms to face him. "Don't be. This is an answer to prayer, a miracle you weren't expecting." Her words were brave, because she was scared, too.

"Will you be there with me?"

She hesitated, but only for a moment. "Of course, I'll be with you, if you want me."

"Oh, I wan you," he stroked the smooth skin of her shoulder. "You told me you loved me last night. Did you mean it?"

"Yes," there was no denying something so important. "You mean more to me than anyone ever has. I am the luckiest woman in the world to have had these days with you."

Zane had to bite his tongue. He was ready to propose. Marriage to Presley was what he wanted more than anything, he couldn't envision spending the rest of his life any other way than with her, but he needed to wait. "No, Baby, I'm the lucky one. You'll never know how lonely my existence was until you walked into my life. You're my miracle."

Waiting to propose was imperative. Zane understood that Presley felt insecure because of the imperfection of her lip. So, if he proposed before he could see – she would always wonder if her appearance would have made a difference in his decision. If the possibility of recovering his vision weren't on the table, he'd be on his knees in a heartbeat. But is he was going to be able to see soon, he wanted to look in her eyes when he said the words and make sure she knew that he loved her – just the way she was. Presley was beautiful, of that fact there was no doubt in his heart.

Chapter Nine

"Here's your coffee, sexy man." Presley held the warm cup by the rim and bottom so he could clasp the handle. Looking as good as Zane did should be against the law, her eyes devoured him. His perfectly toned, tanned body contrasted with the white sheets.

"Thank you, my love." He had been deep in thought, but looked up toward her face and smiled.

"What are you thinking about?" She sat down beside him, enjoying a moment of quiet time.

Zane ran his hand down the wealth of her hair. The texture was so silky, he smiled remembering that she had described the color as dirt. Soon he would know the true hue and he couldn't wait to see it. A ripple of fear crept up his spine. When all of this started, he had warned himself not to get too worked up about this procedure. What if it failed? Oh, he knew his cousin was a magician with a scalpel and her attitude about this was that it was a done deal. But what if it wasn't? He would be crushed. And Presley would be disappointed, too. He knew that. "I'm just enjoying being with you." And that was true. "We've got a lot to do today."

"Tell me." She knew they had the last two presentations to get through at the conference, one was on fracking and the other was on imminent domain. Both he could do in his sleep.

"I'm waiting on a phone call from Marcus, I called him yesterday and asked him to do a work-up on the McCoy's. I thought it would be smart to know more about them before we jumped completely on their band wagon." It wasn't that he didn't believe a guilty man deserved a defense, but there was more at stake here than a single case. A man was dead and another man was accused of his death. Right should prevail. And if an innocent man had been falsely accused of this murder, there was even more injustice to be conquered.

"I can understand your concern. They seem like upstanding citizens, but we really don't know anything about them."

"To complicate matters, at least for me, these men and their sisters might be tied to Aron and his brothers by more than a common surname. The McCoy's are family to me, and if Heath and

Philip and the others are part of that family, I think we all ought to know."

Absently, Presley rubbed his knee. She was deep in thought. "Do you need me to stay here with Adam and help with this case, or is someone else coming with him?" From what she could tell by the plans he had been making in the last few days, Zane was including her more and more under Adam's team. Although she would rather have worked strictly with Zane, she was savvy enough to understand that her growth as an attorney would be better under the tutelage of someone whose bed she was not sharing. Zane was looking after her, she couldn't deny that fact at all.

With care, Zane set his coffee cup on the bedside table. "We both will be involved in this case, I promised Heath McCoy that I would personally oversee it. But I'm selfish, Presley. I need you with me. If I weren't about to go under the knife, I would ask you to stay. But my life is turning upside down and you are my anchor."

"Zane!" She threw herself on top of him and he grunted playfully as he caught her close. "I have been so afraid," she confessed with a hiccupping sob.

"Afraid? Of what?" If there were dragons to be dispensed with, he was ready to do battle. "Are you crying?" He pulled her head up so he could test for tears. Finding tell-tale moisture, he proceeded to kiss it away.

"I'm so ashamed," she whispered.

"What in the hell do you have to be ashamed about? You are the sweetest woman on the face of this earth."

"I've been more worried about what you would think when you saw my face for the first time than I was about the dangers of your operation." She buried her face in his chest. "I'm so sorry."

"Hey, hey, none of that nonsense." He lifted her up in his lap so he could kiss her properly. "I don't need to see your face to know what you look like."

"You don't?" Presley didn't understand.

"No, I see you in my dreams every night."

Presley forgot to breathe. After years of hurtful words bandied about by careless people, Zane was healing her heart. "I only pray that I never, ever disappoint you," she whispered against his warm, hard chest.

"Disappoint? Now you listen to me, Sweet Doll . . ." From the tone of his voice, she was about to get an earful, but the call he was expecting brought his lecture to a halt. "Saucier."

All the time he talked, he held her in his arms. She could hear most of the conversation, so she knew that Marcus had emailed his report. Slipping from his grasp, she got her computer and opened their email. Just like he said, there it was. Before he could tell Marcus thank you and goodbye, she had the document ready to read to him. "I have it."

"Good, read it to me. He said that most of the information was readily available and he also contacted a few folks that used to work for them or knew them back over in Louisiana."

She could tell that Zane was anxious about what the report would reveal. "Okay, here it is." She began to relate facts and observations about the McCoy family. "Heath, Philip, Jaxson and Tennessee McCoy, as well as their sisters, Ryder and Pepper (Penelope) McCoy are children of Christian and Carolyn McCoy. Christian's father was Isaac McCoy who was married to a woman named Phyllis, but according to the records, Phyllis was Isaac's second wife. His first wife was named Sarah."

"Isaac McCoy, seriously?" Zane laughed. He loved it when a mystery began to unfold. "Okay, go ahead."

"Phyllis and Isaac moved to southwest Louisiana after World War II. They began to amass land and formed one of the bigger cattle operations in the south. Isaac also invested heavily in oil and gas refineries. Their son Christian inherited all of this and passed it on to his family, but hurricanes and the BP oil spill took a toll, so the family decided to move their headquarters and their operations to Texas."

"Heath has taken his knowledge of the oil and gas industry and the money he amassed from it and invested heavily in alternative energy. The conference that you are attending is a direct result of his efforts to move our country away from a dependence on foreign oil and find ways to harness more environmental methods of generating energy, such as wind, solar and water. Heath, as eldest, is the rock of the family. Christian is still alive, but he has taken a back-seat and given Heath full rein. They lost their mother in Katrina and they lost their home which sat only blocks off the Gulf. After the storm had devastated both their lives and their surroundings, they were all anxious to go somewhere that didn't have so many hard memories. Heath has pulled it all together. He has made sure each brother has had every opportunity to develop their talents and strengths. Canyon of the Eagles is one of the ways that the family has incorporated making money with preserving the environment."

"Jaxson, the second oldest, is the one that couldn't get away from his love of the land. He, along with his brothers, has bought thousand of acres around Lake Buchanan and formed Highlands Ranch. Only Tennessee has been married and it didn't last very long, so for now, all the siblings live together in a big rambling house at Highlands. One of their friends in Louisiana was quoting Heath when he said it took all four brothers to keep Ryder and Pepper under control. Apparently the females of the family are giving the males a difficult time."

Presley was adding her own comments to the notes, but Zane listened to all without interrupting. She paused to look at him, but he sensed it, and just nodded for her to continue. "Jaxson doesn't just ranch, he also rides rodeo. So he is gone from the ranch more than Heath is. Last year he was one of the top three PBR contenders and expected to be higher than that this year." Not understanding, she asked. "What's PBR?"

"Professional Bull Rider."

"Oh," Presley shivered a bit. "I'm glad you don't do that."

"I used to. And if I get my sight back, I may do it again."

"I don't think so," she said calmly and went back to reading, but she didn't miss his amused chuckle. "Philip, our defendant, is an Indiana Jones type. All of the boys are college educated but the others have business or agriculture degrees. Phillip's major was archaeology. He has traveled all over the world, but specializes in Native American studies. He has been working for The University of Texas doing research into the history of Enchanted Rock and the lost San Saba Mines."

"That's interesting," Zane mused. "The McCoy's mentioned those two things as soon as they heard who the victim was. Find out everything you can on those two topics. Something tells me that we'll find others who are as interested in that lost mine as

Philip. Greed is as great a motivator for murder as jealousy, maybe more so. Is there more?"

"A little," she tilted the screen so she could see it better. All she was wearing was panties and a t-shirt and Zane had worked one hand up under her shirt and his rhythmic stroking of her back was making it hard to concentrate. But she didn't stop him – who needed to concentrate? She'd rather be petted. "Tennessee, the youngest boy, is more of a loner. He owns a company called Wilderness Way that is called upon in various Search and Rescue operations. Tennessee is a professional tracker and has single-handedly rescued dozens of people lost in the mountains, the swamp and even once the Arctic. He is a member of the International Society of Professional Trackers and has a sterling reputation. In fact, all of the McCoys are model citizens and great philanthropists. Marcus says that you should have no qualms about representing Philip McCoy." And then she laughed. "Oh, there is a post script. The girls are a different story. Ryder and Pepper have both been known to cause their brothers to lose their tempers, sleep and give Heath a few premature grey hairs." She put the computer down. "I think we'll like them."

"Yea, me too."

"So, do you think there's any chance they're related to our McCoys?" Presley hadn't heard anything that would answer that question.

"I don't know, I guess it all depends on what Jacob says. Hand me my phone."

She did, and in a few seconds, Zane had him on the line. Presley got up to get dressed, but she didn't go far.

"Jacob, this is Zane. I have a question for you."

"Hey, buddy! How are you?"

"We're good."

"'We're'? Do you have a mouse in your pocket or are you talking about that black hound dog of yours?"

Zane knew his friend was razzing him, trying to get him to admit he was caught – hook, line and sinker. "No mouse, but I do have a beautiful woman by my side, as do you."

Jacob snorted, "About damn time. I'm proud for you Zane. When's the wedding?"

"Just as soon as I can make it happen." He didn't want to take time to explain about the operation, besides it was just a tad too personal. "How's Libby?" Zane didn't ask if there were any news concerning Aron, because he would have been the first to know.

"She's in bed, Zane. This has all been too much for her. The doctor laid down the law. She has to take care of herself and the babies. We're all worried about her leukemia. Remissions can be tricky things, science doesn't really know what triggers them or what brings them to an end.

"Damn, if there is any justice in the world, Aron will come home. Libby has been through enough."

"I agree."

"Is Jessie still pregnant?"

This time Jacob laughed out loud. Zane was so glad he could do that, despite all of the heartache the family had suffered. "Yes, she thinks she'll be pregnant forever."

"I bet you are catching the short end of the stick. Is she grouchy?"

"A bit, but she's also perfect and I wouldn't trade places with anyone else in the world."

For the first time, Zane could relate. "I understand."

"The shark, Patricia Fuller, called me. As bad as I hate to, I guess you need to process the paperwork to make me head of the foundation until Aron comes home.

Until Aron comes home. No one dared say it any different and Zane understood that.

"I'll do it. Now, let me tell you the reason for my call. I need you to tell me about your daddy's parents." Zane had a suspicion, but he needed additional information before he said anything more.

"What are you up to, Zane?"

"Nothing illegal, just answer the question."

Jacob trusted Zane, so he did. "Sebastian McCoy, my daddy, was a man's man. He was a true cowboy, but I guess you know that Tebow belonged to Mama, Daddy came to town and swept Mama off her feet. He had a talent for making money, I swear the man could smell oil a thousand feet under the ground, but he didn't have any land."

"What can you tell me about his parents?" Zane almost knew what he was going to say, but he needed to hear it from Jacob's lips.

"Well, that's an odd situation. Daddy's real parents were Sarah and Isaac McCoy, yes – that's where Badass got his name from. After Daddy was born, Sarah divorced Isaac and married Arlon Cartwright. Arlon raised Daddy, but Daddy kept the name McCoy. I remember them, but not well."

"What would you say if I told you that when Isaac and Sarah split, I think they each took a baby? I'm almost certain that Sebastian had a brother whose name was Christian."

"How in the hell did you find that out?"

Zane laughed, talk about a dropping a bomb, he was just about to do it. "If I'm not mistaken, I think I've run into your first cousins. Christian had four boys and two girls, and you couldn't deny these boys. They look enough like your clan to be your siblings."

"Why didn't I know Daddy had a brother?"

"I don't know. I'm about to find out if they know anymore than you did. Perhaps Christian never mentioned Sebastian, either. What if Sarah and Isaac never told their new spouses or their sons that they had split up a pair of brothers? Hell, when we check their birth dates – they may be twins. Twins run in your family. It's sad, I guess. Christian is still alive. You might want to meet him. And as for this McCoy clan, it's as wild as you boys are."

"How did you run into them?"

"Heath, the oldest, owns the resort we're staying at. I heard the name, then realized how much their speaking voices made me think of you. Presley verified that the family resemblance was uncanny. But the reason I've been able to find out so much about them is because they have retained my services. I'm defending Philip McCoy for murder."

"Murder?" Jacob was stunned. "Is he guilty?"

"That's the million dollar question, isn't it?"

"Well, I don't have to tell you to keep me informed."

"Will do, friend, will do."

Presley followed Zane into the conference room. He had just finished the last presentation at the conference and now they were meeting with their newest clients. It was hard for her to keep her mind on business; she was on pins and needles about Zane's pending operation. And to complicate matters, she had just gotten the strangest phone call – from her mother. It had been years and years since she had heard from her. Kelly Love wanted to see Presley and Presley didn't know what to think. She was completely shook up.

"It wasn't a problem getting you off on bail, Philip. But now the real work begins. I've got my partner, Adam, driving up here tomorrow and he'll handle some of the leg work of the case. I am not turning loose of it, but I have a medical procedure to get through when I get home."

She watched Heath McCoy pace up and down in front of the window. The man had to be six foot four. He was intimidating and clearly unhappy that his family was going through this mess. "Philip didn't kill anyone. What I want to know is how your fingerprints got on that gun they found by the body and what does Holly McBride have to do with the San Saba Mine?"

"I don't know," Philip was being honest, he sat with his hands folded on the table. "I've never dated Holly; I've only run into her a few times in town. This man, Dalton Smith, who I supposedly killed; he's Holly's boyfriend and I had no quarrel with the man."

"What about this lost mine?" Zane motioned for Presley to come closer and whispered for her to check and see if there were any enquires at the land office concerning that particular piece of property.

Logging on to her computer, Presley set out to contact the agency that Zane recommended. It was hard to keep her eyes off the people in the room, though. There were two women who hadn't said anything as yet, but they looked worried. She wondered which one was Pepper and which one was Ryder. There was no doubt they were McCoy's, but the girls were definitely feminine. Neither one of the came to their brother's shoulders and Presley felt like a mushroom beside of them, they were absolutely beautiful.

"I stumbled upon a site that could be part of the mine complex on Highland Property, but I have no proof as of yet. It's all theory."

"Yes," Zane said, "I realize that, but I'm sure those with the same knowledge and interest as yours would not be that hard to find."

"You're right about that," Philip agreed. "It's a pretty close and closed community. Even amateur treasure hunters use social media to access information and make contacts. So you think this could be connected?"

"The man had to have some reason to be in that hole in the ground." Heath rubbed the scruff of his beard, thoughtfully.

"As far as I know, Dalton had no interest in Indian lore, lost gold mines or any other kind of treasure." Philip interjected.

"We'll find the connection, don't worry."

"What I'm hearing is that Smith had some high up connections. I'm worried about Philip getting a fair trial. We don't have a lot of pull in these parts." Jaxson swung his chair around and sat in it backwards.

"Actually, you may have more than you thought you had," Zane smiled and Presley knew exactly what he was about to do.

"What do you mean?"

"I'm talking about Aron McCoy and his brothers of Tebow Ranch."

Tennessee looked up, he hadn't said anything so far. "I have friends in Blue Hope, Aron McCoy went missing on his honeymoon."

"Yes, he did." Zane felt for his glass of water and Presley helped him with it. "We're still looking for him, though. It is our hope he'll be found."

"What about these McCoy's?" Philip asked, a glint of hope in his eyes. He had to be nervous, any man would be.

"I've been doing some research on your family and theirs," Zane began and Jaxson jerked his head up as if offended and Heath's steady hand on his shoulder quieted him.

"Go ahead."

"I believe your daddy and their daddy were brothers and if I'm right, you have some of the greatest allies you could possibly ever want in the state. You are McCoy's and McCoy's stick together and they fight side by side. If I was in a battle, there is no one in the world that I'd rather have standing next to me than those men. They are my friends and I have no doubt that when they find out you are family, they will step up to help you and heaven help anybody that tries to harm you."

"Hell, I don't know if the state is big enough for more McCoy's." Jaxson didn't seem to like the idea.

"They were here first, Jax. Let's not play Hatfield to their McCoy, if we're family, I want to know. I need all the help I can get." After Philip voiced his opinion, they all nodded their heads in agreement.

"Good, I'll get to work. We'll have one more meeting before I go, and then my partner will be here to help you. But remember, I'm never more than a phone call or an email away. Make sure Presley has all of your email address and cell phone numbers. And I'll set up a meeting with you and Jacob." Zane stood up and gathered his things.

Heath came over to shake Zane's hand. "If there's anything we can do about Aron, let me know. Tennessee is a world class tracker."

"I know," Zane patted the other man on the shoulder. "We just don't know where to look – that's the problem."

The sun was bright, too bright. It hurt his eyes. Blue water stretched out in front of him as far as the eye could see. He raised up and looked around. He was on a boat. Hell, why couldn't he remember how he got here?

Damn! He put his hand to his head. There was a knot on it as big as a hen's egg.

"Could I get you something, Sir?"

He jerked around to see a white coated waiter, ready to do his bidding.

"No, I don't want anything."

"Good enough, Sir."

"Where am I?"

"We're in the Caribbean, Sir."

Shaking his head, he tried to remember – anything. 'Where' might not be the best question. Perhaps the best question would be "Who the hell am I?"

Presley and Zane were on their way home. Sherwood had made the trip north to fetch them and Rex had been ecstatic to see him. "Sir, I have news."

"What would that be, Sherwood?"

"I have asked Rachel to marry me and she's agreed."

"Marvelous! When's the wedding?" It seems he had asked that question before – oh yeah, with Chloe. His life was changing. Clasping Presley's hand, Zane decided it was changing for the better.

"In two weeks, Sir. At our age, there is no need for long engagements."

"I'm happy for you, Sherwood." Presley offered. A little bit of jealousy welled up in her heart. What would it be like for Zane to propose to her? She had imagined it a hundred times, how it would feel for him to go to one knee in front of her take her hand and make her the happiest woman in the world. Oh well, it might never happen. After all, he told her once that he was not the marrying kind and she had told him that she had no intention of marrying either.

"Thank you, miss. I have other news, also, Sir."

"Your voice tells me that I'm not going to like this news quite as well. What is it?"

"You have company, Sir. Your whole family arrived at Whispering Pines this afternoon."

Zane winced, he had been expecting that. "All of them?"

"Your mother, father and two girl cousins drove up at three this afternoon."

"There goes my romantic plans for the evening, Presley. I was planning on us taking a ride on the horses under the moon. Rachel was preparing us a special picnic basket supper."

"That's okay, Zane. Your family are worried about you." She was as disappointed as he was; she needed this time with him before the operation.

"You owe me and your brother, Sir. Perhaps you could give me an extra week of honeymoon vacation."

"Oh really?" Zane laughed. "What did you and Kane do?"

"I called him and Lilibet and told him you had plans and they came and got everyone and took them to their house."

"Ha!" Zane laughed. "Yes, that is worth an extra week of vacation for both of you and Rachel!"

"Well, I should hope so," Presley elbowed Zane. "It would hardly do to give one a week off and not give the other one the same thing. It does take two to have a honeymoon, you know."

He surprised her by wrapping an arm around her neck and pulling her close so he could whisper in her ear. "Do you want to have honeymoon practice tonight?"

Calm down, Presley, she cautioned herself. Until he said the words 'Will you marry me, Presley?' no proposal had been issued. But she wouldn't turn down the honeymoon practice, that sounded too good to pass up. "Yes, please. Since I've never been on a honeymoon, I need all the practice I can get."

"I have news, myself," she had decided to tell him about her mother.

"What's that?"

"My mother called and she wants to meet me."

Zane squeezed her hand. "Is this good?"

"I don't know. I'm nervous about it, though. I put her off, but I think I may call her and arrange a meeting. I'll regret it if I don't."

"Let's make a deal."

"What's that?" she was open to whatever idea he might have.

"If you'll be with me through the operation, I'll be with you through this thing with your mother."

"We're going to have a mutual support system?"

"I think that's what couples do, Presley."

Wow, he just took her breath away.

When they arrived at Whispering Pines, Zane checked on his animals first while Presley did some necessary girl stuff. What that was, he could only guess, but he gave her some space, knowing he would be the one to benefit. Rex was glad to be home so Zane turned him loose and let him run. The horses were all well; Frank had taken good care of them. Tonight was going to be special in more ways than one. Before he took Presley out on for their moonlight picnic, he was going to saddle Shalimar and ride her around the corral. "We're going to have a good time, girl. Are you going to let me ride you or are you going to pitch me off like a sack of potatoes?" He rubbed her velvety nose. Onyx trumpeted from down at the other end of the aisle and Cheyenne and Comanche's mom answered. "Listen, everybody is jealous of you." He made the rounds and gave everybody some special petting time. "I'll be back in a bit, I have to go check on my best girl."

Rachel met him at the door. "Did Sherwood tell you our news?"

"Yes, he did. Congratulations." He gave her a big hug. "I'm so proud for you. But I have to tell you, I could see this coming a mile away."

"I don't doubt it a bit," she giggled like a school girl.

"Where's my sweetheart?" He asked.

"She's in your room, getting pretty for you." Rachel took him by the arm and they strolled through to the kitchen. "All of the picnic items are in the refrigerator or already packed in the basket on the table."

He kissed her on the cheek and left to go where he wanted to be the most – with Presley. As he neared his room, he could smell her – God, he cock got hard just from the scent of her shampoo. She was probably getting all smooth and silky for him. Hell, he couldn't wait till the picnic to make love with her, he needed her now! Shedding his clothes, he left them in a trail on the floor. When he opened the bathroom door, a cloud of steam slicked across his body. "Baby?"

"I'm here." He had come to her! She had been fantasizing that he would. They had made love the night before and this morning, but she couldn't get enough of him. Who would have known she could become addicted to sex? She was addicted to Zane, that was closer to the truth.

Presley was within reaching distance, all showered soft and warm. His body tightened at the thought. "I have some things to tell you."

"What's that?" He was naked – all hard, hot and hung. "You are so damn beautiful, Zane. I will never get tired of looking at you."

"Hell, now I forgot was I was gonna say." Reaching out, he touched her and discovered she was deliciously nude, just the way he liked her. Sinking to his knees, he ran his hands over her long, perfect legs. She had applied lotion and they were as smooth as silk, rounded and too damned sexy to be believed. "I have enjoyed you so much." Reverently, he kissed the top of her mound. "You have given me such incredible happiness. I was so lost before you came to me, so alone." Gently, he spread her legs. "When I bury my mouth right here," he touched her rich, satiny pussy, "I taste the sweetest cream in the world."

Presley was having a hard time standing upright, she placed one hand on his shoulder and the other on his dark, rougish mane. "You could do that again, if you'd like. I wouldn't protest."

"What would you give me in return?" He was in a bargaining mood. If she would give him a kiss, he would offer her the world on a silver platter – seemed like a fair exchange to him.

"A blow-job?"

Zane choked back a laugh. She was the cutest thing. "You said blow-job," he teased. When she talked a little dirty, he went into lust-shock. "Sit on that bench behind you. She did, then he knelt between her legs. Holding her open, he kissed and licked her slit. "I get so drunk on you. You're my drug of choice." She whimpered her approval, her fingers tangling in his hair.

"Please, Zane! Suck my clit!" Pride and love swelled up in Zane. Presley was vocal, she never made him guess how she felt. She was generous, affectionate and more responsive a lover than any man had the right to expect. Cupping her ass, he held her still and pressed his face more fully into her pussy, tonguing and sucking on her hot button. She raised both legs and placed them on his shoulders and he could feel her lay completely back, her head must have been almost touching the floor. What an erotic picture she must have made.

In abandon, Presley milked her own nipples, she was in total bliss. He clit was so swollen, the folds of her pussy were more sensitive than they had ever been. "I need this, Zane. I need you so much!" Slowly, he licked her – oh, so slowly, savoring every square inch of her wet velvet. She stretched, writhed, begged, pleaded – cried out his name. Zane!"

Lord, he couldn't believe how sweet she was. He'd never get his fill of her – never.

"I love it, Zane. I love you!"

His need for her burned like a wildfire. Zane's cock throbbed in time to his pounding heartbeat. "God, you're so sexy." He wanted more – more. Lifting her bottom, he angled her body so he could tunnel his tongue deep into sweetest spot on earth.

Presley succumbed, she yielded to his will and unraveled beneath his erotic onslaught. "Yes! You are my all in all, Zane!" she screamed.

Through the storm of rapture that assaulted her, she saw him rise. "Don't leave me," she begged. "I need more."

"What do you need?" he voice was harsh, dominating. Zane was tanned and hard, strong and dominant, his erection stood out in front of him, rampant and leaking pre-cum.

"You."

She felt weak; Presley didn't know if she could stand, but she didn't have to, he fitted his hands at her waist and picked her up, turned and moved with assurance to his bed. Zane might regain his sight, but he would had no need to regain his dominion over a woman's pleasure, for he never lost it. "How do you want me?"

"Inside of me, you on top of me, take me!" Presley couldn't wait another moment. "Please." She held her hands up to him, beseechingly.

As Zane covered her, lowering himself, he felt her grasp. Her hands were hungry on his body, she wanted him, her desire was his touchstone. Presley loved him, wanted him, cared for him – just the way he was. If he never regained his sight, she wouldn't change or turn her back on him, she was his and he was the luckiest son of a bitch on earth. "Feel me, Presley."

"God!" she gasped as he penetrated her. The wide head burned her pussy with exquisite pleasure as he stretched her tender opening. "I want you, only you," she whispered as he eased his cock in, little by little. She didn't know if he was more engorged or if she were swollen, but Zane felt bigger than ever before, and she felt softer. "This is how it's supposed to be," she murmured. Presley felt more like a woman than she ever had, and he was her man.

Zane ground his teeth together, fighting to maintain an even rhythm. What he wanted to do was take her so hard and so well that she'd never want another man's hands on her as long as she lived. "Does it feel good, Baby?"

"Oh yes," she cried. "So good."

Picking up her legs, he held them up, an arm around each knee. As he fucked her, he licked hot trails on one calve and then the other, making her shiver and quake with pleasure. Presley arched her back, seeking to force him deeper. "You want more?"

"Please," she panted.

Pushing her legs down so they were bent at the knee, he rose over her, arms by her head, like he was doing push-ups and he began to jack-hammer inside of her. The jabbing, pistoning strokes brought their ecstasy into sharp focus. The rest of the world was swept away, leaving only the two of them. Him and her. Zane and Presley. And there was no doubt – he owned her. Without missing a thrust, he bowed his back and nursed at her breast. His tongue licked, his lips closed around the tender nipple and he sucked until she began to thrash beneath him, her climax imminent.

More than anything, Presley wanted to share with Zane. She wanted to share his days, his life, and his home. But if that never happened, at least she could share this with him. "Cum with me, Zane," she urged.

Lush, delicious heaven. Zane laid his head on her breast and gave in to the irresistible impulse to shaft into her, over and over. He could feel her sweet body clasp him tight, her pussy close around him. Every time he drove into her, she did her best to hold him there. "Squeeze me, Baby. That's it, good girl. You are mine, aren't you?"

"Yours." She moved just enough that he loosened his hold on her. She wasn't trying to get away, Presley just needed to hold him close. She wrapped her legs around his waist and her arms around his neck. Lifting her hips, she sought to get as close to him as possible. Clinging to him, totally at his mercy, she felt her body fall over the edge of the world as her orgasm flooded her body with tingling, sizzling shocks of ecstasy. When Zane came, she gloried in his groans and held him tight as his seed spilled into her. "Don't move yet," she asked as he started to pull out. "I want to hold you a minute."

He rolled them over, careful to keep them joined. "How's that?"

"Perfect. Can I close my eyes, just for a minute? I'm so tired."

"We have all the time in the world." She nestled down in his arms, her head on his chest. It dawned on Zane that sex with Margaret and the women who had come before was just that – sex. He had never made love until he made love to Presley, and he never intended to settle for less ever again.

He let her nap for about an hour, even dropping off to sleep for a little while himself, but his cell phone woke them up. "Saucier," it was Heath McCoy. As he listened to the big man's concerns, Presley wiggled around and got up.

"I'm gonna shower," she kissed him on the forehead. "I'll be back."

He got up and cleaned himself up with a towel in the guest bathroom, then made his way to his office so he could conference call with Adam.

Presley didn't dawdle, she had been thinking about the phone call from her mother and she was feeling guilty about it. What if Kelly really wanted to make up for lost time? She shouldn't have pushed her away. Drying off, she thought about what she would say. God, she was nervous. They were about to go riding so she chose blue jeans and a simple shirt that tucked in. When she left the bedroom, she could still hear Zane in his office, so she took her phone and went to the kitchen.

With shaking hands, she pulled out the dining table chair and sat down. How many times had she fantasized about doing this very thing – talking to her mother? Even though she had cut the other conversation short, Presley had saved the number. It had just been a shock. She hoped her mother would understand and forgive her. Taking a deep breathe, she hit the necessary numbers.

"Hello?" the voice was the one she had heard before. This time it was suspicious sounding, that was her fault.

"Kelly?" she couldn't bring herself to call her 'mother', not yet. "This is Presley."

"Oh, really." There was a hint of sarcasm in her voice. "Did you feel guilty hanging up on your on flesh and blood?"

"I didn't hang up on you, I just told you that I was in a meeting." Actually she had cut the phone call short, but she had been polite. "You have to realize it was a shock hearing from you after all these years." There was only breathing on the other end of the line for about forty seconds. Presley was so unnerved, she was folding and refolding a dish towel over and over.

"I debated calling you at all." Her mother's voice was similar to Mabel's. There was a hard edge to it, a careless tossing of words that made her wonder what she had called about to begin with.

"Why did you call me?"

"I'd like to see you in person; you're my daughter after all. I just want to catch up. Don't you think it's time?"

Presley closed her eyes, afraid to trust. She had been burned too many times. "All right, I'd like to get to know you, too. But I have some important things to do in the next couple of days." Namely, Zane's operation. "How about I call you and we'll set up a meeting? I'll take you out to dinner."

Kelly whispered something that Presley didn't understand. It sounded angry.

"What did you say?"

"Nothing." Her answer was short. "If you can't spare a few minutes for your mother, I wonder what kind of a daughter you are?"

Warning bells were going off right and left in Presley's head. "I want to make time for you and I will, but a friend of mine is having an important medical procedure that I cannot and will not miss."

"Very well, I suppose I don't have a choice."

"Thank you," Presley lingered over the phone call, even after her mother had hung up. Was she being foolish?

Zane's voice calling her name caused a thrill to warm her heart. "I'm in here, darling." Whatever the future held with her mother, she had been blessed far beyond measure.

"Easy girl," Zane placed the saddle on the horse's back. Presley stood back and watched him work. He talked to her the whole time in a low, caressing tone, telling her how good she was and how pretty. Presley couldn't help but smile. It was dark outside and she wondered about that, but for Zane it was dark all the time, so it didn't matter. The corral was lit, somewhat, by a security light but the shadows were deep and she edged closer to be able to see what he was doing. "Presley, where are you?" he asked.

"Right over here, about ten feet behind you."

"We're keeping an eye on her, Zane." Frank spoke from the other side of the fence.

"Maybe I should join Frank and Henry," she didn't want to get in the way. Presley didn't know much about horses, but this animal had been abused and although she trusted Zane, Shalimar didn't look calm at all. The horse kept looking from her to the men at the fence.

"Go stand by the gate and if she dances near you, you can slip out."

She moved slowly, keeping her eyes on him as he placed a hand on the saddle horn and his foot in the stirrup. The snow white of his shirt shone in the light, his back was wide and strong and right now it bore the mark of her fingernails. After their loving, she had kissed the faint red marks and he had laughed, saying that he loved to wear her brand.

Swinging a leg over the saddle, Zane settled in. Shalimar shuffled in place. He rubbed her neck, "Good girl, let's try a slow walk. Shall we?" He touched her with his knee and pulled the reins gently to the left. Presley knew Zane was aware of where he was, where the fence was and where she was. She had complete and utter faith in him. Her faith in others wasn't so strong, and she saw it happening and could do absolutely nothing to stop it.

Zane was easing Shalimar around the corral and she was doing fine, until Henry said something he thought was funny and slapped Frank on the back. It was a harmless move on Henry's part, but the horse was nervous and expecting the worst. When the pop sounded, Shalimar reared and no matter how Zane tried to calm her down, she wouldn't. She pitched and whirled, slamming into the fence. Presley was frozen in place. Zane had ridden rodeo, he was staying on and all would have been well, but Shalimar turned and saw Presley standing there and reared straight up, throwing Zane backwards. His landing on the ground only served to scare Shalimar more, so she danced backwards and almost stepped on him. Presley wanted to scream, but her voice was gone.

Zane tried to talk to Shalimar. "Easy, girl," he began to rise. In horror, she watched as the horse pivoted and came down on Zane's body, knocking him back down. This time he didn't move.

"No!" she screamed and ran to him as hard as she could. He couldn't see how to dodge the blows or where to go to get out of the way. Throwing her body on top of his, she protected Zane, providing a shield between him and the razor sharp hooves.

Pain crashed through her as Shalimar came down hard – once, twice – the pressure on her side was excruciating. Finally, Frank pulled the frightened animal back and off of Presley and shouts for an ambulance could be heard.

"Excuse me, miss," Henry barked, his concern for his boss overriding everything else. He grabbed her by her arm and pulled her to one side, she managed not to scream. Her focus, like Henry's was on Zane.

"Hey be easy with her, I think she's hurt, too," Frank came to her, but she directed him to help Zane.

"He's unconscious!"

Presley had to get to him, she held her side and edged near. "Zane? Can you hear me?" Uncaring about her own self, she knelt next to him and kissed his cheek. "I'm so sorry." His breathing was good and he wasn't damp with sweat. All she could think about was a concussion. How was this going to affect tomorrow's surgery?

Even though it was only minutes, the wait for the ambulance seemed like an eternity. Frank called Kane and he beat the ambulance, screeching up in the front yard. A small crunch and a curse was ignored as more important matters were at hand. Presley was grateful Zane's brother had come, she felt helpless. He knelt beside him, checking his head and face. "I don't see any contusions," he turned to her, "are you all right, Presley?"

"I'm fine, just take care of him."

"Willow's meeting us at the hospital."

About that time the paramedics arrived mid a scream of sirens and Zane roused enough to ask for her. "Presley?"

"I'm here," she touched his arm, but was pushed back as two attendants checked his vitals and loaded him on the stretcher. "Can I ride with him?"

"No mam," but Kane intervened.

"Let her in that ambulance. He wants her there." The paramedics didn't argue with the sheriff.

The drive to the hospital seemed to take forever. Ignoring the looks from the attendants, she went to her knees next to him. "Zane? We'll be at the hospital soon, you'll be okay. Shalimar didn't mean it."

"I know, Baby," he whispered. "I'm not mad at her. I just have a headache."

She kissed him on his cheek and said a prayer. When they pulled up at the emergency room door, she saw Lilibet standing with a group of people. Zane's father was unmistakable; he was just an older image of his sons. Estelle Saucier looked regal, and when she spotted Presley, she whispered to a younger woman standing next to her. But there was no doubt which one was Willow, she took charge, ordering that Zane be taken straight to x-ray.

Presley paced around the emergency room entrance. This was a part of the hospital that was unfamiliar to her. The pediatric until was where she spent her time. She was scheduled for another volunteer session next week. Before learning about Zane's operation, she had been about to invite him to go with her. Offering up a little prayer, she asked God to give them both more chances to help others.

Lilibet came to Presley and put her arm around her. She managed not to wince. As soon as Zane was seen about, she'd go to the pharmacy and get something to wrap her ribs tight.

"Should you have come, Lilibet? Do you need to sit down?" Kane's wife looked tired. Everyone handled being pregnant differently. She wondered what kind of mother she would be? With that thought came a shiver of self-doubt about meeting Kelly. What if her mother didn't like her?

"I'm stronger than I look," she assured Presley. Robert Lee held Dwayne and as Zane was taken in, the entire family followed. "Do you see that woman with Kane's mother?"

"Yes, is that Teresa?" she remembered what Zane had said. Teresa was Willow's sister.

"Yea, that's Teresa - watch out for her, she gives me the willies." Lilibet's speaking out of the side of her mouth made Presley smile despite her worry.

"Okay, I will," she whispered back. They all went to a waiting room very near x-ray. Presley was going to sit by Lilibet, but another woman with a child took the seat, forcing Presley down near Zane's mother and her niece. Swallowing a lump in her throat, she sat down slowly in the chair. It would be rude not to speak. "Hello, I'm Presley."

"We know who you are," Estelle spoke, not hostilely, but very, very cool. "I am Zane's mother, Estelle Saucier and this is his cousin, Teresa Upshaw."

"It's nice to meet you both." Thank goodness, she was saved from further conversation by Willow reemerging from the examining room. All eyes turned to her.

"Well, I have good news."

Presley realized she was so tensed up that her muscles were aching, not to mention her ribs.

"Zane doesn't have a concussion. I think I'll keep him overnight to watch him and just be sure, and if all is well, we'll go ahead with the operation as planned in the morning."

Estelle and Teresa rose, "Can we see him now?"

"In a moment," she held her hand out, "but he wants to see Presley first."

A hiss of disapproval came from his mother. "Really!"

She didn't wait around to see what else was said. Moving as fast as she could, she went to the room where Zane was lying in a hospital bed. It looked barely big enough to hold his large frame. Kane stood to one side, keeping an eye on his brother. "He's awake. Zane, your girl's here."

"Presley!" he held out his arms and she went into them.

"I'm so glad to see you. I'm so, so sorry that happened to you."

"I'm fine," he kissed all over her face, hunting her lips. She helped zero him it. But he squeezed her body and she whimpered. "What's wrong?" he immediately asked.

"Nothing," she lied, but she moved away a bit so he couldn't hear her hard breathing.

"I think she's hurt." Zane didn't just try to raise up, he sat up all the way.

"Stop, you need to lie still." She didn't want him to have a set-back because of her.

"What's wrong with her? Willow!" his voice rose and Kane came over before he climbed from the bed.

"It's just my ribs, I think they're bruised." She returned to his bedside.

"What the hell? Call Willow!" Zane demanded. "How did you get hurt?"

Kane didn't let her answer. He did. "After Shalimar knocked you down, the horse went a little crazy. She turned on you."

"It wasn't Shalimar's fault," Zane defended his horse. Then it dawned on him – "What are you saying?"

"I'm fine," Presley reiterated, trying to stop the conversation in its tracks.

"When you went down, Presley covered you with her body till somebody could get control of the horse. Shalimar pounded Presley's back and ribs. I bet she's black and blue, but she hasn't had anyone look at her yet, have you?"

"Presley!" Zane gave her a one word warning, full of emotion.

Willow came in to see what the ruckus was about. "You bellowed? I was just down the hall, everyone can hear you!"

"Check Presley, the horse pawed her."

"You should have said something," Willow spoke quietly to her. "Kane, could you excuse us?" Kane tipped his hat and stepped out of the room.

Willow raised Presley's shirt. "Ouch!"

"What?" Zane asked.

"That was me, not Presley." Willow said as she ran a gentle hand over Presley's side. "How much pain are you in on a scale of one to ten, ten being the most pain."

Whispering in Willow's ear, Presley answered, "seven."

"Seven!" Zane did bellow this time.

"He can hear like an elephant," Presley told Willow conspiratorially.

"It's those big ears he has," His cousin laughed.

"My ears may be big, but they are proportional to my other large body parts," he grumbled.

"Ewwwwww," Willow reacted the way Zane expected. She was glad he was talking, it kept him from hearing Presley's almost silent groans. "We need to get you in the ER, you may have cracked some ribs and I need to wrap you with a compression bandage and get you a pain pill or two."

"I can't," she mouthed. "I don't have any insurance, yet," her eyes begged Willow not to say anything.

"What did she say?" Zane was listening intently.

"I'm sorry," Willow gave her a half smile of apology before she ratted her out to Zane. "She says she doesn't have any insurance. What kind of two-bit outfit are you running, cousin?"

"Damn!" Zane shut his eyes. "The insurance doesn't kick in for new employees until thirty days has passed." And a pay period hadn't passed for her to have collected a check from her new position, so he knew exactly how little money she probably had. Her one room apartment weighed heavy on his mind. Well, it would be but a day or two that he'd propose and she'd belong to him. Hell, she belonged to him, now. What was he thinking? "I'll pay, I'll gladly pay any charges for the ER or whatever she needs. Just help her, Willow."

"Wait!" Presley protested.

"That's all I wanted to hear, come on," she led her out of the door before Presley could argue.

When they had gone, Kane came back in. "I'm glad your little lady is getting seen about."

"She should have been taken care of immediately."

"I'm sorry, you're right. I was in here with you. I thought she would have sought out some help for herself."

"You're sticking close to me, aren't you?" Zane lay back against the pillows. He was a tad dizzy; he didn't like feeling this way at all. He wanted Presley.

"I'm sticking to you closer than a brother."

"I do owe you for all of this, Kane. If this operation works, it will be because of you. You are giving me my eyesight."

"I'm just hoping that you'll have a better outlook on the world, after all – you'll be looking at it through my eyes."

Zane knew Kane was joking, but he couldn't shake the fact of how great a miracle this could turn out to be for him. Willow's long-ago promise might finally come true. He might see the world for the first time in over five years, and his brother had made it possible. "If I am blessed enough to see the world again - to watch a sunrise, to see my family and gaze upon the face of the woman I love – it will be more than I ever expected or deserved. I'll never be able to repay you."

"Ha! Don't get to grateful. Wait till you see the dent I put in your Mercedes when I came sliding into your yard earlier."

"Hell."

Chapter Ten

"Zane has always been stubborn," Estelle sipped coffee and crossed one elegant leg over another. "Men have to be shown the error of their ways. They can't always figure it out for themselves."

"I've called Margaret; she's just waiting on word of the final outcome." Teresa flung down a dog-eared copy of a Reader's Digest that had seen better days. A man with an anxious look on his face paced back and forth in the hall, nearby. Estelle and Teresa ignored him. Some people were just below their notice.

Mrs. Saucier seemed to have all the confidence in the world. "Once he sees Margaret and that unfortunate looking upstart side by side, he will realize which one is more suitable as a companion."

"I hope so. Although if this operation fails like the previous one did, she probably won't stay."

"Hmmm, you'd think our money would be more of an incentive."

Robert Lee held Dwayne's hand, he had been standing listening to the women discuss his son's future like they were pulling the strings. "I think both of you need to mind your own business. Both of my boys are exceptional. They might not have followed the path I hoped they would, but I do believe they are better men for the choices they've made." Neither woman responded, so Robert Lee and Dwayne turned to head back to the nursery and look at the newborns. He talked to his grandson, who was too young to understand. "And as for the women they've chosen, we should all be so lucky. Think before you marry, Dwayne." Dwayne nodded solemnly at his granddad.

Willow helped Presley dress. "No cracked ribs, you are lucky. Just some bruising. You'll be as good as new in a day or two."

"Yes, I think so." She wanted to get back to Zane. "What are his chances to see again?"

Stepping back and marking a chart, Willow twisted her mouth to one side as if in deep thought. "His chances are excellent, in my opinion. I promised him a long time ago that I would help him. To keep my word, I've traveled to Spain and Sweden to study new methods of replacing damaged corneas. In the last five years, there have been great strides in the methodology. We've been through this once before, but the transplanted corneas that I used were rejected by Zane's body. There was no rhyme or reason for it, it was just the way it was. But this time it's going to be different. Using Kane's stem cells is as close to using Zane's own as we're going to get."

Presley looked at Willow. She was beautiful. Her career was fulfilling, she was passionate about helping people, but Presley wondered if she was lonely. "I know my gratitude may not mean much, but I thank you for what you're doing for him from the bottom of my heart. How are you able to practice out of this hospital?"

Willow actually blushed. "I have a friend on staff here. He granted me special privileges."

"Oh really," Presley was about to ask about those special privileges, but Willow didn't give her time.

"Let me warn you."

"Warn me?" Presley was confused.

"Teresa and Estelle don't approve of you. Don't be surprised at what they may pull. They're not above attempting to manipulate the situation."

Presley didn't have a clue what Willow was talking about. "Okay, I'll be on my guard." Right now, she wasn't worried about his family, she was worried about Zane. "Can I go to him, now?"

"Sure, just be careful and take those pills when you need them."

Presley nodded her thanks and gathered her things. "I will. And you do be careful when you are operating on Zane. He's the most important person in the world to me."

"I will." They looked at one another with mutual understanding.

With hurried steps, she returned to his room. Visiting hours was long past and she didn't know how long they would let her stay. A nurse was checking his vitals, so Presley put her things on a chair and stood in a corner. Several bouquets of flowers had been placed on a side table, word had gotten around.

A mirror hung on the far wall reflected her image. Presley looked at herself and tried to imagine Zane seeing her for the first time. What would he think? She soothed her long hair and let her gaze flow from her hair to her shoulders, down over her breasts and waist and hips. All in all, she wasn't an unattractive woman. If it wasn't for her misshapen mouth, she would be presentable. Stepping closer to the mirror, she placed a finger over the dividing red line, picturing what she would look like if it were to vanish. Could plastic surgery make her beautiful? Would Zane want her to have her lip reconstructed?

"Presley?" he called when the nurse had exited.

"I'm here."

"Yes, I knew you were. I recognized your footsteps and the baby sweet smell." He held out his hand. "Do you feel better?"

"Yes, I'm fine. Just bruised." In five steps, she was at his side, her hand in his. "How about you?"

"Never better, I could go home if it weren't for the operation, Shalimar just knocked the wind out of me."

He had on one of his own shirts. She smiled. They hadn't been able to get a hospital gown on Zane Saucier. His arms strained the material, as always. "Do you have to get your shirts special made?" she asked absently. To make herself happy, she kneaded his massive biceps. Touching him was a privilege she appreciated.

"Yes, I get them custom made," he admitted. "You like my guns, don't you? I turn you on." With a smug look, he patted the side of the bed. "Sit by me."

His invitation did not go unanswered. "I love how your arms feel wrapped around me. You make me feel safe and worthwhile."

Holding out one arm, he invited her to lie down beside him. "I'll hold you as gently and carefully as I would a newborn."

She settled down by him, and he cradled her close. "Willow wrapped my ribs with a binder bandage, so I'll be fine. Will I get in trouble for being up here with you?"

"You let me worry about that," he needed to hold her and he'd be damned if some nurse was going to deprive him of the only dose of medicine he needed. The nurse did come in and although she eyed them with a disapproving glance, she didn't do anything but turn down the light. "Is she gone?"

"Yea, but she didn't look real happy."

"Tough. This isn't exactly how I hope we'd spend tonight, but at least I can hold you while we sleep."

Presley soothed her hand over his chest. He was so dear to her. "I'm so nervous for you." The idea of him going under the knife just made ice run through her veins.

He rubbed her neck, threading his fingers through her hair. "I'm nervous about the operation, but the possibility of being able to look into your eyes, to see your face, to share a dream with you that we both can see unfold — I can't let that chance pass me by."

"No, you can't."

"Don't worry," he kissed her forehead. "Everything will be fine. As long as you're with me, I can handle anything."

They came after him early the next morning and it was the longest four hours she had ever spent in her life. Presley had been told what would happen. Willow had taken stem cells from Kane's sclerocorneal limbus and cultured them on an organic contact lens made with amniotic membrane. Now, she was planting that amniotic membrane onto the ocular surface of Zane's eyes in the hope of regenerating the damaged corneas and restoring his sight. It would be about six days before the results would be clear, but there could be some indication right away. Since the procedure was still experimental, there were no hard and fast rules, but it was possible that Zane would have some ability to see very soon.

The waiting room was full of Zane's family and others. Lilibet had brought Presley some coffee, but she had morning sickness and wasn't feeling that well herself. Dwayne was running between his Dad and his Grandpa, and Estelle and Teresa were whispering in the corner. She hadn't even tried to keep herself occupied; her heart and soul were in that operating room with Zane. When the waiting room door swung open, Presley's head jerked up hoping it would be Willow with good news. It was her — Presley held her breath.

Zane's cousin walked in, pulled the mask off of her face and smiled. "I have every reason to believe the operation was a success. It will be a couple of days before we take the bandages off, but the preliminary test was good. His pupils reacted to the light."

Presley sagged against the wall in relief. "When can I see him?" Estelle huffed her disapproval, but Presley didn't care.

"He's resting right now. But he asked for you a few minutes ago. I don't want any more than two of you in there at a time, but Presley can stay with him after the family visits. I think he would want her there."

"Good. Thank you, Willow."

Robert Lee and Estelle went in first. Kane and Lilibet, relieved that the worst was over took Dwayne to get a hamburger before their turn came. When everyone had dispersed, it left Teresa and Presley alone in the waiting room.

"Can I get you a soft drink?" Teresa asked. Presley was surprised at the other girl's friendly smile.

"No, I'm fine – thanks."

"I know you're relieved. We all are." She opened her Prada purse and took out some pictures. "This is Zane during happier times." Presley took the photographs and began to look at them. Zane did look happy. She stared hard at his eyes and how they looked focused on the camera. There wasn't a man in the world as handsome as he was. Flipping to the next photo, she caught her breath.

"Who's this?" There was a beautiful, elegant woman hanging on Zane's arm. She was looking at him with adoration.

"Oh, that's Margaret. She was the love of his life. They were together for almost two years. Everyone knew they were going to get married – but his accident derailed their plans." Teresa huddled over the pictures with Presley, like school girls looking at a yearbook. "She's gorgeous, isn't she?"

"Yes," an ache was forming in Presley's heart. If this was the kind of woman Zane had been considering marrying, he was going to be sorely disappointed with her. "Why aren't they still together?"

"It was a misunderstanding. Secretly, I think they are both still in love with one another," Teresa stopped with a gasp and placed her hand over her mouth. "I'm sorry, I forgot you and he . . ." she winced making much over her supposed faux pas.

"It's okay," Presley lied.

"I know, but these aren't things a current girlfriend likes to hear. You just never know, we all thought they were going to get back together after Zane had the first transplant. But it failed and they couldn't handle the strain. Who knows?" she shrugged her shoulders. "Two beautiful people like that deserve each other though, don't they?"

Presley couldn't decide if the other girl was naïve, stupid or just horribly cruel. She smiled politely, returned the photographs and walked off. Maybe she just needed some air. As she went toward the elevator, she passed Kane and Lilibet returning and told them she would be right back. When she got outside the hospital, she almost collapsed against the retaining wall that sheltered the air conditioning units. Why wasn't this getting any easier? Zane loved her. He said he loved her. Still the fact remained that he would soon see her face to face – would he love her then?

"Knock, knock. How are you, you ole' sidewinder?"

Zane turned his head toward the voice. It was a welcome voice, but not the one he wanted to hear above all. He had visited with each family member and now he wanted Presley. Where was she? Only Kane and Lilibet had been truly welcome. And Willow, of course. The others, he preferred in small, small doses. "Noah? Come over here and shake my hand."

"I'm here too, Zane. It's good to see you." Jacob came to one side of the hospital bed and Noah the other.

"How are things? Any news on Aron?"

"No," Jacob answered quickly. "Nothing, unfortunately."

"There will be – soon." Zane was in a very hopeful mood.

"Since I have the two of you together," Noah began, "I want to ask you something that's been bothering me."

"What's that?" Zane asked.

"Pull up a chair, Noah." Jacob grabbed him one and Zane could hear it scraping across the floor. "We came to see about Zane, not to worry him with our problems."

"Your problems are my problems," he assured his friends and clients.

Noah cursed under his breath. "I hate to even say this out loud."

"Then don't." Jacob cut him off. "If you're just gonna spout negativity, I'd rather not hear it."

"It's not that – I'm not saying he's dead. It's just that one of the PI's asked me if we had considered that maybe Aron didn't want to be found. Is that possible? Is it possible he did this on purpose?"

CRASH! Zane heard Jacob's chair hit the wall. "Dammit to hell! No!"

Zane listened to two big men's heavy breathing. They were like two bulls in a china shop. Something was liable to get broken. "Hey, let's calm down. We're all on the same side, here."

"I don't want to think that way, Jacob," Noah ground out the words. "It's just something that I needed to say out loud. I want you to tell me it isn't possible."

"Well, it isn't possible. Aron would never, ever abandon Libby."

"No, he wouldn't," Zane was as sure as Jacob. "He adores Libby and those twin baby boys that are about to be born."

"He loves his home, his family – hell, he wouldn't leave Nathan or you, you idiot." Jacob whopped Noah on the back of the head – Zane heard the blow. He didn't flinch, Noah needed it. "Why are you so damn negative all the time?"

Zane laughed – partly because it was funny and partly because he needed to diffuse the situation. "One of these days, Noah is going to fall in love and when he does – his attitude about everything is going to change."

"Speaking of falling in love, I can remember not too long ago, you wouldn't even date a girl. Now look at you – have you proposed to that little cutie I saw outside pacing a ditch in the front lawn?"

"Not yet – but I will. I called Sherwood and he's bringing me a ring tomorrow."

"Excellent," Jacob picked his chair up off the floor. "One thing I did want to talk to you about was that phone call the other day. What you said came as a total shock. I want you to know that I started digging up old pictures and I went through daddy's files and I found some information that substantiated everything you said."

Zane ran a hand over his bandages, wishing he could see his friends. "I am convinced they are your first cousins. If Presley comes back in, I'll give you their number, although you could look them up online. They're as much news hogs as you troublemakers."

"I don't need their number. I talked to Heath last night." Jacob laughed. "I'll tell you talking to him gave me the funniest feeling, if he had called me out of the blue – I'd have sworn I was talking to Aron."

"That's what drew my attention at Canyon of the Eagles, I walked by and heard a couple of men talking and I felt like I recognized the voices. What did you find in your daddy's files?"

"I found a letter from Isaac to Sarah that he sent her after the divorce. And inside was a picture of Christian. Daddy and Christian were twins, Zane. It's all true – my family is a helluva lot bigger than we ever thought."

For Jacob to say that, meant something. Zane knew Jacob loved family, he valued it above all things. "If you have some to spare, I've got a couple of mine I'd like to trade you."

Even Noah laughed at that, "I guess we'll keep what we got."

"They're all coming over. We're gonna have a pow-wow, a regular family reunion. It seems we're both in crisis – they have Philip's murder trial and we have Aron's disappearance. It's my hope that we can help one another."

"Of that I have no doubt."

"Nathan is just anxious to meet Pepper and Ryder. He said he didn't know McCoy's could be born girls."

"I bet they're hell-raisers."

"I bet they are too."

"Can I come in?" Presley asked from the door.

"You better get in here," Zane held out his hand. "I was just about to send a posse looking for you." His hand was outstretched until she placed hers within it and he pulled her close. "Did you two hear how my baby protected me? She's done that twice, you know. She saved me from getting bonked on the head at work and from a scared rearing horse last night."

"I'd say you have a keeper in Miss Presley," Jacob laughed.

Presley exchanged looks with Noah. She hadn't met him before. He had been staring at her mouth, then looked sheepish when he noticed she was aware of where his eyes had been focused.

"I do plan on keeping her," Zane kissed her loudly on the cheek.

"Well, we best be going." They said their goodbyes, and Presley was about to question Zane when another knock at the door caused them to pause.

"Can we come in?" Adam poked his head around. He wasn't alone. It was a woman. For a split second, Presley expected it to be Renee, but she realized it wasn't — it was someone much, much better.

"Oh my goodness!" Presley couldn't hold back her joy. "It's Laney!"

"Adam!" Zane called out to his friend. "Bring Laney over here so I can kiss her on the cheek."

Laney looked nervous, but Presley was happy to see she was holding Adam's hand tightly. "Hello," she spoke shyly. "I wanted to come thank the both of you."

Adam hovered over her protectively, the sight of them gave Presley a warm, warm feeling.

"Laney, this is Presley. She, more than anyone, is responsible for our finding you."

"So, I heard. Thank you, Presley. I'm forever in your debt." She accepted a hug from Presley and a peck on the cheek from Zane. "How are you," she asked him.

"I'll be right as rain as soon as I get these bandages off my eyes."

"This is wonderful, man — just wonderful." Adam sat beside Zane's bed. "I remember the last time you tried a transplant, it didn't go so well."

"No, it didn't," Zane agreed. "But this time — when Willow checked my reaction, right after the surgery, I saw her face. It wasn't plain, but I saw my cousin." He reached out for Presley, who gave him her hand. "Now, there are other faces I want to see."

Presley looked at Adam and Laney with a hesitant glance, but she only saw happiness and welcome. "It was my pleasure to help you, Laney. We were all so drawn to you, that video you made at the police station touched our hearts." Adam most of all, there was no doubt of that. He had been captivated by Laney from the start. Presley was so thankful their story had a happy ending; now she wanted one for her and Zane.

They visited a bit longer, but before they left, Adam updated Zane on Philip's case. "We've begun questioning people who can substantiate Philip's whereabouts when Dalton was murdered and I'm also putting together a list of other suspects. Come to find out, there were quite a few people interested in that lost mine."

"I bet there are. Has the McBride woman cooperated with you?"

"Yea, Zane – I am beginning to think that Dalton's death was just a way to get Philip McCoy out of the way. I think whatever is in that mine may be the motive for murder."

"Wow," Presley was intrigued. "I'd love to help you when I can. This sounds like a plot from a movie."

"Presley," Laney said her name, softly. "I have something I'd like to give you," she took her purse in her lap and opened it up.

"For me?"

Laney held her hand out and gave Presley a piece of parchment paper. On the paper was a drawing of a white dove flying free away from the open doors of a cage. "I drew it while he kept me imprisoned. Being free was only a dream, but you and Adam saved me. Would you like to have this?"

Reverently, Presley took the sketch. "I'll treasure it, Laney." She was amazed at the intricacy and passion in the lines that gave the bird life. She could almost feel the air rush over her cheeks from the beating of the wings. "Your being here with us today is an answer to prayer."

"Amen," Adam said as he kissed Laney's hand. "When will you get those bandages off?"

"Soon rather than later if it's up to me," was Zane's reply. After a few more minutes of conversation, Adam and Laney took their leave. Presley walked them to the door, then stood there for a moment just taking in the reality that a woman had been rescued from the hands of a monster. And their law firm had been instrumental in making that happen. "It feels good to make a difference in people's lives, doesn't it?"

"Yes it does, but I think you ought to know something."

"What's that?" she turned to look at Zane. It hurt her to see him looking so vulnerable, his eyes swathed in gauze and tape.

"No one has made a greater difference in my life than you. You, Presley Love, have made my life worth living. Come give me a kiss."

He didn't have to ask twice. ·

"This is different, Margaret. He has his vision back."

"Are you sure? You got my hopes up before and he was still as blind as a bat."

"If you want Zane Saucier, you better get your skinny ass over here. He thinks he's in love with a woman named Presley Love and she's here."

"Zane could never want someone as much as he wants me. He used to beg for my touch," she laughed. "I was stingy with my affection. It's good to keep a man hungry, they're easier to control."

"This woman is no match for your looks, in fact she's, uh – unfortunately handicapped, but she seems to have him wrapped around her little finger."

"A blind man will never touch my body, but if Zane Saucier becomes the man he used to be, I want him. I want his muscular body, but what I want more is his name and all of that yummy Saucier money."

"We're at Breckenridge Hospital on the second floor. Hurry."

The time had come. Willow was on her way and soon they'd know what the verdict was. Zane was on edge and Presley had gone down to the lounge to get him coffee. As she walked by the elevator, the doors opened and an amazing looking woman stepped off. She was golden – her hair, her skin, even her eyes were even a beautiful shade of amber. Presley stared, something about the woman was familiar. And then it hit her – this was Margaret, Zane's ex-girlfriend. She almost dropped the hot cup of coffee. Teresa rose from a chair to greet her and everyone else in the room looked uncomfortable. Estelle and Robert Lee had returned, as well as Kane and Lilibet. The family had gathered to lend Zane whatever support they could.

Teresa and Margaret spoke and then the goddess turned and looked straight at her. Presley didn't know what to do, so she leaned on her southern roots and tried to be polite. She smiled, tentatively, and said 'hello'. Instead of returning the greeting, the woman assessed her – looked her up and down and then she smiled, but it was a fake smile, a cold smile. Without saying another word, Teresa and Miss Icicle walked out.

What was she doing here? Had Zane called for her? Dread filled Presley's heart. She didn't need this strain on top of her worry about Zane. Glancing at the family, she noticed they were as uptight as she was. Kane paced. Robert Lee talked on his phone and kept checking his watch and Estelle drummed her fingers on her eReader. She knew they all cared, but they all handled their stress in different ways. Presley's stomach was tied into knots.

Heading on to Zane's room, she walked head down, keeping the cup steady. Surely, Willow hadn't started without her. Minutes passed and she decided to see what was going on. What if something had happened? As she turned the corner, she almost walked right into Margaret. "Excuse me," she sidestepped, but the woman blocked her progress.

"Do you know who I am?"

"Yes, I do, and I'm pleased to meet you. Please let me introduce myself, I'm Presley Love, Zane's girlfriend," she held out her hand.

"Hahahaha," the other woman laughed, ignoring Presley's extended hand. "You are Zane Saucier's girlfriend? That's a joke. Yes, I am Margaret Fenmore, I was practically Zane's fiancé and as soon as he is whole again, I will resume my rightful place. He deserves a woman as beautiful as me. You are an embarrassment to him, he just doesn't know it yet – but he will." Presley just stood there in shock. Glancing around, she hoped no one was listening.

"I guess that will be up to Zane."

"Presley, it's time." Willow motioned from the door of Zane's room.

"Excuse me," she said again, but this time, she escaped. The coffee wasn't so lucky, she sloshed it liberally on the floor and had to stop and clean it up with a napkin to keep someone from slipping.

"Presley!" Zane called and she answered.

"Coming!"

"I love it when she says that."

Presley darted in the room and blushed when she saw he was talking to his brother while teasing about her orgasms. "Be nice," she fussed. God, how normal she sounded when all she wanted to do was get in a corner and scream. So, she did the only thing a good girl did at times like this – she prayed. "Lord, please give Zane his sight. I want that more than anything. Please!" And because she was taught that you have not because you ask not, she added a couple of extra requests. "And please, Lord, let him love me, even when he sees how I look and please send that she-devil Margaret back to whatever hole she crawled out of." Part of her prayer was selfish and probably wouldn't be answered, but at least she was honest.

"Stand by me, Presley."

She stood on one side and Kane on the other while Willow snipped at the bandages. Slowly, she unveiled his eyes and Presley held her breath while Zane blinked.

"Close the blinds," Willow instructed when it became apparent the light was hurting his eyes.

"I'm all right, dammit!" he fussed.

"What can you see?" his cousin pushed for information.

"I see shapes. Everything is still blurry."

Presley bit her lip, stiffened her spine and stepped into his line of vision. "Can you see me?"

Their eyes seemed to meet. Behind her, Kane didn't say a word. Zane stared at her, blinked his eyes and looked again. "Baby, I see your outline, but I can't make out your features very well. I'm sorry. Willow?" He sounded worried.

"It's okay, Zane," the doctor spoke in a soothing tone. "Give yourself a little time. Let me get some dark glasses. You can see, and soon you will see well." He started to rub his eye and Willow stopped him. "No, you'll mess up the stitches. Let me put some eye-drops in. Presley will you run down to the nurse's station and ask for a pair of glasses that they give to patients after cataract surgery."

"Good Lord," Zane fussed. He was getting frustrated.

"Hush, it's just for now."

Presley was shaking as she exited the room. How well could he see? Would he get any better? Teresa was coming down the hall, "How is he?"

"His vision is blurry."

"I'm going in," she made her way to the nurse's station. In order to get there, she had to walk past Margaret.

"Teresa's going to tell him I'm here. What do you suppose is about to happen?" The woman's superior, know-it-all attitude made Presley sick. She retrieved the glasses and started back. When she returned to the door, Margaret was right there. Before she could enter, Kane came out.

"Zane wants to see you."

Presley takes a step forward. "He wants to see Margaret, I'm sorry Presley."

"Here's his glasses," she held them out – helplessly. Her whole body was shaking with nerves. What did this mean?

In a moment, she knew, Teresa came out with a smug look on her face. "You'd might as well leave. He's chosen. I guess his vision wasn't as blurry as he led you to believe."

Presley backed away. She stood there a moment. Her whole world was behind that door. Walking away was the hardest thing she'd ever do, so she didn't walk – she ran.

"What are you doing here, Margaret?"

"I have come to take you back, Zane."

"Kane, leave us, and make sure my Presley is okay."

"Presley? Do you mean that hare-lipped wonder that's been hovering by the door?"

Zane literally growled. "I want you out of here and I never want to see you again as long as I live. You disgust me."

For once in her life, Margaret was speechless – momentarily. Finally, she hissed like a snake. "If I leave this time, I'm never coming back."

"Who in the hell asked you to come back this time?"

Margaret flounced out the door and left.

"Kane! Tell Presley to come in please," His shoulders felt lighter, like a weight had been lifted.

His twin stuck his head in the door. "I can't find her. I'll look around." Zane waited – and waited. After about half an hour, he returned. "She's gone."

"What do you mean?"

"Mother said she saw her running out of the building crying?"

"Crying? Why didn't she go after her?"

Both were silent.

"Nevermind." Zane was miserable, he wanted to get up. "I have got to go find her."

"I don't think so," Kane said. "Willow said if you tear those stitches in your eyes that all this will have been in vain."

"FUCK!" Zane yelled at the top of his lungs. Being blind was preferable to this! "What happened Kane? Why did she leave?"

"Hell, I think it was Teresa and Margaret, there's no telling what they said to her."

"Find out, Kane. I want to know how many minutes until I get up and walk out of here. I swear to God, there's going to be hell to pay. Presley's precious, she's gentle – by God, she's mine and I want her back!"

Presley got a cab. She didn't even know where to tell him to go. "Take me to The Horseman," she finally said. Chloe and Frasier would welcome her.

But when she got there, it was closed, or rather it hadn't opened – it was too early. She could have gone to their apartment, but that didn't seem right. Feeling extremely vulnerable, she dialed Kelly. If she ever needed her mother, it was now.

"Hello?"

"Kelly – uh, mother, it's Presley. Could we meet?"

"What time is it?" she sounded groggy and sleepy. Hopefully she wasn't hung over. Presley hated to think such a thing. She needed to give her mother every consideration. This could be a time of healing and a new beginning for them.

"It's nine-thirty in the morning. Could I come where you are?" Lord, she knew she sounded desperate.

A big sigh. "I guess so. Could you bring me a carton of cigarettes and a six-pack of beer?"

"No, I can't," Presley didn't even blink before answering. Not only did she not have the money, she didn't want to think of her mother using those products.

"Shit." After a few garbled words, she was finally able to make out an address.

"Thanks, I'll be there soon." Considering her options, she decided to take the bus. Twice, Zane called. Twice, she ignored it and then she turned off the phone and dropped it in the bottom of her purse. What a difference a few hours could make. She was now afraid to hear what Zane might say to her. In fact, she was petrified.

As the big, belching bus made its way from downtown Austin to the lower east side, she considered what she was going to do. There was no way she could continue working at Saucier and Barclay. But she'd have to go back, leaving without giving proper notice was unthinkable. They had been too good to her to treat them so abominably. Zane couldn't help because his feelings for her had changed. After all, he had been in the dark, so to speak.

What could she do? She didn't want to go back to Work Force or make pastries again. Zane had given her an unbelievable opportunity, he had legitimized her legal career, and she wasn't going to waste his gracious act. Professor Maddow. She would call Professor Maddow and take him up on his job offer. Perhaps Adam would let her fulfill her two week notice with online work.

With a gust of expelled air, the bus put on its air brakes and came to a halt at the intersection near to Kelly's apartment. Presley stood and made her way down the aisle of the bus. Several people jostled her and she had to steady herself by holding on to the back of the seat. "Why don't you get out of the way, ugly!" The man's harsh words startled her. She looked up to see who he was talking to, wanting to defend them. Then she met his piercing glare and it dawned on Presley that he was talking to her.

As quickly as she could, she climbed off the bus and fled down the street. Trying to see through a haze of tears, Presley had gone half a block in the wrong direction before she came to her senses and turned around. With crossed arms over her breasts, she held herself tight and walked stiffly toward the run-down apartment building. Cautiously, she walked up the stairs. This was the type of building where one could get mugged or raped – in her case, more likely mugged. Hell! Now, she was thinking stupid. Rapists weren't that discriminating. The hallway was damp and dark and she had to strain to see the numbers on the door. Two forty-one, two-forty-two – ah, here is was, two forty-four. Presley pressed the door bell, but it was broken. So, she tapped. Again.

"All right, all right," the door was thrown open and there before her stood – her mother. She was old looking. Time hadn't been kind to Kelly Love. Or maybe it was Kelly who hadn't been kind to herself. "Well, look at you. Come in," she made a broad gesture.

Presley walked in and she was transported back in time to the small trashy trailer where she had spent her childhood. This could have been the same place. The kitchen was littered with dirty dishes and congealed food was stuck to the plates. Dirty clothes were strewn about and cigarette butts filled every possible container. Half empty glasses of liquid sat about like the set of the movie Signs. "Thank you, mother."

"Sit down," Kelly said harshly and Presley looked for a suitable spot. "Don't be so damn picky. Sit down!" Presley jumped, but she sat down.

"I'm glad to see you," she offered a verbal olive branch to her mother.

"Well, I'm glad you got to see me, too." It was a second or two before Presley realized she had been vaguely insulted.

"How have you been?"

"My life has been a series of misfortunate events, beginning with the day I found out I was pregnant with you."

Every word out of her mother's mouth was an insult. "Why did you want to see me, Kelly?"

"I need money."

Well, that was blunt.

"Money?"

"Yea, I heard about you dating that rich blind lawyer. I checked up on you. Presley, I have to hand it you – a blind man, good for you." She laughed. "You found somebody that just suits you."

Never would she have thought it, but Presley got satisfaction from telling her mother the sad truth. "We're not dating anymore, because he's not blind anymore."

"Ha! Of course." She nodded like it made sense to her. "Shucks, just my luck."

"Yea, so I don't have any money."

"None, how about from that fancy job you have?"

"No, I haven't been paid and I'm having to quit, because we're not dating anymore." The facts seemed cold and hard. She felt frozen and lifeless.

"Hell, you have to have some money, somewhere. I figure you owe me."

"I owe you?" she couldn't help but sound skeptical. "For what?"

"You owe me for letting you live. I tried to abort you once, you know."

"What?" The words coming out of her mother's mouth just floored her.

"You weren't wanted. I tried to abort you." She said it like it was the simplest thing in the world. She wasn't wanted. Well, she knew that. What was so wild was that she had thought about it when she was growing up, when things were really, really bad. Presley would wonder what it would have been like to just not have been born. Now, she laughed – out loud.

"What happened? What did you mess up?" Was letting her live, messing up?

"Mother said I messed you up with drugs and alcohol. It was my fault that you are the way you are. So when I was twenty-four weeks pregnant, I went for an ultrasound and I saw you. I saw how you looked and I knew you'd be better off dead. The doctor told me a cleft was a good enough reason for an abortion so they gave me some drugs – the word started with a 'p', I don't remember what it was called. But it started my labor, but it didn't work and they wouldn't try it, again. They said it was a one shot deal, so you were born and I took you to mother's at the first opportunity."

Presley just listened. Now, she knew what her grandmother had been referring to all those years when she would talk about how lucky she was to be alive and how grateful she should be. Six months! Her mother had tried to abort her when she was six months in the womb.

Not thinking, not feeling, not really seeing – Presley got up and walked out.

"Where are you going?" When Kelly saw that she was leaving, she yelled at her, but Presley didn't answer. She just left.

Putting one foot after another, Presley walked until she got to The Horsemen Club. She knocked on the still locked door until Frasier finally came to answer it. With sobs and gasps, she finally got her tale told. How much sense she made, she didn't know. Zane's surgery, Margaret's appearance, the rejection – her mother's abortion attempt – it all got mixed up in her heartbreak and the only thing she knew was that she had no place to be. Presley didn't belong anywhere. She wasn't wanted and she had no home. Oh, she could sit down and reason that she had an apartment – such as it was – she was an adult and could make her own way in the world. She could provide herself with a place to live, to exist, but that wasn't a home. A home was a person to belong to and Presley didn't have that. She might never have a home.

Chloe came and held her, she rocked her. "I want you to quit crying now, girl. There must be some mistake. Zane would not choose Margaret over you. At one time he might have been that stupid, but he's not anymore. Zane Saucier is a smart, kind, sensitive man and he will come after you. You mark my word."

"No, I don't want him to come," she wailed.

"Oh Honey, I understand. You just need some time to think things through. Why don't you stay with us for a couple of days?" Relying on others was not Presley's habit, but Chloe and Frasier comforted her and right now, she needed to feel less alone. Over the next twenty four hours, she slowly began to regroup. Frasier let her use his office and his phone and she placed two difficult phone calls. Even though they hadn't expected her at work, she called in sick at Saucier and Barclay, giving them a verbal two week notice. Adam came on the line and questioned her, but she was evasive. Promising to come in the next day and explain, she hastily cut the conversation short. After that, she called Professor Maddow and set up a meeting. He was surprised, but happy.

She tried, in vain, to keep her mind off Zane. But she wondered and worried over his condition. Taking a risk, she called the hospital to check on him and was told he had checked out. Well, that must mean he was okay. For that, she was grateful. Now, she just needed to stay busy – anything to occupy her attention and keep her mind from dwelling on the tremendous ache in her heart. There was only one thing she could do automatically that gave her some relief from her despair – she could cook. So Frasier turned over a section of the kitchen to her and she began to make pastries – fried fruit pies, loaves of pumpkin bread, cheese-filled Danish – soon the kitchen was filled with aromas and people were placing special orders in the kitchen for the unexpected, yet welcome desserts.

Two days had passed since she had seen Zane – two terrible days and Chloe reported than he had phoned the restaurant looking for her. "He sounds worried. You've got to talk to him."

"It would be best if I didn't. He's just being nice. Zane is a gentleman. Even if we're not together, he's just concerned for my welfare. Did you tell him I'm okay?"

"Yes."

"But you didn't tell him I'm staying with you, did you?" A small hint of panic entered her voice. She took the apron off that had been covering her clothes and straightened the simple sheathe dress she wore underneath. A dusting of flour adorned the dark red material and she brushed it off.

"Sheriff Kane is outside eating your fried pies. I don't think it's a secret anymore," she said dryly.

"Dang!" Presley folded the apron and turned her back to Chloe. "I guess it's time to go home. I appreciate everything you've done for me, Chloe." As she spoke, she put ingredients back on the shelf and organized the big spoons and spatulas in proper order. "The thing I'm most grateful far is your getting me a chance to work for Zane and to meet him. I enjoyed him so much. I'll never forget him, but Zane will be happy. Margaret is as beautiful as he is. They're a perfect match. He'll be better off without me."

"I don't want to live a day without you."

Zane's husky voice, rough with emotion, sounded just over her left shoulder, Presley froze. She didn't move a muscle and she certainly didn't turn around. Her hand automatically went up to cover her mouth.

"Turn around. Look at me, beloved."

"No, I can't. Please don't make me."

"I know what you look like, Presley. Like I told you before, I've seen you in my dreams."

"No, my mouth . . ."

"I've kissed that precious mouth a thousand times. Don't you think I know what it looks like?" She heard him move closer, she could feel the heat from his body on her back. Presley quaked with the need to go to his arms. Her whole body was responding to his, the need to be held was overwhelming.

"Zane . . ." she whispered his name – wanting, needing – yet, so very afraid to take a chance.

"Turn around and look at the man who loves you."

She did. After the first tiny move, it was the easiest thing she had ever done.

"There's my kitten." Zane's heart contracted, seeing the tears in her eyes and the uncertainty on her sweet face. "Do you know who you look like to me?"

"No," she searched his face for how he was feeling. As always – he was perfect, except this time, he was looking back at her. There was total comprehension and total focus in his eyes.

He held out his hand and she placed her palm on top of his. The touch of their skin sent tingles up her arm. "You look like the woman I love."

His declaration set her free and she closed the distance between them with a strangled sob. "Zane, I missed you so. Are you okay? I was so worried. I'm sorry I left, so sorry."

"God, don't ever leave me again. Don't you know it was your face I wanted to see most of all – only your face. Let's go home." He picked her up and walked out of the kitchen, through the restaurant and out into the street. Chloe and Frasier waved and several in the restaurant clapped. It was like the famous scene from an old movie that she had watched over and over, wishing her prince would come and carry her off to his waiting steed.

Her hero wasn't a prince, but he was the sexiest cowboy lawyer in the world. And even though he owned beautiful horses, his steed was a Mercedes with a new dent, she noticed. "Well, hello Miss Presley," Sherwood greeted her. "I'm relieved to see you back where you belong." Presley smiled at the chauffeur over Zane's shoulder. "Where to, Sir?"

"Home, Sherwood and make it speedy." Presley didn't sit in the seat. She lay in his arms and Zane just kept staring at her, touching her face and kissing her lips. So, Presley stared back and they smiled and giggled at one another. It was pure joy. She could see her image reflected in his eyes and she just wanted to drown in them.

"I've gazed into your eyes so often, longing for you to be able to see. I was afraid for you to see me," she bit her lower lip, "but I wanted that for you more than I wanted anything."

"I know, Baby. I could look at you forever and be happy. I love you so much, Presley. Will you marry me?"

"Hallelujah!" Sherwood voice from the front.

They laughed, it was easy to forget they weren't alone. "Are you sure?" she asked. "I only want you to be happy. You don't have to marry me. I'll stay with you for as long as you want."

"Oh yes, you do have to marry me. I want you to be my wife more than I want to see. I, Zane Saucier, want to spend all my days with Presley Love." He sealed his promise with a kiss, weaving his fingers in that beautiful hair of hers and taking that sweet mouth over and over. The first thing he wanted to do was take inventory of his blessings. He was going to inspect Presley – inch by glorious inch – and pay homage with his hands, his lips and his tongue. Other parts of him were clamoring to be included and he promised his cock that it wouldn't be long before it was back where it belonged – deep inside of his beloved's sweet body.

"We're here, Sir."

"Good." Without looking to the left or the right – there'd be time for that later, he carried Presley over the threshold like a bride. This was his first return to Whispering Pines since he regained his vision, but he was more interested in gazing upon the woman of his heart than anything else. Later, they'd share his rediscovery of his home, but not now. Now was reserved for pleasure.

Zane strode through his house, barely seeing all the familiar – yet unfamiliar – details. It was his home, yet he had not surveyed it in years. But he knew where he was going and he knew what he was going to do when he got there. Kicking the bedroom door shut, he sat her down and stood over her, relishing the moment.

Presley couldn't keep her hands off of him. She rubbed his big arms, his shoulders – so glad that she was back where she belonged. "Thank you for coming after me."

"You never answered my question." He put one finger under her chin and tilted her face up to his.

"What question?" Presley brought her palms around to rest on his chest.

"THE Question." He emphasized the words.

"I can feel your heart beating." She hadn't taken her hands off of him, and she might never, if she had anything to say about it.

"It beats for you, Pretty One."

"Oh, my," Presley lost her ability to breathe when the big man went down on one knee. He took her hand in his and kissed her palm. Reaching into his pocket, he took out a ring. "Zane?"

"Presley Love, love of my life, will you do me the honor of becoming my wife?"

He looked at her so expectantly. He was so sweet. "You rhymed," she smiled and he widened his eyes – waiting for an answer, so she gave him one. "You are the dearest thing in the world to me and there is nothing I want more in the world than to be your wife." She watched in awe as he slipped a sparkling diamond on her finger. "Zane, that is the most beautiful ring I've ever seen."

"It's not as nearly as pretty as you are." He stood up and touched her face, feathering his fingers over her brow and high cheekbones. "You may not believe me, but you look exactly as I pictured you. I know you, Presley. You are the very best part of me." He lifted her hair and ran his fingers through it, caressing the strands.

"Never did I ever expect anyone like you to come into my life. You are the greatest gift I will ever receive." She smiled at him then, a smile that lit up her whole face – it lit up his life. Hell, his body responded to the warmth of that smile.

"I can't wait, Precious. I have to see you." He began to undress her, marveling at every inch of her gorgeous body.

Since he had accepted the imperfection of her face, Presley had no qualms about him seeing the rest of her. She helped him shed her clothes and his.

His body temperature rose. She stood before him, naked and soft and smooth. Her curves were lush and welcoming. Her breasts were two sweet mounds of perfection. He couldn't take his eyes off of her, his eyes feasted on the banquet of her beauty. "This – this is what I was longing for. I could have lived in darkness, but I will be forever grateful for the joy of seeing the woman who has given me more pleasure and joy than I ever expected." He let his hands follow his gaze, relearning every sweet inch of her body. "I've just begun to touch you," he growled, "and I'm already completely lost. You are my one desire." Taking her hand, he covered his cock. "See how much I want you?"

No longer did she doubt that he desired her. Zane could see her plainly and he still wanted her. "I want you more," she gave him a challenging little grin as she rubbed her thumb over the head of his cock, spreading the precum.

"I seriously doubt that." Before she could see it coming, he picked her up and laid her on the bed. "Fulfill a fantasy for me. I want to watch you touch yourself."

His request shocked her, but it also made her hot as heck. "You want to see me masturbate?"

Lord, her even saying the word 'masturbate' did it for him, "Presley you are a perfect combination of innocent and sexy and I have craved to see what you look like when you cum. Tonight, I'm going to get that privilege more than once."

He was hers. She could do this. Presley came to her knees and looked her man right in the eye. "Do you want me to show you how much I want you?" She ran both palms up her body and under her hair, lifting it, her breasts rising with the motion. His cock throbbed at the sight.

"How much do you want me?" he countered her question.

She was absolutely delectable. Presley's skin glowed golden in the lamplight and as she caressed her own thighs, teasing her body with little rubs, he sank to a chair in front of her – mesmerized. In the last few weeks, she had given him so much. As he lay in the hospital bed, he had relived the moments when she had opened to him – giving herself to him in the most generous way possible. Open arms, open legs and an open heart. Her mouth on his cock was any man's wet dream and when he would work his cock into her tight little pussy, he had felt like a fuckin' superhero. Now, she was before him – making him want her more than ever.

Keeping eye contact with him, she laid back, watching him as he fisted his cock. Presley was a little self-conscious but more turned on than anything. With a calculated move, she opened one leg, giving him an unimpeded view of her pussy.

Zane couldn't be still. He left the chair and went to her, kneeling at the bed. "Sweet Lord" he breathed as he got his first glimpse of her pink, wet flesh. "I've kissed you there, it is the sweetest flavor in the world."

She felt like a goddess. His eyes were focused on her with a heated, intense gaze. So, she rewarded him by lifting her hips and swirling her fingers through her pussy and around her clit. He groaned and she felt herself grow wet. "Yes," she moaned.

Damn! He didn't know where to look; her gorgeous face, her luscious tits or between her legs. The blood was pulsing in his cock, he couldn't hold out much longer. Just a taste, he promised himself. Catching one leg, he opened her up further and caught her hand, holding it to one side. Was there a prettier sight in the world? Slowly, he lowered his head, placing a kiss right over her clit.

"Oh, yeah! I love that!" she bucked up toward his face, wanting more.

"Uh-uh, continue. I just needed a little something to tide me over."

"Zane, you can't be serious," but he was, she could tell by his expression. He felt he had missed out on some things and she felt privileged that he wanted her to help him make up for it. He would not be sorry. Her own touch felt good, but that wasn't what made her body writhe or bow with ecstasy – it was him, all him. She watched his eyes glaze with passion, a red flush of arousal color his skin. His breathing became shallow and fast, and when he groaned, she only gave him more. With one hand she played with her breast and with the other she caressed the wet folds.

"Fuck!" he hissed. He couldn't keep his hands off of her. Lying down beside her, he just took it all it – touching her leg, her arm, kissing her anywhere she pleased. His hips were bucking sympathetically, the head rubbing sensuously on her leg.

She let her fingers flutter against her clit. "You'll make love to me, won't you?" This felt good, but he would feel so much better. Honey flowed. Her thighs tightened, and with rhythmic abandon she plunged two fingers inside of herself, whimpering, "Fuck me, please. Fuck me, Zane!"

When she gasped his name, he had to act. This was his woman! Her pleasure was his pleasure. Pulling her close, he cradled her head and covered her mouth with his. Pushing past her lips, he mapped the hot cavern of her mouth – licking, branding – tangling his tongue with hers as he possessed her, totally. Zane's whole body burned and tingled, he rubbed himself against her, wanting to get as close to her as possible.

Presley ran her hands down his body, loving the ripples and bulges of his muscles, the flat, lickable six pack. How could any woman resist him? He was sex itself. Reaching between them, she found his erection and palmed it, this was what she needed.

"Presley, I need to tell you something," he panted, "I never knew pleasure like this existed. I want you to belong to me, forever." Taking a breast in one hand, he plumped it and sucked on the nipple like he was starving to death. "I can't live another moment without being inside you. Before was perfect – wonderful, but being able to see you adds another dimension – I want you more than my next breath. Now, look at me."

She tried, but when he covered her body and surged inside of her, burying as much of his cock as he could in the first thrust, she closed her eyes and moaned in complete surrender.

"Let me in, Sugar," he flexed his hips, working his way in. "God, you fit me so well. You were made for me, Presley."

Letting out a breath, she willed her body to relax and let him in. A delicious feeling of fullness – completion – swathed her body in quivering ecstasy.

"That's it," he pumped again, burying himself to the hilt. "Christ!"

She melted around him, accepting his thrusts. Wrapping her legs around his hips, she kissed his chest and shoulders while he set a hard rhythm. Yet every time she looked into his face, his eyes found hers. He was taking all that she had, drawing it from her body and remaking her into something more beautiful than she was before.

An incredible rush of feeling spread throughout her body as his pelvis moved over hers, creating a constant friction, a sublime rolling of heated ecstasy that pulsed in her clit and reached all the way to her hard, sensitive nipples. Every movement of his body rubbed his chest against hers and she pushed up into him wishing she could merge her very soul into his.

God, he was gonna come first, Zane thought as Presley lifted her hips off the bed, sliding herself up and down his cock. Excruciating pleasure was overtaking him and when she screamed his name, "Zaaannne!" and clamped her body down on his, he exploded. They held one another and rocked together, prolonging their orgasm and celebrating the miracle of love they had been granted.

A good while later, after they had dozed, talked and celebrated; he climbed from the bed and pulled on his jeans, shirt and boots. "Let's go see our horses,"

"You're like a little boy on Christmas morning." Presley dressed hastily, there was no way she wanted to miss this.

"Come on, Rex," he called. Rex's job description was about to change, but he didn't seem to mind. Guard-dog during the day and lap-dog at night would suit him fine.

As Zane walked out into the clear light of day, he held the hand of the woman he loved and took in the wonder of the world around him. The colors of the trees were richer than he could have dreamed, the sky was a brilliant blue – even the grass was greener than he remembered. In the pasture, the horses were running in the crisp air and the cattle were grazing in the distance. He wanted to throw his arms up in the air and hug the world. But all the blessings surrounding him paled next to Presley. "Stop, I want to look at you."

"What?

"The love shining in your eyes is the most incredible sight. I never want to forget it."

"You won't ever have to remember, Zane. The love won't ever dim from my eyes or my heart, I'll love you forever."

He wrapped his arms around her and pulled her close, cradling her in the warmth of his body. "You know, Baby, being able to see you, to look at you is a dream come true. But I want you to know that my love for you is unchanging. I loved you before I saw you, and I love you now. I didn't need eyes to see your beauty. No eye sees as clearly as the heart and my heart belongs to you."

Presley laid her head on his chest. She was home.

ABOUT THE AUTHOR

Sable's hometown will always be New Orleans. She loves the culture of Louisiana and it permeates everything she does. Now, she lives in the big state of Texas and like most southern women, she loves to cook southern food - especially Cajun and Tex-Mex. She also loves to research the supernatural, but shhhh don't tell anyone.

Sable writes saucy romances. She lives in New Orleans. She believes that her goal as a writer is to make her readers laugh with joy, cry in sympathy and fan themselves when they read the hot parts - ha! The worlds she creates in her books are ones where right prevails, love conquers all and holding out for a hero is not an impossible dream.

Visit Sable:
Website: http://www.sablehunter.com
Facebook: http://www.facebook.com/authorsablehunter
Amazon: http://www.amazon.com/author/sablehunter

3244154R00152

Made in the USA
San Bernardino, CA
18 July 2013